ALSO BY LUCY GILMORE

The Lonely Hearts Book Club

THE
LIBRARY OF
BORROWED
HEARTS

LUCY GILMORE

sourcebooks
casablanca

Published by Sourcebooks Casablanca, an imprint of Sourcebooks
P.O. Box 4410, Naperville, Illinois 60567-4410
(630) 961-3900
sourcebooks.com

Cataloging-in-Publication Data is on file with the Library of Congress.

Printed and bound in the United States of America.
VP 10 9 8 7 6 5 4 3 2 1

"It was not the thorn bending to the honeysuckles,
but the honeysuckles embracing the thorn."

—EMILY BRONTË, *WUTHERING HEIGHTS*

PART ONE

1

—

CHLOE

FOUND THE BOOK HIDDEN BEHIND A box of rusted plumbing parts.

The faded green cloth cover had been eaten away by damp and mites. The binding was loose and the corners broken. To all outward appearances, the thing belonged in the nearest dumpster—if not a hazmat facility three layers of yellow rubber deep.

Naturally, I kept it.

So far, it was the only book I planned on rescuing from the basement storeroom where I'd spent the better part of the past week, clearing out what my boss called "the unwanted masses." For decades, the Colville Public Library had been storing stacks of old and outdated books down in these subterranean hallways. Although many of them went on to good homes in one of the library's monthly book-sales-cum-purges, the piles had been growing higher and higher as the years progressed.

People just didn't hoard books like they used to. They especially didn't hoard books that had long since passed their sell-by date.

The more fools they.

I felt almost giddy as I ran my hands over the cover of the book, my fingers tracing the embossed title. Even though I wasn't technically a librarian here—you needed a degree for that—I *was* an employee, and a damn good one at that. Some days, I functioned as janitorial staff. Others, I filled in at the checkout counter. This week, my sole responsibility was to do the thing that no one else had the stomach to do: say goodbye to the past fifty years.

Goodbye to the dog-eared romance novels boasting the faded flowing locks of Fabio. Goodbye to the poorly aged self-help guides full of body-shaming advice. Goodbye to cookbooks that were *way* more obsessed with aspic and gelatins than the modern-day digestive system could handle.

I was good at the task, too. I'd always excelled at doing the dirty deeds no one else wanted to tackle. If I'd lived in a big glamorous city or had ties to the high-powered political world, I might be known as a "fixer." As it was, living in a town with a population of five thousand residents, an hour's drive south of Canada, deep in the forests of Washington state, I was…what, exactly?

A cleaning woman? A general factotum? A drudge who had to do what she was told or risk losing the closest thing to a bookish job she'd ever get?

Okay, maybe that last one was a touch dramatic, but my back hurt from hauling all these stupid boxes up and down the stairs. Also, there were cobwebs in my hair and so many paper cuts that my fingers looked like they'd just escaped a miniature slasher flick. Drama was the only thing keeping me going.

"'*I have no money, no resources, no hopes,*'" I read aloud as I lifted the book's cover and scanned the first lines. "'*I am the happiest man alive.*'"

I knew what would happen if I kept turning the pages. Despite the fact that I was little more than a drudge in my small Washington town—or, more likely, *because* of it—most of my free time was spent deep in the pages of a book. Unless you were super into hunting or fishing, there wasn't much else to do around here. I worked and I took care of my family. I did the things no one else wanted to do.

And I read. Always, I read.

Which was why I chuckled and tucked the book in my tote bag where no one would accidentally stumble across it. *Tropic of Cancer* wasn't the sort of novel you wanted to keep lying around the break room—especially a break room like ours, where the fridge sat stuffed with homemade meals in Tupperware containers and the community billboard was tacked with colorful reminders about prayer meetings. If one of my coworkers were to pop the book open and start counting the number of times the words *prick* or *rosebush* or—sorry, literary censors—*cunt* appeared, I'd probably be charged with assault with intent to kill.

It was that kind of workplace—and that kind of book. In fact, *Tropic of Cancer* was most famous for having been banned in the United States for decades after it was first published. I had no idea when or how the Colville Library had gotten its hands on a copy, but I could see why someone had tucked it away in the basement. In the fifties and sixties, people had gone to literal jail over this book.

"Hey, Chloe." A head popped in through the basement doorway. It belonged to my coworker Pepper, the library's bookmobile driver and the only other person I'd trust with my illicit treasure. "Gunderson says he's giving you a reprieve. He's not going to make you throw away any more books until garbage pickup. Apparently, we're creating a fire hazard."

I gave a grateful sigh and wiped my hands on the seat of my jeans. I didn't normally dress so casually, but like I'd said, I was on special basement-cleaning duty this week. My shoulder-length red hair was swept up in a bandanna, an oversized T-shirt tied in a knot at my waist.

Not exactly glamorous, but then, neither was I.

"I thought the fire department was more concerned with the fire hazard down here," I said, kicking at one of the dusty boxes. "They can't have it both ways."

Pepper shrugged. "I don't make the rules. I just abide by them." She nodded at one of the boxes overflowing with discarded Fabios. "Most of the time, anyway. What are you planning to do with those beauties?"

"Toss them out with all the rest. As much as it hurts to throw all these books away, I'm under strict orders not to let anything slip through my fingers."

"Mind if I take a stab at slipping them through mine? My grandma is obsessed with all those old Harlequins. I keep telling her there are way more diverse romances these days, but she likes the way these ones smell."

I'd known Pepper's grandmother my entire life, so I could easily accept this as fact. Lonnie Pakootas was as hard-core as they came—a woman committed to tradition when it suited her and absolutely in defiance of it when it didn't. Pepper was the same, though I wasn't allowed to say so. I'd tried pointing out the similarities once—the ones that went beyond their wide-set brown eyes and impossibly long black hair, the buoyant laugh that could chase even the darkest thoughts away—but Pepper had refused to speak to me for a week afterward. Pakootas women valued their unique-ness, thank you very much, and woe to the best friend who said otherwise.

"I'd be happy to save these poor rejects, but we'll have to sneak them past Gunderson first," I said. "You know how weird he gets about following library protocol."

Pepper dropped her voice in an exact imitation of Gunderson's, all stuffy and nasal. "An employee of the Colville Public Library is a com-munity leader, a model of decorum and dignity," she said. She even managed to purse her lips so it looked like she had a mustache similar to the one he'd been trying to grow out for the past two months. "We can't be seen carting contraband around the streets."

"Speaking of contraband…" I reached into my tote bag and fished out the copy of *Tropic of Cancer*. "Take a look at this bad boy. Emphasis on *bad*."

She glanced curiously at the book before allowing it to fall open to a page somewhere in the middle.

"'*He is about to walk away when suddenly he notices that his penis is lying on the sidewalk. It is about the size of a sawed-off broomstick. He picks it up nonchalantly and slings it under his arm.*'" A grimace twisted Pepper's lips as she read aloud. "What the hell, Chloe? Ew. *Ew.*"

I couldn't help giggling. "I know. It's a terrible book. But it's, like, super famous for being terrible. You couldn't even get a copy in the United States for fifty years after it was published. Not to buy from a bookstore and *definitely* not to borrow from a public library."

I could tell I had her interest. "And you found it here?" she asked. "In the basement?"

"Yep." I took the book back and flipped it open to the last page. I tapped my finger on the small print: *Imprenta de Mexico, 1940.* "Unless I'm mistaken, this is one of the bootleg copies that circulated back in the book's heyday. This company called Medusa Publishing printed them in Mexico and then smuggled them here. This book is probably worth a thousand bucks, even in this condition."

"Ohhh." Pepper nodded as though that made perfect sense. Which, considering how much she knew about my life, was true. "That'll help a ton. New roof?"

"A down payment, if I'm lucky. Or I might just throw caution to the wind and get a dishwasher instead." I tried not to dwell too much on the prospect of such luxury. No point getting my hopes *too* high. "I'll have to wait and see how much this little guy nets me first... *Oh, crap.* Never mind."

"What's wrong?"

Both my expression and my spirits fell as I caught sight of a scribbled note in the margin at the end of the book. For all its obscenities, *Tropic of Cancer* ends on a surprisingly sweet note: The sun is setting. I feel this river flowing through me—its past, its ancient soil, the changing climate. The hills gently girdle it about; its course is fixed.

There, in a scratchy hand, I could make out a message that some long-ago reader had left behind.

Good idea. I'll meet you at our river when the sun is setting.

In a different hand, this one much more florid, the message continued.

When the sun is setting? But I thought The Sun Also Rises?

No. No more Hemingway. You promised.

"That's cute," Pepper said, reading over my shoulder. "Someone left notes."

"It's *not* cute." I thumped the cover shut. "That'll cut at least half off my sale price. Doesn't anyone respect library property anymore?"

"Are you asking the woman who's about to smuggle out a box of thirty-year-old Harlequins for her grandmother?"

"Good point." I tucked the book back in my tote bag. Half a treasure was better than no treasure at all.

"So how do you want to play this?" Pepper asked. "If Gunderson finds out, it'll mean your job, not mine. He can't get rid of me. I'm the only one who knows how to work the clutch on the bookmobile."

I ran through several scenarios in my head until I landed on the easiest one.

"It'll be best for me to carry the box out like I'm adding it to the pile out back," I said. "You just need to keep Gunderson distracted long enough for me to slip it under the bookmobile's passenger seat. Then you can drop it off wherever you want on your rounds tomorrow."

Pepper pulled a face. "That's disappointing. No pulling the fire alarm? No secret handoffs in the break room? I thought you were supposed to be devious and resourceful."

It was true. I *was* devious and resourceful, but only because I had no other choice. Necessity could drive a person to do strange things. Sometimes, it meant slapping on a bandanna and breathing in basement toxins for the sake of a paycheck. Other times, it meant petty not-exactly-theft of ancient, crumbling treasures that were being thrown away *anyway*.

"It's a box of dusty old books, not a Kandinsky," I said. "Look, do you want my help or not?"

"Fine. Some fun you are." Pepper rolled her eyes, but in an exaggerated way that I took to mean she understood.

The nice thing about Pepper was that she understood a lot of things: That I needed the money from the sale of that broken-down book more than I was willing to admit. That I'd liberate a dozen copies of a dozen broken-down books if it meant I could keep a roof over my family's head for one more day.

Also that if there was one person she could count on to see her through, well, *anything*, it was Chloe Sampson.

A fixer. A general factotum. A drudge.

And, apparently, the proud new owner of a bootleg copy of *Tropic of Cancer*.

2

—

CHLOE

OUR HEIST WENT OFF WITHOUT A hitch.

Distracting Gunderson was easy enough for Pepper to do, since he was the sort of man who took twenty minutes to read off his grocery list. A great stickler for detail, our Gunderson, which made him a great librarian but not so great whenever we sat down for a staff meeting. He once put together an entire PowerPoint presentation on alphabetizing when using hyphens and apostrophes—all good and important stuff in the world of books, don't get me wrong, but nothing that couldn't have been shared in a quick two-sentence email.

Anyway, Pepper asked him a question about the new metadata requirements for our online catalog system, and he was off on one of his monotone tangents for the next half hour. As I walked out the back with my stolen books, Gunderson did no more than give me a quick glance before returning to his beloved keywords and ISBN-13s.

Poor Pepper got the short end of that stick, for sure. I jimmied open the passenger door to the bookmobile, slid the Harlequins underneath the seat, and tossed *Tropic of Cancer* into the glove compartment of my huge rusted station wagon until it was time to head home for the day.

Which, blissfully, was now. Eight hours of clearing out books wore on a body a lot more than you'd think, even when that body was only twenty-four years old. Unfortunately, as soon as I stepped up to my front door, half-painted in seafoam green and half-rusted where the paint had run out, it swung open with a bang.

"Chloe, *finally*!" cried the oldest of my siblings as she came barreling up.

Even though Trixie was an absolute knockout of a fifteen-year-old who defied all the rules of adolescence with her clear skin, naturally straight teeth, and a level of self-confidence usually reserved for mediocre men forty years her senior, she always seemed to be barreling. She also flounced, traipsed, somersaulted, and crashed. Unless it was an active verb in its most active tense, she wanted no part of it.

"You won't believe what happened today," she said, beaming. That was another thing she did—she beamed. She was the only person I'd ever met whose sunny disposition went so deep that it was a physical part of her. "Guess which second alternate just landed herself a starting position on the debate team?"

"Penny Harlow?" I guessed. Even though I already knew the answer, I couldn't resist playing the game. As we spoke, I stepped past our tiny entry into the living room, doing my best to ignore the piles of shoes and backpacks and the other inevitable detritus of the young.

"Ugh. Obviously not. Penny can't even raise her hand in class without breaking out in hives."

"Jacob Jarabecki?"

"Chloe, Jake can't string together a full sentence unless it's about football—and even then, he only makes sense half the time." My sister's lower lip came down in a pout. "Are you *trying* to be mean?"

"A little bit, yeah," I confessed, but not before swooping in to press a kiss on her cheek. She smelled, as she always did, of fresh grass clippings and her general air of joie de vivre. Don't ask me what joie de vivre smells like, because I couldn't tell you. All you need to know is that it's chic and effortless, and if anyone finds a way to bottle it up and sell it, they'll make a fortune. "That's fantastic news, Trixie. You deserve it."

She hooked her arms around my neck before I could let go. "I don't— not really. I only got a spot because Sonya and Sasha's mom made them drop out. She says the travel expenses are too high, and that there's no need to pay good money for them to argue in public when they do it at home for free all the time." She pulled back a little and scanned my face. "That's okay, right? We can afford it? The team only travels every other week, and I can participate in the fun runs and stuff to help with the costs."

I thought about the stolen book sitting in my glove box and groaned inwardly. So much for my new dishwasher.

"Sure thing, Trix," I said. "Don't sweat it."

I kept the smile on my face until I felt sure she wouldn't see anything but my pride in her. Help arrived in the shape of my two other siblings, who came dashing into the living room a few seconds later. To be more precise, Theo dashed. Noodle came out with slumped shoulders and a heavy tread I recognized well.

"Is Trixie telling you about her stupid debate team?" Theo asked. At eleven, he was the baby of the family, but he was bidding fair to outgrow every last one of us. It was almost impossible to keep any meat on his bones, so he was all gangling limbs and awkward angles. He ate a whole box of cereal (off-brand Cheerios) by himself every morning, and finished his day with a second box (off-brand Cinnamon Toast Crunch) for dessert. And that didn't even touch the mass quantities of calories required to sustain him the rest of the time.

"Ugh," he muttered. "No one cares about debate. Who wants to talk about politics in front of a bunch of grown-ups?"

"Lots of people," I said. "Especially the kind who plan to *work* in politics with a bunch of grown-ups one day."

He waved me off as only an eleven-year-old blithely unconcerned with anything but the contents of his own stomach could do.

"Whatever. I forgot to tell you—my science project is due tomorrow. Do we have any nitrous oxide?"

I blinked at him, his head level with mine. "Of course we don't have nitrous oxide. Isn't that laughing gas?"

"*Fine.*" His lower lip shot out, but as was the case with Trixie, his optimism ran deep. "What about ammonium nitrate? That's not hard to get, is it?"

"Yes, it's hard to get. They use it to make explosives. What on earth are they teaching you at that school?"

I felt a tug on the bottom of my shirt before I could ask any follow-up questions, most of which revolved around the likelihood of our house still standing by dinnertime. Theo was a bright kid, and I was inordinately proud of him for landing a coveted spot at a local charter school, but I was getting tired of putting locks on every cabinet containing anything even remotely flammable.

I glanced down to find Noodle's fingers twisting my T-shirt between anxious fingers.

"It happened again," he said in the simple, quiet way he had—wholly unlike our siblings, but equally disastrous in the end. "With the Frisbee. We were working on fetch."

I bit back a groan. This was the part I'd been dreading the most. "I thought we decided you'd only work on training at the park from here on out."

Noodle rolled a shoulder in his usual half shrug. He rarely came into full animation unless he was working with our dog, Gummy Bear.

Gummy Bear, who'd never fetched a thing a day in his life. Gummy Bear, who was virtually untrainable. Gummy Bear, who ate almost as much as Theo did on any given day.

Even though Noodle was older than Theo by ten months—Irish twins, my mom always called them, and *not* in reference to the bright red hair we all shared—he was considerably shorter in stature. He was also wary of anything that didn't scamper about on four legs. He spent hours every day trying to teach our slobbering, wheezing bulldog to perform the most basic of tasks, but woe to the older sister who tried to get him to step any further out of his comfort zone than that. When he'd been a toddler, he'd lived almost entirely on buttered noodles, which was where his nickname had come from. It was easier to call a sweet, shy, pasta-loving kid Noodle than it was to call him Aloysius.

Actually, it was easier to call a kid pretty much *anything* other than that. I honestly don't know what my mom had been thinking when she'd filled out our birth certificates. Clotilde, Beatrice, Theodore, and Aloysius were bitter pills to swallow for kids living in a place with exactly one drugstore.

"How long ago did it happen?" I asked, since of all the disasters facing me right now, this one was the most pressing. Money was only material and scientific experimentation inevitable, but a rogue Frisbee had the potential to bring the sky down upon our heads.

Noodle shifted from one foot to the other. His deeply freckled face was covered in streaks of mud, his fingernails so dirty that I felt sure he'd spent the entire afternoon sitting out back, trying to drum up the nerve to go get the Frisbee on his own.

"About an hour," Trixie informed me. She grimaced, her nose wrinkled at the tip. "I was gonna offer to get it before you got home, but…"

"She's a scaredy-cat," Theo finished for her.

"Oh, yeah? I didn't see you stepping up to volunteer," Trixie countered. "All you did this afternoon was pull every cleaner out from under the bathroom sink and read through the ingredients."

Theo stuck his tongue out at her. "I was *researching*."

"You were making a mess." Trixie turned to me with something like triumph. "He left them out. Every last bottle. Trying to go pee in there is like playing a game of hot lava with containers of bleach."

I started to pinch the bridge of my nose, but the sight of Noodle's anxious expression stopped me. "Okay," I said with a deep, fortifying breath. I even managed a smile, though I was pretty sure my insides were quaking just as much as his were. "First things first. I'll get the Frisbee from Mr. Holmes. When I get back, I expect the cleaners to be put away—and I mean *all* of them, Theo—so Noodle can shower. Then… science experiment? Debate practice?"

"*Dinner*," all three kids announced, and with so much force that I recognized it for the nonnegotiable it was.

"Okay. Dinner. It's a plan."

I paused just long enough to press a kiss on Noodle's dirt-encrusted hairline before heading back out the front door. It would have been hyperbole to say that my legs *actually* quaked at the task ahead of me, but there was no denying the twist in my stomach. I'd lived inside this house for twenty-two of my twenty-four years. For every single one of those years, Jasper Holmes had been our next-door neighbor. I'd always considered myself a no-nonsense sort of person, but I had nothing on Jasper. The man was blunt to the point of rudeness and terrifying in ways that only children living in a neighborhood likes ours would understand.

In the area where we lived, west of town, the houses were small and ramshackle, the lawns covered in weeds rather than grass. More than one front yard boasted a car up on cinder blocks, and you could practically hear the collective group pulling out the pots and pans whenever it rained. We were all holding on by a single thread, and with each passing day, you could hear that thread starting to unravel more.

Everyone except for Jasper Holmes, that was—the one man in the world I didn't want to see today, and the one man in the world I had no choice but to tackle head-on. When it came to Noodle, a lost Frisbee was right up there with a retainer accidentally tossed in the trash or a baby thrown out with the bathwater. He'd feel miserable and guilty until he had the cheap plastic toy back in his care.

Granted, there was a greater likelihood that the sky would open up and rain down gold bullion than that Jasper would give the Frisbee up, but I had to at least try.

———

I could feel the watchful eyes of my siblings as I made my way to the end of the drive and ducked under the broken trellis that separated our property from Jasper's. As soon as I set foot across that barrier, it was like being transported to another world—a magical world where oleander shrubs sprang fully formed from the land and mums continued thriving well past the first frost. A white-columned birdbath stood in the center of the yard underneath an arch of purple wisteria vines, and even though I'd never seen anything other than a pack of crows hovering over our own house, there was some kind of yellow-billed bird splashing playfully around in it.

If *I* were a miserable old man who considerably worsened the lives of everyone around me, claiming every wayward toy thrown over the fence as my personal property, my garden would be a tangle of poisonous weeds and hidden trapdoors, but what did I know? Maybe this was Jasper's way of luring people in, transforming his home into gingerbread and sweet treats for the unsuspecting.

His shadow crossed over the window, so I knew he was watching as I knocked on the door. Naturally, that didn't stop him from making me wait a full sixty seconds before finally opening up.

"What the hell do you want?" he barked.

"You know the answer to that, Mr. Holmes." I stretched my face in a smile and infused a note of false cheer in my voice. It was the same voice I used at the library whenever a patron tried to convince me to turn the SafeSearch function off the public computers. "Noodle accidentally threw a Frisbee over the fence earlier today."

"And he made you come all the way over here to get it back? Typical," he said by way of reply. Then, "You're not doing that boy any favors, you know."

"I *do* know," I agreed, still in my bright voice. "But he's just a kid, so let's skip this part, shall we?"

This wasn't the first time I'd made such a request, and I strongly doubted it would be the last. People who didn't know Noodle would never understand him. They were always trying to push him deeper into childhood or all the way out of it, as if he either had to be a developmental failure or a wise old soul born with the weight of the world on his shoulders.

Give him a break, my heart screamed at them. *He's only twelve years old. He likes crossword puzzles and to suck on ice cubes made from lemonade. He gets along with animals more than people. He wants the world to be a softer, kinder place, but he's smart enough to recognize an effort in futility when he sees one. That makes him scared and sad and, yes, a little bit sensitive. Deal with it.*

I never said any of that out loud, of course. I just kept smiling my too-tight smile.

"I know I should've sent him over here to get the Frisbee himself, but I wanted to personally apologize," I added. "I'm trying to get him to train Gummy Bear at the park instead of our yard, but he doesn't like going there without one of us to keep him company. Some of the kids can be really mean."

Jasper Holmes looked me over with a twist to his upper lip. He had one of those faces that was easy to read, his heavy features so weighed down with time that they seemed to show every passing minute. Despite his advanced age, he still had a good head of snowy-white hair, his shoulders so strong and wide that you could practically feel the power emanating off him. In his youth, I imagine he was a highly attractive man. Too bad his heart was made of stone—if he had a heart at all.

"I wasn't talking about the Frisbee, you fool," he said. "I was referring to the name."

I blinked. This was new. Conversation wasn't something Jasper and I shared very often. Our interactions ranged almost entirely around the property rights associated with childhood toys and the land onto which they fell. Somewhere inside this man's house lived about thirty soccer balls, an equal number of plastic Frisbees, and an old baseball I'd scrawled with a barely legible *Babe Ruth* before I'd tossed it over to see what he would do.

"What's wrong with calling him Noodle?" I asked, refusing to let that *fool* part get to me. "Lots of kids have nicknames."

"Not ones named after food." He narrowed his eyes at me. Like the rest of him, they were powerful, their brilliant blue unwavering. "I knew a boy named Beef once."

I blinked again, even more taken aback this time. This wasn't just conversation. If I didn't know any better, I'd say we were bordering on chitchat.

"That's a fun nickname," I said. "Was he a vegetarian?"

Jasper scoffed so hard I could practically see the spittle flying from his mouth. "Of course not. No one was a vegetarian back then. You ate what was put in front of you, and you were grateful for each mouthful."

I got the feeling I was being insulted, and even though I knew *why*, I wasn't exactly sure of the how.

"And before you ask, no, Beef wasn't a large kid," Jasper added. "He was the scrawniest scrap of a human being I ever met. Hell of a fighter, though, which is how he got the name. He had a beef with everyone, even if he'd never met them before."

"I'm not sure I understand the moral of this story," I said. "Is your problem with Noodle's nickname that it's too…weak? He needs something stronger?"

"I'm saying the world takes you at your word. Make sure the thing you're telling them is what you want them to hear." His lips pulled down in a frown. "And I'm not giving you that Frisbee. It's mine now."

I bit back a groan. After all that, he was *still* going to make me beg for it? The door started to close, so I slipped my foot in through the crack.

"Please, Mr. Holmes?" I asked. "I know I promised it wouldn't happen again, but the truth is, I *need* that Frisbee."

"Don't be ridiculous. No one needs a Frisbee. Throw plates if you're desperate."

He tried to close the door around my foot, but I wasn't backing down. If he wanted me to believe that the trick to success was simply standing up and telling the world what you wanted it to hear, then I was ready to give his approach a go. After all, what was the worst thing he could do to me? Steal *more* Frisbees?

"I know it seems like a little thing to you, but it'll cost me five bucks to replace," I said, my irritation mounting. "That's five bucks I could put toward Trixie's yearbook costs. Five bucks to put a gallon of gas in my guzzler of a car. Five bucks I could use to buy the name-brand cereal instead of a sad off-brand replacement."

He stared down at my foot and back up at my face, his gaze equally displeased with both.

"How you waste your money is your problem, not mine," he said with a grunt. "You kids today are all the same. If you knew anything, you'd realize those off-brand cereals are just as good as the real thing. Half the time, they make them in the same factories."

As far as I was concerned, that was the final straw. This man, with his marble birdbaths and well-sculpted gardens, his hoard of stolen soccer balls, his kitchen with only one mouth to feed, had *no idea* what a tiny thing like name-brand cereal meant to a family like mine.

Yes, Theo would eat it in one sitting. And, yeah, technically speaking, it would satisfy the same nutritional needs in the end. But eating that cheap cereal in a cheap bowl every day wore a person down. Not in a way that you could quantify, but by tiny degrees. Each bite was a reminder that no matter how hard we worked or how far we stretched our dollars, some things would never change.

We'd always be starting at the bottom.

"Tell me something, Mr. Holmes," I said, my voice tight. "You've lived in this house for—what—forty, fifty years?"

"Thereabouts," he agreed, grumbling. "So what?"

"So then you've seen my entire life unfold before your eyes," I said. "My mom's, too, probably. You saw her hitch herself to a succession of rotten boyfriends, desperate for someone to lift her up and take her away from this place. Watched those same rotten boyfriends come and go, only staying long enough to knock her up before moving on to greener pastures. Saw her bring home four squalling babies, saw how much she struggled to keep them in formula and diapers and cereal—knockoff brand or otherwise."

I could tell from Jasper's growing frown that he wasn't expecting this direct attack, but I was on too much of a roll to stop now.

"You also saw me go off to college, only to return two years later with nothing to show for it but half a degree and a load of student debt," I added. "And I bet you know why, too. I bet you were the one who called CPS."

The fact that his gaze shifted to a few inches above my head told me everything I needed to know. Since I was, in all honesty, *grateful* for that particular intervention, I didn't press too hard. According to the woman who'd called me, my mom had been gone for over two weeks before the kids had been scooped up and placed in foster care.

Trixie had been eleven at the time. Theo and Noodle had only been seven.

"You know it all," I continued, eyes blazing. "She left them alone. She walked away from her own children. So, yeah. A five-dollar Frisbee might not mean much to you, but it means a lot to Noodle—a kid whose name you may not think is *macho* enough, but who's doing the best he can with the hand he's been dealt. I can always buy another one to replace it, and I will, but I literally stole a library book from work today to help us get by. *That's* what I'm dealing with. *That's* what five dollars means to me."

Instead of immediately going inside to get the Frisbee, Jasper tilted his head. It wasn't much of a reaction—in fact, it was disappointing considering how much of myself I'd just laid bare—but it was enough.

"*Which* library book?" he asked.

I was so startled that I answered without hesitating. "It's called *Tropic of Cancer*. It's old, and it's not in great shape, but there are collectors out there who'll pay a pretty penny to get their hands on it."

"*Tropic…of Cancer*?" he echoed, his hand coming up to clutch at the doorframe. I was afraid that maybe the word *cancer* was the cause, but he shook his head as if clearing it. "Are you sure about that?"

"About its title or about how much it's worth?" I returned. Without waiting for an answer, I added, "Yes to both. I may have only finished half my library science degree, but I'm not without my uses. I can both read and accurately assess the value of historic documents."

He grunted. It was such a judgmental sound that I was suddenly worried about the crime I'd just confessed to.

"And before you go tattling to the library, I found the book abandoned in the basement, so it's not like anyone is going to miss it. Someone had taken pains to hide it decades ago—probably along with copies of *To Kill a Mockingbird* and *The Color Purple*. You know how uptight a town like this can get."

By this time, I'd decided that (a) I'd already said more than was good for me, and (b) there was no way I was going to get my hands on that Frisbee. I gave Jasper Holmes two more seconds to do the right thing. When all he did was continue staring at me like I'd just pulled my bleeding heart out of my chest and offered it to him as a snack, I gave up the fight.

With a sigh, I turned around and went back the way I came. The yellow-billed bird gave a rattling cackle as I walked by, not unlike the sound my car made on cold mornings when it wanted to get going about as much as I did.

"I know, buddy," I said as I trailed my fingers playfully in his bath-water. "But what else can we do? This is technically his property. As long as we keep coming back, he's free to treat us however he wants."

3

—

CHLOE

F I WERE AN INTELLIGENT WOMAN, I'd have followed the age-old advice for new parents everywhere and gone to bed when the kids did.

Trixie, Noodle, and Theo were long past the napping age, but they had a tendency to hit their mattresses hard when they went down for the night. I liked to think it was because they lived each day to the fullest, their bodies and minds wearied by the fun they managed to pack inside each twenty-four rotation, but the truth was that we all lived in a state of perpetual exhaustion.

In the general way of things, I strove to keep my anxieties to a minimum—about the bills and the fact that Theo had come perilously close to mixing ammonia and bleach *just to see what the fuss is about*, about Noodle repeating the sixth grade because his teachers refused to accept that intelligence was more than filling in bubbles on a Scantron. Most days, I managed to do a decent job of it, but the kids must have noticed something off about me when I'd returned empty-handed from Jasper's house. Again.

Theo had begun wordlessly setting the table. Trixie had grabbed a bag of mixed vegetables from the freezer to make a stir-fry. And

Noodle had coaxed Gummy Bear into a corner to work on sitting and staying—an activity that mostly involved Gummy Bear rolling onto his back in a bid for belly rubs.

So, yeah. After dinner, they'd all crashed and fallen into the deep sleep of the weary while I sat in the living room with my old college laptop propped on my legs, a drooling bulldog and *Tropic of Cancer* sitting next to me.

"Let's see," I said aloud as I started typing. "One very old, very used copy, battered and torn, defaced with writing on several pages... *Ugh.* Who am I kidding? No one is going to jump at the chance to get their hands on that."

I quickly erased what I'd written.

"Think, Gummy Bear," I said as I ran my hands over the soft flaps of his ears. He groaned and let me, but I could tell that even he wasn't impressed by my copywriting skills. Or by me. Since I was the Sampson who forced him to go through the rigorous demands of a daily walk to the mailbox and back again, I'd never been his favorite member of the family. "We need to add panache. How about... *One-of-a-kind annotated bootleg copy? A hidden trove of scandal and intrigue just waiting for you to take it home?*"

As good as the words sounded, they weren't exactly truthful. The annotations I'd read had sounded more like a couple of teenagers passing notes in study hall than a deep literary analysis. Setting my laptop aside, I flipped through the book until I found another of the notes scrawled in the margins.

"'To have her here in bed with me, breathing on me, her hair in my mouth—I count that something of a miracle,'" I read aloud. Next to the line in the book, I could see that same scrawled, almost indecipherable hand from before: *Say what you will about the main character's morals, it sounds as if he really loved his wife. I can respect that.*

And, once again, the elegant lines underneath it.

It's not love if you write about the lice crawling over her hair in the very next paragraph. See?

I look at her again, closely. Her hair is alive. I pull back the sheet—more of them. They are swarming over the pillow.

True love doesn't care about lice.

You're just saying that to be contrary.

I'd love you no matter what kind of bugs you carried. I'd give anything to have you breathing on me, your hair in my mouth, your lice lying down to sleep with mine.

The conversation stopped there. Despite myself, I felt a certain kinship with the author of the neat, tidy hand. I liked how matter-of-fact she was, how she didn't hesitate to call out her lover for being contrary. He *did* sound contrary. He also sounded kind of sweet, if I was being honest. The whole point of *Tropic of Cancer* was that the filthy, slovenly animal lust of being a human meant something. Not necessarily something *good*, but something. And the guy with the scratchy hand seemed to sense it.

Hooked now, I flipped faster, my eyes scanning for more messages between the two. After a few chapters, I found them—and I found myself sitting up straighter as I read through.

She'll want to look for a studio with a garden attached—and a bathtub to be sure. She wants to be poor in a romantic way. I know her. But I'm prepared for her this time.

I know you in the same way, C. You think there's romance in poverty, but that's only because you've never lived it.

That's not fair.

Neither is being forced to watch you go to the dance on W's arm. Did you think I wouldn't find out? Try page 131.

"Ohhh, it's a love affair gone wrong," I murmured, my eyes wide. I sat back against the couch cushions, my heart doing a strange flip-flop in my chest. Gummy Bear grumbled but allowed me to shift. "What do you think, Gummy Bear? Should we keep going?"

He didn't have an answer for me. It felt wrong to be reading these private notes, as if I were a voyeur on a wild choose-your-own-adventure ride, but the book had technically been found in the library. Even if someone had shown the foresight to hide it deep in the basement, library books were public property. I had every right to keep turning the pages.

So I did. And once I reached the page 131, there was only one sentence deeply underlined: <u>There's something perverse about women... they're all masochists at heart.</u>

I chuckled aloud at this obvious play, but all communication stopped there. My girl C had no witty comebacks, no page numbers sending her annoyed lover to other quotes by way of reply. My interest in the laptop and my eBay listing now at an end, I settled deeper into the sagging cushions of the couch to read. I had zero interest in the book itself, but the marginalia were starting to *seriously* intrigue me.

Which was why the sound of a sudden knock startled me into a yelp. Gummy Bear cocked a quizzical ear, but he was so inured to the sounds of a young, chaotic household that he closed his eyes and drifted back to sleep.

I, on the other hand, wasn't so easily comforted.

"Who on earth could that be?" I asked as I swung my legs down and glanced up at the clock. Ten thirty on a school night. Not *dangerously* late for visitors, but certainly out of the ordinary.

The knock sounded again, sharper this time. Since the last thing I wanted was all three of my siblings tumbling out of their beds and demanding to know what was going on, I hopped up to answer it. As soon as I swung the door open to find who—and what—was on the other side, I stopped cold.

"Here." A neon-yellow Frisbee was thrust through the gap at me. "I brought your brother's thingamajig back."

I accepted the toy with a blink. I blinked again as I took in the sight of Jasper Holmes standing in his full six-foot-tall glory on my front porch.

In theory, I knew Jasper wasn't *really* a hermit. He could be seen buying his groceries every week in town, his black 1940s Ford truck cruising the streets almost as loudly and gas-guzzlingly as my own. He spent quite a bit of time at the garden and seed store, as his flowers could attest, and we'd even seen him at the annual Christmas pageant once, though he'd stormed out as soon as the baby Jesus started screaming for a diaper change. But he didn't make social calls, and he definitely didn't make them in the middle of the night.

Yet here we were.

"Do you…want to come in?" I asked, trying not to sound as unwelcoming as I felt. The four of us tried to keep the house in a habitable state, but I hadn't yet mustered the energy to do the dishes and there were piles of unfolded laundry spilling over the love seat. That didn't include the schoolbooks lying open on every surface or the dismantled old radio sitting frazzled on the coffee table. Bereft of even his toxic ammonia-and-bleach gas, Theo had been forced to strip the radio of parts to make a lemon-powered battery for his science project. Unless he could be bothered to put it away, the leftover parts would be sitting on that coffee table for months.

Jasper looked over my head and took it all in at a glance.

"Absolutely not," he said.

I couldn't help but laugh. Most people would have at least pretended not to notice. "Well, I appreciate this all the same." I waved the Frisbee. "Next time, you can just toss it over the fence. We'll figure it out from there."

Instead of accepting this polite dismissal, Jasper hesitated. He worked his jaw a few times, as if chewing on the words he didn't want to say.

"That book," he eventually said. "The one you mentioned from before."

There was no inflection in his voice, just a curt summation of the facts. I decided to respond in kind.

"What about it?"

"I came to buy it from you."

"You want to…buy it? From me?" I echoed. I couldn't have been more surprised if he'd claimed to be Henry Miller rising from the grave to claim its authorship. "What for?"

He grunted. "Does it matter? You said you could get good money for it. I have good money. That's all you need to know. Name your price."

I'd been waiting my whole life to hear those words spoken aloud. I'd always dreamed of being the kind of person who could write a figure on a scrap of paper and slide it across the table, the kind of person who could walk into an office and say, "Give us the room," with a complete absence of irony. In my head, I always played it cool, as if money wasn't the one thing that I always feel a desperate, clawing yearning to possess.

Naturally, I didn't play it cool at all. Instead, I said the first thing that came to my mind.

"One million dollars."

A cracking sound that might have been a laugh escaped Jasper's mouth. "Nice try. No book is worth *that* much."

Ever the literary scholar, I was quick to correct him. "Actually, there are early illustrated Bibles that fetch that much all the time. And several unfinished manuscripts from Jane Austen recently sold at auction for—"

"You know what I mean. Name a *reasonable* price." He peeked over my head at the inside of the house again and frowned. "Beggars shouldn't be choosers. How does five thousand sound?"

"Five thousand *dollars*?" I practically squeaked. It was no million-dollar windfall, but there were so many things I could buy with that kind of money. A dishwasher. A new roof, no down payment required. All the debate team escapades Trixie's heart could desire. "Are you serious?"

"Do I look like a man who's not serious?" He thrust a hand into the breast pocket of his jacket and pulled out a check folded neatly down the center. It was only then that I noticed he'd dressed up for this little meeting of ours. Whenever I normally saw him, he wore the traditional attire for rural Washington men well past retirement age: heavy-duty work pants and flannels, the occasional puffy vest when dignity required. The suit jacket he had on now was out-of-date but well pressed, his slacks equally tidy. "Here. It's blank but I signed it. Fill it in with whatever you think is fair."

"But you can't just give me a blank check—"

"Do you have the book in the house with you?"

"Well, yes. But—"

"Then I'll take it with me. *Now.*"

He shoved his hands into his armpits and stood staring down at me, his lips pressed in a flat line. Like the rest of his features, his lips were a little too large even when they were tucked tightly together like that.

I was tempted to tear up the check and tell him that the book wasn't for sale—that a man couldn't terrorize his neighbors for twenty-odd years and then start making demands to buy the only thing of value they had. Besides, I wasn't sure I wanted him to have the book. I was just starting to get to know my star-crossed message writers. He'd take one look at those sentimental, heartfelt ramblings and—

"Well?" he demanded. "I'm not getting any younger."

That was when it clicked. If I hadn't been so flabbergasted by the sight of Jasper Holmes standing on my front porch or the dizzying prospect of a blank check with my name on it, I would have put the pieces together much sooner. As it was, I could only stare in wide-eyed astonishment as his words sank in.

He's not getting any younger.

This was undeniably true, but he *had* been young. Once upon a time, he'd even been my age—young and hopeful, his head full of dreams, his heart ready for the same. If my mental math was correct, that would have been sometime around the 1950s and 1960s.

The exact time that bootleg copies of *Tropic of Cancer* would have been floating around a backwoods town like ours. With a gulp, I glanced down at the check in my hand. Sure enough, the scratchy signature grabbed me with its familiarity.

It's him. He's the contrary lover.

"Gimme a sec," I said as I moved inside to grab the book. I picked it up with more care than I'd shown it before, as if I was afraid the whole thing might go up in a puff of smoke if I handled the binding too roughly. I felt a sudden itching to skim through the pages again, this time with a fine-toothed comb, but Jasper was watching me with an intensity that made me itch even worse.

I was pretty sure he knew what was written inside that book—and that he knew I knew it, too.

"It's all yours," I said as I handed it over.

Instead of grabbing it with a reverence similar to my own, he snatched it greedily. He then tucked the book under his arm as if he cared no more for its contents than he did the weeds he pulled ruthlessly from his garden every morning. Now that he'd gotten what he wanted, he turned to leave with the same curt disregard he always showed me.

But for some strange reason, I was reluctant to see him go.

"Wait," I called. He paused but didn't turn, so I decided to shoot my shot. Well, *a* shot, anyway. "How do you know I'm not going to write myself a check big enough to take every penny you have?"

"You won't," he said as he continued on his way. "If you were *actually* a thief, you'd be living in a hell of a lot nicer house than this."

———

"I think you should take him for the full five grand."

Pepper handed me the last box from the library basement and wiped her hand across her brow. It left a streak of dust behind, which blended poorly with her winged eyeliner. After trudging up and down the stairs with me for the past two hours, she looked as dirty and exhausted as I felt, but the job was finally done.

One basement, cleared of its ancient trove of old and unwanted books, the mystery of Jasper and *Tropic of Cancer* sitting unresolved at the center of it.

"I can't do that," I complained as I climbed the stairs and tossed the last of the books into the dumpster. "Even if the copy I sold him had been in mint condition—which it wasn't—it would only be worth about half that."

"Yeah, but you're not counting sentimental value. If Jasper Holmes really was the guy who wrote all those love notes, then the book is priceless." She grinned. Ever since I'd told her about the additional messages I'd found and Jasper's late-night visit shortly thereafter, she'd been practically thrumming with the romance of it all. Pepper might have been a bit of a hard-ass, but she was a softie at heart. All those Harlequins probably accounted for it.

"To think of him writing secret notes in a dirty book like that," she added. "Who knew the old devil had it in him?"

I shook my head and went to the sink to wash my hands. I was once again dressed for utilitarian purposes, but not for much longer. Now that the basement was cleared, it was back to my usual not-quite-a-librarian status. Half a degree wasn't enough to land me the real position. Eighteen bucks an hour and a decent healthcare package were about all I could ask for.

"Who's an old devil, and why are you guys talking about me behind my back again? I thought we covered that at the last HR meeting." Gunderson, our boss and a man who always dressed in a three-piece suit and tie, popped out from behind the checkout desk. He wore a smile to show he was kidding, but neither of us was fooled. Poor Gunderson had never fooled anyone a day in his life. He was both the best and the worst person to run a library in that way.

The best? He loved rules and lists. He was an organizational wizard. And despite his uptight outlook on, well, just about everything, he genuinely cared about serving the community.

The worst? He desperately wanted to be none of those things. In his head, he was one of us: a part-time employee of the library, here for the paycheck and to occasionally get frisky in the stacks. In reality, he was a fortysomething father of three who was so risk-averse that he made his kids wear helmets when they were out walking the dog.

"Don't worry, Gunderson," I said as I dried my hands. "We weren't talking about you." Since he was watching, I was careful to wipe down the sink and add an extra squirt of sanitizer just to be safe. My job security wasn't so high that I was willing to get on Gunderson's bad side. "Can I ask you a quick question?"

"I don't know," he said. "*Can* you?"

I could hear Pepper groaning behind me, but I didn't mind Gunderson's cheeseball attitude as much as she did. There were a lot worse things for a man to be in this world. My mother had dated most of them.

"You've worked here for a long time, right?" I asked.

At that, he puffed up. "Fifteen years and counting."

"Can you remember ever helping a guy named Jasper Holmes? Older gentleman, robust for his age, unpleasant enough to strip paint from a barn?"

"Now, Chloe. That's no way to talk about a patron."

"That's the thing… I don't think he *is* a patron. He lives next door to me, but I've never seen him set foot inside the library. I don't think he believes in community services. Or the joy of reading."

"Or any joy at all," Pepper muttered.

Gunderson frowned to show what he thought of this levity, but he was too interested in all things library related to chide me for showing an interest. "I think I know who you're talking about. He drives that vintage truck around town, right? Has a garden like a page out of a landscaping textbook?"

When I nodded, his frown only deepened.

"If you want my advice, I'd steer clear of that one," he said. "In fact, I'd pack up those brothers and sister of yours and move as far away as you can get. You don't want anything to do with a man like that."

"Why?" I asked. I didn't point out that moving my family of four was not only financially difficult, but laughably impossible. Our roots weren't very illustrious, but they ran deep. They had to; it was the only way we could remain standing. "What's wrong with him?"

Gunderson leaned close. His breath smelled like the celery-infused water his wife packed for him every day—not unpleasant, but not exactly pleasant, either. "You know I don't believe in gossip."

I did know that. I also knew that he didn't believe in Bigfoot, crop circles, or the Illuminati, though he was still on the fence about chemtrails. "But?"

"*But* you weren't too far off about that whole stripping-paint thing," he said. "From what I understand, he's done a lot more damage than that in his lifetime."

I scanned Gunderson's face for signs that he might be cracking a joke, but he looked the same as he always did—a little stern, a little worried, and so desperate to be liked that he didn't notice either one.

"They say he killed a girl back in the sixties," he added in a low voice. "Some girl from the radar base. The reason his garden is so lush is because he buried her on that very land."

4

—

1960

GROWING UP, CATHERINE MARTIN WAS REQUIRED to follow exactly three rules:

Rule #1: Do what your father says.

Rule #2: Talking back regarding Rule #1 will result in swift and decisive punishment.

Rule #3: Please, Catherine, for the love of everything, just do it and stop arguing. Your father has a lot on his plate right now.

Since these rules had been established early in her childhood (one might even say they'd been established *swiftly* and *decisively*), it was to be inferred that her father always had a lot on his plate—which, as Major Gene Martin would have been the first to tell you, he did.

"Catherine Winifred Martin, at what hour do we breakfast in this house?" he asked the first morning of their first day of his new commanding post. It didn't occur to him that since they'd arrived in Colville sometime after midnight, at which point Catherine and her mother had been forced to unpack the essentials and make up the beds, sleeping in would have been a welcome—if not necessary—treat.

"Oh-six-hundred hours," she said, yawning behind her hand.

"And what hour have we reached at this precise moment in time?" he continued. Since they hadn't yet made it to unpacking any of the clocks, she recognized this for the rhetorical question it was.

"Past oh-six-hundred hours," she said. She plopped onto a red vinyl chair at the kitchen table and reached for the carafe of coffee before remembering how her father felt about young women drinking caffeine.

"Stimulants aren't ladylike," he always said.

"I'll make us a fresh pot when he leaves, Catherine," her mother always countered. "Just be patient. What he doesn't know won't hurt him."

Catherine dropped her hand and allowed it to fall in her lap. Despite being late to the breakfast table, she was dressed in a yellow fitted sundress with a full skirt, her mousy-brown hair flared in a neat bob. Her mother was similarly dressed and coiffed, thanks in large part to the salon they'd both visited in Dallas before getting dragged to this rural outpost. From their Dazzling Coral lipstick to their low-heeled pumps, they were identical. The one exception was that her mother looked about as tired as Catherine felt, with heavy bags under her eyes and a tightness around her mouth that no amount of Pond's Cold Cream could erase.

Not that Major Gene Martin would have noticed. Military precision was the only thing that mattered to him. As long as the cottons were pressed and the shoes polished, he was satisfied. The body inside the uniform was merely a means of transportation.

"I'm glad to see you up and ready to tackle the day," her dad said. Since he followed it up by nodding at the grapefruit sitting in front of her, Catherine took it to mean she was being forgiven for her tardiness. "Are you heading into town to take a look around?"

"Am I ever," she replied as she started sprinkling heaps of sugar over the top of her grapefruit. She couldn't stand the dratted things, but her mom swore by their slimming effects. Fortunately, Catherine had learned that with enough sugar, anything was palatable. "I noticed the local library when we drove in last night. You know that cute little brick building across from the post office? I'm surprised they have such a nice one. I hope they have the new Shirley Jackson, but I'm not holding my breath. I doubt they even know who she is this far away from civilization."

"We're stationed in northern Washington, not the Antipodes," her dad reminded her. "It's much livelier than you think. My squadron alone has over a hundred and forty men."

She recognized this as the reprimand it was. "Yes, sir."

"It's a highly coveted position and a great opportunity for our whole family."

"Of course, sir."

"I'll take you on a tour of the base as soon as you and your mother are settled in. You'll like that."

Catherine grimaced, but it was easy enough to pretend her breakfast was the cause. "That sounds fun. Thanks."

Truth be told, a tour of the 760th Radar Base sounded about as fun as stabbing herself in the eye with her serrated grapefruit spoon, but she wasn't about to say so. Radar scanning and cryptography were all well and fine for people like her father, who thrived in an environment where seeking out enemy planes and missiles on U.S. territory was a tense, important business, but she'd never been one for technology.

Give her a good book, some lively company, and—*oh, please, just one*—cup of coffee, and she was content.

Her poor father. He'd always wanted a son to follow in his footsteps. One who was taller than he was, strapping in ways that he'd never be, and interested in things like vacuum tubes and SAGE systems. Instead, all he'd gotten was Catherine: short and slight, interested only in the newest Shirley Jackson, the taste of her morning grapefruit forever bitter on her tongue.

Her father finished up his breakfast and pushed back from the table. "I'd better get going. It's a half-hour drive out to the base. I wouldn't want to be late on my first day."

He leaned forward and dropped a kiss first on her mother's cheek and then on Catherine's. Underneath this affectionate farewell, she could feel him practically vibrating with excitement. Even a post as small and isolated as this one was fun for him, what with the new systems to organize and people to order around. It was less fun for Catherine and her mother.

Her mother, because she was the one who had to do all the unpacking, and Catherine, because she once again found herself back at the start.

How am I supposed to build a life for myself if I'm constantly being shuffled from one town to the next? How do I make friends when I'm always the person who's just passing through?

Fortunately for Catherine, half of that answer was easy. Towns would come and go, and so would the people in her life, but there was always a friend inside the pages of a book.

To the library she would go.

———

Catherine felt a little guilty for abandoning her mother to the work of settling in, but not so guilty that she was willing to forgo a morning's exploration. Especially since she hadn't been kidding about spotting the library on the way in. It was located just off Main Street in an area that included the sheriff's office, the post office, and some other bland government building that she felt sure her father would later explain to her in painful detail.

"Your bike is on the side of the house," her mom said as she tied an apron around her midsection and set about tackling the boxes labeled KITCHEN. "I made sure we pulled that out straightaway."

"You're sure you don't mind my leaving?" Catherine asked, one foot already out the door.

Her mom laughed. It was a bright, tinkling laugh, and the best thing about her. Even her dad, with all his stern rigidity, was unable to resist it.

"If I said yes, what would you do?" her mom asked.

"I'd grab you an Agatha Christie," Catherine promised. Like her, her mother preferred her reading to be grim, bloody, and as full of murder as possible—the only difference being that her mother had the wisdom to pretend otherwise. Catherine's besetting sin—of which, if you were to ask her father, she contained multitudes—was that she'd never been very good at either wisdom or pretending.

Which was why, with a grin and a backwards glance, she added, "*Two* Agatha Christies if you'll be a doll and let me stay out past lunch."

Her mom waved her off with a dish towel. "Then let me see neither hide nor hair of you until three at the earliest."

Catherine didn't have to be told twice. She bustled out and found the bicycle exactly as promised. It leaned against the clapboards, the floral basket affixed and already holding a collection of her favorite tomes, just in case she wasn't able to get a library card today.

The house they were living in while her father began his new duties as commander of the radar base was very large, very white, and very inconveniently located a mile from the town center. Such qualities might not seem like they were connected to one another, but Catherine had moved around enough times to know that those three things had been the top priorities for off-base housing since time immemorial. The size bestowed prestige. The color was a mark of distinction. And the location meant that they remained aloof from the general riffraff.

Fortunately, Catherine enjoyed getting out into the air, her feet pedaling gently as she took in the sights and sounds of what was to be her new hometown. Swinging her leg over the center bar, she veered a sharp right, her eyes taking everything in.

Unfortunately, the town of Colville was…not impressive. When she'd first heard the destination of their newest station, she'd actually cried. Sat down on her twin bed, dropped her head to her hands, and sobbed as though her heart were breaking. On a map, Colville was a dot in the middle of the forest, a nothing place surrounded by wilderness and trees.

Catherine didn't like wilderness. Or trees. When your life was as small as hers—confined to home and family, dependent on the whims of the Air Defense Command and a man who'd dedicated his life to serving it—location mattered. In cities like Dallas and Grand Rapids, she'd at least had access to culture. Plays and the theater, the occasional opera or ballet. Out here, she didn't have anything except a few hardware stores, a feed store, and a tiny speck of a grocer.

She did, however, spot a tiny art deco movie theater with posters for *The Hound of the Baskervilles* pasted out front. Catherine was so distracted by them—of all Arthur Conan Doyle's stories to be made into film, that was her favorite—that she didn't notice the car taking the corner at a clipping pace. She was just about to turn down the street that would deliver her to the library when a red Mustang convertible whizzed too close and set her skirt fluttering. The fabric caught in the spokes, and she was down before she even knew what was happening.

"Don't try to get up," a low, gruff male voice said as Catherine struggled to get out from underneath her bicycle, the wheels spinning almost as hard as her head. The back of her skull ached, and there was a stinging on her palms that felt as though skin had been scraped clean away, but that was as far as she could assess her own damages.

"You went down hard," the man added.

"That's because you ran me over," she murmured as he lifted the bike off her as though it weighed no more than a matchstick. As she watched him gather up her scattered books, she put a hand to her head and, despite his warning, tried to get up. "Do you always take a street corner like you're in the Grand Prix?"

He didn't answer. Instead he pulled out a handkerchief and handed it to her. The white square of fabric was clean and smelled like a combination of soap and pine needles, so she didn't hesitate to start dabbing at her hands with it.

She also peeked up to make a better assessment of the man who'd run her over. If he was any indication of the population around here, then she was in for a much more rustic time than she'd anticipated. Not only was he dressed as though he'd just come down from a six-month stay at the top of a mountain, but he looked more like a bear than a person. His shoulders were wide and his chest shaped like an oil drum; a patchy growth of hair scraped across his jaw. He was a far cry from the men she was accustomed to, the clean-shaven boys of the military, all of them baby-faced and—in her father's squadron, at least—more interested in science and technology than physical strength.

"Do you feel woozy?" he asked with a grunt.

"No." She started to tenderly test her limbs. "I feel like I just got clipped by a reckless driver with no regard for the safety of others."

He reached for her again. "Here, let me—"

"No, don't," she said, feeling anger starting to replace the shaking fear that had been holding her dazed. As much as she enjoyed *reading* about damsels being butchered on street corners and evil spirits that went bump in the night, she liked to keep her real-life body parts intact. "You've done enough already. I can get up on my own. It's just a few scrapes and bruises."

"Your bike looks broken. If you want, we can put it in the back of my truck and I can—"

"What?" She laughed. "Drive me off the nearest cliff at full speed? Thank you, but I'll take my chances on two broken wheels."

He rocked back on his heels and studied her with a lowered brow, his expression so quelling that she wondered whether she should scream for help while she still had the chance.

"Your blood coagulates beautifully," he said.

She gave a start of surprise. "I beg your pardon?"

He rose to his feet and nodded down at the bloodstained handkerchief. "You can keep that. Are you sure you're all right?"

"Of course I'm sure," she said, but with a kind of dazed detachment that made her suspect she bumped her head harder than she'd thought. Had he really just said what she thought he'd said?

"You might want to stick to side roads from here on out," he said. He took a moment to right her bicycle and fiddle with the gears before stepping away. "Colville is a small town, but some of the drivers here still think they're in big cities."

It was then and only then that Catherine realized that the vehicle pulled off to the side of the road was neither red nor a Mustang convertible. The black Ford truck was covered in dust, and the bumper showed no signs of having recently clipped a bicycle. She was just about to call out to him—an apology? her thanks?—but she bit her tongue to stop herself.

She might have still been befuddled from her fall, but his words from before were starting to echo somewhere deep inside her brain.

Your blood coagulates beautifully... Your blood coagulates beautifully.

"Did that mountain man just quote Hemingway at me?" she wondered aloud. Since he was already sliding into the driver's seat by that time, he didn't hear her—not that she'd have expected much by way of reply. Whatever he'd said was probably a fluke, a random combination of words not unlike a room full of monkeys on typewriters eventually churning out the full works of Shakespeare.

But something about the *way* he'd said it, and the way he'd been so careful to gather up her books...

Catherine shook her head and forced the entire interlude to the back of her mind. Whatever the man had done to her bike had turned it operational again, so she was able to swing a leg over and gingerly begin picking her way the last block toward the tiny brick library.

Even if she *had* been the type of girl to dwell on every chance encounter with a man, what she saw would have pushed all thoughts of him into oblivion. There, propped up in the front window, was a sign—and not just any sign. The white cardboard and black block letters spoke directly to her heart.

NOW HIRING. INQUIRE INSIDE.

She gave a small squeak as she propped her broken bicycle against the front wall. Even with the stiffness in her step and the stranger's hand-kerchief still tucked in her hand, she lost sight of everything but that sign as she bustled up the library steps.

How could she care about something as silly as a man when the books were what she'd really come to see?

5

—

CHLOE

"OKAY, THIS IS EVERYTHING WE HAVE that's not checked out right now." Pepper bounded forward with her arms full of old cloth-bound books. She dropped them to the counter with a loud bang—a thing she'd never do while Gunderson was around, but he'd already left for lunch. According to the clock above the checkout counter, we had exactly forty-three minutes before he returned and we needed to get everything back where it belonged. "*The Old Man and the Sea* and *For Whom the Bell Tolls* were in the bookmobile. The rest—*The Sun Also Rises, A Moveable Feast*, and *To Have and Have Not*—were on the regular shelves."

I started greedily opening the covers and flipping through the pages. "And how many were checked out?"

"Just two. *A Farewell to Arms* and *The Torrents of Spring*." Pepper paused and wrinkled her nose, considering. "I didn't know people still read Hemingway. Not for fun, anyway."

"You'd be surprised how timeless and relatable some of his stuff can be." I stabbed a finger at the opening line to *The Old Man and the Sea*. "'*He was an old man who fished alone in a skiff in the Gulf Stream and he*

had gone eighty-four days now without taking a fish.' I can think of at least
three of the regulars at the Acorn Saloon who go fishing every morning
without catching a single thing. They might get a real kick out of this."

Pepper snorted. "If one of the regulars you're talking about is Freddy
Wilson, the reason he never catches anything is because he only goes
down to the river to smoke weed without his brother finding out. I don't
think you'll find *that* in Hemingway."

I laughed obligingly, but my interest was taken up in scanning the
pages for any sign of the two now-familiar scrawls: one that almost
definitely belonged to Jasper Holmes, and one that—maybe, possibly—
belonged to the young woman who was dead and buried in his garden.

Which, okay, was a stretch, but *come on*. If anyone in this town was
hiding the bodies of his enemies, it was my grouchy neighbor. Even if I
didn't end up finding literal bones, I was sure my search would yield a
skeleton or two in his closet.

I could hardly wait.

"I can't believe it never occurred to us before," I cackled as I set
aside the first book and reached for another. "Jasper always acts like my
brothers and sister are trespassing if they so much as *look* at his garden
the wrong way. We should have started digging years ago."

Pepper plucked the copy of *The Sun Also Rises* out of my hands and
tossed it aside. I was about to open my mouth to protest, but she spoke
up before I could say anything.

"There won't be anything in that one, remember?" she said. "The
note in *Tropic of Cancer* said, 'No *more* Hemingway,' so they must have
been talking about reading a different one together. Besides—this is
a reprint from the '90s. There's no way your dead girl was writing in
this one."

I plucked it back out of her hands. "It's still worth checking. It only
takes a sec."

It did only take a second, but Pepper was right. There was nothing inside the book except a receipt for sixteen gallons of gas back when it cost $1.73 a gallon. *$1.73?* People had no idea how good they'd once had it. I'd paid almost three times that amount this morning. Pretty soon, I was going to have to start farming out my ovaries just to fill the tank.

"This is fruitless," Pepper said as she jumped up to sit on the counter. That was another thing that only happened when Gunderson wasn't around, but there weren't any patrons in the library right now, so it wasn't as if it mattered. "Even if our two mystery writers had been talking about a Hemingway they checked out from this library, what are the chances it's still around after all these years? Or even that they wrote similar notes inside it? For all we know, we may have even tossed it out with all those other books yesterday."

I shook my head. "No, I'd have remembered seeing a Hemingway." And probably would have tried selling *it* on eBay, too, but that part went without saying.

In my heart of hearts, I knew that searching an entire library's worth of books for signs of Jasper's torrid love affair was a waste of time. I also knew that there was very little truth to Gunderson's claims of murder. Still, I couldn't shake the feeling that strange things were afoot.

If I were to take my motivations out and examine them under a microscope, I felt sure the findings would come back inconclusive. Part of me was interested for the sole purpose of being interested—curiosity killing the cat and all that—but I suspected these particular waters ran deeper. That Jasper Holmes, a lonely grouch of a man, could have once fallen headfirst into love, and a *literary* love at that, touched something deep inside me. And, no, not because I was a lonely grouch of a woman.

At least…not entirely. It was hard to be lonely when you were surrounded by the endless pull of three living, breathing, vibrant kids. Then again, it was hard *not* to be lonely under those conditions. There was a reason my mom fell into the habit of hooking onto every handsome face to offer her a respite, however brief.

"I still think you should cash that check for something like twenty thousand dollars just to see what happens," Pepper said, grinning in the way that always pulled me back to reality. "If Jasper finds out and comes at you with a shovel, then you'll know he's a killer for sure."

"That's very supportive of you, thanks," I said as I continued searching through the Hemingway books. By the time I was done, my hands were coated in dust and I was no closer to an answer than before. Either my missing notes were in one of the two checked-out copies, or Pepper's hunch about the book being long gone had been right.

"So what's next?" Pepper asked. "I know you. You aren't going to stop until the writing on the wall is in permanent ink."

"I think we need to shift our focus," I said, clicking over into fixer mode once again. "If there really was a missing girl from the sixties, shouldn't we have heard about it before? Especially if she was connected to the radar base? That's the sort of thing that makes national news."

Pepper shrugged. "Who's to say it didn't? It's probably buried deep in the police records somewhere. When the base closed, the whole town stopped being relevant. Even if there *had* been a scandal, it was probably sealed up and forgotten about along with it."

She spoke no more than the truth. Everyone who grew up in Colville knew about the old radar base that had once stood about twenty miles outside town. Before it closed down in the early sixties, it had been a part of the U.S. military warning system that went up during the Korean War. Terrified of a repeat Pearl Harbor, the government had spent a pretty penny putting up warning stations near any and all international borders. The hope was that they'd catch incoming danger before the damage was done.

To my knowledge, the base had only lasted a little over a decade, but it left a mark all the same. Not only was the abandoned structure a favorite hangout for teens, paintballers, and aspiring graffiti artists, but we still had an Air Force survival school in these parts. Apparently, the Air

Force had fallen so much in love with our surroundings—and the many natural hazards, which emulated the worst places a pilot might be forced to land—that they'd decided to set up a permanent training facility.

"Are you thinking what I'm thinking?" I asked suddenly.

Pepper grinned and cracked her knuckles. "If what you're thinking is digging through a decade's worth of microfiche, absolutely. I never get to put my librarian skills to good use anymore. Most people only ever ask me how to send documents to the printer."

I laughed and started stacking up the books to return to the shelves. As much as it pained me to admit it, Pepper was more suited for that kind of research than I'd ever be. In fact, she was a better librarian than me in almost every respect. Not only had she *finished* her degree, but she understood the technology way better than I did. I could stock a shelf with the best of them, but the additional training needed to move forward in our increasingly digital age always seemed to be just out of reach.

Physically. Financially. Emotionally.

I *wanted* to care about e-book lending and online content curation, I really did, but I also wanted to sleep sometimes. Everything in this world was a trade-off—at least for me. Pepper, on the other hand, never did anything she didn't want to. I tried not to be jealous of her, but it was a struggle. She'd actually *turned down* a research library job in Seattle to start driving around in the bookmobile instead. She'd always preferred the close feeling of life here, the way everyone's stories played out on a small stage like an intimate off-Broadway experience.

Which, now that I thought about it, was probably why she'd started hanging out with me back in grade school. Every detail of my life had been on display since the moment I'd been conceived.

The phone rang before I could dwell too much on that depressing thought. Pepper jumped down from the counter and reached to answer it before I could snag the handset.

"Colville Public Library, could I interest you in a book by Ernest Hemingway? We have several in search of a good home."

"Pepper!" I hissed as I kicked playfully at her leg. Pepper was ready for it with a neat sidestep. "What if that was Gunderson calling in to check on—"

"Wait. He did *what*?" Pepper glanced quickly at me before turning her back so I couldn't hear her conversation. I recognized the ruse for what it was: right after I got custody of the kids, I used to catch Trixie doing the same thing. Every incoming call had the potential to be Mom with a rational explanation, full of tearful apologies that would make up for the wrongs she'd done us.

She'd never once called, but that hadn't stopped Trixie from dashing to answer the phone anyway. Or me from wishing there was *anything* I could do to ease the sting for her.

"You'd better give it to me." I waggled my fingers in front of Pepper's face. "Whatever Theo's done now, it can't possibly be as bad as the time he set fire to—"

"Yeah. Uh-huh. Yep." Pepper ignored me and continued with her terse, one-syllable replies. "She'll be right there. First floor? By the ambulance station?"

At the sound of that word—*ambulance*—my stomach turned over.

"But it's lunchtime," I protested. I didn't know who I was protesting to, but I felt it needed to be said. "He should be at school. He's safe there. They don't let any of the kids near the science equipment unless they're supervised."

Pepper hung up the phone and turned to look at me. "It's not Theo this time. It's Noodle." Her lips pulled into a frown so serious that the churning in my stomach stopped cold. "They said you're going to want to get to the hospital straightaway."

The hospital was located less than a mile from the library as the crow flies. Even though I was no crow, I got there in record time.

"I'm here for Noodle—I mean Aloysius—Sampson," I said, breathless as I ran up to the first person in scrubs I could find. She looked to be all of eighteen years old and no more qualified to practice medicine than I was, but her name tag proclaimed her Dr. Letitia Underhill, so she was good enough for me. "He's twelve years old, has red hair, isn't very tall, and—"

She held up a hand to cut me off. Since she smiled while she did it, I found it in me to obey.

"You must be the sister," she said in a voice that sounded as young as she looked. "I'd have recognized that hair anywhere."

"His sister *and* legal guardian," I corrected her, lest there be any confusion. I also fought the urge to put a hand to my head. A flaming head of red hair always sounded good in books, but the real thing wasn't nearly as glamorous. People could spot my family walking down the street from space. "Is he okay? What happened? Why isn't he at school? What—"

"Whoa, there," she said, still smiling. "He's fine. Just a broken leg, that's all."

I felt my knees growing weak. "*Just* a broken leg?"

"Well, his ribs are pretty bruised, too, but kids tend to heal fast. He'll feel like he fell off a cliff for a few days, but that's because, well, he fell off a cliff."

The weakness in my joints traveled to the rest of my limbs. "I think I need to sit down," I said.

"I'll say you do," a cheerful male voice said from behind me. "You look like you just swallowed a ghost."

I felt rather than saw a chair materialize underneath me. Too grateful to care how or why it had appeared, I sank into it.

Childhood ailments and injuries were nothing new to me. Trixie had once hit her head so hard on the door of the station wagon that she'd gotten a concussion and five stitches for her trouble. Noodle was prone to sore throats and got them so often that the pharmacist no longer needed a prescription for his antibiotics. And Theo…well. Theo had, in no particular order, burned off his eyebrows and eyelashes (twice), removed the top quarter of his pinkie finger (he claims it was an accident), and gotten his tongue stuck to an icy metal pole (also twice).

But to my recollection, no one had yet fallen off a cliff. *Especially* not Noodle.

"He's a tough little chap, I'll give him that," the male voice sounded again. This time, it was accompanied by a body as the man squatted in front of me. He was dressed in head-to-toe camouflage, with leather boots up to his knees and a cape that seemed to be made of some kind of thatch. The dark stubble of five days' growth roughened his jawline, his hair color impossible to determine under the knit cap he wore. He smelled exactly the same way he looked, with wafts of bark and earth rising up from his clothes in ways that would defy explanation, if the explanation weren't already well known to me.

"You're from the survival school," I said—unnecessarily, since the truth was obvious for all to see. If ever a man looked as though he trained crashed Air Force pilots how to survive using nothing but their wits and a single piece of string, it was this guy.

"What gave me away?" he said with a laugh and a flash of teeth that looked incongruously straight and white against his mud-caked skin. "No, don't answer. I can tell you're in shock. You'll say something you'll regret, I'll tease you mercilessly about it, and then we'll be forced to tell our grandkids all about it at our fiftieth wedding anniversary. How boringly predictable."

If my thoughts had been in a whirl before, they were downright jumbled now. "Our…grandkids?" I echoed with a helpless glance up at the doctor. She smiled with what I thought was understanding, but the man laughed as though he hadn't a care—or a beloved sibling—in the world.

"I should probably mention that Aloysius has decided you and I are going to be married. Apparently, he likes the way I take charge of a situation. He says you could use more of that in your life."

The man smiled again, more gently this time. It was a good smile, and I was starting to realize that under the layers of wilderness getup, he was inordinately attractive, but I still bristled under it. I resented any and all implications that I wasn't fully capable of handling things on my own.

I was handling things. I was *always* handling things. There was no way I was letting a perfect stranger rob me of the only thing that kept me going.

If the man noticed my annoyance, he didn't let it show. "I didn't have the heart to let him down, so I think that makes us officially betrothed. I hope you don't mind."

I ignored the part where my heart fluttered uselessly in my chest and focused on what really mattered. "Wait. He *said* all that to you? Opened his mouth and spoke the words aloud?"

"We had a nice chat while I carried him down the mountain. I gave him a few pointers on training that dog of yours." He leaned forward and winked—as in, *actually* winked. I'd never seen a man under the age of eighty do that before. "Between you and me and the lamppost, you can't teach an elderly bulldog to do much of anything but what he damn well pleases, but the experience won't hurt Aloysius any. Or Gummy Bear, come to think of it."

I could only goggle at him, my heart still fluttering wildly. This time, the fluttering wasn't caused by the man himself so much as the words coming out of his mouth. Noodle didn't talk to *anyone* until he knew them for at least three weeks.

The man must have taken my shocked silence as worry because he reached for my hands and chafed them between his own before realizing that he was mostly just transferring dirt from his palms to mine.

"He's all right, I promise," he said. "A little shaken up but in excellent spirits, considering. He's lucky I came along when I did. That part of the forest doesn't normally see a lot of foot traffic. He could have been down there for a while before anyone thought to look for him."

"Zach's right. All things considered, this story turned out pretty well." The doctor nodded toward the opposite hallway. "Would you like me to take you to see your brother? He's resting, but I think he'd appreciate a friendly face. He's not too keen on all the bother of the doctors and nursing staff."

"He doesn't like strangers," I said as I got to my feet. As I stood, the man kneeling at my feet—Zach—got up with me. He towered over me by well over half a foot. I glanced up at him and gulped. "At least, he usually doesn't. You must have some kind of magic powers."

"That's me." Zach agreed cheerfully. "A genie someone accidentally unleashed in the forest. Sorry about all the dirt, by the way. I didn't want to waste any time getting your brother to safety."

At this reminder of Noodle's close call, a wash of heat rushed to my cheeks. The man saw it, I felt sure, since my freckled skin made every blush stand out like grape juice on a white carpet, but all he did was salute cheerfully before jamming his hands deep in his pockets. Then he took himself off with a whistle on his lips and a spring in his step, pausing just once to wink back at me.

And then he disappeared through the sliding hospital doors.

"Who *was* that guy?" I demanded of the doctor as she led the way down the sterile hall. Despite her young appearance, she moved with the neat, quick step typical of those with a lot of work to do and no time at all in which to do it.

"Who, Zach?" She laughed and handed me a visitor's badge to clip to my shirt. "He's been an instructor at the survival school for about a year. He steps in sometimes when we're down an EMT. He's the most capable person I've ever met, extremely handy in an emergency, and—in case you couldn't tell—an incorrigible flirt."

She accompanied that last one with a sideways look at me—not that I needed the warning. My life was a small one, but I could recognize danger when it winked playfully at me. That Zach guy had a definite whiff of sulfur about him.

"He saved Noodle's life today, didn't he?" I asked.

Her smile disappeared. The moment it did, she seemed to age about twenty years. "Almost definitely. It's only September, but the part of the forest where Zach found your brother doesn't get much sunshine this time of year. If he hadn't stumbled across Noodle the way he did, it would have been a very cold, very uncomfortable night."

I nodded my understanding as we approached a closed door. I tried to keep a shiver from moving down my spine, but there was no hiding the goose bumps that broke out in prickles across the back of my neck. In this part of the state, "very cold" and "very uncomfortable" were code for near-freezing temperatures and bears eagerly stuffing their bodies with enough food to settle them into hibernation.

Several more questions arranged themselves on my tongue—*Did she know what Noodle had been doing out there in the woods all alone? How far was the fall from the cliff? What on earth was I going to do about all the co-pays?*—but they fled the moment I stepped into my brother's room.

"Noodle!" I cried. He looked so small in the hospital bed, his lower leg in a cast and bandages wrapped tightly around his midsection. His face was bruised and he had a gash above his mouth, his little expression so woebegone that I knew no word of censure would ever leave my lips. Whatever he'd been through had been punishment enough. "Thank goodness you're all right."

I rushed forward to embrace him but he flung up a hand to stop me.

He did that sometimes, preferring to indulge in physical affection on his own terms, so I was quick to submit.

"I broke my leg," he said, and with so solemn an air it almost broke my heart. No kid should have to carry as much of the world as he did—as much as *all* of us did. "I was running in the woods and I fell."

"I know you did, love," I said as I sank to the chair next to his bed. "Don't do that again, okay? Let's leave Theo to do all the bone breaking from here on out. He's had a lot more practice."

The doctor laughed, but my words didn't bring so much as a glimmer of a smile to Noodle's face.

"It gets worse," he informed me.

I didn't see how things could be much worse than a near-death experience and all the costs associated with it, but I didn't say so.

"Whatever it is, whatever's wrong, we'll get through it together," I said as I slipped my hand in his. His fingers lay limply in my own. I squeezed gently. "It's okay, Noodle. It was just an accident."

"No, it wasn't," he said. He lifted his hand away, leaving only its warm impression behind. "I was running away from school. I hit a boy so hard they suspended me. They said I can't go back for a month."

6

—

CHLOE

"DO YOU WANT THE GOOD NEWS or the bad news?"

As soon as I swung open my half-faded, half-painted front door, Pepper brushed past me and joined me inside the house. My relief at seeing her was so strong that I almost started crying.

Almost. The last thing this place needed right now was more tears. Ever since Trixie had come home from school to find me tucking Noodle into bed, she'd been in and out of hysterics. In true Trixie fashion, she'd gnashed her teeth and wrung her hands and otherwise acted out the most melodramatic response humanly possible, but that was only to be expected. In all honesty, I wouldn't have minded a little teeth gnashing of my own.

Fortunately for the household, Theo *hadn't* cried, but he did demand every gory detail of Noodle's mishap, which was almost as bad. Mostly because Noodle had told him. There were some things an eldest sister was never meant to hear. A fifty-foot fall into a ravine and the tumbling rocks that had pinned him into place at the bottom of it were at the top of the list.

"I don't want news of any kind," I said as I ushered Pepper into the living room. The house was even messier now than it had been before, but Pepper was one of the few people I trusted not to judge me for it. "I want a stiff drink and a good night's sleep, in that order."

"I thought you couldn't keep any hard liquor in the house," she said. "The last time you bought a bottle of vodka, Theo swiped it from the freezer and used it to make a Molotov cocktail."

"I didn't." Theo didn't look up from the computer screen where he sat in intense concentration. He'd been building the same castle fortress in his *Minecraft* game for the past three years and showed no signs of flagging. "I was making an ethanol rocket. It's different."

Pepper reached over and ruffled his hair. "I hate to break it to you, kid, but flames are flames, no matter what you call them."

He turned to her with a grin. "It *was* pretty cool. The fire burned in midair, even though you couldn't actually see the fuel. Wanna watch me build my underground lava tubes?"

"Absolutely not," she said good-naturedly. "The only thing worse than playing *Minecraft* is watching other people play it. Where's our invalid?"

I hooked a thumb over my shoulder. "Trixie's in the boys' room reading him *The Lord of the Rings* out loud. I can't decide whether she means it as a special treat or a punishment."

"That twelve-hundred-page monstrosity?" Pepper asked with a shudder. "Punishment, no doubt. Do you really not want to hear any news? Not even the good part?"

I glanced over at Theo, the tip of his tongue sticking out from between his lips in an effort of concentration. To all outward appearances, he was absorbed in his game, but I knew better. That boy could easily juggle twelve tasks at once, all of it processing through his energetic brain at once.

Lifting a pair of cushioned headphones, I slipped them over his ears before leading Pepper to the couch. "He can read lips, but only if he's paying attention," I said. Then, because bad news and I were long-standing friends, I forestalled her before she could speak. "There's no need to tell me the bad news, by the way. I checked my work email about an hour ago. Gunderson already told me how disappointed he is that I walked out in the middle of a shift."

Pepper winced. "You know how he gets about following protocol."

"Yeah," I agreed. "Only it gets worse. His wife offered to take Noodle for the next few weeks while he rides out his suspension."

"Oh."

I nodded and relaxed into the couch cushion. One of the nicest things about having a friend as long as I'd had Pepper was that I rarely had to speak the words between the lines. Like the hasty notes scrawled in the margins of a beloved book, she and I had our own way of communicating. As kids, we'd even had a set of military-grade walkie-talkies that we'd found at the abandoned radar base. The mile between our houses was nothing compared to the range on those things, which meant our late-night conversations about which Hardy Boy we were destined to marry sometimes got interrupted by the people discussing hunting locations or what hour was best to get up and hit the fishing boat.

"What are you going to do?" Pepper asked. She cast a glance at the shut door to the boys' bedroom, where Trixie could be heard reading aloud in her deepest Gandalf voice. "About the suspension, I mean?"

I splayed my hands helplessly. The thing we weren't saying—the thing that didn't need to be said—was that Noodle would rather stand up in front of a crowd of three hundred people and recite "Jabberwocky" from memory than spend his days with Gunderson's wife. Babs was a lovely woman, and their three elementary-aged kids even lovelier, but no matter how many times I tried explaining that Noodle was just reserved, she insisted on speaking to him in an overly enunciated, painfully slow voice that left little room for doubt about how she viewed him.

"He insists he can stay home and take care of himself, but he can't even hobble to the bathroom without help," I said. "Both Trixie and Theo offered to stay home, of course, but Trixie has debate practice and Theo…"

We both glanced over at where my brother was slaughtering pixelated cows with shouts of bloodthirsty glee.

Pepper laughed. "Theo would burn the house and all its contents down before you made it to the end of the driveway?"

I ignored the knot of anxiety that had been lodged in my stomach all evening and focused on Pepper's laugh instead. As long as she could find something amusing in all this, I felt sure I could, too.

"I'll call the school first thing in the morning and see what I can do to get him reinstated. He won't tell me anything about what happened. Just that he hit another boy and the school has a zero-tolerance policy for violence." Even though I didn't think Theo was listening, I lowered my voice to a near-whisper. "Poor Noodle. No wonder why he ran into the woods like a bat out of hell. He once accidentally pushed Theo on the swing so hard that he fell off and almost broke his nose. Remember that?"

Pepper nodded. "Didn't Noodle refuse to come from under the porch for like three days?"

"We had to slip tuna-fish sandwiches underneath just to keep him going. He felt so terrible that he sobbed every time he even looked at Theo's black eye." It was so many years ago now that I could even laugh about it. "Meanwhile Theo begged him to do it again so he could get a matching shiner on the other side."

We sat back then, the two of us thinking through my options and systematically discarding each one. Staying with Babs was out of the question for obvious reasons. I couldn't leave Noodle here alone, and taking him to work with me was equally impossible. And there was simply no way I could afford to call in sick for the next few weeks. Not only would Gunderson take it as a personal affront for me to reject his wife's offer and then stay home, but I didn't have any paid sick leave left.

"What about your grandma?" I asked. "I *did* steal her all those Harlequins, so she kind of owes me…"

"No can do, I'm afraid. She's in Spokane for the next week. She's seeing that specialist again."

"Not—" I began, but Pepper shook her head in warning.

"It's just a routine follow-up. Nothing major."

"But—" I began again. This time, Pepper's warning was more like a threat.

"Don't, Chloe. She'd be pissed at me for even mentioning it. Forget I said anything."

I added that hot brick of frustration to the wall I was currently building inside my gut. Lonnie's struggles with thyroid cancer were no secret, but the one thing the Pakootas family had been adamant about from the start was that I wasn't allowed to contribute to their situation in any way. I couldn't offer a drive to see the specialist in Spokane. I couldn't make a dish to feed the many guests who paid visits. I couldn't even bring a bouquet of flowers unless they were wild and I just happened to pick them on a regular walk through town.

Those kids keep you busy enough as it is, Lonnie would say.

You can't afford anything more, Pepper would add.

They were both right, of course, but that didn't make me feel any better about it. These days, my friendship with Pepper was almost entirely one-sided. I took and took and took—and until the kids graduated from high school and could stand on their own two feet, taking was all I'd be able to do.

The pair of us fell silent once again.

"I could always use my vacation days," Pepper began, but I cut her off with a sharp shake of my head.

"Absolutely not. Noodle's my responsibility, not yours."

I fell silent again, this time allowing my mind to wander to the emergency phone number I carried in my wallet, nine digits scrawled on a scrap of paper that I hadn't yet gotten up the nerve to tell my brothers and sister I'd found in the interlibrary loan system. I hadn't tested the number, so I couldn't say for *sure* that the woman on the other end belonged to our mom, but according to the records, that particular Ravenna Sampson had checked out William Goldman's *The Princess Bride* no fewer than seven times from various libraries across the state.

That had been, hands down, my mom's favorite book. Back when it had just been the two of us, when she'd promised me that we could tackle the whole world as long as we did it together, she used to read it aloud to me. I'd loved the swashbuckling sarcasm of it, the layers upon layers of storytelling that my seven-year-old brain hadn't been able to unravel.

It still sat in the box of her things wedged under my bed. I liked to think that she left the book here on purpose, that she'd wanted to remind me that "Life isn't fair, it's just fairer than death, that's all," but I think she probably just overlooked it when she'd packed. She'd taken her clothes and the family emergency fund from the cookie jar, a single photo of the five of us on picnic at Crystal Falls, and that was all.

A whole life—four whole human beings—left in the dust.

I'd sworn to myself that nothing short of the direst of circumstances would compel me to call her. Although these circumstances were grim, the literalist inside me refused to call them *dire*.

"If all else fails, I can cash the check from Jasper and hire a private nurse," I said with what I hoped was a casual shrug. "It's not how I wanted to spend that money, but I might not have any other choice."

"Ooh, speaking of." Pepper's eyes lit up as she turned to me, one leg tucked underneath her. "That's your good news. You don't have to pack up the kids and find a new place to live. Jasper *isn't* a killer. I poured through every news story between 1950 and 1961—all the years the radar base was open. Not one of them mentions a dead girl, an accusation of murder, or even Jasper Holmes at all. Gunderson is full of hot air, as usual."

Contrary to expectation, I didn't appreciate the reassurance. The moment my search for Jasper's sordid history ended, the moment I'd have to focus on the present: *mine*.

"Technically, that doesn't prove anything except he didn't get caught," I said hopefully.

Pepper grinned and dug around in her pocket. She pulled out a printed page and handed it to me. "True, but I also found *this*. I thought you might want to have it."

I wasn't sure what to expect as I unfolded the page, but it wasn't a grainy printout of a black-and-white photo from the fifties. Two rows of men stood in front of a pile of felled trees, all of them virtually indistinguishable from one another. In addition to wearing the same rough clothes, they all bore the robust, hungry look of those who regularly performed manual labor. A huge two-man saw was propped up next to them, its metal teeth gleaming in the bright patch of forest sunshine where they stood.

"These look like a bunch of old-timey loggers," I said.

She tapped one of the men standing off to one side. "That's because they are a bunch of old-timey loggers," she said. "But check out that strapping specimen on the end. Look familiar?"

"No way," I breathed as I drew closer to the image. Sure enough, I recognized the frowning, heavy-featured face, though most of it was hidden behind a scratchy growth of beard. "Is that Jasper Holmes? And is he...hot?"

Pepper's peal of laughter was loud enough to cause Theo to pull down his headphones and glare us into quieting down.

"I know, right?" she said, lowering her voice to a hush. "Who knew a man like that could've been such a dish? If he *did* kill a girl, it was probably with that smolder."

"'The Neilson Logging Corporation celebrates a hundred years with its latest crew,'" I read from the caption. "I guess that makes sense?

Almost everyone who lived around here back then was involved with either the radar base or timber in some form or another. He had to make a living."

"It also explains why he was having a love affair with some random chick in the pages of a library book," Pepper said. "Try telling me you wouldn't fall head over heels if a guy like that starting talking Hemingway to you. I know you, Chloe. All it takes is one line of poetry, and your panties practically fly right off."

"Pepper!" I cast a look over at Theo, but he was once again absorbed in the computer. I lowered my voice to a hiss. "That's not true. These days, a guy could read me the whole of *The Iliad* in original Greek, and all it would do is make me annoyed at him for wasting my time. If he brought me a trunk full of groceries, however..."

I thought about Zach as I trailed off. Much to my annoyance, a flush of heat rose to my cheeks. I knew, deep down, that all that flirtatious nonsense from earlier had been his way of putting me at ease, to distract me from the fact that I very nearly lost Noodle today. I also suspected that Zach probably didn't read anything except the occasional wilderness survival guide. Hemingway quotes were way out of the question.

Pepper grinned. "I'm just saying. The sooner we get our hands on whatever copy of Hemingway that Jasper and his mystery ladylove doodled in, the better. I'm dying to know what happened between them."

"Knowing Jasper Holmes, he probably grunted and growled at her until she had no choice but to run screaming for her life," I said, but I was careful to refold the picture and tuck it safely away.

"You think?"

"Absolutely," I said. "It's what any sane woman confronted with a curmudgeon like that would do."

7

—

1960

CATHERINE HAD BEEN WORKING AT THE Colville Public Library for almost three weeks when she stumbled upon the copy of *A Farewell to Arms*.

Of all the books that moved through the shelves in this town, Hemingway's works were some of the most popular. According to Mrs. Peters, the woman who'd hired her and who treated all her employees as if they were attending a wayward school for fallen women, it was because Hemingway was one of the greats.

"A master of restraint," she'd intoned in the pompous, ceremonial drawl that was already starting to work its way into Catherine's dreams. "It's what he doesn't say that says the most."

While Catherine agreed with this literary analysis, she suspected that Hemingway's true popularity had more to do with his subject matter. Anything war or military related was beloved in these parts. When a town's entire economy revolved around the local military base—and when almost every social activity involved the hundred or so single men who worked there—that kind of interest was inevitable. *All Quiet on the Western Front* and *The Red Badge of Courage* enjoyed equal popularity.

As did the numerous young men who wandered inside the library to check out books, kill time and, more often than not, ogle the librarians.

"Don't look now, but William McBride is giving you googly eyes from the nonfiction section," said a low, hissed voice from behind Catherine. "That makes the fourth time he's come in this week."

"The fifth," Catherine said with a sigh. She ducked out of the way so as not to fall under the direct gaze of those googly eyes. "You weren't here yesterday, but he came in right before closing to look up something about Egyptian sun goddesses."

Lonnie groaned. She was one of the four other part-time librarians on staff and rapidly becoming Catherine's favorite person in the whole of Colville. Catherine had already witnessed the gorgeous Native American girl put several patrons in their place when they questioned her knowledge of all things bookish—and she did it with such a bland, unassuming smile that they had no idea how quickly she'd shown them to be the narrow-minded fools they were.

"Don't tell me," Lonnie said, laughing. "He told you that if you couldn't find anything in the archives, he'd worship you instead."

Catherine decided right then and there that Lonnie was, in fact, her *most* favorite person in the whole of Colville. Possibly even the entire West Coast.

"That's pretty close, actually," Catherine admitted. "Is it just me, or does he have an abnormal amount of teeth? I swear, when he smiles, it's like looking at the Cheshire cat."

"From what I understand, his parents paid a fortune for those teeth. You should learn to appreciate them better." Lonnie glanced over her shoulder at where Second Lieutenant William McBride stood lurking. He held a book open in his hands as though deeply enthralled, but Catherine could tell that his eyes weren't moving across the page. "Poor guy. He's besotted with you."

Catherine pulled a face and turned her back on the young officer.

Even with all the teeth, he was a handsome enough young man, his features proportionate, his hair perfectly slicked back, his uniform in a state that she was pretty sure would have her father salivating with approval.

Unfortunately, she'd met his like before. She was *always* meeting his like.

He'd be faultlessly polite to her father, flatteringly impressed by her mother, and patronizingly protective of her. Their first date would be to the local diner and maybe a movie at the drive-in a few miles north of town, where he'd have a flask of gin ready and waiting to keep them warm. He'd try to slide his hand up her leg. She might even let him. But at the end of the day, he'd take her safely home again.

Yes, sir. No, sir. It's an honor to take your daughter out, sir.

And underneath those bland nothing-sayings would be the unspoken part she always felt simmering under the surface.

I'd be happy to take her out again, sir. Shall we discuss it over my next promotion?

"He's besotted with the idea of becoming a first lieutenant," Catherine said. She grabbed the returned copy of *A Farewell to Arms* she was supposed to be shelving and sighed. "Unfortunately for him, I'm not stupid enough to fall for it."

She wasn't sure what caused her to flip through the pages of the book in her hand, but she suspected it was partly due to the googly-eyed attentions of William McBride, and partly due to the tidy square of a handkerchief she carried tucked into her favorite bullet bra. It had taken her mother three washings to get the blood out, but Catherine had wanted to return it to her bicycle savior in good condition. After the initial shock of her accident had worn off and she'd settled her nerves inside the library, she'd realized how unpleasant she'd been to the poor guy. Giving him his handkerchief back was secondary only to the apology she owed him.

But first a week had gone by without seeing him. Then another. Now she was on a third. If it weren't for the light pink scars on the palms of her hands, she might have even suspected she'd imagined the whole thing.

"Except I was right," she breathed as her gaze landed on the quote she was looking for. "It *is* from Hemingway."

"What is?" Lonnie popped up to read over Catherine's shoulder. The girl's light lavender scent tickled her nose; yesterday's perfume had been more like an overdose of orange peel. Apparently, Lonnie had ambitions to sell Avon products, and this was her testing phase. "Why did someone underline the words, 'Your blood coagulates beautifully'? And what does it say in the margin next to it?"

Catherine's heart gave a small stutter as she glanced at the message. The words were written in a scratchy hand, but she could still make each one out.

I didn't mean to scare you. I hope there was no lasting damage.

"Uh-oh," Lonnie said. "Don't let Mrs. Peters see that. One time, a kid practiced his letters inside a copy of *Charlotte's Web*, and she made us track down the culprit and force his mom to pay for the damages."

Catherine flipped through a few more pages, searching for another message, but there was none to be found. Just those two sentences sent off into the void—two sentences meant for her and her alone.

"Do you know what it means?" Lonnie asked. "The message?"

"Oddly enough, yes. I do." Catherine grabbed the yellow borrowing card from the front and read it. "The last person to check this book out is someone named Jasper Holmes. Do you know who that is?"

Lonnie's eyebrows flew up. "Jasper? Sure. Everyone knows him. He works for the logging company."

"Youngish guy?" Catherine prodded. "Tall and loose-limbed, a little rough around the edges?"

"A *little* rough?" Lonnie shook her head with a laugh. "Jasper Holmes looks like a nineteenth-century fur trapper who accidentally stepped into a time machine. My grandparents say this place used to be lousy with them."

Based on Lonnie's description, Catherine felt pretty certain this Jasper Holmes was her bicycle savior. What she *didn't* know was why he'd left her a message. Had he known she'd recognize the quote? And that curiosity would compel her to eventually seek it out?

"Wait. Do you think *he's* the one who wrote that message?" Lonnie asked. "Because to be honest, I never took him as the writing type. Or the reading type. We get his kind on the reservation all the time. All they want is to hide off in the woods somewhere, alone with their bad attitudes and fishing poles."

"You remember how my hands were all scuffed up the day I put in my application?" Catherine asked.

Lonnie nodded, her dark eyes rapt as Catherine pulled the handkerchief out.

"Someone sideswiped my bike with their car, and he sort of came to my rescue. He gave me this to stanch the bleeding, quoted that line at me, and then left."

"He complimented your *coagulation*?" Lonnie held up a hand, laughter shaking her body. "I take it back. That sounds exactly like something Jasper Holmes would do. Most of the kids in town run to the other side of the street when they see him coming. They think he's some combination of Bigfoot, the bogeyman, and Jack the Ripper. He's not exactly known for his charming personality."

"Poor guy," Catherine murmured. "He was nice enough to me."

Lonnie swept an obvious gaze up and down Catherine's body. Since she was once again dressed in one of her mother's hand-me-downs, her silhouette a perfectly commercial feminine shape, she interpreted this as it was intended. A hot flush touched her cheeks.

"It wasn't like that," she protested. "It's what anyone who witnessed the accident would have done. My bike was all bent out of shape."

Lonnie grinned. "And I'll bet he straightened it right out." She must have sensed Catherine's growing sense of discomfort because she dropped the grin and nodded down at the book in her hands. "Are you going to write him back?"

Catherine took her lower lip between her teeth. "Do you think I should?"

"Why not? What's the worst that could happen?"

Mrs. Peters walked by at that exact moment, her stern face set in a frown. She was a small woman—both of stature and of mind—her beady eyes magnified behind a pair of glasses so thick they outstripped the bottom of Coke bottles everywhere. She liked decorum and dictatorship in equal proportions, and if it weren't for the fact that she'd given Catherine a job without even bothering to check her references, she'd have found her intolerable.

"Chitchat on your dime, ladies, not the library's," she chided in a singsong voice that fooled neither of them. "Time to lean means time to clean."

"Sorry, Mrs. Peters," Lonnie said, her eyes brimming with mischief. "We were just discussing whether or not it's appropriate for William McBride to spend all his time lurking in the back and catcalling the librarians when we walk by."

"Lonnie!" Catherine gasped, but Mrs. Peters pulled herself up by her virtual bootstraps, gaining a good half inch in the process. They could practically hear her girdle creaking under the sudden strain.

"Is he harassing you girls?"

"Gosh, I don't want to get him in any trouble," Lonnie said. "But it makes me feel so embarrassed, knowing how close he's watching. I can hardly remember my alphabet."

"I'll take care of him right now," Mrs. Peters announced with an increasing air of self-importance. "These young men have to realize that my library isn't a USO show. We're here to educate, not fornicate."

Both Lonnie and Catherine found it difficult to suppress the snorts of laughter this remark elicited, but they managed it. They also moved quickly away so as to avoid the spectacle of Mrs. Peters reducing the young lieutenant to proverbial dust.

"You owe me now," Lonnie said as she rummaged behind the checkout desk. She handed Catherine a pen and gestured at the copy of *A Farewell to Arms*. "Write him something short and sweet. Just to see what happens."

"What's going to happen is either Mrs. Peters will catch me and give me the sack, or this book will sit on the shelves for a few weeks before some random stranger comes to check it out."

"Then there's no harm, is there?" Lonnie countered brightly. She propped her chin on her hand and waited. "You'd better hurry. 'Time to lean means time to clean.'"

Catherine nibbled the end of the pen for a moment before putting the tip to the page.

I'll live, which is more than I can say for the poor C in this book. I'll never understand why all the literary greats insist on killing female characters off in order to redeem a man.

"Oooh, I like it." Lonnie nodded her approval as Catherine blew a light breath across the page to dry the ink. "Playful yet intelligent. He'll agonize over that for weeks."

Catherine felt a spasm of alarm as she closed the book and returned it to the cart for shelving. "I don't want to *agonize* him. I just want to…" She let her voice trail off, uncertain what, exactly, she was trying to do.

Start a conversation? A *flirtation*?

Lonnie forestalled any of Catherine's attempts to explain herself with a laugh. "Share deep literary analysis with a local logger who rarely strings two words together and whose frown could curdle milk?" She tapped the side of her nose. "Don't worry, Cath. Your secret's safe with me. And until then…"

They both glanced over at where Mrs. Peters was leading William McBride out the library doors. The older librarian held her head as proudly as if guiding a prisoner down death row.

"Until then, you can always leave a note or two inside a book about Egyptian sun goddesses," Lonnie said, still with that laugh on her lips. "It'll be interesting to see who writes back first."

8

—

CHLOE

YOU'RE TO KEEP THE PHONE NEXT to you at all times, got it?"

I handed Noodle my cell phone, which I'd programmed with all the numbers a twelve-year-old kid stuck at home with a broken tibia and a badly bruised rib cage might need.

The library, obviously. Our family physician. That nice Dr. Underhill from yesterday. The local pizza place, which promised to deliver to the house on credit.

And after careful and agonizing deliberation, the number from my wallet.

"That last one is only in case the whole world starts burning around you," I warned him. Noodle nodded solemnly and tucked the phone into his pocket. "I mean it. For emergencies with a capital *E*—as in full apocalypse, Theo and Trixie turned into zombies, me trapped inside the library holding back the second wave of the undead, and Gummy Bear foaming at the mouth."

I hesitated a moment before adding, "And even then, don't expect her to pick up on the first ring."

"Or at all," Trixie said as she slid her feet into her shoes and slipped her backpack over her shoulders. I'd warned her ahead of time about the phone number I'd found—confessed my crime, as it were—but she hadn't reacted as I'd expected. I assumed she'd be furious at me for keeping our mom's contact information a secret from her for so long, but so far, she was only upset that I'd uncovered it at all.

She was careful not to look at me as she spoke. "Sorry, Chloe, but I've got five bucks of lunch money left that says the number doesn't even belong to Mom. It probably goes to some automated government survey or one of those places that'll tell you sloth facts for three ninety-nine a minute."

"Sloths can lock their hands onto a branch so hard that they sometimes stay attached even after they die," Theo said without looking up from his giant bowl of cereal.

Noodle winced as he settled more comfortably on the couch, where I'd arranged him on top of about twelve pillows with enough graphic novels from the library to keep him entertained for a full month. He was particularly into the Nightwave series, a gory but surprisingly upbeat collection of books that we had a hard time keeping on the shelves.

"Don't worry, Chloe," Noodle said with a pained smile. "I'll be fine."

Theo scooped another bite of soggy cereal into his mouth. "Sloths only poop once a week, and when they do, it's a giant pile that weighs one-third their body mass."

"You're better off giving Noodle the number to the White House," Trixie warned. She was still avoiding my gaze, still speaking with a bitterness that caused my heart to clench. "Or even a phone without a battery in it. A dead carrier pigeon would reach her faster than one of her kids calling for help."

"The oldest sloth in the world lives at a zoo in Germany," Theo announced as he started slurping the milk from his bowl. "His name is Jan, and he's over fifty years old."

I closed my eyes and did the same thing I did every morning when trying to corral this herd out the door—I addressed their issues one at a time. Sometimes I moved in order of age. Other times I opted for the old librarian standby, alphabetical order.

Today, I started with the easiest and worked my way up from there.

"Theo, those had better be facts you read about on the internet and not the result of a hundred-dollar sloth hotline bill I'm going to be hit with next month."

Theo giggled and tossed his breakfast things in the sink. "I guess you won't know until next month, will you?" he asked.

I assumed—and hoped—the question was rhetorical, so I moved on to the next task. Pressing a kiss on Noodle's forehead, I said, "Please call me as many times as you need today, okay? Don't feel like you have to hold back because I'm at work. Gunderson won't like it, but he *will* understand. If you need anything—anything at all—I can drop what I'm doing and come running."

Noodle nodded solemnly. "I will. I promise."

Drawing a deep breath, I turned to Trixie next. She was already halfway out the door, but she stopped long enough to fling up a hand. "Don't say it. I was just blowing off steam. I didn't mean it."

"Trix," I said.

"I can't have this conversation right now. We're already running late. If I get too many tardies, they'll kick me off the debate team."

"She did the best she could with a bad situation," I said, unwilling to accept my sister's attempt to wriggle out. For once in our lives, we were actually running ahead of schedule. The adrenaline that had been running a nonstop course through me since yesterday was doing wonders for my time-management skills. "I know you haven't forgiven her, and I'm not asking you to, but—"

Trixie turned toward me in full-tilt Trixie fashion, every one of her hackles up. "I will *never* forgive her. Not in a million years. Not if she showed up on the doorstep with a million dollars."

The tight feeling in my chest clamped harder. I was a long way from forgiving our mother myself, but it had been a while since I shared the sharp edge of anger that Trixie held clenched in both hands. I'd learned the hard way that responsibility would do that. All the things that used to fire me up a few years ago—a passion for justice, the absolute certainty of right versus wrong, a desire to go out and follow my dreams to the bright, brilliant future that awaited me—had grown dull and weathered. I'd grown old before my time, and not in the fun way that some women did, turning into eccentric aunts who may or may not be secret witches on the side. Most days, all I wanted was a nap.

"You can't hold on to your anger forever," I said.

"Watch me."

I gave up the fight. I knew, from a handful of conversations with Trixie over the years, that she'd done everything in her power to keep the household going after Mom had run out. Even at age eleven, she'd known enough about the system to recognize that the safest route was to pretend that all was well. As long as the kids showed up to school at their regular times, moderately bathed and fed, the state wouldn't intervene.

For more than a week, she'd kept up the pretense—feeding the boys whatever she could find and walking them the bus stop, making sure they looked the part of happy, healthy children whose mother was just at home sleeping off too many drinks at the bar the night before. I had no idea how she managed it for as long as she did, but I suspected it was the boundless certainty that characterized all her actions.

"You should throw that stupid phone number away," she muttered now. "We're doing fine without her."

"Of course we are," I agreed blandly. The lie rolled easily off my tongue. "But it's a good fallback plan. No matter what happens, she's still technically our mother."

Trixie's look of derision spoke loudly, but I pretended not to hear it and ushered her and Theo out the door instead. Nothing about this situation was ideal, but as I clicked the lock behind me, I refused to let myself dwell on the quiet of the house or the way Noodle's mouth was set in a firm line against it all: the pain, the boredom, the loneliness of the day stretching out ahead of him.

And, underscoring everything, the realization that there was very little any of us could do about it.

———

Gunderson took pity on me and put me on shelving duty for the day. There'd been talk of lending me to the parks and recreation janitorial staff for a few months, since they were short of workers and my government paycheck kept me at the mercy of any and all municipal offices in need of labor, but he must have sensed that I was nearing the end of my rope.

The library, with its hushed interior and quiet efficiency, the books laid out in neat, organized rows, was the only kind of order I had in my life right now. Sure, I might have to check the bathrooms every fifteen minutes to make sure the kids weren't indulging in the new TikTok trend of covering the seats with clear plastic wrap. And, yes, I was the one who had to answer the phones and listen to irate patrons complaining about late fees, but I still appreciated the gesture. Gunderson didn't even hold it against me that Noodle turned down the offer of his wife's company.

I pushed my cart down the nonfiction aisle and groaned to discover that someone had moved all the dystopian fiction to current events.

"This was cute the first time it happened," I muttered as I pulled out a copy of *The Handmaid's Tale* and stacked it on the cart alongside *1984*, *Battle Royale*, and *Parable of the Sower*. At least whoever was responsible for the prank had good taste. "People need to start coming up with better ways of participating in civil government."

"*Psst.*"

The sound of a very obvious, very indiscreet whisper assailed me from behind.

"Psst," it sounded again, this time accompanied by a low male voice. "Come here. I have something I want to show you. It's a library emergency."

I was careful *not* to turn around.

"Sorry, buddy, but that only works on librarians one time. Then they wise up and call security." I pointed at a black semicircle embedded in the perforated ceiling panel above my head. "And you should probably tuck it away before you get caught on camera. That's the kind of public embarrassment that stays on the internet forever."

Instead of the hastened sounds of retreat, the man laughed.

"It's not that kind of library emergency," he said, the chuckle so ingrained in his voice that I suspected he always carried it. "And do men *really* try that? Surely there are more creative ways to flash poor unsuspecting women who are just trying to do their jobs."

With a comment like that, I felt it was safe enough to turn around. Imagine my surprise to find myself staring up into the face of Noodle's rescuer from yesterday—Zach of survival school fame, once again both looking and smelling as if he'd spent the night on a bed of pine needles, though he was much cleaner this time.

"That sort of thing happens more than you'd think," I said, the words leaving my mouth before I could stop them. "The first porn director who decided to make 'sexy librarians' a thing ended up ruining community services for everyone."

A handsome smile lit his face. I only noted its attractive quality because he accompanied it with a flutter of his long dark eyelashes and a casual lean against the bookshelves. That kind of move was so nonchalant and cool that it *had* to be on purpose.

"I don't think you can blame the porn directors too much," he said, still fluttering those eyelashes at me. "You're very cute when you're muttering to yourself in the library aisles."

Now I *knew* he was purposely provoking me. I'd been so preoccupied this morning that I'd thrown on the first clean item of clothing I could find. My tiered linen dress fit more like a potato sack than a tailored garment, and my hair was in a sloppy pile on top of my head. I looked like something the cat dragged in, forgot about, and then decided to drag back out a few days later.

I scowled at him. "Can I help you with something?"

"Yes, actually." He wasn't the least bit discomposed by either my tone or my frown as he reached into a rucksack slung casually over one shoulder and extracted a book. "I came to return this, but I wanted to make sure you knew that I wasn't the one who damaged it. The writing was already inside."

I knew, in an instant, what he was talking about.

It's them. Jasper Holmes and the mysterious C. The Hemingway title we couldn't find on the shelves.

"Is it *A Farewell to Arms* or *The Torrents of Spring?*" I asked, reaching greedily for the book. In my eagerness to discover the title, I gave too much of myself away. Zach yanked the book up out of my reach and tsked.

"Nuh-uh. Not so fast. I want something from you first."

Since this was accompanied by another of those too attractive, too obvious smiles, I dropped my hand.

"Unless that something is directions to the reference section or my opinion on how they choose which books to put on the *New York Times* bestseller list, I'm not sure I can help you," I said coldly.

The ice in my voice didn't faze him. "I know where the reference section is, and I'd love to hear your opinion on lots of different things, but that's not what I meant," he said. Playful lines of amusement crinkled around the edges of his eyes. "I was hoping you could tell me how the little guy is getting on. He was trying to put a good face on it yesterday, but I could tell he was rattled."

"Noodle?" I asked blankly.

"I know it's none of my business, but I always get emotionally attached to the kids I rescue from peril. It's a personal failing of mine." The eye crinkles deepened. "Well, that and my attraction to pretty librarians, but everyone has his faults."

He spoke of Noodle with such sincerity that I was willing to overlook the rest. I also spoke a lot more honestly than I normally would have.

"He's being brave about the whole thing, but I had to leave him home alone today. Physically, I think he'll be fine, but emotionally…" I allowed my voice to trail off. The less said about his emotional state, the better. At least while I was at work. "Let's just say he's never gotten into a fight at school before. Or anywhere. He's the sweetest, most peaceable person I know. He's taking it really hard."

Zach nodded along with so much friendly concern that I faltered even more.

"He didn't tell you anything about what happened at school yesterday, did he?" I asked. "I tried talking to the principal, but she doesn't know any more than I do. Just that Noodle snapped, punched a boy in one of the bathrooms, and immediately turned himself in."

She'd also said that the other boy hadn't wanted to lodge a complaint, and that if Noodle had simply kept quiet about the whole thing, it would've blown over without any follow-up, but that part wasn't worth mentioning. Explaining Noodle's strong moral compass and deep aversion to violence was too monumental a task, even for a man who seemed as understanding as this one.

"Sorry," Zach said with a roll of one shoulder. "I didn't press him for details. In my experience, anyone running through the forest to try and escape the things they've done has a very good reason for doing so."

I blinked, startled by this piece of reasoning. "Even when they're only twelve years old? And when they're so upset they tumble down a ravine in the process?"

"He's tougher than he looks, your brother. I think it'll take a lot more than one fall to break him." He looked at me a little strangely, a tilt to his head. "You, too, come to think of it."

"But you don't know anything about me," I protested. For some reason, his easy air of assurance was starting to seriously unsettle me. "For all you know, I'm broken in a thousand different places."

"'If people bring so much courage to this world the world has to kill them to break them, so of course it kills them,'" he said as if reciting a quote. It only took me a second to realize that *a quote* was exactly right. "'The world breaks every one and afterward many are strong at the broken places.'"

"*A Farewell to Arms*," I said, my words coming out in a long breath. "I should've guessed it."

He grinned and handed me the book that he'd been holding out of my reach. "I don't normally memorize book quotes, but that's what I was trying to tell you. Someone wrote a bunch of messages in the margins. That was one of the sections they highlighted."

The moment he placed the blue book in my hands, I felt a tingle of electricity. Not—as Lonnie and Pepper and their hoard of Harlequins would tell you—because of the gentle brush of Zach's fingers against mine, but because of what I knew I'd find when I opened the cover. The copy was *definitely* old enough to be part of my growing Jasper Holmes collection; the faded cloth cover and gilded lettering belonged to a much earlier era.

"You read the whole thing?" I asked as I flipped through the pages. I paused when I got to the end of the ninth chapter. Next to a line about coagulation, I found the writing that was starting to become as familiar to me as my own.

I didn't mean to scare you. I hope there was no lasting damage.

I'll live, which is more than I can say for the poor C in this book. I'll never understand why all the literary greats insist on killing female characters off in order to redeem a man.

Because you terrify us.

I've never terrified anyone a day in my life.

That's not true. You terrify me.

Is that why you ran away without saying anything when I saw you in the drugstore yesterday?

"You don't look surprised," Zach said, watching me as I eagerly devoured the lines. "Do you know these people?"

"I'm starting to," I said as I traced the words with my fingertip. The bit about the "poor C in this book" stood out the most. Thanks to Jasper's handwriting on the check, I'd already confirmed that the barely legible scrawls were his. But the other writing, the pretty writing, told a much more detailed story. Namely, that the C in *A Farewell to Arms*—the main character, Catherine—wasn't the only C we were dealing with. In fact, it sounded to me like the two of them may have shared a name.

Catherine and Jasper. Jasper and Catherine.

"The quote you just recited," I said hurriedly. "The one about breaking people—what page is it on?"

"I don't remember," he said. "Somewhere near the end. Why?"

I wanted nothing more than to take my treasure to a back room and pore over each of the lines in private, but I sensed that Zach was watching me more closely than I cared for.

"Thank you for bringing this to my attention," I said in my primmest librarian voice. "Vandalizing library books, even ones as old as this one, is highly frowned upon."

Then, because it seemed odd that this level of vandalization would have gone unnoticed for the sixty-some odd years that this book had been sitting on the shelves, I flipped open the cover and looked for the barcode. It was there, but the edges were peeled up in a way that would cause Gunderson to prepare an hour-long lecture on maintaining standards.

"Wait," I said, suspicious. "You checked out an ancient Hemingway from *this* library?"

He shrugged. "The nights can get pretty long out under the stars. Reading helps pass the time."

"And you found it on the regular shelf?" I persisted, trying not to picture this man spread out in a makeshift bed of leaves and twigs, reading Hemingway under the light of a full moon. I wasn't a woman given to romantic sentimentality—when would I have the time?—but there was something about the image that left me shaken. Pepper had been right about that part, for sure. "Not…hidden behind some rusted plumbing or anything?"

"What would you do if I said it was given to me by a fairy godmother who holds the secret to true love?" he asked, a smile lurking at the corners of his mouth.

I let my own mouth form a flat line. "That I don't believe a word you say."

"Fine." He heaved a playful sigh. "Then I found it on an ordinary shelf on an ordinary day. You're no fun."

I didn't dignify this with a response, which was my first mistake. My second, I soon realized, was letting this man trap me in a quiet corner of the library in the first place.

"Now me, on the other hand," he added mischievously, "I'm tons of fun. If you let me take you out on Saturday night, I'd be happy to show you."

A low cough interrupted our conversation before I could reply. This was good for a lot of reasons, most of which had to do with how quickly and vehemently the *no* rose to my lips. Dating was as out of the question for me as packing my family up for a whirlwind getaway to Disneyland. Especially dating a guy like this one, who probably asked out every personable woman he ran into in our small rustic town. But he *had* saved my brother's life, and he *had* brought me this book, so I figured I should let him down gently. At the very least, I could give him a peek inside the hot mess of my life so he realized how much better off he was not touching it with a ten-foot tentpole.

"I'm sorry to interrupt what looks like an important literary discussion, but I need you to cover the reference desk for Daisy's break," Gunderson said. He leveled his sternest glare at Zach, though he needn't have bothered. Zach was as impervious to him as he appeared to be to everything else. "Perhaps there's something I can help you find, young man?"

"Actually, you can," Zach said without batting an eyelash. Well, technically that wasn't true—he winked at me, but only when he was sure Gunderson wasn't looking. "I work over at the survival school, and I've been hoping to build up a reading list of survival stories for the men and women who pass through. Shackleton's expedition, *The Martian*, *Lord of the Flies*, that sort of thing. Do you think you could help me come up with some titles I might not be familiar with?"

I had no idea how Zach knew *exactly* how to win Gunderson over to his side, but I suspected it was all part of the pickup-artist charm that practically oozed out of him. With a roll of my eyes, I turned to leave. As far as I was concerned, these two could have each other and welcome to it.

"Oh and, Chloe?" Gunderson asked. I clutched tighter at the copy of *A Farewell to Arms*, fearful that he might order me to damage it out or, worse, put it on hold for someone else. I had every intention of tucking this beauty away until I could properly pore over the pages.

"Yes, Gunderson?" I asked politely.

"Babs made a casserole for you. She figured you'd have more than enough on your hands taking care of your brother." He smiled in a way that made me feel like a jerk for every time I'd been ungenerous to him. "It's in the break-room fridge. She wanted me to tell you that we're all rooting for him."

Feeling like a villain of the worst degree, I thanked him and started to wheel my cart back to the reference section. I was so focused on this task that I didn't even notice the piece of paper tucked into the Hemingway until Zach was long gone.

In a scrawl that reminded me a lot of Jasper's illegible hand, I saw Zach's name followed by a nine-digit phone number. And underneath that:

I also respond to the bat signal, but don't tell anyone. I wouldn't want my secret getting out.

9

—

CHLOE

RETURNED HOME IN AN EXHAUSTED BUT strangely upbeat mood. Not only was dinner taken care of, courtesy of a cheese-covered dish that both looked and smelled delicious, but the only emergency phone call I'd received all day was from Theo's school reminding me that every child was required by law to keep his shoes on in the classroom, even if he *had* chosen *onychocryptosis* as his Science Word of the Day.

Fortunately for both me and the school secretary who'd been forced to make the call, I was at the reference desk at the time. It had taken me all of five seconds to log in to Google and come to the conclusion that Theo had decided to share his ingrown toenail with his fellow classmates. It took five seconds more to write myself a note reminding me to make him an appointment with our general practitioner. If his toe was getting bad enough to pull out and frighten his classmates with, then it was probably time to get the inflammation looked at.

Unfortunately, my mood took a turn for the worse when I parked the station wagon in my usual spot and slid out of the seat. Even though it was too early for Trixie and Theo to be home yet, Noodle and Gummy Bear were nowhere to be seen.

"Gummy Bear?" I called as I stepped through the house. On any given day, there was only a fifty percent chance the dog would answer, but I had to try anyway. "Noodle? Where are you guys?"

No one answered, and the more time I spent looking around the house, the less likely it seemed that someone would. There was no sign that my brother had touched any of the snacks or ordered a pizza like I'd told him to. His bottle of water was untouched, the television remote exactly where I'd left it. Most damningly, however, was that his graphic novels were nowhere to be seen.

There were only two things in this world that Noodle treasured most: the Nightwave series and that slobbering, useless lump of a dog. If he were to run away into the forest again, those were the exact two things I'd expect him to take.

Not food. Not water. Not a sleeping bag. Not anything even remotely useful to sustain life.

I dashed out the door with my heart in my throat. I had no idea how far a preteen with a freshly broken leg and a rented pair of crutches could get, but he had at least a six-hour head start on me. I didn't like my odds.

Nor did I like how the road stretched off in two different directions with half a dozen walking paths thrown in for terrible measure. In Colville, the national forest was never more than a stone's throw from any given location. For the longest moment, I toyed with the idea of dashing back inside and pulling that slip of paper from between the pages of *A Farewell to Arms*. Of everyone in the world who could track and hunt a missing kid, Zach seemed like the most qualified candidate. I had no doubt that he'd be able to drop his nose to the dirt, sniff a few times, and tell me exactly where to find my missing brother.

"No," I said aloud. I wrapped my arms tightly around my midsection—partly to stop the acid feeling in my stomach from taking over, and partly because I was cold. The fall temperatures were already dropping earlier and earlier with each passing day. "That isn't an option. I'm sure I can find him on my own. I just need to *think*."

That was when I heard the howl.

At first, the sound was only a faint one, and I barely recognized it. Gummy Bear wasn't a dog given to howling in the normal way of things. Not only did it require too much effort, but bulldogs treat the process of creating a howl like summoning a demon. There's chanting and crackling and *way* more saliva than seems necessary. The longer the sound went on, however, the more I realized what I was hearing. And, more important, where it was coming from.

"Gummy Bear?" I called as I ran to the edge of the lawn, where the trellis beckoned me into Jasper Holmes's garden of good and evil. "Is that you, boy? Are you hurt?"

"Noooooo!" came a scream. *That* one I recognized just fine. Noodle's anguish was unmistakable. So was the shriek that followed.

Tearing through a shrub I couldn't identify, I dashed toward the back of Jasper's house. I had no idea how—or why—Noodle and Gummy Bear had made their way over here, but I knew that there was nowhere on earth the pair of them would be less welcome. The glimpses I was getting into Jasper's past through the book notes made him seem *slightly* more human, but I wasn't willing to stake anything of value on it.

Especially not my brother.

"Whatever's going on back here, I—oh! Noodle? *Jasper*?" My feet dug into the soft, cushiony lawn as I came to a halt. There, in front of me, sat Noodle, kingly in an Adirondack chair and with his leg propped up on a log. In one hand, he held a stick with a string dangling off the end, a literal and proverbial carrot bouncing back and forth. A bite had been taken out of it, courtesy—I assumed—of Gummy Bear, who was actually *prancing* across the grass in front of him.

As if this sight wasn't startling enough, Jasper Holmes himself sat in an identical chair, a steaming mug of tea in one hand and a paperback copy of *North and South* in the other.

Of all these things—my brother relaxing in Jasper's backyard, Gummy Bear disporting himself like an actual dog, and Jasper reading a romance—the last one was what alarmed me the most. *North and South* wasn't just romantic fiction; it was also deeply religious and full of saccharine sentiment—all things I never would've associated with this man.

"Hey, Chloe!" Noodle cried before I could say any of the things I was feeling. "Watch this!"

He proceeded to bob the carrot in front of him as Gummy Bear wheezed and snapped in an effort to clamp the garden-fresh vegetable in his hungry jaws. The poor old bulldog couldn't get much air, but that didn't stop him from heaving his chubby body as high as it could go.

"I'm fishing for Gummy Bears," Noodle added, beaming at me. "Did you know dogs can eat carrots? And that they *like* them? Mr. Holmes says it's good for him. It'll make his breath smell less like death warmed over."

"I don't… I'm not…" I cast a bewildered glance at Jasper and back at my brother, my confusion giving away to a different sensation. Shock, maybe? Prostration? I hadn't heard Noodle speak that many words in succession in years. "Mr. Holmes, did you do this?"

"You already called me Jasper once," he grumbled as he slipped a bookmark between the pages and set the book carefully aside. "You might as well keep doing it."

"I don't understand. What are you three doing out here? Did Noodle come to pay you a visit?"

"You didn't cash the check," Jasper replied.

It took me a moment to realize what he was saying. "The book check?" I asked, blinking. "No. I haven't had a chance to stop by the bank yet."

I also hadn't decided on a proper sum of money—partly because I feared Jasper might end up demanding my soul if I took too much, but also because I was waiting to see what kind of medical bill the hospital planned to slap me with.

"You were supposed to cash the check," he echoed, this time with a curl to his lip that made me take a protective step in front of Noodle. Not that my action was appreciated. Noodle let out a grunt of frustration.

"You're in the way, Chloe. Gummy Bear can't jump over you."

"Oh. Sorry." I immediately stepped aside, but the damage had already been done. And by damage, I mean Jasper Holmes had somehow gotten the upper hand despite having kidnapped my brother and his not-very-guarded guard dog.

"You can't leave a boy with a broken leg home alone all day," he said, that curl still in his lip. "Do you have any idea what could have happened to him?"

Yes, I could. Hence the fact that I'd dashed over here like my whole life depended on it. In many ways, it *did*.

"He could have fallen or tripped over that blasted dog," Jasper said. "He might have slipped into shock or taken too many pain pills. Hell, for all you know, someone could have broken in and taken everything you own."

This last one gave me the courage to speak up. "Sorry, but anyone breaking into our house is going to be *very* disappointed. Unless they want a cracked laptop, a set of mismatched dinner plates, or a pile of laundry so deep I think there might be baby clothes at the bottom, there's not much to be had."

I could have kept going, but Noodle gave a low cough. His voice dropped down to its customary whisper. "Don't be mad, Chloe. Mr. Holmes said I can keep him company for a few days. Did you know that he's never read a graphic novel before? He says he likes gory stories, so I loaned him one of mine. I hope that's okay."

"Of course it's okay," I said, ruffling his hair in what I hoped was a soothing manner. My hands still shook as I came down from the adrenaline, but I don't think he noticed. "But we can't ask Mr. Holmes—"

"Jasper," the man in question grunted.

"We can't ask *Jasper* to babysit you. I'm sure he has lots of things he should be doing—"

This time, Jasper didn't grunt so much as laugh. It was a rough, coarse sound, almost like Gummy Bear summoning demons with his howl.

"I don't have anything to do, and you know it," he said. Then, more hesitantly, "Until you make alternate arrangements, you can send the boy here in the morning. I'll make sure he eats and doesn't get into any trouble."

Just in case I got the wrong idea about this generous offer, he made a motion as if to spit at my feet. "I won't do more than that, mind. I don't change diapers, and I won't do any dressing changes. I'm not a nursemaid."

I doubted anyone would ever accuse Jasper of being a nursemaid, but Noodle only grinned.

"I don't wear diapers," he said and then cast an expectant look my way. "Well, Chloe? Can I?"

Every fiber of my being balked at this arrangement. Not only did I loathe the idea of owing this man a favor for, well, *anything*, but I'd noticed a particularly flourishing patch of crocuses and lilies in the shape of a rectangle near the back of the garden. A quote from the burial scene in Hardy's *Far from the Madding Crowd* immediately sprang to my mind.

The crocuses and hyacinths were to grow in rows; some of the summer flowers he placed over her head and feet, the lilies and forget-me-nots over her heart. The remainder were dispersed in the spaces between these.

Now that I knew Jasper was an avid reader, it seemed possible that he'd read the same book and took it upon himself to festoon Catherine's burial ground with a flower for each part of her body. Murderers could be weird like that.

Although it wasn't the best justification I'd ever come up with, it wasn't the worst, either, so I held on to it with both hands. When you were grasping at straws, you couldn't be too particular about how flimsy they were.

But then Jasper ruined it.

"It's not as if you have any other choice," he said with something like a sneer. "Or did you want me to call CPS over this, too?"

His words hit me like a blow to the chest, staggering me backwards. Walking out on three kids under the age of eleven wasn't the same as leaving a twelve-year-old home alone for a six-hour shift at the local library, but that didn't seem to matter to my heart. The guilt I'd been grappling with all day was lodged there as solidly as a stone wall.

"That was uncalled for," I said, my voice deceptively quiet.

"I know it was. Is that a *yes* on my offer?"

I was getting close, but I couldn't seem to force the words out. Giving Jasper the care of my brother was almost as bad as handing Noodle the phone number none of us wanted to call. You didn't just open the gates and invite the enemy in. Shakespeare didn't say it first, but he certainly said it best: That way madness lies.

"Chloe?" Noodle prodded. The longer I took to respond, the more his face balled up in a worried pinch. "You don't mind, do you? I promise to be good and not get in the way. I like Jasper. He doesn't pick."

Noodle's remark gave me pause. My brother didn't like very many people, and he *admitted* to liking even less. And that small concession—that Jasper didn't "pick"—carried a lot more meaning than either of them realized. Every day of his life, Noodle was surrounded by adults who chipped away at him. At his confidence and his courage, at all the things about him they refused to understand. I suspected that Jasper's restraint in this arena had more to do with his lack of interest in his fellow human beings than softhearted sentiment, but I wasn't about to attempt an explanation.

"Okay. Fine. Whatever." With each concession, I felt myself moving closer to the dark side. "But I want to state for the record that I don't like any of this."

"Yes!" Noodle said.

"Awwooo!" Gummy Bear agreed.

Jasper was the last to react. "There's no need to be so dramatic," he said. He came as near to rolling his eyes as I imagined he was capable. "I won't hurt the boy. Contrary to popular legend, I wasn't always the village outcast."

Since this was very much in line with what was scribbled in the margins of the library books, I felt emboldened to speak.

"If that's true, then what *did* you used to be?" I asked.

I could tell I'd caught him off guard. He blinked at me a few times before managing a grunt. "The problem with young people," he said in a tone that oozed sarcasm, "is that you believe you're the only ones to experience life. You think everything that came before you walked onto the scene is just make-believe."

"Is this where you tell me about your friend Beef fighting his way through life again?" I asked. "Because I'm not sure that metaphor is going to work a second time."

Jasper picked up his book and flipped it to the bookmarked section. I craned my neck to see if there was any writing in it, but the pages were as crisp and clear as a new Scholastic Book Fair purchase.

"No," he said and started to read. "This is where I tell you that a librarian should know better. If you aren't aware of the power of a good piece of fiction by now, you never will be."

10

—

1960

JASPER HOLMES WAS THE MOST DIFFICULT man Catherine had ever encountered.

After *not* running into him in the drugstore, she continued *not* running into him at various locations across town.

Early one Saturday morning, when her mother sent her to the feed store with instructions to pick up the tomato seedlings she'd ordered, Catherine saw him buying a dozen bags of fertilizer. His body was bathed in sweat as he hoisted the heavy ammonia-scented bags into the back of his truck. She'd lifted a hand in greeting, but all he'd done was turn around and start hoisting faster.

With the tomato plants perched in the basket at the front of her bicycle, she'd immediately pedaled over to the library and flipped through the pages of *A Farewell to Arms* until she found what she was looking for.

> It is never hopeless. But sometimes I cannot hope. I try always
> to hope but sometimes I cannot.

She no longer felt a twinge of conscience when she picked up her pen and wrote in the margins. If Jasper refused to talk to her in anything but the pages of the book, then the pages of the book it would have to be. Half a loaf was better than none.

For a minute there, I thought you were going to wave back. That was silly of me, wasn't it?

I don't know what you want from me.

Hope, obviously.

...why?

Their method of communication was a necessarily laborious and time-consuming one, so it took almost a week for the entire conversation to unfold. In the interim, Catherine saw Jasper at the movie theater (he didn't buy a ticket), the gas station (he was helping old Mrs. Winters fuel up her station wagon), and once, hanging off the back of a logging truck as it wound its way down Main Street with a full load rattling on its bed. (That time, she was willing to give him the benefit of the doubt. He'd looked so exhausted, he'd barely noticed the air around him, let alone her furtive attempts to catch his attention.)

In all that time, Jasper never waved, never smiled, never so much as nodded at her in greeting. She'd have suspected she'd fallen prey to a *Cyrano de Bergerac* switcheroo, if not for how completely he avoided her. That level of disregard could only come from a determined campaign.

As the daughter of a major, she knew a determined campaign when she saw it. One might even say she was waging one. She lifted the pen and scrawled:

Try chapter seventeen. Near the end.

Catherine returned for her shift a few days later to find a gap where the book was usually found. Her heart leapt to her throat as she scanned for any signs that it had been misplaced or put away on the wrong shelf. It beat even faster when she noticed Mrs. Peters watching her every movement like a hawk fixed on its prey.

"If you're looking for your young man, I asked him to take a peek at the filing cabinet in my office," she said, her nostrils pinched so tightly they were all but invisible.

"M-my young man?" Catherine asked, trying to not to look as rattled as she felt. Mrs. Peters *knew?* About Jasper? About the book?

"I don't approve of him spending all his free time hanging around the library, but he promised to take care of that sticky lock for me," she said. Catherine could almost feel the warning tone in Mrs. Peters's voice reverberate in her bones. "So I'll let it pass. *This* time."

Catherine ran her sweat-slicked palms down the tops of her thighs, grateful she'd defied convention and her father's wishes for the day by wearing a fitted pair of capri pants. If Mrs. Peters had Jasper trapped inside her office, then there was nowhere he could run—and nowhere he could hide.

It was perfect. This was her chance.

"I'll just see if he needs a hand, shall I?" she asked brightly.

She didn't wait for an answer, but that didn't stop Mrs. Peters from calling one out at her anyway. "Keep the door open! One inch for every temptation of the flesh!"

Catherine was careful not to meet Lonnie's eye as she scuttled past and made her way to the office. She was afraid she might burst into laughter otherwise. She also blamed her distraction for why she spoke up before she got a good look at the man squatting in front of the metal cabinet of Mrs. Peters's oversized desk.

"Aha! I've got you now," she called in as singsong voice. Then, with a silent apology to Hemingway for the slight alteration, she quoted from their book, "'*We are all cooked. The thing is not to recognize it.*'"

The man jumped to his feet, his smile so wide and bright that it shocked her into a state of immobility. Actually, her immobility was due to the smile *and* the fact that she wasn't looking into the ruggedly saturnine features of the man who was rapidly coming to haunt her dreams. Nothing about William McBride was rugged, saturnine, or haunting.

"Catherine!" he said. "You're here at last."

Catherine fought to keep her dismayed expression from showing. Years of training in the role of the perfect military daughter helped, but she was no match for the sight of *A Farewell to Arms* sitting askew on the desk behind him.

"What are you doing with that?" she demanded as she reached for the copy. He stopped her with a neat side step.

"It's my cover story," he said with a knowing look at the open door. They could both hear Mrs. Peters tut-tutting to herself on the other side. With a carefully lowered voice, he added, "I had to come up with an excuse to keep visiting the library. Mrs. Peters is starting to catch on to us."

For the longest moment, Catherine's heart stopped beating and all of her *Cyrano* nightmares came rushing back. William McBride was the one writing her those notes? William McBride was the one who made her heart go pitter-patter every time she walked by that book on a shelf?

"No," she whispered, but so quietly she wasn't sure William heard her.

"I can't say I'm much of a dab at literature, but there's no rule that says I have to *read* the books I check out, is there?" he said. "This one looked pretty short, so I figured it would give me an excuse to come back in a few days to pick out another one."

"Wait." Her heart slowly started pumping again. "You haven't read it?"

He picked it up and glanced at the spine. "*A Farewell to Arms?*" He grimaced. "No offense, but I get more than enough military drilling at work. Not that your father isn't a good commander—he is. A great commander. An even greater man."

Relief rendered her more careless than usual.

"So you just picked it up at random? Oh, thank goodness. You almost gave me a heart attack." She held out an imperious hand. "Give it to me."

William McBride may have been a buffoon, but he was no fool. He immediately stepped between Catherine and the desk. "Why? What's so special about this book?"

"Nothing. It's not for you, that's all."

He tapped the cover. "Have *you* read it?"

"Of course."

"And do you like it?"

She took her lower lip between her teeth and considered the question. Truth be told, she'd never been much of a Hemingway fan. In fact, she'd only read this one because someone had told her father it wasn't appropriate for a young unmarried woman like herself. Nothing piqued her interest faster than a determination to keep her away. She'd immediately converted her mother to her cause, quoting the book's literary merit and military accuracy until her father had no choice but to give in.

In the end, the book wasn't nearly as scandalous as she'd been promised. All the love scenes were hinted at rather than shown, and the moral of the story ended up being the *exact* kind of thing her father approved of.

A loose woman killed in childbirth. A man going on to live a full, active, happy life without any punishment for his half of the sin. *Ugh.* Give her Bram Stoker's ...tall old man, clean shaven, save for a long white mustache and clad in black from head to foot, without a single speck of color about him anywhere. Range her on the side of Mary Shelley's ...figure hideously deformed and loathsome.

She preferred it when authors had the nerve to give their monsters a physical form.

"It's fine, I guess," she said, trying to downplay her interest in the book. "A little pedantic, but perhaps that's the sort of thing you like."

William's bright smile dimmed by a fraction—enough so she felt bad, but not so much that he handed the book over. It was like she'd said; he was no fool.

"If I give this to you, will you do something for me?" he asked.

"Of course," she replied, the words popping out before she could stop them.

And just like that, the light was back on in William's eyes. He held the book tantalizingly out of reach. "Then I'd like you to go out with me."

Her heart gave another one of those convulsive pangs. "What? Why?"

"This book obviously means something to you," he said, speaking with the smooth, unironic confidence of a man who had no idea he was about to commit what amounted to a moral crime. "And *you* obviously mean something to me. One date, Catherine. That's all I'm asking. They're showing Gidget out at the drive-in. We could grab milkshakes at the diner afterward."

This was so similar to the bland, unimaginative date she'd pictured him offering that she almost betrayed herself with a laugh. She also realized that she needed to play her hand *very* carefully if she wanted to keep the book safe.

"Sure. Fine. If you want."

"Really? This Saturday?" His face lit up with such an ecstatic expression that she almost felt guilty for getting the guy's hopes up. Fortunately, the blackmail angle stopped her from going too far down that path. A *real* gentleman would have asked her for some innocuous favor instead, like helping him select a new book to read or telling him the phone number for the weather update. Not her literal flesh.

"Saturday sounds perfect," she said with a sweet smile. "And to show you I mean business, you can go ahead and check out that book if you really want it. You might even enjoy the read. It's all about how the main character deserts his post and shames himself as both a soldier and a man."

To anyone else—say, Jasper Holmes—this would sound like the obvious ploy it was. To William McBride, it worked like a charm.

"Nah. Like I said, it was just my excuse." He handed her the book, still grinning like the Cheshire cat floating in a tub of cream. "I was starting to run out of ideas for coming in here. Don't tell anyone, but I'm not actually interested in Egyptian sun goddesses."

"You don't say," Catherine said dryly.

If William caught on to her sarcasm, there was no chance for him to indicate it. A low cough sounded in the open doorway, and Mrs. Peters popped her head inside. From her tightly pursed lips, Catherine was guessing she'd heard that bit about goddesses.

"Is that lock fixed yet, young man?" Mrs. Peters asked.

"As good as new, ma'am," William said with a polite nod that Catherine prayed her mother would never have a chance to see. Her mom could be counted on to brew clandestine pots of coffee and look the other way when Catherine walked out the door in indecently tight pants, but if there was one thing she loved more than anything else, it was a young man who had manners.

"I should get back to the base anyway," he added. "But if you have more work that needs to be done around here—any work at all—I'd be happy to pop in during my off time to see what I can do."

Mrs. Peters tutted and swooned in a way that Catherine took to mean she approved of this offer. However, as she also took William by the arm and started to escort him on a tour of the various rusted hinges and broken bricks that could use a man's touch, Catherine didn't worry too much about it. If anything could be used to keep William from haunting the library—and, by proximity, *her*—it was the length of the library repair list.

As soon as their voices receded in the distance, Catherine shut the door and flipped the pages of the book until she found the end of chapter seventeen—the last place she'd directed Jasper, and to a quote she was more than a little curious to hear his thoughts on.

In a heavy underscore, she'd highlighted the passage she intended for his eyes only. To her relief—and delight—he'd been quick to catch on.

"I'm your friend."
"I know you are."
"No you don't. But you will some day."

If you really want to be my friend, this is the part where I should probably confess that I don't like Hemingway very much.

Catherine barely managed to tamp down her outburst of delight in time. He hadn't actually *agreed* to a friendship with her—or indicated in the slightest that he felt the same way—but he'd returned her message. That was enough for Catherine. For now.

She dashed off a quick answer before Mrs. Peters could return and demand an accounting of events inside this office.

I won't tell anyone if you don't. But if you don't like Hemingway, why did you pick up the book in the first place?

Her hands trembled as she slid the novel in her pocket to be shelved later, but not with fear. This was anticipation, pure and simple. There was a good chance that one of them was going to get caught in this little game, and that the fault for it would land squarely on her own shoulders, but Catherine didn't care.

Life in this town might not contain ballets and museums, but it was turning out to offer more excitement than all the glittering cities and their untold mysteries combined.

She had romance and intrigue. She had a job and something to hide. But most important of all, she had a friend.

11

—

CHLOE

W E NEED TO FIND EVERY OUTDATED copy of *The Haunting of Hill House* located within a hundred-mile radius," I announced to Pepper as I came into work the next morning, my arms laden with the empty casserole dish, the copy of Hemingway, and a printed-out list of all the used bookstores in the area.

Unless I wanted to trek all the way to Spokane, the pickings were slim, but we weren't *completely* without resources in our neck of the woods. Several of our thrift stores boasted well-stocked book sections, and garage sales were always an option. Besides, when it came to holding on to items until they literally fell apart, a town like ours pulled out all the stops. Bookcases became garage shelves before being torn apart and turned into fire starters. Sheets doubled as curtains until they needed to come down to make a faded floral toga for Spirit Week at the high school.

Even Theo had his ways and means. Just this morning, he'd informed us that we were expected to hunt down every back alley for discarded cigarette butts. Apparently, he'd learned in detention (five days, courtesy of the Toenail Incident) that the filters could be soaked in water to create a kind of antirust concoction. Theo planned to make gallons of the stuff and increase our family fortunes by selling it to local farmers.

I wished him well, as I always did, but politely declined to participate in his excavation efforts. Parenting already came with more terrible, disgusting tasks than anyone had warned me about. I wasn't about to add more, family fortunes or not.

"Shirley Jackson?" Pepper asked as she came to relieve me of my burdens. She only grabbed the Hemingway book, so she wasn't much help, but I could hardly blame her. I'd been up well past midnight reading and rereading the notes scrawled in the margins. It was more captivating than a Lucy Foley thriller, which was saying a lot considering how quickly I devoured every new thing she wrote. "Why? Is she our next stop on the Jasper Holmes literary tour?"

"End of chapter seventeen," I said. Then, because I could see Gunderson making a beeline straight for me, I staved him off by handing him the empty casserole dish. "I bet you're surprised to see this again so soon. My family devoured every bite. Apparently, I've been starving them. Please thank your wife again and let her know that we really enjoyed it. Was that cauliflower in there? Instead of pasta?"

I couldn't have said anything better suited to put him in a good mood than if I'd asked him to share his celery water with me.

"The whole family's doing keto." He patted his stomach with the air of a proud mother-to-be. "I've lost eight pounds already. I'll ask Babs to make you a few more to get you through the weekend."

"Oh no. That's not necessary. We're doing really well. Great, actually." I spat the words out like a machine gun. "Please don't ask your wife to put herself out on our account. We wouldn't be able to enjoy the food."

"She only wants to help," Gunderson said, a little hurt. "We all do."

"It's no use, Gunderson," Pepper said, barely glancing up from the book. I could see the handwriting from here, but Gunderson didn't seem to notice. "The only thing more difficult than getting Chloe to accept a helping hand is getting Chloe to admit that she needs one in the first place."

"Says the woman who refuses to let me visit her ailing grandmother."

"Oh, you can visit," Pepper said without missing a beat. "You just aren't allowed to bring anything with you when you come. By the way, Gunderson, she's really enjoying the juice press you guys got for her. She's not sure it's doing anything about her thyroid, but she's obsessed with sticking all the kitchen scraps in there and seeing what pops out. Yesterday, she made us a potato peel and onion juice that weirdly tastes like hash browns."

"That's not what we meant—" Gunderson began, but he gave up the fight with a sigh. "I'm glad she's getting some use out of it."

"How is this fair?" I cried.

Pepper turned a purposely obtuse gaze at me. "Did you want some of the hash brown juice? I'll have her whip up an extra batch and bring it in tomorrow. I think you have drink it fresh, though, or the potato starts turning a weird shade of brownish-gray. You should ask Theo. I bet he knows why."

"Pepper," I said.

"Chloe," she replied.

"Gunderson," Gunderson said. He grinned and added, "I was feeling left out."

Now it was my turn to give up the fight. I wasn't nearly as gracious about it as he was, though. "Fine. Yes, Pepper, I'll take some weird juice if she needs to unload it, but I can't promise to drink any. And yes, Gunderson, a few more casseroles would be wonderful. I don't want Babs to bend over backwards, but if she—"

"Say no more," he said as he turned to leave, the casserole dish clutched to his chest. "She'll be so excited. She has this new egg roll in a bowl recipe she's been dying to try."

We watched him go—me with relief, Pepper with a knowing grin.

"That's not the route I'd have taken, but it worked. Was the food really good, or did you just say all that to get rid of him?"

"It was delicious," I said, still feeling annoyed. "But that's not the point. Pepper, I know how to accept help."

"Sure, you do."

"I literally exist on a combination of GoFundMe campaigns and state assistance."

"Your last GoFundMe was to get enough money to fix Theo's broken molar, and you closed it because he decided to pull the tooth out with a pair of pliers and save everyone the trouble. That's not existing. That's barely squeaking by."

As Theo still had that tooth in a jar and liked to show it off anytime he was accused of not doing his part to help the family, Pepper wasn't wrong. Too bad for her, I had a counterargument ready to go.

"If I'm so bad at accepting help, then why did I agree to let Jasper babysit Noodle for the foreseeable future?" I asked. At her sudden gasp, I laughed. "That's right. You heard me correctly. I handed my beloved brother over to the meanest man in the world, and I did it without regret. *That's* how desperate I am. *That's* how willing to accept a helping hand."

Instead of the capitulation I'd hoped for, Pepper tossed me the book. "You're such a bad liar. You don't think Jasper is mean at all. You kind of love him. You and this Catherine chick both have it *bad*."

"You found the passage? You see what I mean about Shirley Jackson?" I was so excited I could barely keep the vibration out of my voice. "I'm almost certain *The Haunting of Hill House* is the next piece of the puzzle, but I already checked the library database. We haven't carried any copies of it for years."

"I found the passage," Pepper agreed. "But if you and Jasper are besties now, I don't see why you can't just talk to him about it. If you want to know the ending to his romance, all you have to do is ask."

"Are you kidding? That's the worst idea I've ever heard." I could hardly believe that Pepper—romantic, intelligent, literary Pepper—didn't see things as clearly as I did. "He's every brokenhearted book curmudgeon come to life. Archibald Craven from *The Secret Garden*? Heathcliff from *Wuthering Heights*? Arthur McLachlan from *The Lonely Hearts Book Club*? Come on, Pepper. I taught you better than that. He obviously suffered a terrible romantic tragedy in his youth, and he's spent his whole miserable life trying—and failing—to get over it. It's why he's so unhappy now. Maybe she broke his heart. Maybe she really did die—not from murder, obviously, but the normal way."

"You sound awfully gleeful about the prospect of your beloved C kicking the bucket."

At the thought of such an untimely end for a woman I was rapidly becoming obsessed with, a pang of guilt assailed me. As strongly as it tugged, however, it was no match for the curiosity that was taking over all my other worries. It had been so long since I'd felt excitement—or anything other than stomach-churning, helpless anxiety—that I found myself falling under its spell.

"Fine," I capitulated. "Maybe she's alive and pining for her lost love somewhere, and all I want to do is reunite them in their golden years."

Pepper's only response to this was a flat, sarcastic stare, so I flipped open the book and read the words that were already imprinted on my heart.

If you really want to be my friend, this is the part where I should probably confess that I don't like Hemingway very much.

I won't tell anyone if you don't. But if you don't like Hemingway, why did you pick up the book in the first place?

I plead the Fifth.

Only mobsters and politicians do that.

Fine. Someone recommended it to me.

Who? A librarian?

You're very nosy.

And you're very cagey. I bet it was L. She likes sappy, dramatic books. She even likes this one.

It wasn't L. And it isn't sappy and dramatic. It's supposed to be romantic.

Romantic? _Romantic_? If Hemingway hadn't killed C off at the end, their love story would have been doomed. F is a selfish deserter who would have gotten tired of C as soon as the war ended. Poor C would have had to go on to raise her child all by herself. In the 1920s, a fallen woman with no way to support herself. That's not a romance. It's a tragedy.

At this point, their communication had gone on for so long that I was forced to turn the page to keep reading. I had no idea how often this book switched hands or how much time passed between each message, but the well-thumbed pages made me think it had been a lengthy endeavor.

Okay. I get it. You don't like love stories.

And you do? What's your favorite book?

Can I plead the Fifth again?

Only if you promise to wave at me the next time I see you in public.

There. I did it. Happy now?

Getting there. I liked that shirt you were wearing. It brings out the color in your eyes.

Compliments weren't part of the deal.

Then don't wear a blue shirt the next time I see you. If you won't tell me your favorite book, how are we supposed to pick what we're going to read next? Mrs. P is starting to get suspicious of how much time I'm spending near this shelf.

I don't know... What's your favorite book?

Right now? Guess.

Pride and Prejudice?

Ew. Be serious.

Fine. Mysteries of Udolpho.

Getting warmer. I've always loved a good Gothic... Bonus points if it's modern. Horror is so much scarier when it has a possibility of being real. SJ, for *example, knows how to strike the fear of God in a girl.*

Oh, geez. I'm not reading that one. It's too scary.

Did you guess? Good boy. But I should warn you ahead of time...it's not scary. It's terrifying.

Wait. Why aren't you saying anything?

J? J???

Fine. You win. Let's read the terrifying one.

But I thought you didn't like terrifying things?

...I'm starting to change my mind.

And that was where it ended. No more messages, no more literary criticisms, no more developments about Jasper's blue shirt and how it brought out the color in his eyes. Since I'd seen the messages in *Tropic of Cancer*, I knew that things between them must have progressed to the point where they started meeting in public and—1960s sensibilities notwithstanding—discussed things like love and lice and lying down in bed together.

I wanted to fill in those gaps. I *needed* it. More than a blank check. More than all the casseroles Babs could muster. More, even, than a faded phone number I didn't have the nerve to call.

"This is really important to you, isn't it?" Pepper asked me, her head tilted as she watched me sigh and clutch the book to my chest. Needless to say, I wouldn't be putting this back on the library shelf—not that anyone would miss it. I'd tried scanning the book to get a glimpse of its checkout history, but for some reason, the battered barcode wasn't in our system.

"I have to know what happened," I said.

She pursed her lips. "He won't like it."

I didn't have to ask who she meant. "I'll give Jasper the whole collection when I'm done gathering it. Word of a Sampson."

"He won't like that, either. He'll know you read everything."

"Then I'll hide it from him and spend the rest of my life making sure it stays hidden from everyone else in existence, too."

"Fine," she said. "I'll help you."

I was so relieved to hear those words from Pepper's mouth that I failed to note the way she held up her one hand in warning.

"But only if you fill out that check for the full five thousand dollars and take it to the bank during your lunch break."

As if I could do that *now*. "Pepper, that's not fair! I just told you that Jasper offered to babysit Noodle for as long as I need him. I can't accept both his generosity and his money. It's too much."

Her lips pursed even tighter. "Then you have to let me call in sick or sign over some of my vacation days to pitch in."

I shook my head, feeling my heart sink with each twist and turn. I knew that look on Pepper's face. That was her determined face, her I-will-not-be-crossed face.

"You need those days for your grandmother," I insisted.

"You have to give me *something*, Chloe," Pepper said. "I'm getting exhausted just watching you try to carry the whole weight of the world on your shoulders. Isn't there anyone you can call to lend you a helping hand? Some unknown hero waiting in the wings?"

Something about her phrasing—that unknown hero, a man just waiting for me to send out a call—caused me to fire up. My instinct was to ignore that warm, liquidy sensation, to push it down until my stomach acid consumed it, but I didn't. How could I, when I was clutching a bona fide romance to my chest? I didn't believe in True Love™, and if I had anything to say about it, I never would, but even my cold dead heart felt a pitter-pattering starting to take flight behind my rib cage.

"You mean like someone who answers to the bat signal?" I asked. "I actually do know a guy like that."

Pepper laughed. "I was thinking more along the lines of your mother, but that works, too. In fact, if it's who I'm thinking of, he'll work very nicely indeed."

12

—

CHLOE

Y OU KNOW, WHEN YOU AGREED TO go out with me, this wasn't the intimate evening I had in mind."

I had no idea how Zach managed it, but he looked as much at home at our local bowling alley, Copper Bowl, as he did a hospital, the library, and the great outdoors. Instinct warned me that he did that everywhere—looked good and wholly at ease, his large form relaxing into the seat as he draped an arm *almost* over the shoulders of the woman he was with at the time—so I was careful not to dwell too much on the heat rising off his bared forearm.

"Yesss! Strike!" Theo came dashing up to us, his hair plastered to his forehead with sweat. "That makes two in a row for me. Don't forget to write it down. Chloe, are you writing it down?"

"I'm the one keeping score," Noodle said with a shy look up at Zach. He tapped his small stub of a pencil against the sheet in front of him. "Am I doing it right?"

Zach glanced briefly over it before nodding. "Perfect. You're a natural scorekeeper. Remind me to take you with me next time I hit the horse races."

"You go to horse races?" Noodle asked.

"Will you take me?" Theo asked before Zach had a chance to answer. "I've always wanted to be a jockey. Hiyah! Giddyup!"

"Nah. You're too tall to be a jockey. They like 'em small and compact like Aloysius here."

"I'm small and compact, too," Trixie said from her seat on the other side of the lane. She batted her eyelashes in a way that made me lose all hope that we'd get out of this evening alive.

Since the moment Zach had pulled up to our house, surprised but not dismayed to find that he wouldn't be taking just one Sampson out for the night, but all four of us, Trixie had decided she was *in love*. Any man, she'd said, who could (a) accept the entire Sampson clan with little more than a blink, and (b) call Noodle by his given name and get away with it, was clearly a hero of the highest order. I was no fifteen-year-old schoolgirl with more brains than common sense, but I was inclined to agree.

However, I was also determined not to show it.

"There's still time for you to run," I told Zach, but not before shooting a warning glare at Trixie. She feigned having something stuck in the long wings of her fake eyelashes and therefore pretended not to see. "Although I *did* warn you that I wasn't a cheap or easy date."

Zach's whole body rumbled with suppressed laughter. "I thought that meant you'd order the nachos with extra jalapeños."

"They have nachos here?" Theo asked. He, too, turned his eyes toward Zach and batted them dangerously. "I'm awful hungry, Chloe. Can't we get an order? To share?"

Trixie gave an audible scoff. "The only thing you know how to share is germs."

"That's not true. I let you use my special dandruff shampoo, don't I?"

"I don't have dandruff!" Trixie flushed bright red to the roots of her hair—which, yes, had a tendency to flake whenever the weather got too dry. "I like the way your shampoo smells, that's all."

"That's the zinc pyrithione, and it doesn't smell good. It smells like wet Gummy Bear." Theo turned to Zach with triumph. "That's because it's killing all the head fungus. I have fungus on both my head and my feet. It's all over me. Trixie, too, but she likes to pretend it's just a rash."

"I can't believe this is happening to me," Trixie moaned as she slunk lower in her seat. "Chloe, can't you make him stop?"

I dug in my purse until I found a handful of change. Most of it was pennies and nickels, and even then they had some kind of unmentionable goo on them, but Theo could work that out later.

"Here," I said, pouring the change into his hand. "Take your fungus to go play some arcade games. I'm sure it would enjoy going head-to-head with you for a few rounds of *Ms. Pac-Man*."

"My fungus prefers *Rampage*, but whatever," Theo said.

"Make him take Noodle," Trixie complained. "Then we can have an actual adult conversation."

"I'm making him take all of you," I said with another of those stern warnings. She forgot to blink that time, so she caught the full weight of it. I threw caution to the wind and my last ten dollar bill into her hand. "Get the nachos. Get the jalapeños. Have a contest to see who can eat the most in sixty seconds. I don't care as long as you don't come back for at least twenty minutes. You're giving me a headache."

Trixie groaned but grabbed Noodle's crutches and helped him to his feet. "Come on, Noodle. I can tell when we're not wanted."

"And I was trying to be so subtle about it, too," I said, laughing. She shot me a look that indicated she was planning to put her all her newfound debate skills to use later, but she was nothing if not a good sport. Besides, she knew as well as I did that Zach was only on loan to us for a short time. Any minute now, he was going to realize what he'd agreed to and go running back to his hills.

"This is the most fun I've had in a long time," he said, his arm still draped in that casual, carefree way that was so close to touching my shoulder. "Thanks for letting me be a part of it. I had no idea that families like yours existed in the real world."

I took this for the insult I felt sure it was. "You mean dysfunctional, hell-born babes who are too smart for their own good? Yeah. They can be a real handful. Feel free to abandon them before they get too attached."

"Before *they* get attached, or before you do?" he asked. He must have seen my Trixie-like blush because he grinned and added, "Uh-oh. On a scale of one to lamprey, how stuck are you? I feel like I should prepare accordingly."

"I know this isn't what you had in mind when you gave me your phone number," I said, refusing to rise to the bait. "But I really needed the night out, and unfortunately, we're a package deal."

He shrugged in a careless way that felt more authentic than any number of reassurances might do. "I don't mind. I've only read about families like yours in books."

"*Which* books?" I asked warily.

He raised his hands in a laughing gesture of surrender. "Only good ones, I promise. *Little Women*, maybe, or *I Capture the Castle*."

"You've read both of those?"

"I'm not just a pretty face, Sampson. I told you—the nights get long out on the mountain. If I didn't have books to while away the hours, I'd go full Robinson Crusoe out there." He paused. "I check out books at the library all the time, but you're usually too busy to notice me. Once, I read the first page of every single book in the True Crime section hoping to get your attention."

I didn't buy this any more than I bought his other nonsense. "Our True Crime section is only like eight books."

"Well, I had a team coming in from Fairchild, so time was tight. I'll linger in Westerns next time. That should keep me on-site for at least four hours. People around here seem to really love their cowboys."

I bit down on my lip to keep from laughing out loud. It was no secret that our Louis L'Amour reading population outnumbered most of the libraries in the country. We were a horse-loving people. "You've really read *Little Women*?"

"I'm a Jo March fanboy," he said solemnly.

"And *I Capture the Castle*?"

"Couldn't put it down," he vowed.

"What about *The Haunting of Hill House*?" I asked, unable to resist.

His brow wrinkled in an effort of concentration. Like most of his other expressions, this one seemed calculated to elicit a reaction from parts of my body wholly unaffiliated with books, libraries, and men who desperately needed a shave. "Why that one?"

I aimed for a nonchalant shrug, but I didn't quite stick the landing. "Just a thought."

His gaze stayed on me so long that I was starting to fear there must be something stuck in my teeth. "Wait. It doesn't have anything to do with it being a modern-day Gothic from the fifties written by a certain SJ, does it?"

I gasped aloud, equal parts annoyed and delighted that he'd worked out the same clues as me. "You mean you *knew*? And you didn't say anything?"

He held up both hands in a gesture of surrender. "I didn't know anything until this exact moment. I saw the same notes as you, but I didn't piece them together until you said something." He paused only a moment before adding, "Does that mean your two scribblers kept writing in *The Haunting of Hill House*? Their little love notes? Can I see?"

I could have kissed him for his easy reading of the situation. Truth be told, I could have kissed him for a lot more than that, but I wasn't going to. I'd already lured him out on false pretenses for a date with my three younger siblings—a privilege he'd cheerfully paid for, and with such a convincing air of good grace that I *almost* suspected him of meaning it.

"I wish," I said. "I haven't been able to track that copy down. We don't carry it at the library, and all the used bookstores I've called only have recent editions on their shelves. I *might* be able to find it at a thrift store or estate sale, but that's like searching for a needle in a haystack— without knowing for sure whether or not the needle even exists in the first place."

"Damn. That's rough. And there's nowhere else it could be hidden?"

"Well, there is *one* place…" My nose wrinkled as I considered a final option. *Jasper Holmes.* If my neighbor was willing to pay five grand per copy for the books that he and his lost Catherine had written in, then there was a good chance he was sitting on that particular one—possibly even that he'd been sitting on it for decades. "Can I trust you with a secret?"

Zach lifted his hand in an unironic Boy Scout salute. Because *of course* Zach would have been a Boy Scout on top of everything else. He'd probably carved his Pinewood Derby cars by hand and painted them with crushed wild berries and fermented lichens.

"I'm a vault," he said. "I carry more secrets than the presidential archives."

"Why do I get the feeling you're messing with me again?"

"Because you're a cynic. A *cute* cynic, but still." At my sudden squeak, he laughed and crinkled his eyes at me again. "You do know what I do for a living, right?"

Grateful for a chance to use my voice for something other than girlish nonsense, I was quick to answer. "Yeah. You contract with the Air Force to provide wilderness survival training to their pilots. Like Bear Grylls but with government clearance."

"Nineteen days," he said without losing a single crinkle. "That's how long I get my hands on each trainee. Nineteen days of grueling, labor-intensive work. Nineteen cold dark nights. Nineteen sunrises and sunsets."

I nodded along, finding myself mesmerized by the way the words were taking shape on his lips.

"You'd be surprised what happens to people after a few days living under those kinds of conditions," he continued. "It's like plugging into a different reality—one where the bullshit just falls away. You eat and you struggle. You make it through each moment, hoping it won't be your last. And when you finally lie down for the night, you turn to the person next to you and say what's in your heart. You don't have the energy for anything else."

I didn't say anything for the simple reason that I *wasn't* surprised. Maybe my daily struggle wasn't a life-and-death one, but it was close. Juggling the lives of three children, each one of them headstrong and brilliant, took every scrap of energy I had. I made it through each moment, hoping I wasn't making their lives worse, and when I finally lay down for the night, I turned to…what, exactly? An empty bed? A flattened pillow? A realization that with everything my heart longed to say, there wasn't a sole living person who wanted to hear it?

"I know you think I come on a little strong, but it's the nature of the beast," he said with an apologetic shrug. "I forgot how to pretend a long time ago. When you've heard as many life stories as I have—the mistakes and the regrets, the missed connections and wasted opportunities—you learn to just go for it. I like you, and I like your family. I'm interested in seeing more of both. I don't see any reason to pretend otherwise."

If I'd been a frank, ruggedly handsome mountain man with the best smile in the world, I might have been able to reply in kind. As an underpaid not-quite-a-librarian college dropout who was holding her family together using nothing but carefully rotating credit card balances and sheer force of will, I changed the subject.

"You must be an only child," I said.

He looked at me through quizzically teasing eyes. "What makes you say that?"

"If you had siblings, then you wouldn't spend an evening with mine and want to repeat the experience. The only charm they have is that of novelty."

"Don't forget the charm of an older sister who's determined not to make this easy on me," he pointed out. He heaved a playful sigh. "But you're right. I'm the only child of two only children. Life doesn't get much bleaker than that."

At that, I felt a flash of triumph—and a stab of something else, something like pity. My siblings were a trial and a menace, but they were everything to me. I couldn't imagine a world without Trixie's determination to cut a swath straight through it, Theo's blithe disregard for convention, or Noodle's gentle acceptance of it. I couldn't imagine a life where I woke up alone in that house without their noise and their joy to get me up out of bed.

Sometimes, I wondered if my mom felt that, too—the people she'd left behind, the children she'd been unwilling to see as anything but a burden—or if all she felt was free.

"That sounds lonely," I said.

"It was. It is."

A shout of laughter came from the direction of the arcade games. We both glanced over to find Theo tipping a pinball machine so far on its side that it was in danger of falling on top of him.

I sighed. "You can borrow mine whenever you want them. Free of charge."

"As long as you come with them, I'm in," he said. I was so flustered by this that I failed to notice when he shifted position. His hand brushed lightly against my shoulder, pushing aside a strand of my hair. "Does this mean you aren't going to tell me the secret?"

"The secret?" I echoed, distracted by that hand and how close it was to the exposed skin of my neck. "Oh. Yeah. That."

"You made it sound pretty juicy, like you know where the copy of *The Haunting of Hill House* might be."

I was so grateful to have something—anything—else to focus on that I ended up blurting out more than I intended. "It's our next-door neighbor, Jasper. Jasper Holmes. He's this horrible, grouchy old man who steals all our Frisbees and soccer balls and gets mad if we accidentally step on one of his roses."

"He steals Frisbees? The nerve."

"You laugh, but he's been my personal white whale for longer than I can remember. Only get this—just last week, I finally bagged him."

Zach put a hand over his chest and gave a mock swoon. "*Moby Dick* references? Be still, my beating heart."

I nudged him with my hip until my thigh pressed up against his. And then, inexplicably, I left it there.

"This is serious," I said. "It all started when I found a ratty old copy of *Tropic of Cancer* down in the library basement. It's this dirty book that—"

"There's no need to explain *Tropic of Cancer* to me," he interrupted, his hands up in a gesture of surrender. "I spend half my life alone on a mountain, remember? If there's even one mention of a marital bed inside a piece of literature, I've read it, placed it under my pillow, and let it carry me off to dreamland."

A burst of heat rose to the surface of my skin. "No decent human being admits to reading that book, let alone enjoying it."

"Yet here we are, discussing it like two hot-blooded, consenting adults." He took pity on my flaming cheeks and pulled his leg away from mine. Only when the press of his thigh was gone could I breathe normally again. "Okay, you found a copy of *Tropic of Cancer*. So what? *Fifty Shades of Grey* is way more descriptive, and people read that at their kids' piano recitals. In this day and age, it's not a big deal."

I bit down on the urge to ask him if he'd read the entirety of the Fifty Shades series up there among his trees and focused on what really mattered: the romance of Catherine and Jasper Holmes.

"There were notes inside it," I explained as I filled him in on the rough details. "Notes written by the same two people who scribbled inside your Hemingway." In the short amount of time we had, and with the booming clatter of bowling pins falling down around us, I couldn't go into as much detail as I wanted, but Zach was quick to catch on—about Jasper's blank check and greedy snatch at the book, about his strange kindness in offering to keep an eye on Noodle, at the hint dropped by Gunderson that something catastrophic happened in Jasper's past. All of it seemed to indicate that the next page of my personal mystery was behind his closed doors.

"That settles it," Zach said as soon as I was done.

"Settles what?"

We could see the kids finishing up with their games and heading back with demands to be further entertained, so Zach spoke quickly.

"We have to get inside his house somehow and take a look around. Between the two of us, I'm sure we can uncover something good."

13

—

1960

"WHO IS THAT YOUNG MAN IN the blue shirt, and why does he keep staring at us?"

"What? Who? Where?" Catherine stopped in the middle of the grocery store with her basket hanging over one arm, her heart suddenly feeling like a bird taking off in the middle of a windstorm. She tried to act calm, but she was pretty sure her mother could tell that she was a wreck. "What I mean is, which young man are you talking about?"

"I think he's trying to get your attention. He waved."

Catherine bit down on her bottom lip as she glanced across the aisle to find Jasper Holmes on the other side—not staring or waving, as her mother suggested, but looking as though he'd like to do a little of both. He also looked like a man who'd spent the whole day chopping down trees in the forest.

"He's a patron from the library," Catherine said. "I've helped him choose a couple of books."

"*That* man?" Her mom tsked and returned her attention to the shelf of tinned fruit. "He doesn't look as though he's read a book a day in his life. You must be mistaken."

"Mom, don't be a snob."

Her mom plucked a can of pears and set it in Catherine's basket. "It's not a good idea to encourage his type, love. Let Mrs. Peters direct his course of reading. She'll know just how to depress his pretentions."

Catherine tried to step in front of her mom, but she was too late. Jasper either heard the words or was able to read enough of her mom's lips and expression to get the gist. With a grimace, he turned away.

"Now look what you did," Catherine hissed. "You hurt his feelings."

"Don't be silly. Men like that don't have feelings. They have urges."

Catherine bit back a sigh as her mom continued grabbing groceries and loading the basket down. Every instinct told her to run after Jasper as he made his purchase and headed out the door, but she knew that would only make things worse. Jasper Holmes, for all his size, was more like a skittish deer than the bull in a china shop he appeared to be.

The library book currently jumping along in her pocket was all the proof she needed of that. It was her turn to leave a message in the margins, but she wasn't sure how far she was willing to push him.

That she *wanted* to push him was clear. That he was willing to be pushed was becoming equally evident. But Catherine had never been good at knowing when to stop. She was more like a bull in a china shop than the skittish deer she appeared to be.

In fact, the messages from *The Haunting of Hill House* were so well known to her at this point that she had them memorized.

I could live there all alone, she thought, slowing the car to look down the winding garden path to the small blue front door with, perfectly, a white cat on the step. No one would ever find me there, either, behind all those roses, and just to make sure I would plant oleanders by the road.

This is me in about ten years. All I want is a house, a

cat, some oleander, and to be left alone. (Without the murder-y ghost bits that come later, obviously.)

Nice try. You'll be happily married with six or seven kids by then.

Why, J. Is that a proposal??

No.

That was fast. You sound awfully sure about it.

Because I am.

If marriage is out of the question, does that mean we're running away like Romeo and Juliet instead? I can tell you right now, I'm no Hemingway heroine. I'm not dying at the end of the book for the sake of a good redemption arc.

We're not doing anything. It would be a crime for you to throw yourself away like that. You can do a lot better than me.

How much better? No one ever gave me a guidebook. Can he at least be a shy, well-read logger? I'm partial to those.

No. Can we please go back to discussing the book now?

And that was where she was stuck. The thing she *wanted* to say—that throwing herself away was her decision and her decision alone—got jammed every time she picked up her pen. And the thing she *should* say—that none of it mattered because every town she'd ever lived in came with a two-year expiration date—only made her feel depressed.

"By the way, how did your date with that nice William McBride go the other night?" her mom asked in a bright, obvious voice as they continued walking down the aisle. It might have been Catherine's imagination, but she could almost swear the scent of pine needles and leather lingered in the air where Jasper had been standing only moments before.

William McBride hadn't smelled like pine needles and leather. He'd smelled like Aqua Velva and desperation.

"It was fine. He tried feeling me up at the drive-in."

"Catherine Winifred Martin!"

"What? I didn't say I let him. Just that he tried. His sort always does."

Her mom gave up on the pretense of grocery shopping and lowered her voice to a sharp hiss. "This is neither the time nor the place for that kind of discussion, young lady." Then, with a reluctant smile, she said, "And don't think you shock me with your brassy tongue. I was young, too, once upon a time. I know the sort you're talking about."

Catherine felt an answering smile of her own take shape. One of her favorite things about her mother was how primly un-prim she was under the surface, even if she refused to admit it. "Mom! Are you trying to tell me that Dad took premarital liberties with you?"

"Of course not. Your father is and always has been a perfect gentleman. But I know how young men like William McBride can be." She paused before adding, "That young man who just left the grocery store, too. This is a small town, Catherine. People talk, and your father listens. Be very careful to ensure you control the dialogue."

It was advice like this that always made Catherine want to throw off the shackles of her upbringing and force her mother to step out into the sunlight with her. She didn't want to control the dialogue. She didn't want to eat grapefruits for breakfast and date men like William McBride. She wanted to live her life the way her father did.

That was the quiet part that no one in their family said out loud—how much richer his life was than theirs, how much fuller. Every day of his life, her father woke up knowing that his orders would be carried out to the letter. At work, because of his rank. At home, because that was simply how things were done. Yes, her mother found ways around it in tiny acts of rebellion, things like a shade of lipstick that was a little too red or the pack of cigarettes hidden behind a yellow box of SOS pads under the sink, but how was that living? How was that fair?

Catherine was allowed to have a job for the sole reason that being a librarian was one of the few feminine professions her father approved of. He didn't know that Catherine used her position to check out every new horror book that crossed her path, or that she spent her breaks with her head bent over the gory, macabre tales of H. P. Lovecraft and Daphne Du Maurier. He had no idea about the copy of a brand-new book called *Psycho* in her bag, or how she planned to stay up late reading it.

And he *definitely* didn't know that she was carrying on a flirtation with a local lumberjack in the margins of yet another horror novel—this one rife with ghosts and horrible visions and strange writings on the wall.

Catherine looked at her mom through suddenly clear eyes. She was such a beautiful, vibrant, *extraordinary* woman—or rather, she could have been, if she didn't have to hide her beautifully crooked smile behind her hand.

"Don't look at me like that, Catherine," her mother said. "I don't make society's rules. I only follow them."

Even that—the sharp, intelligent mind that could interpret every twitch of Catherine's stare—was extraordinary. And it was being used to, what? Get mustard stains out of cloth napkins? Continue in a relentless pursuit of the perfect little black dress?

"Do you think you can finish the shopping without me?" Catherine suddenly asked, shoving the basket into her mother's hands.

Her mom accepted the basket, but not without another of those shrewd looks. "Why?" she asked sharply. "Are you going after that young man?"

Catherine drove her hand into her pocket and fingered the familiar edges of *The Haunting of Hill House*. The library copy had been fairly new when they'd gotten their hands on it, but their repeated correspondence meant that the pages were already starting to show signs of wear. They were careful not to leave anything incriminating behind, but if someone ever found these books in the library, that person would have one heck of a story to unravel.

"Yes, actually. I am. His name is Jasper Holmes, and he's my friend."

"Catherine…" her mother warned, her lips tightly pursed.

"I know. Control the narrative. Don't let Dad find out." *Hide who I am for the sake of a man who's never once tried to see me.* She got up on tiptoe and pressed a kiss onto her mom's talcum-scented cheek. "It's all right, Mom. This isn't the first time I've had to sneak around to meet up with a boy from the wrong side of the tracks."

"Catherine!"

She waggled her fingers in a playful farewell and dashed out the door before her mom could say more. There was a good chance she'd be forced to endure a womanly heart-to-heart later, followed by a list of even more ways to lead a double life of espionage under her own roof, but that was a small price to pay for freedom.

Especially since she knew exactly which direction Jasper had gone.

———

"There's no use looking. I haven't put it back yet."

Catherine watched with satisfaction as Jasper jumped, grunted, and did his best to tamp down his reaction to finding her standing on the other side of the library shelf. She was a good six inches shorter than him, so she had to stand on tiptoe to peek at eye level, but she didn't mind. He looked so scared to see her—and so happy—that she had to choke back her giggle. Never had a man shown such an endearing conflict of emotions whenever she entered his sphere. He liked her, but he didn't *want* to like her—and even better, he didn't know how to stop himself from either reaction.

Catherine had never known that kind of power before.

"But you always put it back in the mornings," he accused as his hand dropped from the shelf. Like her, he spoke in the hushed whisper that both the library setting and Mrs. Peters required. He must have noticed her struggling to hide her smile, because he narrowed his eyes. "You're supposed to be at the grocery store."

"I had to leave. I find broccoli to be tedious."

"Of course it's tedious. All Cruciferae are tedious. They take up too much space and attract more pests than any other vegetable. Most amateur gardeners don't find them worth the effort."

At this terse recitation of gardening facts—the most words he'd ever said to her out loud—Catherine's grin only widened. "You seem to have awfully strong feelings about broccoli."

"In case you haven't noticed, I have strong feelings about everything." He stuck out his hand. "Give me the book. It's my turn."

Even though he was standing on the other side of the library bookshelf and the copy of *The Haunting of Hill House* was tucked safely in her pocket, she jumped back. "Not yet. I'm not done talking about vegetables. I'd like to know what else you find offensive about them."

He scowled. "I don't find *all* of them offensive. Just that particular type."

"The kind that takes up too much space?"

"Yes."

"The kind that demands regular attention?"

"Exactly."

"The kind that causes nothing but bitterness and distaste any time you put them in your mouth?"

That one gave him a moment's pause. It also caused his gaze to fall quickly to her lips before shooting back up to her eyes again. "I never said that."

He didn't have to. He'd revealed more in that brief flicker than in the entire past three months of literary correspondence. As much as Catherine enjoyed the slow pace of their communication, of the anticipation and excitement every time she saw that book on the shelf, the danger in knowing that anyone might stumble upon the copy and burst the iridescent bubble in which the pair of them were encased, she was too much a living, breathing woman to stay in that bubble forever.

A careful, quiet courtship was all well and good when you were reading about it in the pages of a book. She liked an epistolary novel just as much as the next girl—she'd thrilled over every page of Dorothy Sayers's *The Documents in the Case* and had even managed to make it all the way through *Anne of Windy Poplars*—but there were times when a scribbled note wasn't going to cut it.

This was one of those times.

"I haven't had a chance to write a response yet," she said with a knowing pat at her pocket. "But if you come with me, I'll tell you what I was planning to put down."

Jasper couldn't have looked more alarmed if she'd brained him over the head with the entire shelf of Shirley Jackson books.

"Come with you where?" he asked, his voice hoarse.

She had to think fast. For one thing, she knew that she only had about thirty more seconds before Jasper made a break for it. It didn't seem to matter that he was a tall strapping bear of a man with hands that looked as though they could crush baseballs, or that despite his rough exterior, he was incredibly intelligent with an almost encyclopedic knowledge of plants and literature. Nor did it seem to occur to him that he had Catherine practically eating out of the palm of his hand. She knew that one wrong move—or one loud sound—and he'd dash back out into the woods, never to be seen again.

For another thing, she could hear the heavy footsteps and even heavier breathing of Mrs. Peters heading their way. That woman could sense a man lingering in the aisles faster than a bat echolocating its way to dinner.

"This way." She tilted her head toward the back of the library, where the stairs down to the basement stood. There wasn't much down there but an unused coal scuttle and a big empty room they used to store old books, but like Jasper Holmes, that was a large part of its charm.

It was quiet. Tempting. And wholly underappreciated by the world at large.

He looked as though he wanted to argue, but he was even more terrified of Mrs. Peters than he was of Catherine. With a duck of his head, he followed her to the end of the bookshelf.

That was when Catherine made her move. Dashing out a hand, she wound her fingers through his, locking his palm in place. As expected, his hand felt rough against hers, his calluses formed through hard work and determination. Her own palms were silky smooth and slightly infantile, thanks in large part to the Vaseline that her mom insisted she slather all over her hands before shoving them inside a pair of cotton gloves before she went to bed every night.

Jasper must have felt the difference as keenly as she did because his whole hand flexed and tried to pull away.

"No, don't," she whispered as she began leading him toward the basement door. "I won't hurt you, I promise."

Jasper found nothing strange in this remark. He only ducked his head and followed her, his eyes watching for any sign of Mrs. Peters. The two of them fumbled and bumped as they made their way down the dark hallway and the even darker stairs, but no one came after them.

There were several light bulbs with dangling strings that Catherine could have pulled, but she didn't want to risk it. Instead, she kicked aside a box of shiny new plumbing parts and wrapped her arms around Jasper's neck. And then she read the one thing that was better than a new book: the soft, scared, *hungry* look in Jasper's eyes.

So she kissed him.

As an attractive young woman whose adolescence had been spent around military youths who went weeks at a time without seeing any other females, Catherine was no stranger to kisses stolen in the darkness. She'd always liked the way a man's lips molded to hers, the way their bodies, emboldened by her eager response, often did the same.

However, nothing could have prepared her for this kiss. The moment her lips touched Jasper's, he sucked in a sharp breath that seemed to steal all the air from her lungs. And then she didn't remember breathing again.

That oxygen must have been hitting her brain, she knew for a fact. She didn't pass out or swoon, didn't asphyxiate in the heated embrace of a man who was determined to prove he was no military youth. But as his mouth moved over hers, she became every clinging miss and shy damsel of romantic nonsense. She'd been the one to give herself to him, but he was the one who *took*, and she had literally no idea how much time passed before Jasper finally yanked himself away, his panicked expression discernible even in the shadows.

"Catherine," he said, her name taking shape on a long exhalation. The sound of it contained censure and wonder, both of these things underscored by a longing she felt reverberate down to her very bones.

"Well?" she responded. "I didn't hurt you, did I?"

His only response was to stare at her. Emboldened by the glimmer in his eyes—and the fact that no one had come to the door demanding they account for themselves, Catherine reached up and turned on the light. They both blinked against the sudden flood of illumination, but she was the first to recover. Reaching into her pocket, she pulled out the book and the pen she always carried in case inspiration struck. She found the section she'd left off on and read through the last messages.

> *We're not doing anything. It would be a crime for you to throw yourself away like that. You can do a lot better than me.*

> *How much better? No one ever gave me a guidebook. Can he at least be a shy, well-read logger? I'm partial to those.*

> *No. Can we please go back to discussing the book now?*

Underneath that, she finally wrote the words she'd been longing to say.

> *There. Do you still want to talk about the stupid book?*

She handed him both the book and the pen, trying not to smile as his eyes scanned the line. A soft grunt escaped him, but he didn't look up as he rifled through the pages until he found what he was looking for: a new passage, a fresh page.

Catherine longed to peek over his shoulder to see what he was underlining, but if there was one thing she was learning about this man, it was that he required vast amounts of patience.

"Here." He finished and handed her the book. Sure enough, he'd underlined a section about halfway through.

> "We have only one defense, and that is running away. At least it can't follow us, can it? When we feel ourselves endangered we can leave, just as we came. And," he added dryly, "just as fast as we can go."

Any other woman might have taken that as a commentary on her technique, but not Catherine. Not when it came to *her* Jasper. Her own emotions were running high, her blood pounding hot and heavy through her veins. She could only imagine how overwhelmed he must feel. He didn't like to take up too much space under the best of circumstances. Under these circumstances, he'd grown practically invisible.

Fortunately, she knew exactly how to find him.

Hiding a smile, she settled herself on top of the box of plumbing parts and wrote.

I'm a nineteen-year-old librarian, not a house of evil and doom. Don't you think you're being a little dramatic?

You're exactly like that house.

Is this where you call me terrifying again? Because I thought you liked that about me.

And I'm exactly like Eleanor.

You're a young woman who spent the last decade of her life caring for her invalid mother? Strange. I didn't pick up on that.

YOU KNOW WHAT I MEAN, C.

Catherine had to hide her smile behind her hand when she read that one. An increasingly irritated Jasper Holmes was a sight to behold. He looked as though he wanted to wring her neck and also like he wanted to kiss her. Maybe even at the same time.

She also took pity on him. Mostly because she *did* know what he meant.

Eleanor is anxious. Driftless. Unmoored. At least, until she goes to Hill House and lets it suck her in. The house scares her, but she likes it. She likes the idea of giving herself over to it and letting it possess her. Even if it destroys her in the end, it's a destruction she wants. Maybe even needs.

As soon as he read the words, he relaxed. He also handed her back the book without writing anything in it.

"You *do* know," he said, sounding so relieved that she tucked the book in her pocket. She also took his hand again, this time letting herself glide her smooth palm over his rough one, enjoying the way his skin caught against hers. It was as if his very being was reaching out to her using any means at its disposal.

"Of course I know, Jasper. Why do you think I like this book so much?" She paused and lowered her voice before adding, "And why I like you?"

This time, he was the one doing the kissing. Catherine had no idea how such a large man could move so swiftly, but she was crushed against his chest before she even realized what was happening. The book wedged awkwardly between them, but neither one of them seemed to care as they fell deeper and deeper into one another's arms.

She had no idea how long they might have stayed entwined like that—Catherine Martin and Jasper Holmes, Hill House and Eleanor Vance—if not for the scuttling sound of footsteps approaching the top of the steps.

"This is a terrible idea," Catherine said as she jumped back. Jasper's hand shot out and caught the book midfall.

"I told you that already," he muttered. "You didn't listen. I'm starting to think you *never* listen."

She didn't miss the adorable flush to his skin or the way he clutched the book like it was the most precious thing he'd ever held. She also didn't miss the thump of Mrs. Peters heading toward the stairs.

"Not about the kissing, silly," she said as she grabbed his arm and began dragging him toward the coal scuttle. There was a back door that led to the street from there—and, if they were lucky, to freedom. He tried to dig his heels in, but he was no match for her determination.

No man was, but most of them never had a chance to find that out.

She lifted his hand to her mouth and pressed a kiss on the roughest of his calluses. And then she pushed him out the door. "I only meant that we need a more secure place to meet."

He hesitated. At first, she feared he was going to push back—against this thing they were doing, against *her*—but then he spoke.

"I know a place," he said, blushing, his words slightly stammered. "It's not much, just a little cabin by the river, but—"

A thrill moved through her. To be able to cause a man like this to blush so profusely, to bring such a strong, stoic being to his knees—it was heady stuff, and she wasn't impervious to the power of it.

"Take me there," she said before he could think the better of it. "A little cabin by the river is exactly where I want to go."

14

—

CHLOE

ZACH STOOD UNDERNEATH THE TRELLIS BETWEEN our house and
Jasper's, his tall head grazing the top and snagging the tendrils of
a particularly flourishing clematis. It had been almost a week since I'd
roped him into hunting for *The Haunting of Hill House* with me, but
instead of losing his fervor, he was throwing himself heart and soul into
the effort.

"I still don't see why we can't just knock on his door and ask to use
the restroom or something." Zach pushed aside the clematis. "I'm sure
it won't take long to search his bookshelves. It's not a very big house. I
could pretend to be violently ill while you look around."

"He'd see right through you," I said, shaking my head. "If you were
going to be violently ill, you'd do it at my house."

"No, I wouldn't. I'm trying to make a good impression on you. I'd
be *mildly* ill, at the very most."

I choked on the laugh that had been bubbling in my throat ever since
Zach had rolled up to the house in full heist black. It was a difficult task,
mostly because the more time I spent with the man, the more I wanted
to laugh about everything.

"It doesn't matter because it's not working," I said. "My only impression of you is that you'll say anything if you think it'll get a reaction."

That only made him grin. "Does this mean we're going with my plan? The only other idea I have is to let Aloysius look through the house when he's—"

"Absolutely not," I interrupted. "I don't want Noodle involved in this. Sending him to Jasper every day for supervision is bad enough."

I expected a pushback, but all Zach did was shrug. "Then we'll have to sneak in under cover of night and steal every book he owns like we're coming after the Declaration of Independence. That's all I've got."

I snorted. For all his apparent resourcefulness, Zach wasn't much of a criminal mastermind. I imagined it was the Boy Scout within him; as far as I knew, there was no merit badge for breaking and entering. Fortunately for our mission, I had more than enough training. You didn't grow up in a neighborhood like this without learning a thing or two about petty theft.

"We need to come up with something less obvious," I said. "Jasper's not likely to let you inside without a full background check and several reference letters. He doesn't like strangers. He doesn't like friends, either, but I think that's mostly because he doesn't have any."

As Zach tilted his head to examine the house, the clematis tickled his ear. His gaze wandered from the vibrant purple bloom to all the others dotting the yard.

"It's kind of late in the season for a lot of these flowers, isn't it?" he asked as he reached up to finger the flower. "What's his secret?"

"According to my boss at work? Dead bodies."

Zach's laugh came as a quick, staccato burst. "What's the answer according to you?"

Strangely enough, I had an answer ready to go. "Time and attention, mostly. I know he used to be a logger back in the day—Pepper found a picture in the library archives—so he's always been a bit of an outdoorsman. Add in an entire lifetime spent holding people at bay, and this is what happens. His garden gets all the love he's never been able to give anyone else."

Zach paused to look at me. "I thought he loved that girl from your book."

"Her name is Catherine." As I said her name out loud, my heart gave a small pang. Of sympathy, maybe. Or possibly just sadness. "At least, that's what I assume from some of the things she wrote. And he *did* love her—I'm sure of it. That's why I'm so determined to figure out what happened. Somewhere along the way, something terrible happened to tear them apart. It's what turned him into such a sour, miserable old man."

"And you want to fix it? To fix *him*?"

This time, the answer was much slower in coming. Mostly because I didn't know this man well enough to admit the truth. Pepper knew, though. She might have been the only person in the world who did.

The truth was that Jasper Holmes wasn't the only one who held people at bay. I hadn't lost a grand romance the way he had, but I *had* lost out on a dream. To make something of myself and get out of this town, to build a life that extended beyond the mountains that ringed our little patch of God's green earth. Sure, I could go back to college again, or maybe even take a few online classes, but it wouldn't be the same. Every day that passed with my hands in a sink full of dirty dishes and my bank account in the red brought me one step closer to the inevitable.

Growing old in a place like this, using my youthful disappointments as a reason to hide. Turning into a sour, miserable old woman whose only solace could be found between the pages of a book—or a garden like this one.

Solving the mystery of Jasper's misery was as close as I could come to solving my own.

"I just want to know the truth," I said. It was as good as I could do in the current situation. "Look, if you don't want to help, I won't hold you to it."

"Oh, no you don't." He brought his hands up in a gesture of surrender, his grin as easy and effortless as it always was. "You're not robbing me of my adventure now. I need this."

"Your whole life is an adventure," I pointed out. "You literally kill things with your bare hands and then eat them."

"Yeah, but that's just action-flick levels of adventure. This is intrigue. This is mystery." He waggled his eyebrows at me. "This is *romance*."

The fluttering of my heart recognized this ploy for what it was, but something about the way he spoke sparked a memory—two of them, actually, both of which tied up together in a realization that made my heart flutter even more.

The first was that in the pages of my Hemingway, Catherine had accused Jasper of being a romantic. Considering the rollout of their courtship thus far, I felt deep in my bones that she was right. Only a romantic would take the time to get to know a girl in the pages of a book before he made a single move, and then continue flirting with her through that medium for as long as possible.

The second was that when I'd walked into the backyard to find Noodle and Jasper together that first day, he'd been reading a copy of *North and South*. That book was arguably one of the best pieces of romantic fiction to have emerged from the nineteenth century (with all apologies to Jane Austen and the Brontës, of course), but it wasn't exactly topping the required reading list at the library. Anyone relaxing with a copy of that was doing it for pleasure, pure and simple.

These clues could only mean one thing: Jasper loved love. Somewhere underneath those deep frown lines and angry mutterings lay a man whose heart was as fragile and delicate as glass.

"I think I know how to play this," I said suddenly.

"Really?" Zach cracked his knuckles. "Please tell me it involves scaling that back wall. I've been itching to show off ever since we got here."

I snorted but refused to let myself be charmed any further than that. "I think I'm just going come out and ask Jasper the truth."

"Wait." His arms dropped to his sides. "Just like that?"

"Why not?" I turned to study the house and its gardens anew. Instead of seeing his home as the wide-eyed child who'd grown up next to it, fearing the angry giant atop the beanstalk, I imagined it as the quiet oasis of a man who was clinging desperately to the one thing of beauty remaining in his life.

"I'm pretty sure he already knows I'm on to him," I said. "We could spend weeks tiptoeing around and planning heists, or I could roll up to his front porch and put it all out there." I nodded and took a step forward, my decision made. "You know what? I'm going in. What's the worst he can do to me? Shut the door in my face? Throw books at me? Refuse to babysit Noodle?"

That last one actually did have the potential to derail me, but I didn't let it weigh on my decision. I marched forward instead, only pausing to look back when it appeared that Zach wasn't following.

"What's wrong?" I asked. Zach hadn't moved from his spot under the trellis, though he'd narrowed his eyes to watch my progress across the lawn. "Scared of what he might do to you? Don't worry. I'll protect you."

"You have no idea, do you?" he asked.

I blinked. The total summation of all the things I didn't know in this world would have filled the Library of Alexandria. "Know what?"

"How many women—how many *people*—would just walk up to someone and ask a question like that? 'Excuse me, sir, but did you once love a young woman named Catherine so much that you wrote messages to her in the margins of a library book? If so, would you be willing to let me read any of the other books the two of you wrote in?'"

I felt a flush of color touch my cheeks. "You think it's too much?"

He released a long, silent laugh that left me feeling dizzy. The feeling didn't abate when he crossed toward me in three easy strides.

"I think it's exactly the right amount. And I think you're exactly the person to do it. Let's go put it all out there and see what happens."

———

"What do you mean, you found this on the shelf? The *library* shelf?"

Jasper stood in the doorway to his house, his massive frame blocking the way inside. Over one of his shoulders, I could just make out the interior—white walls and white carpeting, both of which were offset by so many houseplants that it looked like a tropical jungle in there.

From the way his body trembled as he stood holding the copy of *A Farewell to Arms*, I felt pretty sure a strong breeze would send him toppling over and get me through the door, but I wasn't going to push it—or him. His face was already so white that it almost matched the walls.

"Technically, Zach was the one who found the book." I tilted my head at the man standing at my back. "But don't worry about him. He's safe."

"I can't decide whether to take that as a compliment or an insult," Zach murmured in a voice I suspected was only for my ears. He brushed past me with his hand outstretched. "It's an honor to finally meet you, sir."

"I'm not paying you for this one," Jasper said, completely disregarding both the hand and the man attached to it. He fixed his gaze on me instead. Already, he was starting to regain his color and his bearing—and, I need hardly add, his bad attitude. "So if you've come here peddling literature like it's a box of Girl Scout cookies…"

"This one's on the house," I assured him. "But we'd like to come in and chat, if it's all the same to you."

He set his jaw. "It's not."

"I read through the book," I warned him. I didn't want to have to resort to threats, but they were one of the only things Jasper seemed to react to, so I didn't have much choice. "I also flipped through most of *Tropic of Cancer*. You might as well let us in. I'm not leaving until you tell me about Catherine."

Instead of him growing pale again, a seeping red color started to move up his neck. "Catherine," he echoed, no hint of a question in his voice.

"That's her name, right?" I persisted. "You only ever call her C in the books, but I put the rest together on my own."

"That's her name," he agreed. His shoulders came down a fraction. "*Was* her name, I should say. She died a long time ago."

My first feeling of triumph—I *knew* their story was tragic, and I *knew* Jasper had built a whole life around that tragedy—was quickly quashed under a muffling wave of sadness. She must have been awfully young when it happened.

And so, I realized, had he.

"I understand if you don't want to talk about her," I said, fighting every urge I had to reach out and pull Jasper into a hug. I had the distinct impression it would only ruin my chances of making it through the door. "But it would mean a lot to me if you'd at least let me inside."

"Why?"

Jasper's question was a simple one, but there was no simple answer. "Because I'm curious," I admitted. "Because we've lived next to each other my whole life, and I know less about you than I do the guy who only comes into the library once every six weeks to re-checkout *Dune*."

The last one took a little more to get out.

"Because I've only known your Catherine for a little while, but she already feels like a friend."

Behind me, Zach was being awfully quiet. Before I had time to wonder why, Jasper threw open the door. He turned and shuffled inside, pausing only after he was halfway across the foyer. "Fine. You can come in. But take off your shoes first. And shut the door. The aphids are coming out in full force this year. I don't want them in here mucking up my plants."

I was so surprised that it took a gentle nudge from Zach before I slipped out of my worn Vans—the last shoes I'd bought before I'd moved back home, and likely the most expensive pair I'd own for a very long time.

I turned to find Zach looking at the space recently vacated by Jasper. "I thought you said this old guy hated you," he said as he began carefully undoing his laces.

"He *does* hate me," I said. Since Zach's shoes were hiking boots that went halfway up his calves, getting them off was taking some time. "This is probably a trick to get my guard down. We need to act like every word out of his mouth is double-edged."

The thud of one boot hit the floor. "Want me to tie him to a chair while you interrogate him?"

"If I said yes, could you actually do it?"

"Could I, as in am I physically capable of it?" Zach shrugged. "I once did the same thing to a black bear who kept trying to eat my trainees. Could I, as in would I be willing to take the risk because a pretty girl asked me to?" This time, he smiled. "I guess there's only one way to find out."

I examined Zach out of the corner of my eye, but he was being careful not to look at me. I had no way of knowing how much he said was the truth and how much was hyperbole, but I had the feeling he was a man who rarely gave anyone a straight answer.

The other boot hit the floor. "If you don't like the chair idea, I could always whip up a truth serum using natural herbs from his garden," he offered.

"Don't tell me," I said dryly. "You once had to do the same thing to a colony of rabbits you suspected of being enemy spies."

"*Now* you're getting it."

Shaking my head, I stepped the rest of the way into the house. As I'd seen from the doorway, it was neat, tidy, and crawling with plant life. Vines, ferns, potted flowers, and a string of spider plants seemed to connect every room in the house. Oddly enough, there wasn't a single book or bookshelf to be seen.

There was, however, a lonely old man sitting hunched on a kitchen stool, a smile touching his lips as he flipped through the pages of the book in front of him.

"She always did have a way of making me say and do things against my will," he said as he ran his fingers over the scrawled lines in the margins. "Imagine me, carrying on like this with a librarian, of all things."

"Wait," I said, and with that, all my plans to handle Jasper with tact disappeared. "Catherine was a *librarian*? Here in Colville? At the same library where I work?"

"She was way out of my league. I knew that from the start." He glanced up at me with an unreadable expression. "And if I'd had my way, that would've also been the end."

It seemed as much of an answer as I was going to get. I blew out a long breath. "So she worked at the library. That's why you guys left each other notes inside books."

"We left each other notes because we didn't have any of this new-fangled technology you kids seem to put so much value in," Jasper corrected me, his voice like a rap to the knuckles. "We didn't have the option of texting naked pictures or those stupid yellow circles back and forth."

I was careful not to look at Zach at the "naked pictures" part, but the second half got my attention. "Stupid yellow circles?"

Jasper waved an impatient hand. "The ones that smile and drool and fart. I don't know what you call them."

"Emojis, sir," Zach said.

Jasper pointed a warning finger at him. "Call me 'sir' again, and you'll find yourself wishing you'd never set foot inside this house."

"Yes, sir," he said with a bland and—in my opinion, at least—bold disregard for Jasper. "I'll work on that."

Jasper looked as though he was contemplating making good on his threat, but he sighed and waved around the kitchen. "You might as well sit down," he said, sounding irritable. "I can see you won't be easy to dislodge."

Since he'd been the one to invite us in, I ignored the comment and made myself comfortable on a wooden stool. Zach waited only a few seconds before joining me.

"It was 1960," Jasper said, unprompted. "That was when we started…corresponding. Her father got put in charge of the radar base during its final years of operation, so she took a post at the library to pass the time."

This was already way more information than I'd been expecting—and offered up free of charge. I sensed a trap.

"And before you ask, no, you can't have *Tropic of Cancer* back." Jasper turned a sharp pair of eyes on me. "You still haven't cashed that check, but that doesn't mean the transaction is void. It's not my fault you refuse to go to the bank like a normal person."

I could see Zach looking curiously at us, so I was quick to turn the conversation. I had no way of explaining why that check still sat uncashed in the bottom of my purse. The more I needed that money, the less willing I was to take it. Pepper would have been quick to point out my inability to accept help, but there was more to it than that. To cash in on this man's pain, to reduce his life story to a series of zeros and dollar bills—it felt wrong.

People *had* to be more than a number in their bank account. Life *had* to carry more meaning than that.

"So, you and Catherine started by writing to each other in *A Farewell to Arms*," I said, phrasing it as a statement of fact.

Jasper's hands moved reverently over the cover. "That we did."

"And then you moved on to *The Haunting of Hill House.*"

"Did we make it that easy to figure out? That was indiscreet of us." A smile touched his lips as he rifled through the pages. "Now that I think about it, a lot of the things we did were indiscreet, but that's the nature of youth. None of you are as good at hiding things as you think you are."

I was sensing an attack now rather than a trap but Jasper wasn't done yet.

"If the book says we moved on to Shirley Jackson next, then I'm sure that's what we did," he said. "It's so long ago now that I don't remember everything we put to paper. Catherine loved horror books—the darker, the better. She was always happiest when people were being torn limb from limb."

"Sounds like my kinda girl," Zach murmured.

"You wouldn't have lasted five minutes in her company," Jasper returned as easily as batting a tennis ball at high speed. "She'd have had your measure, chewed you up, and spit you out before you could put the twinkle in your eye."

"My measure?" Zach echoed. He looked at me and, even though I had no idea how, put a twinkle in his eye. "Should I ask?"

"You're everything that's wrong with modern youth," Jasper said without waiting for an invitation. I was so happy not to be the one under attack anymore that I actually found myself enjoying the exchange. "You're too aware of your own worth. All you kids are. You make endless videos of your exploits, preen in front of mirrors, and get a blue ribbon every time you join a sport."

Zach chuckled and waved a hand over himself. Although he'd washed his customary dirt away, he still looked weathered and—to my eyes, at least—appealing in the extreme. "You think *I* preen?"

"Of course you do. You wouldn't be following this girl all over town, swaggering about like a pig in his sty, if you didn't think she had a thing for barnyard animals. There's no *humility* in any of you."

This was taking things too far, even if Zach was the last person who needed someone rushing to his defense.

"Now wait just a second," I said. "A few weeks ago, you told me I needed to give Noodle a stronger, more dignified nickname. You said he had to present himself to the world in the guise he wanted to be treated."

All at once, Jasper softened. It was like watching a hot-air balloon deflate after a long, arduous journey. "Ah, yes. But Noodle is different."

My throat felt suddenly too thick for speech. If any other person had dared to say those words to me—*Noodle is different, Noodle is other*—I'd have gone full *Haunting of Hill House* and, like Jasper's beloved Catherine, torn them limb from limb.

For once in his life, however, Jasper wasn't speaking from a place of judgment. He and Noodle had only been together for few days, but those days had been enough.

He saw. He knew.

"Do you happen to have the copy of *The Haunting of Hill House* that you wrote in?" I asked, pushing the sharp prick of tears back from my eyes. The last thing I wanted to do in front of either of these men was break down. "The library database was a bust, and I haven't been able to find anything in the shops around town."

Jasper blinked at me. "Of course I don't have it."

"Oh." Disappointment added to all my other swirling emotions, leaving me bereft of anything to say.

Zach gently cleared his throat and filled the breach. "We figured it was a long shot, but since the other two books were easy enough to find, it seemed worth a try. Maybe we could just skip over that one for now…" He let his words trail off.

"Is this the part where you ask me to write you out a list of all the books that Catherine and I corresponded in so you can get your filthy, irreverent hands on my love story?" Jasper asked.

Since this was *exactly* what I wanted to ask, I held my breath and waited for the answer.

"Too bad. Those are mine. *Catherine* is mine."

I feared this might signal the end of his frankness, but he kept going.

"If it makes you feel better, I doubt any of those old books are still around. Why would they be? She's the one who kept them all. And when she died, I…" He shook his head as if to rid himself of the memory. "Never mind. It doesn't matter what I did. Let's just say I'm surprised you were able to find the two books you did. Catherine must have hidden them so her parents wouldn't find them—one in the library basement, the other in plain sight on the library shelves."

Instead of dashing my hopes, these words filled me with a sudden burst of optimism—not just that there might be more books out there, but that they'd been saved for a reason. It was as if Catherine had known how much the discovery would mean someday…not necessarily to Jasper, but to me.

A librarian more than sixty years in the future. Someone lost and looking for answers to questions she didn't even know she had.

"Does this mean you think she hid them on purpose?" I asked, knowing I was pushing too hard but unable to stop myself. "Because she wanted them to be safe from prying eyes? Or because she wanted them to eventually be found?"

Jasper cast me a pained look. "She didn't hide those books for a nosy, meddling not-a-librarian to start a wild-goose chase, if that's what you're asking."

"Technically, it's not a wild-goose chase if you catch the goose in the end."

"I knew it was a mistake to let you two in here." Jasper groaned and got to his feet, though I noticed he was careful to keep the copy of *A Farewell to Arms* close at hand. "Go home. Leave me alone. Stop poking your nose into a past that's gone, buried, and already mourned."

Since Jasper had clearly reached the end of his patience, I gave in and stepped toward the door. My steps were helped along by the gentle press of Zach's hand on the small of my back.

We'd made it to the door and were in the act of slipping our shoes back on when Jasper spoke again.

"*If* she hid the rest of them, it was because she knew her parents would have found a way to destroy them," he said, his tone so soft that I could barely hear him over the beating of my heart. "They didn't approve of the two of us."

The question popped out before I could stop it: "Because you were a logger?"

A flicker of surprise crossed his face. "*Someone's* been doing her homework," he said. Then, "Yes. Because I was a logger and she was the daughter of an Air Force officer. Because I didn't have money and she did. Because the only thing I had to offer was a windowless one-bedroom apartment above the hardware store, and she deserved the world."

This was so sad that I had to pause a moment and remind myself to breathe. To most people, those barriers didn't sound insuperable, but I wasn't most people. Books were always trying to teach us that the power of love could overcome any hardship and that money didn't buy happiness. In many ways, I believed those things to be true—I really did.

But crossing that line was a lot to ask of someone. Especially someone you loved.

"I'm sorry," I said and meant it.

Jasper must have sensed my sincerity because he offered me one final gift.

"Ask Lonnie Pakootas," he said as he swung open the door and pointed us out through it. I nearly stumbled on the frame, saved only by Zach's ready and waiting hands.

"Lonnie?" I echoed. All of a sudden, that passage about L liking sappy, dramatic books was starting to make sense. Like Pepper, she'd once been employed by the local library—a thing that I, in my fervor to get to the bottom of this whole mystery, seemed to have forgotten. "You mean Pepper's grandmother?"

"If anyone would know where to find that book, it's her," Jasper said by way of answer. His eyes took on a dreamy, faraway look, and I realized he was no longer standing with us. Not in any way that counted. "Once upon a time, Catherine and Lonnie were best friends in the whole world."

15

—

CHLOE

LONNIE LIVED IN ONE OF THE most beautiful houses in Colville. It wasn't very big—few houses around here were—and it didn't have many modern upgrades—a serious drawback in the heat of the summer—but the home sat on a huge patch of acreage near the top of Crystal Falls. On cold, clear nights, you could hear the cascading water from the back porch.

To be fair, you could also hear the teenagers who went there to party and drink when boredom offered no alternatives, but you couldn't have everything in this world.

"Chloe!" Lonnie came out to greet me the moment my station wagon rambled up the drive. She looked well, all things considered, if a little thinner than the last time I'd seen her. My visits to Pepper's grandmother didn't happen as frequently as I would have liked, so I was never sure what to expect. Her cancer wasn't an aggressive kind, and she'd had several successful surgeries on her neck, but she was under no illusions about how precious her last remaining years were. "Please tell me you brought your brothers and sister with you. I have a Kentucky butter cake inside that needs to be eaten. Theo's the only one I trust to do the job right."

"Theo would eat the quills off a porcupine's back if you gave him the chance," Pepper said. She slid out of the passenger seat and joined me as I made my way up the steps.

"No, he wouldn't," I countered. "He'd turn them into darts or throwing stars and terrorize the whole neighborhood."

As soon as I reached the top step, I found myself engulfed in a hug so strong that I found it hard to imagine Lonnie not standing on the same porch offering the same comfort for the next three hundred years.

"I'm sorry I couldn't help you out with Noodle's accident," she said. "That poor kid. What was he doing, running through the forest without looking where he was going?"

I was glad she hadn't yet let me go. The longer I went without answers about what was going on with Noodle, the worse I felt. Jasper's mystery was turning out to be the much easier one to solve.

"I don't know," I said. "He won't talk about what happened. All he'll say is that he's sorry for being a bother."

"That's a Sampson for you." She clucked her tongue and started ushering me inside the house. "Always running full speed at the wall and then apologizing when they don't do anything but break their own backs in the process."

"I don't run full speed," I protested. "In fact, I don't run at all. I used to get last place in the mile in gym all the time. Ask Pepper."

"Since I know very well that my grandma is talking in metaphors, I'll do no such thing," Pepper said. She took one look at the tidy, welcoming front room—and one deep inhalation of the sweet scent of baked goods—and relaxed. Today was obviously one of Lonnie's good days.

"What wall have I ever apologized to?" I demanded.

"The wall of life," Pepper was quick to respond.

"The wall of honest feelings," Lonnie added.

Pepper went again. "The wall of ambition."

So did Lonnie. "The wall of other people's mistakes."

Pepper held up her hand for a high five. "Oooh, good one, Grandma."

Lonnie chuckled as she playfully swatted her granddaughter's hand. She let her palm linger there and laced their fingers. An ache filled my throat at the sight of such easy, nonchalant warmth between the two women. I'd always been intensely jealous of the bond they shared, and of the bond the whole Pakootas family seemed to have with one another. Although I had plenty of siblings to go around, Pepper was an only child—not that there was anything *only* about it. She had heaps of relatives. Aunts, uncles, cousins, people who weren't related to her by blood but who were as tightly bound as if they'd all shared a womb... Pepper couldn't walk anywhere in town without being accosted by someone who claimed kinship with her.

That kind of network—of people who loved her, of people who cared—was something I'd never known. It was as if she'd been born with a safety net stretched tight underneath her. She could run off a hundred different cliffs in the woods, but no matter how hard she fell, she'd never touch the ground.

I, on the other hand, had never known my father, and any grandparents I might have had were lost by my mom's inability to maintain a healthy relationship for longer than a few years at a time. From the moment of my birth, my mom had been my only safety net—a wispy, unreliable thing with more holes than support.

Somewhere in there was another metaphor about how one person couldn't be a safety net alone, how they'd eventually get spread so thin that they were reduced to a bundle of loosely tied threads, but I wasn't about to examine it too closely. Lonnie and Pepper could discuss the details after I was gone. For now, I was going to keep stretching, give my brothers and sister *something* to hold them aloft, however flimsy I might be.

"Thank you for all those old Harlequins, by the way," Lonnie said as she let go of Pepper's hand. We followed her to the kitchen, where the promised cake glistened in a buttery ring in the center of the table. She cut us both generous slices and placed them in front of us. "I'm in the middle of a really good one where the heroine is pregnant and has amnesia, and she has to be saved by a retired Navy SEAL who does repo work. It's called *Pregnesia*."

Laughing, I held up a hand. "You can stop making things up. I'm not falling for that one. There's no way that's a real book."

"It is! I'm only about halfway through, but I'll finish it tonight. I can't put it down."

"Lonnie!" My outburst was slightly muffled by the mouthful of cake I was trying—and failing—not to spray across the kitchen. "That can't be true."

"Oh, it's true," Pepper said. "It was a hot commodity a few years back—I think it was when you were away at college. I couldn't keep it in the bookmobile for longer than a few hours at a time."

Pepper moved across the kitchen to the wall of bookshelves along the far wall. Since both Lonnie and Pepper had devoted themselves to the librarian career, their book hoard was an impressive one.

"Wasn't there another one you liked with an even more outlandish title?" Pepper asked as she scanned the spines, most of which were worn with repeated use. "*Blackmailed by the Prince's Wanton Waitress* or something like that? I swear it was here when—"

I was too busy shoving more of the Kentucky butter cake in my mouth to notice Pepper's sudden halt. And then I was too busy enjoying the way it practically melted on my tongue to realize what that halt meant.

"Uh, Chloe?" she said, her voice sounding as if from afar. "Want to come here for a second?"

"If this is about the collection of erotica your aunt Raylene gave me, I don't want to hear it," Lonnie said. "What I choose to read in my own free time is—"

"It's not that," Pepper said. She pulled a book from the shelf and rejoined us. In her hand sat a black hardcover with faded yellow flowers across the front. I recognized it almost at once. Especially since it still bore the ancient stickers from when it had been a part of the library system. "Grandma, is there something you want to tell us about this copy of *The Haunting of Hill House*?"

The moment Lonnie's eyes went soft, I knew we'd found more than just a book. It was the same light that had flooded Jasper's when he'd talked about Catherine—the same light that no amount of time seemed able to erase.

Oh, to be the sort of woman who inspired that kind of sentiment after sixty years. To know that no matter how much the world changed, a memory could carry that much weight.

"That old thing?" Lonnie said with a dismissive wave of her hand. "It's older than your father. I barely remember what it's about anymore."

"It's about a girl who visits a haunted house and gets sucked into it forever," I said. "And about a pair of star-crossed lovers who read it together back in 1960."

Instead of trying to fob me off, Lonnie laughed. The sound was as rich and delicious as the cake, and so much more precious because I knew it had an expiration date.

"So you know about that, do you?" she said as she lifted the book from Pepper. She ran a hand reverentially over the cover as if smoothing away its rough edges. "Did Jasper tell you?"

Instead of answering, I tossed her a question of my own. "I wasn't aware that you and Jasper knew each other."

She glanced at me over the top of a pair of bright-pink readers. "There are all of twelve people in this town over the age of eighty, Chloe. Of course I know Jasper, the miserable old codger. He was as unpleasant back in his youth as he is now, if that's any consolation. The world has never known a more determined grouch."

This was so much in line with everything I knew to be true that I laughed. "I wish you'd have said something years ago. The boys have lost several dozen Frisbees and soccer balls in the past six months alone. Jasper steals them the moment they touch his precious grass."

"That sounds about right," Lonnie agreed.

"If you knew Jasper, then you knew Catherine, too, right?" Pepper asked. "And about their love affair?"

"Ah, now Catherine is something else," Lonnie said, once again with that softening around her eyes. "She was the light to his dark, the sun to his moon. To be honest, I never really understood what she saw in him, but I suppose that was the whole point."

"The point of what?" I asked.

Lonnie flipped open the cover and turned the pages until she reached a section somewhere in the middle. The moment I caught sight of the writing, I felt my heart take flight. Stifling the urge to snatch the book out of Lonnie's hands, I let her read the passage aloud.

"'*It is my second morning in Hill House, and I am unbelievably happy. Journeys end in lovers meeting; I have spent an all but sleepless night, I have told lies and made a fool of myself, and the very air tastes like wine.*'"

The cadence of Lonnie's voice was so soothing that I could have listened to her read for hours, but I was dying to know what the margin notes said.

"And?" I prompted.

"And I'm not done yet. Hold your horses." She cleared her throat and kept going. "'*I have been frightened half out of my foolish wits, but I have somehow earned this joy; I have been waiting for it for so long.*'"

"Grandma, now you're just being mean," Pepper said. "We don't care about the book—we just want to know what kind of naughty things Jasper and Catherine wrote to each other."

This time when Lonnie peeked over the top of her glasses, it was to glance at her granddaughter instead of me. "They didn't write anything naughty. Do you really think Catherine would've given me this copy if they had? This is *romance*, child. Pure, unadulterated, real-life romance."

"Then let us read it already." Pepper grabbed the book and, sensing that her grandmother was likely to fight back, tossed it to me. "Make a run for it, Chloe! Save yourself! I'll distract her until you get to the good parts."

Even though I knew she was joking, I scooted a little out of the way before I picked up where Lonnie had left off.

You are happy, Eleanor, you have finally been given a part of your measure of happiness.

I hate to say it, C, but I'm starting to feel like we might be cursing ourselves with this book.

How do you figure?

Because I'm happy. Because I've finally been given my measure of happiness. And considering how this book ends, I'm not sure that's a good thing.

Hmm. Interesting. Did you spend an all but sleepless night last night?

You know I did. You were there.

Shhh. I'm trying to be philosophical. Did you tell lies and make a fool of yourself?

I'm not sure about the lying, but the second part is true. I started reading that Psycho book you told me about, and I've never been so scared in my whole life. Why do you like the dark stuff so much?

I can't help it. It matches my true nature. But you're getting off course: What about the air? Do you find it tastes like wine?

No, but your lips do. Does that count?

"I thought you said this wasn't naughty!" I squealed. The idea of Jasper reading a book he didn't like for the sake of a woman—and of Jasper telling someone her lips tasted like wine—was almost too much for me. "Did Jasper and Catherine really spend the night together? Before they were married? In *1960*?"

Giving a sad shake of her head, Lonnie clucked her tongue. "Lord save me from the youth of the world. Every generation thinks they invented sex and everything that goes along with it. If that's the case, missy, then how did you and Pepper come into being? Or those many siblings of yours? Immaculate conception? The Great Spirit?"

Although I did my best *not* to imagine the various ways in which my siblings and I had been conceived, I couldn't stop a sudden image of my mom's face from flashing through my mind. It was never very far away since every line of Trixie's beauty had come from that woman. The flawless skin and gorgeous smile, a body that seemed to mold itself to current trends without the least bit of effort.

A stunner, I'd heard my mom called more than once. *A hot piece of ass*, also (unfortunately) more than once. *An absolute waste* had been another common refrain from my childhood, *a beauty like that on a woman without the common sense God gave a cow.*

I sometimes caught a glimpse of that face in the mirror, though it was more like a trick of light than any of my actual features. I could see her lingering under the surface, but only briefly, and usually when I was too distracted to remember to put up my guard.

"I don't know all the details of what happened between Catherine and Jasper, so it's no use asking me," Lonnie said, forestalling me from making the attempt. "I remember their love affair as being very fast, very hot, and very catastrophic. The best ones usually are."

This compelled Pepper to put up a protest. "Grandma! You were married to Dada for fifty years before he passed. How can you say that?"

She tsked and waved her granddaughter off. "Your grandfather was a good, solid man, but he never wooed me in the margins of a book. I think the most he ever wrote was a note reminding me not to forget to pick up a bag of potatoes on my way home from work."

Since I'd watched Pepper's grandparents live and laugh and love together, I knew this for the lie it was. I also knew that since his death a little over five years ago, she refused to poke too hard at the wound his loss had left behind. So when she gestured for me to turn the pages, I obeyed. It didn't take long before I found another section with the writing.

"These others need your protection so much more than I," she said. "I will do what I can, of course. But they are so very, very vulnerable, with their hard hearts and their unseeing eyes."

It's strange, isn't it? To think that a hard heart could make you more vulnerable instead of less?

Not really. It's the whole point of the book. The house kills those who don't love it. The entire conflict is their inability to accept the house as it is, so it takes revenge.

Is this the part where you compare me to the house again? If you don't love me, I'll kill you?

You'll kill me either way, C. I think we both know that.

A sigh escaped me before I could help it.

"Oh dear," Lonnie murmured. "I recognize that sound."

"I know," Pepper said, grinning. "She's got it bad. If Jasper were a hundred years younger, she'd probably steal him for herself."

Lonnie pointed a gnarled finger at her. "Watch yourself, child. We aren't *that* old."

I pointed a finger of my own. "And I don't *have* anything—good or bad. I'm just interested, that's all. The Jasper Holmes I know is exactly like this passage here: a man with a hard heart and unseeing eyes. But Catherine saw the vulnerability. She knew exactly how to handle him."

"You're not wrong about that," Lonnie allowed, her lips pursed with sudden thoughtfulness. "I've never seen anyone handle a man the way Catherine did Jasper. She took one look at him, decided she wanted him, and then didn't stop until she had him on his knees. You two could learn a thing or two from her."

"I know I can," I admitted. "That's why I'm trying so hard to piece together the rest of their story."

I paused then, unwilling and unable to say the unspoken part aloud. The truth was, I was much less like Catherine than I was old, closed-off, hard-hearted Jasper. To know that someone had been able to tear down his walls, to force him to feel the love that every fiber of his being balked at—it meant something to me.

If I was being honest, it meant *everything* to me.

I knew I had to approach my next question carefully. If not for Lonnie's sake, then for my own.

"If you knew Catherine back then, then you know what happened to her," I said. The words felt oddly thick inside my mouth, but I gave each one the weight it needed. "Gunderson claimed Jasper killed her and buried her body in his garden, but—"

Lonnie's bright peal of laughter interrupted me before I could finish. "Gunderson gets nine-tenths of his information from that wife of his. She's the moderator on half a dozen different conspiracy websites. Don't believe a word out of their mouths."

"I don't," I said. "But Jasper was always so mean to us, and Catherine's death was so sudden and tragic. It made a certain kind of sense."

Pepper nodded along. "And I tried searching the microfiche for stories about disappearing women around that time, but there weren't any. This place was kind of dull back in the fifties and sixties. All anyone ever seemed to do was clip coupons and hold sock hops at the radar base."

"Wait." Lonnie looked back and forth between the two of us, a heavy pucker drawing her brows. "What do you mean, her death was sudden and tragic?"

My own forehead mirrored hers. "Wasn't it? I mean, any death is tragic, obviously, and since she was so young, I figured it must have happened out of the blue. Otherwise, why would Jasper have been so brokenhearted?"

"Chloe, honey, Catherine didn't *die*."

My whole body went still, and for the longest moment, I felt sure my heart had, too. "What do you mean, she didn't die?"

Lonnie looked at me so strangely that I started to suspect I hadn't spoken the question out loud. Pepper had to step in and repeat it for me.

"If she's not dead, then what happened to her?" Pepper asked. "What are we missing?"

"You're not missing anything," Lonnie said with a tsk. "I never heard the whole story, but there was some sort of scandal with another man— one from the radar base. She gave me this book, told me to protect it, and left. That's the last I heard from her."

"What about Jasper?" I asked, feeling faint. "What about their tragic love story?"

A sad smile touched Lonnie's lips. "It ended, child, as all things do. Their whole story was nothing but a brief, tempestuous chapter in a book that no one ended up wanting to read."

PART TWO

PART TWO

16

—

1960

JASPER RECEIVED A PAYCHECK EVERY FRIDAY afternoon at three o'clock on the dot. By three thirty, he'd already spent half of it.

"Same as usual?" asked the cheerful blond behind the counter at the city hall office. She served as the bank teller, wire transfer operator, and postmistress all in one, which meant she held most of the town's secrets in the palm of her well-manicured hand. "Forty in cash and forty to Aberdeen?"

"Yes, please," Jasper said, his attention only partially on the transaction. It was taking every ounce of his self-control not to pull the copy of *The Haunting of Hill House* out of his pocket and find where he and Catherine had left off. They were supposed to meet tomorrow night at their usual spot down by the river, but he was itching to hear her thoughts on the passage he'd highlighted yesterday.

The book was scary as hell, and he'd lost hours of sleep to tossing and turning as he tried to shut out the images it evoked, but that was nothing new for him. Jasper had been scared almost every day of his life—of how brightly the sun shone in this part of the state, of the people who smiled and waved and went about their business as though life held nothing but joy, of beautifully laughing girls who made him feel things he thought he'd taught himself to suppress.

"Earth to Jasper," the blond said as she slid four crisp ten-dollar bills across the counter.

"What? Oh. Sorry." He took the money and shoved it into his wallet. "I wasn't paying attention."

"No kidding," she said, but with a smile he assumed was meant to reassure him. "I was just saying that your family must really appreciate everything you do for them. My only brother doesn't care what becomes of us. He left to work in the stockyards in Spokane a few years ago and never looked back. We don't even get a Christmas card."

"Oh," Jasper said, feeling his cheeks grow warm. He couldn't remember the last time he'd sent a Christmas card, either. Was that a thing you were supposed to do? When you already sent every available penny home? "That's...unfortunate."

The blond—Samantha, he thought her name might be—lifted her brows in a perfect arch. She also slid the receipt for the wire transfer across the counter. "You must get lonely without your family to take care of you," she said with a pointed look down at the receipt. Jasper followed the line of her gaze to find that she'd scrawled a six-digit number across the top. "If you ever want to talk about it, you can give me a call."

"Oh. Um. Thanks." He fought the urge to crumple the receipt into a ball and throw it in the nearest garbage. He was no master of the social graces, but even he knew an insult like that would be hard for her to swallow. "I'll do that."

"You won't, but I figure it can't hurt to try." She winked. "See you next week."

Jasper mumbled something even *he* couldn't interpret and ducked his head as he left the city hall. Across the street, he could just make out the beige brickwork of the tiny library, but he didn't direct his steps toward it. There was no point. He already had the book in hand, and Catherine wasn't on shift right now anyway.

Once upon a time, the library had been his happy place, his sanctuary. He'd been able to duck in there any time of day, grab a book off the shelf, and walk away without anyone engaging him in discussion, conversation, or—worst of all—banter. Now, every time he entered those hallowed walls, he became acutely aware of his every breath.

In and out: Lonnie would be watching him with a mischievous twinkle in her eye.

Out and in: Mrs. Peters would step in the way whenever he tried to scrawl a note in the book's margin without getting caught.

In and in and in: There she'd be. Catherine. *His* Catherine, her head bent over a book, the wisps of her hair trailing over flushed, softly rounded cheeks.

She always knew when he came into the library, though she never gave any indication of her awareness other than a brief flutter of her eyelashes. Jasper knew because he felt it, too. Anytime they stood in a room together, the air shifted to make space for them. It had no other choice—the world wasn't designed to hold them in close proximity for long. Like a chemical reaction, they were unstable, combustible, and, most dangerous of all, *explosive*.

Unable to wait another second, he ducked into an alleyway and pulled out the book, hoping no one would walk by and see him. The streets of Colville were annoyingly wide, built to accommodate the sixteen-horse logging carts that used to clog the throughways. The extra space was nice in the winter or for the annual parade that wound up and down Main Street, but terrible when a man wanted a little privacy—and privacy was the one thing Jasper wanted most in the world.

At least, it *used* to be.

His fingers fumbled as he searched for the correct page. As soon as he saw his own illegible scrawl followed by Catherine's pretty, sloped writing, he felt the air leave his lungs.

Each was so bent upon her own despair that escape into darkness was vital, and, containing themselves in that tight, vulnerable, impossible cloak which is fury, they stamped along together, each achingly aware of the other, each determined to be the last to speak.

If you've ever wondered why I sometimes find it hard to say the words out loud, it's this right here: fury and despair, both of them binding me tight. I wish I could offer you a whole heart, but I can't. Not while those two things still exist within me.

You're so dramatic sometimes, J, she'd written, and he could almost hear the laugh in her voice as he read the words to himself.

That was the thing he liked best about her—the thing that attracted and repelled him in equal proportions. From the top of her shining brown hair to the tips of her dainty, well-shod feet, Catherine was the poster child for everything bright and beautiful in this world. Her main trials and tribulations were parents who cared too much about her; her biggest worries centered on how far to push the boundaries that chafed her at every turn.

He didn't want to resent that about her—he didn't want to resent *anything* about her—but when you were a man with only forty dollars in his pocket, it was hard to quash those feelings. Thirty of those dollars would go to his weekly room and board, five to the savings bundle he kept hidden in his mattress, and five to everything else.

Five dollars didn't afford much of a life, even in a backwoods place like this. A book or a night out at the cinema, a new potted plant to brighten up the dingy walls that no amount of decoration could make feel like a home.

He heaved a sigh as he flipped a few of the pages, searching in vain for more writing. Either Catherine had been forced to move quickly, or she was running out of things to say, because he didn't find anything.

Just those five words: *You're so dramatic sometimes, J.*

The worst part was, she wasn't wrong. He *was* dramatic. He always had been. For as long as he could remember, he'd always reacted to situations in the worst possible way. He laughed when he should have smiled, cried when he should have sucked it up, curled into a ball when what the situation needed was a stiff upper lip.

I'm sorry, he wrote back. *I wish I knew how to turn it off.*

He shut the book and dropped it into the library's return box. With any luck, Catherine would see the message and understand: that he was a man who felt things too much, too quickly; that every day was a struggle to find the balance between what the world expected of him and what his heart demanded of himself.

With his head bent low to the ground, he shuffled along the sidewalk toward his apartment. The forty dollars felt uncomfortable in his pocket, as if it had no right to be in his possession. In many ways, it didn't. He'd promised his mom a long time ago that he'd send his earnings back to her and his brothers and sisters. It was a promise he'd kept for three long years—first as a sixteen-year-old away from home for the first time, and now as a nineteen-year-old taking on the rigors of a job that regularly ground fully grown men down to skin and bone.

He wasn't skin and bone—not yet anyway—but every day, he felt himself grinding further and further away. Six hungry mouths to feed would do that to a man.

"Hey. You. Lumberjack boy."

At the sound of that voice, Jasper kept his gaze fixed on his feet, hoping he could feign ignorance or, at the very least, stupidity.

A pair of booted feet planted themselves in front of him. "It's Jacob, right? Or…Jeremy? Jerome? I'm sorry. I know it's something with a J."

Jasper sighed and glanced up. "Jasper," he said in the surly voice that had won him so many enemies in his short lifetime.

"That's right. Jasper." The man—William McBride—smiled brightly at him. "I'm good with faces but not with names. Mind if I walk with you for a bit?"

Jasper did mind, actually, but he couldn't think of a way to say so. He tilted his head in a gesture of assent.

"I don't think we've formally met, but I'm William McBride. I work at the radar base." He said this with all the air of a man conferring a treat on a young schoolboy. "Second Lieutenant McBride? Maybe you've heard of me?"

Jasper grunted. "I know who you are."

"Good. Then you won't think this next part is odd."

He already felt that this whole situation was odd, but there was little he could do about it. He slowed his steps to match that of the other man.

"You're a big reader, right? Spend a lot of time checking out books at the library?"

Jasper's step faltered. "Who told you that?"

"No one. I just always see you hanging around this part of town, and you always seem to be eyebrows deep in some new book or other. What's the one you were reading the other day? It had a green cover." He snapped his fingers as though the answer was incoming. Jasper could have easily enlightened him—it had been Daphne du Maurier's *Rebecca*, and he'd enjoyed every minute of it—but he wasn't about to encourage conversation. Especially not about his deep, highly abashed love of anything containing a hint of romance.

That was the one thing he never told anyone—not even Catherine. She could poke and prod all she wanted, but he was determined to be a fortress. She'd never let him live it down otherwise.

"Anyway," William said. "You read a lot."

"Yes," Jasper agreed when it appeared some answer was required.

"Would you…? Could you…?" William paused, his steps pausing with him. Jasper had no choice but to do the same. "The thing is, I'm trying to get in good with one of the librarians. Catherine Martin. She's the daughter of my commanding officer, and the only thing she seems to like is books."

Jasper had to fight every urge to stalk away from this conversation. He could have easily enlightened this young man about Catherine's interests. She liked books, yes, but she also liked movies—the gorier and bloodier, the better. She ate a single apple for lunch every day when what she really wanted was a cheeseburger with extra pickles and a dark chocolate milkshake on the side. She loved her mother more than any other person in the world, and even though she was outwardly obedient to her father, her heart yearned to cast off every rule and reprimand in his playbook.

But most important, she longed for a bigger, brighter life than this town had to offer. And since she wasn't likely to get it, she was taking solace in an affair with a man who had no right to touch any part of her.

"Have you tried reading a few?" Jasper suggested.

To his surprise, the young officer laughed. He flashed a set of white teeth that seemed unnatural in the full light of day. "Of course I have. I've read more in the past two months than the rest of my life combined. It doesn't seem to do any good. She thinks I'm boring."

Jasper found himself nodding. That sounded exactly like Catherine. She didn't want the ordinary things in life; she wanted drama and terror, excitement and joy. Everything about her burned bright. It was as if the day she'd moved to their town, the sun had come out from behind a cloud and was threatening to blind them all.

"I was just wondering…" William kicked at the ground. "I dunno. If maybe you'd ever overheard her talking about her favorite books, or have ideas about what I should read to get her attention. I took her out to the drive-in a few weeks ago, but I don't think she had a good time."

Jasper started walking again, mostly so he could avoid punching this guy in the face. Catherine had gone out with him in public? No sneaking around, no hiding behind the pages of a book? And he'd *wasted* it?

"Wait—don't walk away." William jogged to keep up, his long, sloping strides easily catching up to Jasper's. Jasper was in good physical shape—when you worked ten-hour shifts felling trees, you had to be— but he'd never been able to make his movements seem even remotely natural. "Just one book title. That's all I want. I've seen you watching her. I know you could help me if you wanted to."

"Watching her?" Jasper echoed, his mouth dry.

"Like a dog staring at a bone. Don't worry. You don't have to explain yourself to me." A smirk touched the edges of the young officer's mouth. "You should be careful how obvious you are, though."

Jasper's skills at reading people had never been particularly strong, but even he knew when a man was trying to threaten him.

"She likes scary books," he said, more for Catherine's benefit than his own. *Not* because he thought this bag of wind and hair pomade deserved a chance at her, but because he had the feeling William could make life very uncomfortable for Catherine if he wanted to. "Try *The Woman in White* or 'The Legend of Sleepy Hollow'. Or anything by Poe."

William wrinkled his nose. It made him look like a petulant baby. "Seriously? You're not just pulling my leg?"

Jasper just managed to refrain from throwing up his hands. He had neither the time nor the energy to continue this conversation. "You asked for my opinion," he said gruffly. "I gave it. What more do you want?"

He started to walk away then, but the young lieutenant's voice stopped him before he made it more than a few strides.

"She won't look twice at a man like you, you know," William said, and without raising his voice. He didn't have to. He knew damn well that Jasper was listening to every word. "Do you have any idea who her family is? How well-connected they are?"

He didn't—not in the way that William was implying—but that didn't matter. Jasper understood all too well the point he was trying to drive home. Not that Catherine was military royalty who could have any man she wanted, and not that she came from the kind of money that meant she'd never have to worry about the source of her next meal, but that Jasper wasn't worth the snap of her fingers.

As if he didn't already know that. As if he didn't feel it down to his very bones.

"If she won't look twice at me, then you have nothing to worry about," Jasper said, his own voice matching the other man's for pitch and keel. He wouldn't give anything of himself away—not for free, anyway. A man in his position couldn't afford it. "Read the books. Don't read the books. I don't care what you do, just so long as you leave me the hell out of it."

17

—

JASPER, PRESENT DAY

JASPER HEARD THE RUMBLE OF THE car pulling up next door before he saw it.

At first, he thought it might be the guy from before—the one Chloe had dragged behind her the day she'd stopped by. Zach, he'd been called, a young man who looked as if he'd crawled out of the forest only to stand in the middle of Jasper's house with his hands tucked in his armpits, his gaze never straying far from Chloe's face. Jasper had recognized the smitten, stupefied look too well to expect never to see him again. That boy would be back to visit the Sampson house, and he'd be back often, or Jasper missed his mark.

It was a strange feeling, the pulse of jealousy he felt when he considered the task Zach had ahead of him. His battle was an uphill one, to be sure. Chloe Sampson wasn't the sort of girl to make things easy on a suitor. She'd laugh and smile and flash the dimple in the middle of her right cheek at all the right moments, but she wouldn't bend without putting up a fight first. If Zach wanted to get anywhere, he'd have to throw his whole heart into the task of wooing her, and even then it wasn't a sure thing.

Not that Jasper was the least bit interested in Chloe for himself. He just missed the uncertainty of it all—the fluttering, uneasy feeling that he was in over his head, the secret smiles that meant more than a touch.

It had been a long time since he'd felt that. More than sixty years, if he was willing to do the math, which he wasn't. At his age, math was never a good idea. The sums and subtractions always ended up being depressing.

He peeked out the window above his kitchen sink, the one that looked out over into the Sampson's front yard, offering him an unbroken view of the house. The car that pulled up wasn't one he recognized. It was dark blue and sleek, the windows so tinted he couldn't see any signs of life inside.

The last time a car like that had pulled up, it had belonged to Child Protective Services. It had gone against every instinct Jasper possessed to put in that call when he had, handing those poor kids over to a system where there was no guarantee that they'd be treated fairly or even kindly, but what other choice had there been? Sneaking in a few groceries while the kids were at school and sitting out on his porch to keep a nighttime vigil had worked for a few days, but he was an old man—and a tired one. There was only so much help he could offer from behind a closed door. He'd waited as long as he could, and even then, he feared he'd waited too long.

He braced himself as the door swung open and a man's legs stepped out of the car. They were too short to belong to Smitten Zach the Mountain Man, and the shoes were much too fussy. So were the shoes that got out the passenger side—a pair of high heels that would ruin a lawn faster than you could say "aerator spikes."

That was when he realized who it was.

"No," he said, even though there was no one to hear him but a hundred different plants that never, no matter how much he talked to them, talked back. "No, no, no, no."

His words were as futile as the rest of him. As he watched the woman emerge from the car and shake out her flaming-red head of hair, he knew that everything good he'd been working toward was at an end. No more Chloe barging over and handing him books that made his heart flip over in his chest. No more Noodle sitting shyly in the yard, reading aloud to him from the Nightwave graphic novel he was obsessed with. No more of those other two kids, so loud and clamoring and *alive* that it sometimes hurt to watch them.

Ravenna Sampson was back. And from the size of the suitcases she started instructing the short man to pull one by one out of the trunk, she looked as if she planned to stay.

———

Jasper waited ten minutes before deciding to act.

For the first five minutes, he listed all the reasons why he shouldn't get involved in the drama he could hear unfolding on the other side of the fence.

1. It wasn't his business.
2. He hated drama.
3. The Sampson kids could take care of themselves.
4. He was already too involved with them.
5. Seriously. He'd managed to go sixty years without emotional entanglements. There was no reason to end the streak now.

For the last five minutes, he'd paced up and down his living room, wearing a tread in the thick white carpet. No matter how many times he tried to tell himself that he didn't care, that they'd survive without him, that no one needed him or even wanted him around, he couldn't rid himself of the feeling that something terrible was going on over there. It was too quiet. Those kids were *never* quiet. Between the dog barking, the television playing at full volume, the occasional explosions that rocked the whole neighborhood, and always—always—the Frisbees whizzing into his quiet retreat, it was like living next to an active volcano.

He'd just hit on a plan to head over with a few of those Frisbees when a loud knock at the back door interrupted him.

"Mr. Holmes?" called a female voice. "Please, Mr. Holmes. We know you're in there. Let us in. It's an emergency."

Jasper's first thought, that Chloe had come to beg for his assistance, was quickly replaced by the realization that this voice was higher in pitch. His second thought was that it made perfect sense for *Trixie* Sampson to be the one shaking his whole house. Chloe wasn't the sort of person who asked for help. She wasn't the sort of person who asked for anything. She reminded Jasper so much of himself at that age that it sometimes hurt to watch her.

"What's going on?" he grumbled as he pulled open the door. Sure enough, the younger Sampson sister stood there with those soulfully big eyes and spattered freckles like something out of an L. M. Montgomery novel. He suspected he'd have been able to hold out longer against the family if not for how alike they all looked. Their similarities were damnably charming, if only because not one of them gave it a second thought. They were forever tied by the bonds of blood and affection, and it never once occurred to them how valuable—and rare—that was.

"Finally," Theo said as he pushed his way past both his sister and Jasper into the house. He moved in a hurricane of long limbs and prepubescent body odor, but stopped short once he reached the interior. "Why do you have so many plants? Are you growing herbs in here? Vegetables? *Poison?*"

This last one seemed to fill him with a sense of excitement that vibrated so strong it rattled Jasper's bones by proximity.

"Theo, you can't just barge into someone's house without asking," Trixie said. Then she turned her eyes on Jasper, and he realized he was done for. "You'll let us in, right? You don't mind? Since you're already taking care of Noodle and everything?"

Jasper, who had long ago closed his heart off to anything but the simple act of *lub-dub, lub-dub*, swung the door open with a sigh. "Fine. You can come inside, but I'm not feeding you. And don't touch anything." He glanced quickly out after her. "Where's Noodle?"

A grimace flashed across Trixie's face. "He didn't want to come. He's...visiting."

Jasper didn't have to ask *who* he was visiting. Even if he hadn't witnessed the prodigal mother returning, the expression of distaste on the girl's face told him everything he needed to know.

"Is your sister also 'visiting'?" he asked, aiming for polite disinterest and falling painfully short of his goal. Fortunately for him, Trixie and Theo were too caught up in their own emotions to notice.

"She almost cut her finger off," Theo announced in a delighted voice that showed what he thought of such a treat. He turned until Jasper could see the sleeve of his T-shirt, where a patch of red showed. "Look. She got blood all over me. She was cutting up carrots for dinner. No one even likes carrots. But then in walks Mom, and BAM!"

"Don't you dare call her that," Trixie said, her voice low and dangerous. "She is *not* our mom. I don't care how many presents she brings or who this fancy new guy—" She cut herself off, her lower lip between her teeth, and dropped a bag to the floor with a thud.

It was only then that Jasper realized what she was carrying—what they were *both* carrying. Backpacks, and ones that were stuffed so full that there was no way they'd just stopped by for some help with their homework.

Trixie followed the path of his gaze and bit her lip even harder.

"I know you don't like us very much," she said. "And I know it's a lot to ask, but pretty please can we stay here for a few nights? Me and Theo both?"

"No." The word shot out before Jasper could stop it.

Instead of taking this sharp denial at face value, both of the Sampsons seemed to draw strength from it. Theo clasped his hands in front of him and put on an expression that could only be described as that of a fallen angel. Trixie, conversely, narrowed her eyes with a shrewd understanding that belied her tender years.

"We'll be so good, Mr. Holmes," Theo begged. "You won't even know we're here, honest. Unless that flower over by the window is nightshade, like I think it is. I might take an eensy-weensy clipping so I can—"

"Stop it, Theo. You aren't helping." With a determined tilt of her chin, Trixie cleared her throat and launched into speech. "*Webster's Dictionary* describes *community* as a *feeling of fellowship with others*. In the following argument, I will relay to the audience not only that community extends beyond the mere—"

"Absolutely not," Jasper said, cutting her short.

She blinked up at him. "But I haven't gotten to the good part yet. You have to at least let me get past the opening statement."

Jasper was about to point out that he didn't *have* to do anything he didn't want to when Theo dug a hand deep into his pocket. The boy pulled out a crumpled, well-worn slip of paper and held it out.

"Here," he said as he slipped it into Jasper's hand. "Maybe this will help. I stole it from Chloe's purse. It's the blank check you gave her."

"The devil it is," Jasper muttered as he uncrumpled the paper and laid it flat. Sure enough, his own signature winked up at him from the bottom. From the looks of it, no attempt had been made to name a figure—not the five thousand dollars he'd offered, not the million dollars she'd threatened to steal, and not even a five-dollar fee to cover a single box of name-brand cereal.

"If I give it back to you, it's kinda like paying room and board, isn't it?" Theo asked, a look of anxiety causing lines to form around his mouth. Of all the Sampson children, Theo was the one Jasper had always felt himself to have the least in common with; he was too exuberant and boisterous, his confidence off the charts. Something about those lines, however, struck home.

"I don't have any money of my own, or I'd add it to the pile," Theo said. "I tried having a paper route once, but there are only like six people in the whole town who get newspapers anymore."

"You don't understand," Jasper said, his words almost a plea. He started taking a few steps back, as though putting space between him and these two kids might help him stave off the inevitable. "You can't stay here."

"We won't take up much space," Theo promised with another of those woebegone looks.

"And we're at school most of the time anyway," Trixie added. "You'll barely notice us."

Jasper reached for the only available lifeline he saw. "But what about your sister? You're just going to abandon her?"

The two kids shared a look so intense that Jasper could practically feel the current flowing between them. He doubled down.

"She gave up everything to take care of you, and this is how you repay her? By running away at the first sign of trouble? Some brother and sister you're turning out to be."

His words were cruel and his tone even crueler, but that was the problem with kids who'd grown up the way they had. Few things had the power to scare them.

"Chloe can handle anything," Theo said with a determined jut of his chin.

"She knows how I feel about that woman," Trixie added, stopping herself just short of spitting in disgust. As if sensing how close Jasper was to the brink, she started to unzip her backpack. "I can pay you, too, if it helps."

"I don't want your money—" he began, but he cut his words short when he saw what she was pulling out. As with the past two books that had recently been returned to him, this one was as recognizable as his own face. As *Catherine's* face.

"This is yours, right?" Trixie said, holding the book—a first-edition library copy of *The Haunting of Hill House*—out of Jasper's reach. He could have easily snatched it from her despite his advanced age, but he didn't.

I was right. Lonnie actually had it. That old bat's been holding on to the book for all these years.

"Where did you get that?" he asked, even though he knew the answer.

"I took it from her room. I'm not stupid. I know you and Chloe are doing some weird literary scavenger hunt."

He almost laughed out loud at how totally wrong—and devastatingly right—Trixie's assessment of the situation was. To all outward appearances, Chloe was merely interested in tracking down a series of library books that had been damaged sixty-some-odd years ago. To Jasper, however, what she was doing was tantamount to resurrecting a corpse.

"Did you read it?" he asked, his voice sounding strained.

"Nah. Books are Chloe's thing, not mine, and they turned this one into a Netflix series anyway." Trixie dangled the book closer. "What do you say? Do we have a deal? I'll give you this smelly old book, and in exchange, you'll let me and Theo stay here until the hosebeast leaves?"

"Hosebeast?" he echoed in an effort to buy himself some time. What he planned to do with that time, however, was anyone's guess.

"She-Who-Shall-Not-Be-Named?" Trixie suggested. "The devil incarnate? The Great Disappearing Ravenna? I don't care what you call her just so long as you don't call her *my mother.*"

Theo sniffled. "She didn't even say she was sorry. She just walked in like nothing had happened."

"She's married now," Trixie added. "She changed her last name. She's not a Sampson anymore."

Each of these was uttered like the clincher to an argument that had long since been won. Which, to be perfectly honest, it *had*. Jasper wasn't sure when he'd become such a pushover where this family was concerned, but he suspected it was the day that Ravenna had first brought Chloe home from the hospital. That red-faced, wriggling baby had taken one look at him and screamed as though she'd give anything to crawl back into the warm cocoon she'd come from.

Me too, kid, he'd thought at the time. *Me too.*

"Let me see the book," he said, reaching for it. Trixie didn't balk as he snatched the book from her hands and turned greedily to the last page. He didn't remember *all* the things he and Catherine had written in the margins, but those final words were imprinted on his heart.

In the unending, crashing second before the car hurled into the tree she thought clearly, Why am I doing this? Why am I doing this? Why don't they stop me?

Serious question for the definitely-not-Eleanor in my life: If someone tried to stop you now, what would you do? Would you walk away? From me? From us?

You know I wouldn't. I can't.

But why are you doing this? Why are you doing this?

Because I love you, C. You know it as well as I do. I've loved you since the moment I first laid eyes on you.

Yes, but you've read the book now. It didn't end well for Eleanor, and it's not going to end well for us, either.

I know.

Jasper ran his fingers over that last line, his hastily scribbled *I know.* Oh, that he could reach back through time and shake the young man who'd committed those words to the page. He didn't know. He *couldn't* know. The kid he'd been—only a few years older than Trixie and Theo, his eyes burning just as hopefully—had no idea that he was in for a lifetime of heartbreak and regret and loneliness.

Loneliness most of all.

"Does this mean you'll let us stay?" Trixie asked eagerly.

"Yes," he said, suddenly feeling too exhausted to fight back. He'd been fighting since the day he was born, and what had it gotten him? A house full of plants but no pictures. Empty halls and emptier holidays. A closet crammed with Frisbees he didn't need or want, but that he held on to because those bright spots of color were the closest thing to a life he had.

"Yes!" Theo cried.

"Thank you!" Trixie sighed.

Both kids made a move as if to tackle him in a hug, but Jasper was quick to step out of the way.

"Don't even think about it," he warned. He hadn't felt the affectionate pull of another person's arms in too long. He was pretty sure that breaking the streak now might actually kill him. "I don't have a guest room, so you'll have to sleep on the living room floor."

"I can sleep anywhere," Theo boasted.

"We'll make a fort," Trixie agreed.

"And if that family of yours comes knocking, I'm not lying. I'll tell them exactly where you are and how you coerced me into taking you in."

"We don't care," Theo said with a mulish set to his mouth.

"It doesn't matter anyway," Trixie added with much less belligerence. "I told Chloe what we were going to do."

That got Jasper's interest. "And she let you walk out the door? Without a fight?"

"She told us to do our worst." Trixie grinned in such a wide, engaging way that Jasper *almost* found himself grinning back. "She said there was no way under the sun you'd ever agree."

18

—

1960

N HIS SHORT LIFETIME, JASPER HAD read no fewer than three different books on etiquette.

The first had been more of a pamphlet than a book, given to him by his mother after he'd been invited to a children's birthday party where he'd known zero of the guests and even less about the many different forks he was likely to encounter there. The second had been Emily Post's *Etiquette in Society, in Business, in Politics, and at Home*, and he'd only picked it up because someone had left it on the train when he'd moved to Colville. The third had doubled as a cookbook, and the only thing he'd gleaned from it was that any and all modern dinner parties required a generous investment of aspic, but he still counted it on his list.

Nothing, however, could have prepared him for the delicate situation of telling a young woman that he was being threatened into helping an up-and-coming lieutenant under her father's command to win her love.

"Out with it," Catherine hissed as they sat in the back of the darkened movie theater, carefully separated by a row in case anyone walked in and discovered them. "What's so important that it couldn't wait for a note inside our next book?"

He glanced over his shoulder to find the flickering lights of the movie casting a brief illumination across her face. The film was one they'd both already seen—*Some Like It Hot*—and they'd carefully chosen a time when they knew the theater would be empty, but Jasper still wished they could watch it like two people on a real date. Sitting side by side, sharing a bucket of popcorn, her thigh pressed warmly against his… Jasper knew her parents would never allow these things, but he still wanted them.

He still yearned.

"We need to pick a new book anyway," he said as he settled back in his seat, buying himself time. "I've run out of interesting things to say about *The Haunting of Hill House*."

Her soft sigh reached him. So did one of the Sugar Babies, courtesy of her surprisingly good aim. It thwacked the back of his head before falling to the sticky floor with a plop. "You're such a liar," she teased. "You loved that book."

He grunted. He'd actually disliked it quite a bit, finding the lack of romance and meandering sentences not to his taste, but he wasn't about to say so. Not when the book was so clearly her favorite.

"Don't worry," she said, still in the teasing tone he didn't trust. He *liked* it, obviously, and was in serious danger of falling irrevocably under its spell, but he trusted it as much as he did a coiled snake. "I have a new one for us to read. I think you're going to enjoy it."

"What is it?" he asked.

"I can't divulge the title. It'll shock your maidenly senses."

He felt himself stiffening into an upright seated position. "My senses aren't maidenly," he said. "They're…sensitive."

"You almost passed out when I took off my top the other day."

"Catherine!" He whirled around, unable to continue the pretense of holding this conversation while speaking to the space in front of him. Sure enough, her face was lit with laughter, her lips parted to show a flash of her teeth. "You can't say things like that in public."

"Why not?" she asked. "I'm only telling it like it is. If I hadn't had the foresight to push you up against the wall of your cabin, you'd have fallen flat on your face."

He groaned and sank down in his seat, feeling his cheeks flame. While it was true that she'd pushed him up against a wall—and that she'd done it while his hand was cupping the most glorious bit of flesh ever to be crafted by God or humankind—he hadn't been shocked.

He'd been excited, obviously. Delighted, yes.

But he'd also been aware of a truth more terrible than anything contained in her stupid horror books: there was no way he was getting out of this thing alive. He was in too deep, too fast, so lost in her that he was in danger of drowning forever.

"If it's D. H. Lawrence, you're too late," he said, feeling petulant. "I already read *Lady Chatterley's Lover*, and my maidenly senses didn't flutter once."

A gurgle of laugher escaped her. "It's not that, but tell me more. *When* did you read this masterpiece of titillation?"

He ignored this and stared at the screen, where Marilyn Monroe sashayed to and fro.

"I've read all of Walt Whitman, too, so don't even try," he added. "*And* the Marquis de Sade, though the translation was bad, so I didn't understand most of it."

Much to Jasper's surprise, Catherine climbed over the back of the seat next to him. She slid into the empty spot, her eyes sparkling. "Why, Jasper Holmes. You're a bit of a dirty bird, aren't you?"

He could only be grateful that the dark lights of the movie theater made it impossible for her to see his blush.

"I just wanted to know what the fuss was about, that's all," he explained.

Instead of teasing him further, Catherine sighed and settled into her seat, allowing no more touch than the light brush of her forearm against his. She was good at that—at knowing when to push and how hard, at pulling back before he got too overwhelmed by the scent and feel of her. He sometimes thought it was her restraint rather than her forwardness that intrigued him the most.

It was as if she knew, on an instinctive level, that the empty spaces were where people like him thrived. The lull in a conversation that neither one of them felt compelled to fill, the electric space where their thighs didn't touch, the lines of a page where she sometimes scrawled a single word—those things meant more to him than all the rest. It was quiet there, and he could be alone in his thoughts without feeling lonely.

"And what, in your estimation, is 'the fuss'?" she asked.

Jasper didn't have to answer her. The question had been uttered in rhetorical spirit, and she wouldn't think it strange if he sat back and watched the movie for a few minutes while he regained his bearings.

But he wanted to tell her. He wanted her to know.

"I know I'm supposed to read those books for the scandal of it," he said as he settled more comfortably in his seat. The side of his oversized work boot brushed the curve of her red patent leather pump. "I hear some of the other guys snickering over stuff like that sometimes, like a few words strung together on a page is supposed to be the same as feeling a woman come undone in your arms."

She sucked in sharp breath, her foot still pressing up against his. "It's not the same to you?" she asked.

He almost laughed out loud. There was no combination of letters in *any* language that could match the way it felt to have Catherine's body next to him—her heart beating against his, her mouth open to let him in, her very spirit escaping and wrapping around his insides until he could no longer tell where one of them ended and the other began. He could read every book in existence and never come even close to that.

"No," he said.

She held her breath in anticipation of more, but Jasper didn't attempt an explanation. There was no point. He wasn't a writer or a poet, and he had nothing to say that hadn't already been said in a thousand different, better ways.

He was just a shy, awkward, overly sensitive man who could never seem to make the world inside his heart and the world he was forced to live in fit together. That Catherine was some sort of bridge, he knew. He'd known it from almost the first moment he'd laid eyes on her, yelling at him from underneath her broken bike, so full of fire that simply being in the same room with her brought him to life.

Her fingers slipped into his. "Okay," she said.

As she rested her head comfortably on his shoulder, her attention fixed on the movie screen, he found himself once again crossing that bridge—however temporarily.

"What if someone comes in and sees us?" he asked.

"Then I get grounded for life," she said as though it were the most natural thing in the world. "Or sent back east to live with my grandparents. Or married off to the first handsome officer to cross the threshold."

That last one caused Jasper to slide his hand out of hers—or at least, to *try*. Catherine's hold on him was too firm for him to slip easily away.

"Don't," she said. "It was a joke."

He was well aware of that, but there was no part of him that felt compelled to laugh. "He likes you," he said, choosing his words carefully. "William McBride."

"I know. His kind always does."

"He approached me in front of the library the other day."

"He did?" That got her to pull her hand away. She cast an anxious glance at him, her brow furrowed and her nose wrinkled. "What did he want? What did he say to you?"

Jasper tried not to let her tone get to him, but her worry cut through him like the slice of a freshly sharpened sword. It had been on the tip of his tongue to divulge everything—the threats and the mockery, the fear that they weren't being as discreet as they should—but he didn't want to add to her troubles.

"He wanted me to give him a reading list," Jasper said, since it was no more than the truth.

Her peal of laughter came at an opportune time, matching that of the silver-screen goddess. "That's cute. Did you do it?"

"I had to. He wanted to know what you liked to read. So he could... woo you. Over literature."

"You didn't tell him about our books, did you? Because if he finds them—"

"No, of course not," he said roughly. "Those are for us."

"And for anyone else who checks them out and finds the notes," Catherine pointed out.

Jasper grunted his agreement. They both knew it was only a matter of time before someone found one of their books and discovered the communication inside them, but that was the whole point. Jasper would never be one of the literary greats. His education had been cut too short, his time too taken up in physical toil. He'd never be able to say even a fraction of the things he felt in his heart.

But for a few lines, for a little while, he got to pretend. In his own meager way, he got to write his love story down.

"Just don't be surprised if he starts quoting Edgar Allen Poe at you," Jasper said by way of warning. "And don't—"

She glanced up at him, her head tilted in an innocent query. "Don't what?" she asked.

It had been on the tip of his tongue to tell her not to fall for it—not to fall for William—but he knew better than to make the attempt. He'd read enough of the books to know how the *real* stories ended.

Not with happily ever after. Not for a man like him.

"Don't encourage him to pick up D. H. Lawrence," he said with a huff. "He's the exact sort to think the scandal is the point."

19

—

1960

THE SPOT BY THE RIVER WHERE Jasper and Catherine met on the sly was as rustic as it sounded.

Jasper had discovered it on one of his many walks through the forest, a habit he'd gotten into when he'd first moved to Colville and hadn't known a single soul outside of his logging crew. The habit had stuck during the three years he'd continued in his post. It wasn't that he didn't *like* the other guys on the crew, but he had a hard time finding a common ground with them.

To be fair, he had a hard time finding common ground with anyone, but that wasn't the barrier. The barrier was that the people he worked with were rough men, tired men—men who'd been forced to trade their strength and youth for a paycheck that, more often than not, fell short of a living wage. They drank and fucked like tomorrow could very easily be their last day on earth, preferring the shortsighted perks of the coarse-minded over the long-term benefits of a well-read mind.

"I had no idea you were such a snob." Catherine laughed as she lay in his arms, sipping from a thermos filled with strong coffee and even

stronger spirits. "How can you look down on men for drinking and
fucking when it's the same thing you literally just did?"

Jasper shook his head as he watched some of the whiskey-laced coffee
slide down the side of Catherine's lipstick-smeared mouth. She dashed a
quick tongue out to catch the drop, but she missed a spot. Naturally, he
had to finish the job she'd started, so it was a good five minutes before
they were able to get back on topic. By then, he'd not only forgotten the
question, but he was pretty sure he'd forgotten all the answers, too.

"How did you find this place, anyway?" Catherine asked with a
crooked smile made all the more lopsided for the lipstick that was even
more smeared now. "A cabin like this must belong to someone. What
makes you so sure the owners won't come back?"

Jasper cast a look around the dilapidated shack—he refused to buy
into Catherine's optimism and call it a *cabin*—and snorted. It had a
roof and four walls, it was true. There was a bed and a fireplace and,
thanks to Jasper's painstaking efforts, enough chopped wood and supplies to survive for a few weeks, should the need arise. He'd also built a
bookshelf where he kept the few books he actually owned. He dreaded
the moment when Catherine's curiosity took over her languid, feline
sleepiness and she looked closer at his collection. He felt pretty sure she'd
laugh outrageously over each of the titles he'd gathered over the years—all
his favorites, and all books she was likely to eschew as romantic nonsense.
Unless you counted Beth March succumbing to scarlet fever or Matthew
Cuthbert being carried off by a heart attack, there wasn't much death
anywhere in those pages.

"The owners won't come back because no one in their right mind
would want to live here," he explained when she cocked an inquisitive
eyebrow at him.

"You would."

He gave a small start.

She giggled. "You can't fool me, Jasper. You'd give up everything to come live out here in the woods like a hermit, chopping wood and growing your food and refusing to have any communication with the outside world." She paused before adding, "In fact, I'm curious why you haven't done that already. You're already nine-tenths a hermit. Why not take the final step?"

"I can't," he said simply.

Just as simply, she answered. "Why?"

Jasper sucked in a sharp breath, wondering—not for the first time—why this woman's soft, sweet brevity so unnerved him. In anyone else, her ability to cut straight to the heart of the matter would send him running for the hills. In Catherine, he only felt himself to be at peace for the first time in his life.

She didn't play games, his Catherine. She teased and taunted. She pulled him so far out of his comfort zone that he was pretty sure the only thing holding him up at this point was a wisp of a cloud that would disperse at the first strong wind. She made love easily and joyfully, and for no reason that Jasper could discern other than because she wanted to. But never, in all the time they'd been writing back and forth, had she been anything but herself.

So even though it pained him—even though his heart suddenly started beating as though it would grow wings and fly straight out of his chest—he told her the truth.

"My life isn't my own," he said. "It never has been."

"What do you mean? Like the company you work for? Are you… indentured?"

"In a manner of speaking," he admitted, scrubbing a hand over the rough landscape of his jaw. No matter how many times he shaved, his shadow seemed to reside at a permanent five o'clock. The trick came in handy when he needed to give off the air of a man who didn't want to be bothered, but he sometimes wished he didn't *always* look so weathered. He'd barely been able to hold on to any sort of childhood as it was.

"Do you owe them money or something?" Catherine persisted. "Because if you do—"

He interrupted her before she went any further down that particular road. "I have a family back home," he admitted. "A big one."

All at once, she sat up. As she did, the faded floral sheet that had been covering the upper half of her body slipped away. Jasper had to dig his fingernails into the palm of his opposite hand just to sit in the same room with such perfection.

The fact that she'd given herself to him—and without once showing a glimmer of regret—was bad enough. That she continued to do so despite the state of this cabin and Jasper's personal situation was worse.

He didn't deserve this. He didn't deserve her.

"What do you mean, you have a family?" she asked, heedless of her nudity. "You mean…a wife? *Kids*?"

He released a silent laugh. "How old do you think I am, Catherine?"

"I don't know…twenty-eight? Twenty-nine? It's hard to tell."

This time, his laugh made an actual sound, but there was no mirth in it. "I'm nineteen," he said. "The same age as you."

"Oh." Her eyelids fluttered as she tugged the sheet back up around her body. Even though he could have gazed at her forever, he was grateful to have her shielded from view. He'd never been great at dealing with too much of a good thing.

"Does that mean you *don't* have a secret wife and kids stashed away somewhere?" she added.

He unfolded himself from the bed and reached for his wallet. Pulling out a photograph weathered around the edges and with images that were already starting to fade away, he handed it to her.

"That's my mom," he said, indicating the tall, slim woman standing on the front steps of a dilapidated town house. "The five kids seated around her are my brothers and sisters."

She looked over the photo for a moment that felt prolonged, even to a man accustomed to lengthy silences.

"Where's your father?" she eventually asked.

He took the picture back from her and tucked it safely away again. "He died when I was twelve. She was still pregnant with Bobby—that's the little boy at her feet—at the time." He paused, unsure how to say the rest without making it sound like a bid for pity. "We did okay for a few months, what with the neighbors pitching in and my mom taking in laundry, but the money ran out faster than any of us expected. I had no choice but to leave school and go to work at the lumberyards."

"At age twelve?" she asked, her eyes wide.

He ducked his head in silent assent—not exactly ashamed, but not unashamed, either. It was a strange position to be in, and one he'd inhabited for so long that he no longer knew any other way. His lack of formal education would always weigh on him, especially since school had been the one place where he'd felt truly at peace, but he was also proud of the man he'd become. A poor man, yes. A weary man, certainly.

But also a man who took care of his family. One who made sure that Bobby, Tina, Harriet, and the twins—Uli and Olly—never had to sacrifice anything they weren't ready to give.

"I didn't come to Colville until a few years ago," he said, since Catherine didn't seem disposed to fill the silence. "I'd been working the mills in Aberdeen for almost four years at the time, and the logging company here put out a call for lumberjacks. I didn't want to leave, but they offered a signing bonus as well as hazard pay. So I lied about my age, packed up a few things, and came here. Half of everything I earn goes home. Half of everything I earn will *always* go home. It has to. There are too many people counting on me."

"Your life isn't your own," she echoed.

He rolled his shoulder in an uncomfortable shrug. "It's not as bad as it sounds. I like being outside and working with my hands. I enjoy the forest and how quiet it gets at night." He smiled slightly over this next part. "And we've always had a well-stocked library here in town. That means more than all the rest."

Catherine slid out of the bed, the sheet clutched to her body like a Roman toga. For the longest moment, Jasper feared that he'd said too much—revealed a truth so bleak that she had no choice but to flee—but all she did was make her way over to the bookshelves. He could make out the curve of her naked back as it fluttered through the fabric, his whole body aching at that expanse of skin, but he didn't move.

Running her fingers lightly over the row of books, she peeked over her shoulder at him. "That's why you read so much, isn't it?" she asked, and in a voice so soft that something wild threatened to break out of him. "It's your education. Your connection to the world."

He nodded, not trusting himself to speak.

"I wish you'd tell me your favorite," she said as though it was the most ordinary thing in the world for a man to reveal the inner workings of his heart. She examined the spines with a smile playing mischievously about the corners of her mouth. "*Pride and Prejudice. Their Eyes Were Watching God. Wuthering Heights.* This is quite the personal collection. Very…romantic."

He held his breath, knowing from her light, teasing tone what was coming next. Coming from anyone else, he'd have fought back—fought against the idea that he could be so exposed and still function in a world that sought every day to wear him down. Coming from Catherine, he knew he could take anything she had to give.

At least, that was what he thought before she spoke up again.

"I brought the next book we're going to read together," she said, still with that teasing note in her voice. She sauntered slowly over to her bag and bent to retrieve it, aware the entire time of how exposed her body was. "But remember what I said—it's going to shock you."

The only shocking thing was how unshaken Jasper's hand remained as he accepted the green clothbound book she held out to him.

"*Tropic of Cancer*," he said aloud. He glanced sharply up. "Catherine! Where did you get this?"

If he hadn't already been head over heels in love with her, the smile that curled her lips would have sealed his fate. It was equal parts mischievous and shy, daring and demure.

In other words, it was exactly like her.

"So you *have* heard of it," she breathed. "I was hoping you had."

"This book is illegal in the United States," he said. He hadn't yet opened the cover, fearful that the contents might burn him. He'd felt the way the first time Catherine had kissed him, and he wasn't so sure he'd come away from that encounter unscarred, either. "You didn't check this out from the library, did you?"

Her rich peal of laughter rang out, filling the cabin with the last thing needed to make it truly feel like home. "Of course not. Can you imagine me trying to sneak this past Mrs. Peters? She'd have palpitations just thinking about all those delicious Parisian orgies."

"Then where did it come from?"

She slid onto the bed and lay back against the headboard, waggling her eyebrows as she went. "I have my sources."

"You have underground literary sources? In *Colville*?"

She giggled. "Okay, I got it from Lonnie, but you can't tell anyone. One of her brothers got a whole box on his last trip to Mexico and has been selling them out of his trunk for twenty bucks a pop."

Jasper released a low whistle as he considered the book in his hand. That kind of money was a steep price to pay for a single book, but he couldn't pretend not to be intrigued. There'd been a lot of scandal attached to this book since its publication in the thirties, most of which had to do with indecency laws and the corruption of minors. "And you bought a copy? For *us*?"

She took the book back and started lovingly flipping through the pages. "Well, I would've snagged one with or without you, but I thought it might be a fun thing for us to do together."

"Catherine…"

She cast him a pair of innocent eyes. "What? It's important to be well-read. Consider it the next step in your self-driven education."

He tsked and shook his head, though not without a slight smile. Only Catherine could turn an innocent game of reading into something that threatened to upend his whole life.

"I take that to mean you're in?" Catherine asked eagerly.

Obviously he was in. But what he said was, "Where did you come from, Catherine Martin? Who *are* you?"

She purred and stretched out on the bed, interpreting his questions in the most literal way possible. "I'm a nomad, Jasper. I come from everywhere and nowhere."

"And?"

"And nothing. I'm exactly who I look like. A girl who's spent her whole life doing what her father tells her to." A slight grimace touched her lips. "Just like one of his obedient little soldiers."

Jasper looked at the cabin around them, this nest of vice and virtue, the place that would forever hold his heart, and laughed.

"What?" Catherine demanded, sitting up. "What's so funny?"

He climbed onto the bed with her. The moment his knees touched those sheets, the smell of her came rushing over him. "You're nothing like one of your father's soldiers," he said as he brushed his lips over hers. "Everything you do is an act of defiance."

"You're only saying that because you want another act of defiance out of me before we leave."

He shook his head, unwilling to let her turn this moment into one of her games. Threading his fingers through hers, he said, "I've never known anyone who flips the world upside down as easily as you. You read the books you're not supposed to read. You make friends with the people you're not supposed to befriend." He blushed and stammered a little over the next one. "You seduce the men you're not supposed to seduce."

She squeezed his fingers in her own. "I do, don't I?"

"Promise me you won't ever let anyone make you feel like you owe them anything." He spoke with a violence that was too heated, but since when was that new? Jasper always carried extra emotion wherever he went. It followed him and bound him at the same time. "Not me, not your parents, and definitely not men like William McBride."

"Why, Jasper Holmes. That sounds an awful lot like jealousy."

"It's not." He lifted her hand to his mouth and dropped a soft kiss onto each of her fingers. "I just know how the world works. It's designed to grind people like you under its heel."

"And what about people like you?" she countered, her gaze fixed on each movement of his lips. "What does it do to you?"

Jasper had the answer ready. "I was ground down the day I was born. The most I can hope for is to return to the earth exactly as I came into it."

20

—

JASPER, PRESENT DAY

JASPER FELT THE FRISBEE WHIZZING BY his head before he saw it.

It flew past as a brief flash of neon in his periphery. At first, he thought it might be the goldfinch that sometimes visited his bird feeder, or even one of those strange tricks of light that seemed to interfere with his vision more and more these days, but it was accompanied by an overly loud, overly obvious shout of, "Aw, Gummy Bear! Look what you made me do."

He set aside his book with a sigh. *The Haunting of Hill House* was just as grotesque as he remembered, but he was having a hard time buying into the terror of it the way he had as a kid—for a kid he'd definitely been the first time he'd read it. Nineteen years of age might technically qualify one as an adult, but he'd been a fool to think that he was anything like this Eleanor character.

Was I melodramatic and prone to long, depressed walks in the moonlight? Of course.

Did all reason and rationality flee as soon as darkness fell? Obviously.

Would I drive my car into a tree in a last-ditch effort to flee the inevitable? That part he wasn't so sure about anymore.

In the growing light of dawn, with more than sixty years of hard living at his back and two kids curled up in sleeping bags on the floor of his house, it was hard to remember those feelings. He and Catherine had been so young at the time, caught up in a love affair as brief as it was ill-conceived, that they hadn't stopped to think about the long-term ramifications. Back then, if someone had asked him if theirs had been a love worth dying over, he'd have responded with an unequivocal yes.

These days, however…

"*Psst*, Jasper. Jasper, are you awake?"

"Of course I'm awake," he said as he unfolded himself from the chair. He cast a quick look around the yard and found the Frisbee embedded in a currant bush. Grabbing it, he stalked over to the fence. "What are you doing up so early?"

He knew the answer to that question as soon as he caught sight of Chloe's face. She looked as though she'd slept all of five minutes the night before, her wild flame of hair swept up on top of her head and her freckles standing out from the pale anxiety of her face. She'd thrown a tattered robe over her tank top and pajama shorts, but it didn't provide nearly enough protection against the early morning chill. Already, the fall dew was starting to crystallize into frost, her breath coming out in short, billowing puffs.

"I thought we decided you weren't going to play with that dog in the yard anymore," he said, his tone rough with concern.

She ignored both this comment and the dog himself, who was so uninterested in playing fetch that he'd sprawled himself out by his empty food dish instead.

"Are they okay?" she asked.

He didn't have to pretend to know who she was talking about. "What, are you afraid I killed them in their sleep and buried them out back? Because I don't think you realize how long it would take to dig a grave of that size."

She laughed. It was an uncanny sound, almost frantic, as if was escaping of its own free will. "Do you know, a few weeks ago, I'd have said yes?" She tilted her head toward one of Jasper's favorite flower beds. It was where he planted his annuals—a complete waste of space and effort, but somehow all the more beautiful because of how short a time they had on this planet. "For a while there, I thought that might be the grave of your long-lost Catherine."

The name rolled off her tongue so easily that Jasper felt himself growing weak in the knees.

"But that can't be, can it?" she asked, watching him. "Her grave, I mean?"

Her question sounded and felt like a rhetorical one, but the pause lingered so long afterward that Jasper had to say something. "No," he agreed slowly. "It can't be."

"What year did you say she died, again?"

This seemed strangely like a challenge. "I didn't."

A light flipped on inside the house behind Chloe, at which point she gave a small jump. "Oh, God. She's up. Quick—can I come over?"

Jasper splayed his hands helplessly. She had to know that when he'd allowed her brother and sister to stay, he'd also opened his doors to her. His doors, his home, his whole blasted life—he'd gone sixty years keeping them tightly sealed, only to find that his barriers were made of nothing but hot air.

"Are you sure you should leave Noodle alone?" he asked as Chloe came dashing around the shrubbery. He caught a glimpse of her grimace before she managed to tamp it down.

"Noodle's the reason we're in this mess in the first place. He's the one who called her. Ravenna. *Mom.*"

That surprised Jasper, but not for the reasons Chloe would have expected. From some of the things the boy had let fall, it was clear that he saw more of Chloe's struggles than the other two kids combined. The anxiety over money, the way she fought like a tiger against anyone who said a word against her family, her determination to stand on her own two feet no matter what the cost… Jasper had seen those struggles, too, though it hadn't been his place to intervene.

"He's only trying to help you," Jasper said.

Chloe cast him that curious look again. It was different from the way she usually looked at him, which was warily and with a light sprinkling of contempt. This was more puzzled than anything else, as if she was trying to see something that lay just beyond the surface.

"Does that mean you encouraged him?" she asked. "Noodle talked to you about making that call?"

That made Jasper snort. "You think we're over here all day talking about the mom who walked out on you? And that I gave him grandfatherly advice about how to deal with it?"

An infinitesimal relaxing around the corners of Chloe's eyes was all Jasper needed to know that she understood. Most of the time, he and Noodle merely sat in blissful, companionable silence.

"Are you going to stand outside in your underwear all morning, or did you want to come in for coffee?" he asked. There was nothing about his tone to indicate she was welcome, but he held his breath, hoping she'd know it anyway.

Chloe took her lower lip between her teeth. After casting a quick look back at her house, where lights and footsteps continued to indicate that life was awakening inside, she nodded.

"His name is Todd," she said with a grimace.

At that, Jasper was in danger of laughing out loud. "Todd?"

"Todd Aarons. He works in insurance, but only because his pro football career didn't pan out the way he wanted it to. Apparently, his knees are bad."

"Guys like that *always* have bad knees," Jasper agreed, fighting a smile. From the way Chloe spoke, you'd think the guy was a regular

Bluebeard about to unleash his horde of dead wives. "Is it safe to leave Noodle with them for a few minutes?"

"He's nice, all things considered," Chloe admitted, her lip curling as though "nice" was the worst thing she could say of anyone. She paused before adding, "And I think he's good to my mom. He seems really supportive of her."

Jasper only nodded. He knew what an admission like that must be costing her. "Then come on in. You can see for yourself that Theo and Trixie are perfectly fine."

Her hand touched his arm, the movement so quick that he almost thought it was the rustle of the wind. But then she spoke up, and with the tight pinch of worry that always bound up her expression.

"And you? How are you holding up?"

"If that's your way of asking whether or not that brother of yours has tried burning down the house already, the answer is yes." Jasper turned on his heel and stalked into his house. "But I have excellent smoke alarms and made sure to hide all the accelerants. We're safe for now."

———

They entered the house to find that both children were awake, alert, and making a mess of Jasper's kitchen.

"Chloe, did you come for breakfast?"

"Chloe, look-it! Jasper—I mean Mr. Holmes—I mean Jasper—has *five* different kinds of cereal. And they're the good ones, too."

"Chloe, will you tell Theo that he can't just pour all five kinds into one bowl? Mixing Grape Nuts and Lucky Charms is an abomination against nature."

Instead of answering her siblings, who were apparently unable to exist inside a room without destroying it, Chloe peeked over her shoulder at Jasper.

"You just happen to have five different kinds of name-brand cereal in your house?" she asked.

He rolled an uncomfortable shoulder. "I didn't know how long they planned to stay. I picked up a few supplies while I was in town."

"Cocoa Puffs! Real live Cocoa Puffs." Theo gave up on trying to mix the cereals and poured himself out enough sugary bounty to keep him bouncing off the walls for hours. "Sorry, Chloe, but I'm officially moving in with Jasper."

Trixie snatched the box out of Theo's hands before he could pour it all into a single bowl. "Save some of that for me, you jerk." She had the decency to blush as she glanced at Chloe, but with a determined set of her jaw that dared anyone to contradict her. "If you're here to make us come home, you can save it. I don't want anything to do with that woman or the deadweight she dragged in with her. If you try to make me, I'll run away."

At these clear lines of battle, Chloe held her own.

"Oh yeah?" she asked. "Where will you go? To the forest cliff where Noodle almost fell to his death? Because I feel like that approach is getting old."

Trixie's chin jutted out. "Yes, if I have to. I'd rather die of exposure than share breathing space with that woman."

"She came all the way from Vancouver to help out," Chloe said.

"That woman could have journeyed from Mars, and I'd feel the same way. You might be willing to accept a first edition copy of *The Princess Bride* as a peace offering, but my price is a lot higher than that."

Jasper turned curiously toward Chloe, watching as a touch of red started creeping up her cheeks. *The Princess Bride*, huh? Strange. The tongue-in-cheek narrative style wasn't his personal favorite, but from the way Chloe clamped her mouth shut, he was guessing the book meant a lot to her.

"You keep calling her 'that woman,'" Theo said around a mouthful of Cocoa Puffs. "Shouldn't you just call her Mom?"

"I'll call her Mom when she starts acting like one."

With that, Trixie flounced out of the room. Jasper had no idea where she was going—his house was a small one, so their voices would reach her no matter what—but he didn't bother trying to find out. He was starting to realize that this family had no idea what *not taking up much space* meant. They were like a meteor crashing into the earth: fast and thundering, unable to land without leaving a huge scar behind.

"I'm sorry," Chloe said as she sank to one of Jasper's stools. She accepted the cup of coffee but only sat aimlessly stirring it. "I figured this would be hard on Trixie, but…"

As her voice trailed off, she caught sight of the book Jasper had brought inside with him—the book that had, just yesterday, been in her own possession. Well aware where to lay the blame, her eyes narrowed and her head swiveled to face Theo's.

"Theo," she said warningly. "Did you go through my things?"

He shoveled a spoon of cereal into his mouth. "Yep."

"And did you take that book without permission?"

"Technically, Trixie was the one who did it. I only supervised."

Jasper intervened before their squabble could descend any further. "In their defense, it *is* my book. All they did was return it to its rightful owner." He paused. "I was right about it? Lonnie had it the whole time?"

Chloe turned to look at him, once again with that uncanny light in her eyes. "Yes. We had a nice long chat about you. And about Catherine."

He didn't wince at the sound of her name, but he did feel a sharp pang in the region of his heart. He pushed on. "Interesting. How's old Lonnie doing these days?"

"Dying," Chloe stated baldly.

This time, he really did wince. Despite the connection they'd once shared in the form of Catherine Martin, he and Lonnie Pakootas had never been close. He'd always felt as though Lonnie blamed him for what had happened to Catherine. It *was* his fault, obviously, but Lonnie didn't have to be so judgmental about it. He'd tried loving Catherine. He *had* loved Catherine.

Unfortunately, love wasn't always enough.

"You should visit her," Chloe said. "She might appreciate seeing a friend from her girlhood."

Jasper's only response to this was a nod. He wasn't sure what Chloe was driving at—or what Lonnie had said to put her on her guard—but it wasn't his priority right now. He could only handle one crisis at a time, and even that was a strain.

"How long are they staying?" he asked instead. "Ravenna and... Todd?"

Theo stopped in the act of bringing the spoon to his mouth, his eyes bright as he awaited the answer.

"I don't know." Chloe gave up on stirring her coffee, her shoulders slumped. "A few days? A few weeks? *Forever?* Even though she has no legal authority over the kids, the house is technically in her name, so she can stay as long as she wants."

"And she hasn't said anything?" Jasper persisted. It went against his nature to prod at an open wound not of his making, but he couldn't resist. "About leaving the way she did? About walking out and abandoning three underage children?"

Theo's mouth tamped down in a straight line. So did Chloe's.

"I think the decision of how long she stays is going to be up to Noodle," Chloe said, but not before first reaching over and gently ruffling Theo's hair. "He's the one who called her. He's the one who needs her."

"He doesn't need her," Theo said. He pushed his half-eaten bowl of cereal away. "Not when he has us."

Instead of reprimanding him for waste, Chloe sighed and propped her chin on her hand. "I'm sorry, Theo. I don't like it, either. Unfortunately, I can't just pack everything up and move in with Jasper like you and Trixie. Someone has to be there to keep an eye on Noodle."

Jasper didn't mention that since he'd issued no invitation, she was in no position to live with him in the first place. What was the use? At some point in the past month, the Sampson children had decided he was one of them: a friend, a protector, a *grandfather*, even. He hadn't gotten so caught up in a whirlwind of other people's emotions since, well, Catherine.

Chloe grimaced. "At the very least, Mom might be able to get Noodle to tell her what's going on with all this school and running away stuff. I can't get anything useful out of him."

"Don't look at me." Theo shrugged. "All he says is that he's sorry and he didn't mean to make trouble."

Chloe turned toward Jasper, a not-unhopeful gleam in her eye. He knew what was coming, so he flung up a hand to stop her. "I haven't pried into the boy's affairs, and I have no intention of doing so. If he wanted you to know what was going on, he'd have told you. You need to trust him to work through it on his own."

"That's the stupidest thing I've ever heard. He's a *child*."

"Yeah," Theo chimed in. "Children aren't to be trusted. All we do is eat and make messes."

"Thank you," Jasper drawled with an obvious look around his disaster of a kitchen. "I've been able to piece that much together on my own."

Theo giggled, but Chloe wasn't ready to let the subject drop. "You do realize Noodle's only twelve, right?" she asked. "He's still very much a minor and still very much under my care."

Jasper recognized the heat in her voice but refused to let it sway him. If anything, he found himself warming to it. "Good God, girl. Twelve is old enough to know his own business. Do you have any idea what I was doing at that age?"

"No," she countered. "Tell me."

He had no idea what compelled him to respond. His childhood was none of Chloe's business, and even if it was, telling sob stories about things that couldn't be changed wasn't his style. Better to keep things bottled up tight than splash them around to become someone else's problem.

Still. He answered.

"I was working full-time. I was taking care of my family just like you. So don't sit there and sigh like you're the only person to ever experience hardship. To ever *sacrifice*."

Instead of pushing back, as Jasper expected, the hard line of her mouth softened. "I'm sorry," she said. "I didn't know."

"Why would you?" he shot back—mostly because he was ready to move the conversation along, but also because he didn't know what else to say. It was too early in the day for kindness and understanding. A man needed some time to *adjust* first.

He blamed that unsettled, upended feeling for what popped out of his mouth next. "Very well. If you're that worried about the boy, I'll see what I can find out."

Chloe turned to him in what looked like slow motion, her mouth dropping open in a gentle O of surprise. "You will? How? *Why?*"

"Don't ask me impertinent questions," he grumbled. She didn't have to look *that* surprised. His offer of help wasn't entirely altruistic. How the hell else was he supposed to get this family out of his house and off his lawn? "Do you or do you not want to help your brother?"

"I do," she said.

"And do you or do you not trust me to elicit answers you're too soft to get for yourself?"

A burgeoning smile touched her lips. "I do."

"Then there you go." He grabbed his cup of coffee again, pleased to find that his hands were steady. He nodded first at Chloe and then at Theo, who was watching the whole interaction as if it were a high-wire circus act. "Since I'm already doing nine-tenths of your work for you, I might as well add this to the list. It's not as if I have anything else to fill my days."

"What did you fill them with before?" Theo asked.

"Reading," Jasper said, even though it was a bald-faced lie. Before Chloe's discovery of *Tropic of Cancer*, he hadn't picked up a book in years. Lately, however, he found he couldn't get enough. All his old favorites— those sloppy, sentimental romances that were once the only thing that made him feel alive—were suddenly stacked up on his bedside table.

He'd forgotten how it felt. To hold a book in your hands and know that everything would turn out okay in the end, to lose yourself in someone else's story… That was a joy he hadn't allowed himself to indulge in for a very long time.

He wasn't sure if he did a bad job of hiding his emotions, or if Chloe was always this pushy in the morning, but she cocked her head and asked the one question he'd been dreading: "Why are you doing all this for us? What's changed?"

He didn't say the answer that was in his heart, for the sole reason that to give it voice was to put it on the line. The words were much safer where they lay hidden, protected by the wall he'd constructed a long time ago.

I have, it said. *It's me. I changed.*

Instead, he glowered and began shuffling away to the relative privacy of his bedroom.

"I can still kick the whole lot of you to the curb," he said instead, his words carrying a warning that none of them bothered to heed. "Don't push me too far."

21

—

JASPER, PRESENT DAY

RAVENNA SAMPSON–RAVENNA AARONS–WHATEVER her last name was now—was exactly the same as Jasper remembered.

"Mr. Holmes, I presume?" she asked as she answered his knock on the front door. She smiled sunnily up at him, though he could detect signs of wrinkles starting to develop around her eyes. In many ways, those wrinkles were the only things that differentiated her from her two daughters. The gene pool was strong in this family. "Just kidding. I remember you. Chloe said you might be swinging by today. Come on in."

His only reply was a grunt. To say anything else was likely to open the floodgates of conversation, and neither of them wanted that. Jasper, because he wasn't in the mood for a lengthy chat; Ravenna, because she wouldn't enjoy hearing any of the things he had to say to her.

"I came to get Noodle for the day," he said, trying to peer around her. Even though it hardly seemed possible, the house was in even more disarray than the last time he'd been here. Suitcases lay open, their contents seemingly scattered at random, a pile of untouched gift boxes on the coffee table. "Is he here?"

She frowned, the lines around her eyes deepening. "Didn't Chloe tell you? I've come to take care of Noodle until he's recovered. You're off the hook."

Jasper didn't have an opportunity to respond to this. For one thing, that lazy, stumbling dog of theirs came ambling forward in hopes of a treat. For another, a loud, booming male voice made itself known in a big way.

"Come in, come in!" it called. Despite the deep timbre and how much it rattled the walls, the voice belonged to a man who couldn't have stood more than five foot six, his build slight and his paunch considerable. Jasper had to hold back a snort at the sight of him; if this guy went around convincing people that the reason his football career didn't take off was because of his knees, then he was one hell of a salesman.

"You must be the savior," Todd said.

Jasper felt his hand being grasped in a surprisingly strong grip and wrenched almost from its socket.

"What did you just call me?" Jasper asked, forcibly taking his hand back.

The man didn't even blink. "The savior. The good fairy. The knight in shining armor." When each word out of his mouth only caused Jasper to turn a deeper shade of red, Todd chuckled. "The next-door neighbor."

He made even that last one sound like something out of a fairy tale—a thing Jasper didn't appreciate in the slightest.

"I'm here for the boy," Jasper said with a hard set of his jaw. "Where have you hidden him?"

"I'm right here." Noodle emerged from the hallway, his steps halting from the crutches that propped him up. Ravenna brightened and extended her arms, but Noodle ducked before she could wrap him in a hug. He embraced the dog instead.

"Isn't he such a brave, strong boy?" Ravenna asked.

Even though Jasper felt fairly sure the question was meant for him,

Todd took it upon himself to answer. "A real trouper," he said as if addressing an audience of three thousand people instead of just three. "Pluck to the backbone, just like his old mom."

"Well, really, Todd." Ravenna had the decency to blush, but not for the reasons Jasper supposed. "How dare you call me *old*?"

"And still as beautiful as the day I met you," Todd added with a pat on her behind.

The look Noodle cast up at Jasper was so speaking—and so anguished—that it was all he could do not to haul the kid up in his arms and drag him out of there as fast as he could. Unfortunately, his old bones didn't allow for it.

"You've got to be at least forty-five by now, Ravenna," he said instead. If action was out of the question, then venomous words would have to do the trick. In his experience, they usually did. "I think the adjective fits."

Ravenna's mouth fell open with surprise, but Todd only chuckled. "Now, Mr. Holmes. Is that any way to talk to a lady?" he asked.

"When I see a lady, I'll let you know." Jasper turned his attention to Noodle. "Well, brat? Are you coming with me or not? I've got a field trip planned for today, but with that leg of yours, it's bound to be slow going. We'd best get a move on."

From the way the kid lit up, like a Christmas tree standing alone in the middle of a decimated forest, Jasper realized his duty: he had to get Noodle out of here, and he had to do it no matter what it cost him.

"A field trip?" Ravenna echoed. Her face fell to a comical degree. "Oh, no. Noodle, honey, I thought we were going to spend the day together, just you and me."

Todd gave a low cough.

"And your stepfather, of course," she added. She took her lower lip between her teeth. "We have so much stuff to catch up on."

"About four years of stuff, by my estimation," Jasper said. He pretended to think about it. "Or is it five? The time goes by so fast when they're young. It's hard to keep track."

From the way Ravenna's face went suddenly white, he knew he'd hit his mark. He also knew that he didn't give a flying fig whether or not he'd hurt her feelings. Chloe might be willing to accept this woman for the sake of her family, and Noodle had his own reasons for calling her, but that didn't mean Jasper had to play nice.

In fact, *not* playing nice was an art he'd perfected a long time ago. More people ought to give it a try.

"I'm sure you two will find plenty to keep you busy while we're gone," Jasper added as he grabbed the leash hanging by the door and clipped it to the useless bulldog's collar. It would take three times as long to get anywhere with the dratted animal dragging at their heels, but he knew how much Gummy Bear mattered to the boy. "There's a sink full of dishes you could do, the roof leaks in at least half a dozen places, and I'm sure if you dig around long enough, you'll find a stack of unpaid bills lying around. *Lots* of them."

Ravenna opened her mouth and closed it again, looking exactly like a fish that had just discovered a hook in its mouth, but Jasper didn't wait around to see how Todd reacted. For one thing, he didn't give a damn what that man thought. For another, Noodle was staring up at him with wide eyes that he was having a hard time interpreting. Was that surprise? Anguish? Or, as he allowed himself a brief moment to hope, respect for a job well done?

"Come on, Noodle," he said gruffly as he started tugging the dog out the door. "Daylight's wasting, and you promised to read aloud to me from the next *Nightwave* book."

Noodle ducked his head and hobbled on his crutches as he followed Jasper out the door, but not before first casting an apologetic look back at his mom. Jasper wanted to tell him to save his apologies and emotions for someone more deserving of it, but what was the use?

He knew what it was like to be the son of a woman who struggled, every day, to do the right thing—and a woman who almost always ended up handing the problem to someone else to handle for her.

You suffered and you strove. And even though it hurt, you survived.

———

"Hold on tight, Aloysius. We're taking this next part at full speed."

Jasper braced one hand on the trunk of a ponderosa pine and breathed heavily as young, annoyingly fit Zach zoomed down the path with Noodle slung over his back like a knapsack. The two of them jostled and bounced all the way down, heedless of broken bones and plaster casts and all the other hazards that faced them. Jasper's whole body ached just to watch them—and, considering the groan Gummy Bear heaved by his side, he was sure the dog felt the same way.

They weren't kidding when they said that youth was wasted on the young. What Jasper wouldn't give to have the strong back and legs of his lumberjack days, when lifting a woman was as easy as—

"You coming, old man, or what?" called Zach from the clearing at the bottom of the path. He wasn't the least bit winded from carrying the hundred-pound boy on his back for over a mile, a grin splitting his good-natured features.

"Hold your horses," Jasper grumbled as he pushed off the tree. He and Gummy Bear made their way down to join them, their bones cracking with each step. He'd debated with himself for a full ten minutes before finally giving in and calling the wilderness school to request Zach's help with this little adventure. He didn't *want* the young man's company, but he *needed* it. These days, the two things were becoming damnably intertwined.

"There's no need to be so heroic," Jasper grumbled as he almost stumbled over a rock. "Chloe isn't here to watch you show off."

Zach waggled his eyebrows. He did that good-naturedly, too, as if he was incapable of doing anything without that blasted smile. "Yeah, but Aloysius here can go home and tell her all about it, which is just as good. Why else do you think I agreed to take the day off to be a pack animal?"

Noodle smiled shyly over the top of Zach's knit cap. He also smoothed the waters with a bland disinterest in any and all things related to his sister's burgeoning romance. "This is the most fun I've had on a field trip before," he said.

Zach laughed. "That's because I'm the one doing all the hard work. How much further until we get there?"

"Tired already?" Jasper countered, but without much rancor. Mostly because he was plenty tired himself. "Don't worry. It's just through that clearing. The key's hidden under a mat, but I doubt you'll need it. The raccoons have been making themselves free with the place for years."

"Everyone's gotta live somewhere," Zach said by way of answer as he turned and trotted the rest of the way to the cabin.

Jasper hadn't been here in years—probably close to a dozen of them, if he was keeping track—so he wasn't sure what to expect as he stepped through the aforementioned clearing and up to the one-room log structure that had once housed so many of his hopes and dreams. In his memory, the cabin always seemed to exist in a dappled half sunlight, like an underwater cavern untouched by time or tide.

Like so many parts of his memory, however, the reality was much less exciting. The cabin, once charmingly rustic, was now in danger of falling over. The stacked log walls leaned perilously to one side, the door sunk so low that he had to take an actual step down to make it inside.

And the interior, well, the less said about that the better. If the raccoons had been making themselves free with the place, it had been almost entirely to use the structure as a urinal and nothing else.

"This. Is. Awesome," Noodle breathed as Zach carefully lowered him to the ground.

"It sure is," Zach said, and with an absence of irony that put Jasper on his guard. "This is *your* place?"

"It technically belongs to the Neilson Logging Corporation, but yeah. It's been abandoned for as long as I've lived in Colville." He closed one eye and added, "Which is well over sixty years, so don't push me."

Zach grinned. "I hadn't planned on it, sir." He started moving around the cabin, his hands tucked carefully behind his back as he peered at the artwork adorning the walls. Most of it was just nature sketches and pressed flowers, but a black-and-white photograph of a young smiling Catherine sat slightly askew above the bed.

"Is this her?" he asked, peering at it. "Catherine? The woman who... died?"

Jasper didn't care for younger man's tone, but there didn't seem any way to avoid it. "That's her," he agreed.

Zach released a soundless whistle. "Damn, Jasper. She was a looker."

Something inside his chest turned over. "I know."

Fortunately for the state of Jasper's sad, still-beating heart, Noodle unknowingly intervened once again. "Mr. Holmes, you have a ton of books here. Like, *a ton*."

"I know," he said again. He lowered himself to a wicker chair that looked as though it might hold his weight long enough to get this over with. Gummy Bear, with an affinity that Jasper was starting to find disconcerting, settled next to him with a weary sigh.

"But you don't have any bookshelves in your house," Noodle continued. "All you have are plant shelves."

"That's because plants are alive, and books aren't," Jasper said.

This was only partially the truth. In many ways, books were more alive than most of the people he knew. They were living, breathing entities that changed each time you picked them up. When he was a young man, every book had been an opportunity to see the world from a place of safety and comfort, to travel to exotic destinations he'd been unable to afford and too shy to explore on his own. As a middle-aged man, he'd found books to be less about hope and more about finding the discrepancies between what fiction had promised and reality delivered.

And as an old man…well. He wasn't sure about that part yet. These days, he was finding that damnable optimism creeping back in on agile legs.

Noodle hobbled forward and began running his hand over the damp, decaying spines of what used to be an excellent personal library. Time hadn't been kind to those books—but then, it hadn't been all that generous to Jasper, either. That was exactly why he'd left them out here. Not to rot but to be entombed.

"Have you really read all these?" Noodle asked.

"Several times," Jasper said. He caught Zach turning an interested eye toward the books and quickly changed the subject. "But that's not what I brought you out here to say."

Noodle lowered himself to the end of the mildewed mattress and folded his hands in his lap with an air of expectancy. Zach almost did the same, but he must have decided that the rickety frame wasn't up to his weight because he leaned in the doorway instead.

"Am I allowed to hear this?" he asked. He hooked a thumb over his shoulder. "Or is it better if I make myself scarce? I can, you know. I spotted some chicken-of-the-woods on our way down that I wouldn't mind scooping up."

"There are chickens out here?" Noodle asked. "Where? I didn't see any."

Zach offered him a crooked smile. "Not the kind you're thinking of, Aloysius. I'm talking fungi. Sulphur polypore. Sweet, earthy delicacies that'll—"

Noodle made a face. "Ew. *Mushrooms?*"

Jasper held back his laugh. One of these days, he was going to lose control and actually release one, but he wasn't that far gone yet.

"You can stay if you want to," he said to Zach. "It's the least I can do after you trekked all the way down here with that deadweight on your back—especially since you still have to cart him back up." Jasper pointed a warning finger. "But you're not to tell any of this to Chloe, understand? It's meant to be between us men."

Zach saluted. "Aye, aye, sir."

"Really?" Noodle asked, his eyes widening. "Like a secret?"

"Exactly like a secret," Jasper said. "I don't want your sister thinking I go around offering violence to every young person who gets on my bad side."

Noodle's eyes only got bigger, but Zach turned to him with narrow-eyed interest.

"Violence, huh?" he murmured. "I bet you packed a mean punch back in your heyday. You have the build for it."

"I did." Jasper pressed his mouth into a flat line. "I once punched a man so hard I broke his jaw."

Noodle's response to this was a squeak—of excitement, maybe, or dismay.

"I shouldn't have done it, of course," Jasper said, lest the boy get the wrong idea. "Hurting another human being is never the answer—no matter how strong the provocation or how much you want to do it."

"Did you want to do it?" Noodle asked. He was a bright enough kid to pick up on the subtext—that this story would tie into his own recent skirmish, and that Jasper had brought him out to the middle of nowhere with the sole intent to discuss it.

"Oh, I definitely wanted to." Jasper lifted his hand and flexed as if feeling the crack of William McBride's jaw breaking all over again. "He stole the love of my life."

Noodle pointed at the picture of Catherine. "You mean that pretty lady right there?"

"Her name was Catherine Martin," Jasper said. "And the day I punched him was the day after I found out I was going to be a father."

22

—

1960

I T WAS A TRUTH UNIVERSALLY ACKNOWLEDGED that when two young star-crossed lovers shared a bed and a single copy of *Tropic of Cancer*, their story would end in ruin.

"Jasper, would you please stop pacing back and forth and sit down?" Catherine sat perfectly composed at the small table and chairs sitting outside the secret cabin, her hands wrapped around a chipped mug of chicory coffee. She had yet to take a sip, but the warmth of the beverage seemed to be giving her strength. "You're making me dizzy."

"I knew this was a bad idea," Jasper muttered without slackening his pace. He felt pretty sure he'd never be able to smell chicory again without feeling this same sensation: utter, blinding terror followed immediately by a happiness that was so overwhelming it threatened to topple him where he stood. "I never should've let you seduce me."

Catherine's rich, delicious peal of laughter did much to calm the frenzy of his stride.

"Bless you, Jasper Holmes, for making me the villain of this piece. It's a role I've always had a desire to play." She patted the seat opposite her. "Sit. I mean it."

He sat, but only because he was pretty sure the first rule of ruining a woman was letting her decide when and how to proceed with the fallout.

"How far along are you?" he asked, his voice hoarse. He took the mug from her and kicked back the coffee, wincing at the earthy burn of it. "Or—wait. Do you even know? Have you been to a doctor?" He groaned. "Oh God. Have you told your parents?"

Her hands slid over the top of his, her grip strong despite her smaller size.

"No, I haven't seen a doctor yet, but based on my math, I'm guessing I'm about three months along."

He nodded, even though he had little idea what three months of pregnancy signified. That she probably wasn't mistaken about her condition, certainly, but what else? That he'd be a father in six short months? That he was about to be responsible for the care and upkeep of two more people?

His mouth went dry at the thought. There was enough savings inside his mattress to carry them for a little while, but he'd have to start looking into other revenue streams. A night job at the supermarket, maybe, or a logging contract in Canada where there were fewer safety protocols but—

"Stop it," she said.

He blinked. "Stop what?"

"Making plans and machinations for our future together. I swear on everything you love, if you propose to me right now, I'll never forgive you."

He tried taking his hands back, but she proved herself to be the stronger of them in this as well as everything else. Her eyes crinkled with a smile that made his heart ache.

"You forget that I already proposed to you once, and you turned me down," she said. "You obviously only want me for my body, so there's no going back now."

It took Jasper a moment to realize what she was talking about. And when he did, his heart started hammering uselessly in his chest. If only he'd known. If only he'd had the strength to walk away then.

"Wait," he croaked. "You mean in the margins of *The Haunting of Hill House*? That doesn't count. You were only trying to get a reaction out of me."

"I'd end up with six or seven kids, I believe you said." She heaved a playful sigh. "It's more than I'd like, but if it's what you have your heart set on…"

"Catherine," he pleaded. "This is serious. Please be serious."

"I am being serious," she said, suddenly so quiet that he had no choice but to believe her. She lifted her hands and settled them in her lap. Jasper felt their absence even more than he'd felt their reassuring weight. "I know this feels sudden to you, but it's not to me. I've had a lot of time to think about it, and I don't see any reason why you should have to ruin your life over this."

"It won't ruin my life—" he began, but it was no use. With Catherine, it was never any use. She'd get her way, and all he could do was watch as the entire train of their future together derailed before him.

"Maybe not," she agreed, "but it *would* ruin your mother's life—and the lives of all five of your brothers and sisters."

"It's not a problem. Tina is likely to get married in a few years anyway, and—"

"And that's going to free up enough of your time and resources to support a family of your own?" Since the question was a rhetorical one, she didn't bother waiting for an answer. "You said it yourself, Jasper. There's no romance in poverty."

"There could be. We could *make* there be."

She shook her head then, her gaze fixed on her lap in a way that made Jasper's blood run cold. "I've already made up my mind. Asking you to support both me and a baby is out of the question."

Something frantic clawed at Jasper's throat, but he fought the beast back. For as long as he could remember, money had been a barrier between him and the rest of the world. He knew it didn't buy happiness, and that families had been surviving for generations on whatever they could scrape together, but he also knew that Catherine had never known that kind of struggle.

She'd never heard a child's hungry cries being muffled into a pillow. She'd never felt that gnawing ache that was so much more than the biological need for sustenance. *Tropic of Cancer* did a decent job of portraying what poverty was really like, but even that was hidden behind layers of self-indulgent introspection and an alarming lack of personal consequences.

Catherine had never known that kind of deprivation—and if Jasper had his way, she never would. Even if it killed him, even if it broke him in Hemingway's proverbial thousand different places, he would give her that much.

"Okay," he said, his throat tight. "Whatever you want from me— whatever you need. I have some money saved up if you want to…explore your options, and I won't stand in the way of what you decide."

She eyed him with an intensity that made him feel as though she was peeling away his skin to reveal his inner workings.

"You mean that, don't you?" she asked. "You'd really give me everything you have—even if it means spreading yourself so thin that you disappear in the process."

"Of course I would," he said. He'd never been anything but honest with Catherine before, and he didn't see any reason to stop now. "I love you, C. The only thing that matters to me is making you happy."

She drew in a deep breath. That breath, more than anything else, made him feel as though the world was slipping out from underneath him—and that he'd never again stand on solid ground.

"Then you won't be upset when I tell you that I've decided to accept an offer of marriage from William McBride. I told him about the pregnancy, and he's willing to claim the child as his own in exchange for certain…gifts from my father."

"No." Jasper felt all the blood drain from his body. It started with his head and rushed down in a cascade of emotions, all of which left him feeling cold and empty.

"It's the only way out of this situation, and you know it." She pushed back from the table and stood towering over him. If he looked closely, he could detect the signs that had evaded him before—a slight thickening of her waist, a fullness in her cheeks that hadn't been there before. But most of all, it was the healthy, blooming glow of her that confirmed his worst fears: that she was pregnant, yes, but also that she was *happy*.

"I want you to know that these past few months have been the greatest ones of my life," she said in a voice that didn't waver even once. She extended her hand, but Jasper didn't reach for it. He couldn't. Moving was out of the question, touching her even more so.

"Naturally, William has asked that you and I stop seeing each other. Considering his position and what he's doing for me, I think he may be right." She paused and frowned, her hand still outstretched. "Please shake my hand. I need you to be okay with this. I need you to move on."

"Move on?" he echoed blankly. "Move on to *what*?"

He was on his feet then, standing over her but somehow still so small.

"There isn't anything else for me, Catherine," he said as he raked his hands through his hair, desperate to hold on to something but knowing, despite her proffered hand, that she was no longer an option. "You're it. You're everything. If you leave—"

"Jasper, I was always going to leave," she interrupted, her voice slicing right through him. "You know that as well as I do. The only difference now is that I get to take a part of you with me when I go."

He felt the whole of the world leaking out from the wound her words left behind. Not because what she was saying was wrong, but because she was right. He'd always known that he couldn't keep Catherine, that she was only on loan to him for however long fate decided to smile on him, but he'd always assumed she'd be moving on to the life she wanted—the big city lights and exciting adventures, the world just waiting for her to take a crack at it.

Not the same drudgery her mother had settled for. Not William *fucking* McBride.

"Say something," she pleaded. "I can't leave until I know you're going to be okay."

He wanted to give her what she was asking for—he really did. He knew that the best thing he could do for her was to let her go, to allow her to move on to the next chapter of her life with an easy conscience, but he couldn't. He wasn't going to be okay, and no amount of lying to her—or to himself—would change that.

"Do you remember when you asked me what my favorite book was?" he said. He didn't wait for her answer. "I wouldn't tell you because I knew you'd laugh at me. You'd want to write notes in the margins."

"And that's a bad thing?" she asked, her brows drawing together.

It was the worst possible thing. She was already so much a part of that story that he'd never be able to look at it the same way again.

"'*Be with me always—take any form—drive me mad,*'" he quoted, his throat raw. "'*Only do not leave me in this abyss where I can not find you.*'"

Her eyes narrowed with recognition of the line, pulled straight from the pages of *Wuthering Heights*. Instead of mocking him for his choice—one of the English language's most disastrously romantic works, a book about lovers who destroy each other from the moment of their first meeting—she lowered her hand and took a step back, a frown tugging at the corners of her mouth.

In the long silence that ensued, the rest of the quote stood pulsing between them, so much a presence that neither one of them needed to hear them spoken aloud.

Oh God! it is unutterable! I can not live without my life! I can not live without my soul!

She was the first to break that silence. "That's not fair, Jasper."

He knew it wasn't. None of this was.

"I'm doing this for you—for your whole family," she insisted "You have to understand. If I stayed—if I asked you to—"

She cut herself off and turned away, but not before he saw the angry way she dashed her hand at her eyes. "God, what a fool I am. I should've known you'd turn this into some romantic melodrama instead of seeing it for what it really is."

Her words hurt him, but not nearly as much as the way she held herself, as if poised for flight. It almost felt like she was afraid he'd try to physically restrain her—or, worse, let her go without any kind of fight at all.

"And what is it?" he asked, his voice hoarse. "In your wise, all-seeing, unromantic view of the world, what's happening here?"

It took her a full minute to answer. Jasper knew there were a dozen different ways he could have filled those sixty seconds. With weeping, perhaps, or a Heathcliff-like fury that lashed them both with its sting. By getting on his knees and being every inch the dramatic, lovesick sap she was accusing him of being.

But he didn't. He stood in stony silence and waited for her to say the words out loud.

"It's real life, Jasper. That's all. Not some dark horror story I get to read as a way to avoid my humdrum existence, and not some sweet tale of redemption you can pretend waits for you in the future. It's just two people who made a mess and now have to deal with the consequences."

It was the cruelest thing she could have said to him, and she knew it. So he said the cruelest thing he could think of back.

"He'll make you miserable," he warned, his voice surprisingly calm considering the way his whole soul was tearing apart inside. "He'll make you miserable every day of your life until one day he doesn't. Then and only then will you realize what you've done."

23

—

1960

JASPER FOUND WILLIAM MCBRIDE WAITING FOR him the next day.
He would never know if Catherine had warned the other man
about his imminent arrival—told him about the scene at the cabin so he
could arm himself appropriately—or if William was simply wiser than
Jasper had given him credit for, but when he hunted the other man down
at the radar base, there was no surprise in his expression.

"Ah," William said, turning smartly to face him. "And so we meet again."

William was dressed in full Air Force regalia, and even though Jasper
loathed the very sight of him, he couldn't help but be impressed by the
figure he cut. In another lifetime, with another family and different
burdens to bear, Jasper liked to think he might have followed a similar
path. His own father had served in WWII, though he'd done it as an
enlisted man rather than an officer.

That, more than anything else, proved the differences between them.
Jasper was and always would be what he appeared on the outside: a low-
level nobody, a man for whom bodily strength was more lucrative than
anything else he had to offer. William McBride, on the other hand, was
a shining, gleaming ball of potential.

For the past twenty-four hours, Jasper had rehearsed in detail what he planned to say. In his head, he was a master of articulate superiority, reducing the other man to shreds with his razor-sharp wit.

You're offering Catherine the only thing of value you have—your money and your position—because you know you have nothing else to give her, he'd spit out.

Catherine and the baby might be yours in name, but they'll always belong to me first and foremost, he'd say.

Don't hurt them, he'd beg. *Whatever you do, whatever happens, please just make sure they're happy.*

In the end, he said none of those things. Not only was it impossible to reduce a man to shreds in the bustle and camaraderie of soldiers going about their business, but his tongue was cleaved to the roof of his mouth.

"I suppose I have to thank you," William said when all Jasper did was open and close his mouth, unable to force his tongue to start moving. "That Edgar Allen Poe trick worked like a charm. 'We loved with a love that was more than love.' A little over-the-top, if you ask me, but she seemed to like it."

"Don't you dare quote Poe at me," Jasper said, surprised to find that his hands were balled into fists at his sides. He'd never been a man given to violence, even though some of the guys on the logging crew seemed only to respond to brute force. "It's not a game you'll win. 'Leave my loneliness unbroken.'"

"Oh, I'm no match for you, and I know it," William confessed with a flash of a smile that grated down Jasper's spine. "That's the only line I memorized. Well, that and 'Quoth the Raven, "Nevermore"' but that one didn't seem to fit the moment. Girls like Catherine need a touch of romance, even when they don't have any other choice."

That was when Jasper struck. He'd have been hard-pressed to say whether it was the smugness of the man that drove him to it, or if it was the condescending way he spoke of a woman who was so superior to him that they shouldn't be expected to share the same planet, let alone the same home. Either way, his fist shot up and cracked against William's jaw so fast that neither one of them saw it coming.

"*Gunnhh!*" William staggered back with a grunt, his whole body reeling with the sudden force of the blow. Even though Jasper was horror-struck at his own actions, he lunged again, this time to tackle William the rest of the way to the dirt. He might have done it, too, if not for the half-dozen young men who came running up to hold him back.

"Whoa, there. Take a beat, man."

"He just hit Lieutenant McBride! Did you see that?"

"I don't think he's one of us, is he?"

"Someone had better get the Major."

Of all the sudden babel of voices, it was that last one that caused Jasper to stiffen. *The Major* meant Catherine's father—a man he'd only seen a handful of times, and then with a wary circumspection to be expected of a nineteen-year-old facing the father of a woman he'd recently taken to bed.

"You hit me," William slurred, his hand clutched to his already swelling jaw. "You fucking *hit* me."

"Come a little closer, and I'll do it again," Jasper warned.

All of a sudden, the arms that had been holding him let go. He surged forward and just managed to avoid falling flat on his face. As he regained his bearings and glanced around, he found that all the young men were standing ramrod straight, their eyes trained ahead and their expressions tamped down to give nothing away.

"Someone had better tell me what's going on," a cold authoritative voice announced. Jasper turned slowly, already aware of what—or rather, who—stood behind him.

Major Gene Martin looked exactly like the type of man to have Catherine for a daughter. His stature was small but determined, his expression one that challenged every living entity to even *try* messing with him. His clothes were neat and fit his body like he'd been born wearing them, but more than that, he crackled with the same vitality that characterized everything Catherine said and did. It was as if there was too much life to be contained within them; they were filled with something more than energy.

Catherine found her outlet in sneaking around and breaking the rules, but the Major had obviously chosen rigid discipline instead. Jasper wasn't sure yet whether that made him more or less dangerous than Catherine, but he felt fairly certain he was about to find out.

"Lieutenant McBride, you're making a mess of your uniform. Please go at once to the treatment facility and get yourself attended to. Unless there's a war going on, there's no reason to sully your uniform with blood." The Major cast a careful look around. "As far as the rest of you go, I believe I've made myself clear on the rules and regulations regarding recreational fighting. Do I need to repeat these for your edification?"

The chorus of *No, sirs* that this question elicited might have made Jasper laugh, if he wasn't the next to fall under that eagle-eyed stare.

"And as for you, young man, I can see that you're not one of mine. Do you have clearance to be on the radar base?"

"No, I don't," Jasper said, stopping himself before adding his own sir to the end. He might have a lot to answer to for his behavior, but this man had no power over him.

His daughter, however...

"And is it your custom to show up uninvited and sow disorder among the ranks of the armed forces?"

"Not usually, no," Jasper said. Emboldened by the thought that things literally couldn't get any worse, he added, "But this is a special circumstance."

The Major narrowed his eyes in a way that might, had Jasper been one of his enlisted men, have made him cower where he stood. Instead, he straightened his spine and met the man's stare.

For some reason, this seemed to please the officer. "What's your name?" the Major asked.

"Jasper. Jasper Holmes."

From the way the shorter man suddenly flinched, as if a divine hand had swatted him from above, Jasper knew that he had the whole story. Also that there was about to be serious hell to pay.

But all he said was, "I see," before turning to the man nearest to him in rank. "Captain Lindholdt, be good enough to assume command until I return. Please see that the training exercises are carried out at their usual hour. I'll be escorting this young man home."

"Actually, I drove myself—" Jasper began, but his protest fell on unheeding ears.

"That will be all. You're dismissed."

If Jasper hadn't already been terrified, the speed with which the men dispersed would have done the trick. In a matter of seconds, he was left standing on a dusty patch of earth with only Catherine's father to witness what happened next.

"Come along, then," the Major said as he brushed lightly past Jasper. "I don't have all day."

"Uh...can I ask where we're going?" Jasper asked. He flexed his hand involuntarily, a tight bruising already starting to take shape around his knuckles. He'd pay for that injury at work tomorrow, but he couldn't find it in himself to regret it. "Or would that be an impertinence?"

The Major paused just long enough to cast a look over his shoulder at Jasper. "It is an impertinence, but you might as well know now. You'll have plenty of time to repent when we get there."

"Get where?" Jasper asked.

"To my house, obviously," he said as though it were the most natural thing in the world. "My wife would like to have a few words."

Jasper wasn't sure whether to be relieved or dismayed when he stepped onto the driveway of a pristinely white two-story house to find that Catherine was nowhere in sight.

On the one hand, he quaked to think of what his lover would say if she knew what he'd done—driven up to the radar base in a blaze of impotent fury, attacked the man who was to make an honest woman of her, and confronted her father on his own turf. On the other hand, he was *not* good at parents. Not by any stretch of the imagination, and certainly not when he was handling them on his own.

"Come along, then," the Major said as he closed the door of his green Chevy Bel-Air and started making his way to the front door. He didn't even check to make sure Jasper was following. "Mrs. Martin is eager to meet you."

"I doubt that," Jasper muttered, but he followed anyway.

Now that he was at Catherine's house, he found himself more interested in his surroundings than he'd have previously thought possible. It had never occurred to him before to drive by her family home or even to wonder what her life might be like outside the library and their clandestine meetings. That her parents were overbearing, he knew from their conversations. That she yearned for more than the picture-perfect cutout life of an obedient daughter and wife, he also knew.

That was what made this situation with William McBride so frustrating. Catherine didn't want a life of safety and security, of white picket fences and military precision. She wanted to go on adventures. She wanted to squeeze the most out of every day. She wanted to explore the highest of highs and the lowest of lows, never flinching from either extreme.

He, Jasper Holmes, had taken that from her. He'd robbed her of the life she deserved. And she, in agreeing to marry William McBride, had let him.

Her house was typical of the few upper- and middle-class homes in the town. Anything that could be called "stately" around these parts had been around since the turn of the century, the historical features pristinely maintained over the decades. Unlike his own family home, which was a skinny town house squeezed between too many others along the log-jammed waterfront of the Chehalis River, everything here was picture-perfect. The couches sat at perfect right angles in the living room, a silver tea service tray already set out in expectation of this visit.

This was bad enough, but nothing could have prepared Jasper for the little signs of Catherine everywhere he looked—a copy of *Breakfast at Tiffany's* lying facedown on a side table, a bottle of her light-pink nail polish next to it. A little notebook and a stub of a pencil for jotting down in it, probably for quotes she found meaningful in the book.

And, more damning than all the rest, an exact replica of her standing in an apron at the far end of the room. Jasper knew, from a few chance meetings around town, that this woman was Catherine's mother, but he'd never seen her up close before. Now that he had, he wished the meeting undone. The gently wisping lines around her eyes and the slight strands of gray in her hair hinted at her older age, but the two Martin women were otherwise identical. It was like catching a glimpse into Catherine's future—a future he would make no part of, and a future he wanted so much that it ached.

"Mrs. Martin?" he asked as he came to a halt in front of her. He brought up his hand to shake hers before realizing that his knuckles still bore the imprint of William McBride's face. He tried shoving his hand behind his back before she noticed, but there was no point. Catherine and her mother didn't just share features; they shared the quick, ready understanding he found so appealing.

"Oh, you poor thing," she murmured as she clasped his hand gently between her own. "Let's get a steak on that before it swells up. I have a lovely rib eye that should ease the sting."

"I thought that rib eye was for supper—" the Major began, but he caught his wife's eye and immediately clamped his lips shut. With a curt nod, he began to back out of the room. "I suppose you know your business best. I'll wait in the car until it's time to drive him back."

And with that, he was gone. Jasper had thought that nothing could be more uncomfortable than the long, silent drive from the radar base, but he was wrong.

This was worse. This was so much worse.

"I suppose you had to get it out of your system, didn't you?" Catherine's mother said as she led Jasper to the couch and urged him to sit in it. "I don't know why men always turn to violence in troubled times, but it's good to know you're just like the rest of them."

"I'm not like them," Jasper tried protesting, but she only chuckled and patted him gently on his uninjured hand.

"It wasn't meant as an insult," she said with a smile. "In fact, I expect it will make this next part a lot easier. Relax and pour yourself a cup of tea, if you'd like one. I'll be right back with the steak."

Jasper neither relaxed nor poured himself a cup of anything. Instead, he examined the room for signs of an exit route. There was a promising-looking window toward the back, but what would be the use? Colville was a small town. There was only so far he could run and nowhere he could hide.

"Catherine tells me you're a long way from home," her mother said upon her reentry. Instead of handing him the cold wrapped beef, she took care to rearrange it on top of his knuckles for him. It had been such a long time since anyone had taken such maternal care of him that he could only sit in a daze and let her. "Your people are from Aberdeen? Is that right?"

"Yes, ma'am," he found himself saying.

Her laugh rang through the air. It sounded exactly like Catherine's. "Please don't call me ma'am. It's bad enough that I'm going to be a grandmother." She gave a ladylike shudder and lowered herself to the seat opposite Jasper. "Such a strange idea, isn't it? Me, a *grandmother*?"

"Please, I—" he croaked.

She stopped him with one hand. "I'm not here to yell at you. I only wanted to meet you and to...talk."

"Talk?" he echoed blankly. "About what?"

Already, his hand was starting to feel better, the numbing creep of the expensive cut of steak doing its work. The rest of him, unfortunately, was starting to show serious signs of strain.

Mrs. Martin pursed her lips. "Well, that's up to you, I suppose. I'm sure this all came as a shock to you. It certainly was one to the Major. I don't think I've ever seen him turn that shade of purple before. Aubergine, my mother would have called it, but she always had a flair for the dramatic. All the women in my family do. I'm sure you've noticed by now."

Jasper had the feeling this conversational overload was meant to subdue him, and it was working in a big way. He swallowed heavily and attempted to veer the conversation back on course.

"Does that mean it wasn't a surprise to you?" he asked.

That laughter sounded again, a little quieter this time. "Well, no, to be honest. I know Catherine, and I know what happens in quiet, cozy towns where the only thing to do on a Saturday night is slip out the drive-in with the local bit of rough."

"Oh," Jasper said—just that, just *oh*. That single syllable said everything and nothing.

"And that's just it, isn't it?" she added with a cluck of her tongue. "She was bored and you were interested, and nature took care of the rest. Did you ask her to marry you?"

"Well, no," Jasper admitted, his head spinning with the blunt rapidity of her questions. "I *wanted* to, but—"

"It wouldn't have mattered if you had. She'd have turned you down." Catherine's mother paused and looked at Jasper then—*really* looked at him, her eyes kind but penetrating, her findings clear. "I'm not saying you're a bad man, Jasper Holmes, or even that you bear any more of the responsibility for this situation than she does, but you understand my position, yes?"

He nodded, not only because words were impossible by this point, but because he *did* understand. These people were everything his family wasn't—genteel and well-to-do, more concerned with the appearance of the shameful pregnancy than its actual cause.

They were also determined to see that their daughter carried on the tradition no matter what the cost—to him or to her.

As if to drive this point home, Mrs. Martin tapped a thoughtful finger in the middle of her chin. "Aberdeen... Aberdeen... I think we met a sailor from there once. Lovely young man. Tragic backstory. One of those families that fell on hard times during the Depression and never found their way back on solid ground."

Jasper could tell where this was headed.

"I believe Catherine had a fancy for him, too. Isn't it funny how girls her age have a certain type they come back to time and time again?"

"Yes, ma'am," he said. He knew that nothing more was expected—or, at this point, the least bit necessary.

"Well," she said brightly as she folded her hands in her lap. "I can see that you're every bit as intelligent as Catherine painted you out to be, so this next part will come as no surprise to you. The Major and I are prepared to offer you a lump sum for your troubles, provided you relinquish any and all paternal interest in the child."

The steak fell to the floor with a wet flop. "I'm...sorry? A lump sum?"

"I know it's unseemly to discuss these things, but I'd like to ensure that there are no misunderstandings going forward. It's what Catherine wants."

"What she wants?" he echoed again. He knew he sounded every bit like the oversized doddering lumberjack he appeared to be, but what else could he do? Maternal solicitude and bribery were the last two things he'd expected out of this meeting—if *meeting* it could be called. It was starting to feel more like an ambush.

"Yes. The Major and I were prepared to send her away and find the child a proper home, but she insisted that she'd prefer to raise her son or daughter herself. Marrying William McBride was her idea, and although I can't say I was on board at first, it seems to be working out for the best. He's been a brick from start to finish."

When Jasper couldn't find it in him to do more than goggle at this poised, soft-spoken woman, she nodded and reached for the handbag that sat next to her chair. His heart sank when he saw her extract a folded check and push it across the table at him.

"I think you'll find that we're prepared to be generous. Not just for your trouble, but for your discretion."

He didn't want to look. He tried not to pick up the slip of paper. But when she kept sitting there, smiling at him like an older, wiser, stone-cold version of Catherine, he found he had no choice.

PAY TO THE ORDER OF JASPER HOLMES, $5,000.00

Five thousand dollars. It was more money than Jasper earned in a year, more than he'd ever seen in one sitting, a veritable fortune.

He let go almost at once. The paper fluttered to the floor as if it had wings, joining the steak in its wet, congealing lump. Tsking gently, Catherine's mother plucked it back up and wiped the stains of red around the edges.

"I really am sorry," she said. More determined this time, she pressed the check into his hand. "I know I sound like a horrible old snob, but our daughter asked us to be generous, so we are."

"I don't believe you," he said, suddenly springing to his feet, the check crushed in his fist. "Catherine wouldn't have agreed to it. She wouldn't do this to me."

He saw a flash of it then—that fire that so characterized these women, the core of steel that nothing earthly could touch.

"*You* may be in the habit of lying and sneaking around, Mr. Holmes, but I can assure you that I am not." She smiled then, and even though it was meant to be every bit as charming as her earlier attempts at friendliness, it chilled him to the bone. "In fact, she gave me a message for you—something she said you'd be sure to understand."

"Please don't," Jasper croaked.

"I have to," she returned, a little warmer this time. She fished in the front pocket of her apron until she pulled out a slip of paper. From his distance, Jasper could make out the sloping lines of Catherine's painfully familiar hand. "It's the only way. You don't realize it now, but this is the best solution for everyone."

And then she read the words Jasper knew were coming.

"'*I've no more business to marry Edgar Linton than I have to be in heaven*,'" she read in her soft, firm voice, "'*and if the wicked man in there had not brought Heathcliff so low I shouldn't have thought of it*.'"

Jasper flung up a hand in entreaty. To his surprise, it worked. Catherine's mother stopped in the middle of forming the next line, her lips parted in a perfect *O*.

"'*It would degrade me to marry Heathcliff now*,'" he finished for her.

She blinked. "Why, yes. So you *do* know. She said you'd recognize the line, but I wasn't sure I believed her."

He groaned with the sudden enormity of it. Of the irony of Catherine—*his* Catherine—flinging the only words she knew would get him to back away. Of her quoting a passage from *Wuthering Heights* as though a single stupid book could contain the enormity of his love for her.

And of her obvious decision not to finish the line: He shall never know how I love him; and that not because he's handsome, Nelly, but because he's more myself than I am. Whatever our souls are made of, his and mine are the same.

In the book, the love between Catherine and Heathcliff wasn't enough to overcome the pecuniary demands of the world they inhabited. In real life, it seemed, the love between Catherine and Jasper was doomed to follow along the same lines. And just like the devastating unfolding of Emily Brontë's classic tale, his only recourse was to stand back and watch as the love of his life destroyed him, body and soul.

"You be sure to cash that check, honey," Mrs. Martin said as she led the way to the door. She stepped over the congealing steak, but her heel squelched into the edge. "The Major will take you back now. I trust we'll never see or hear from you again."

And even though his heart was breaking—a thousand china plates crashing inside a wooden box, a thousand times over again—Jasper had no choice but to follow that bright bloody trail out of the house.

Catherine had spoken. She'd made her choice.

It was over.

PART THREE

24

—

NOODLE

T'S WRONG TO STEAL THINGS.

I know that for sure. I know *lots* of things for sure, but not for the reasons I'm supposed to. Other people—most people—understand the rules to things just because. They know when to talk and when to keep quiet, when someone needs a hug and when they need space.

I only know things because I'm good at paying attention. Well, because I pay attention and because my brother and sisters give me lots of practice.

For example, when Theo sets things on fire, everyone around him gets mad, so that one's easy. Don't light fires. And when Trixie smiles, which she does all the time, most people smile back. They also give her things and are super nice to her, so I know that's a helpful trick. Do smile at people. Most of the time, I can count on Trixie to teach me what I should do and Theo to teach me what not to do. They're like one of those good cop/bad cop movies, only it never bothers Theo that he's the bad one. Most of the time, I think he *likes* it.

Anyway. I didn't mean to take the book from Jasper's bookshelf, but I couldn't help myself. When Jasper told us that story about him punching a guy, and how he only did it because his heart was broken and that lady kept quoting sad things from a book called *Wuthering Heights*, I had to pull it off the shelf. And once I did, I saw those notes that Chloe's been obsessed with for the past few weeks.

Only this book has, like, a zillion of them. On almost every page, and just in the lady's handwriting.

"Noodle, honey, did you remember to take your pain medication before bed?"

As soon as I hear my mom's voice, I shove the book underneath my pillow. I don't want her to see it. If she does, she'll ask questions that I don't have the answers to yet. I plan to wait until I have them before I show anyone the book.

That's my other secret, by the way. When I don't know how to act or what to say, I keep things hidden until I'm ready.

"Yes, Mom," I say as I snuggle down under my covers. Gummy Bear is snoring at one end of the bed, so I can't get my broken leg very comfortable, but that's okay.

My mom appears in the doorway to the room I share with Theo, though he's not staying in it right now. He and Trixie have been sleeping over at Jasper's house. I'm kind of jealous, since camping out on the floor with all those plants seems fun, but I'm the one who called Mom, so I figure I should probably stay here to keep her and Chloe company. Todd, too.

Is it bad if I say I like him? I know I'm not supposed to—the evil stepfather and all that—but he's nice and he laughs a lot. I especially like that he laughs the hardest at his own jokes, and he doesn't care if anyone joins him. Whenever he falls into one of his laughing fits, he winks at me and then keeps going like I'm in on the joke with him.

"You look nice and cozy," Mom says as she leans her head against the doorframe and watches me. She's not the same as I remember, but that's no surprise. I was only seven years old when she left, which means she's been gone for almost half my life.

"Can I get you anything?" she asks. "A drink of water? A bedtime story? You used to like Beatrix Potter, didn't you?"

I nod. Theo would get mad if anyone reminded him of the books he liked as a kid—he was so obsessed with the Warriors cat books that he used to draw whiskers on his face with a Sharpie—but I still sometimes read *The Tale of Peter Rabbit* when I'm feeling sad.

My mom takes one look at my nod and sighs. She also slips into the room, careful to snick the door closed behind her.

"You're the only one who can stand the sight of me, aren't you?" she asks as she sits down on my bed, her body weight tugging at the mattress until we both sink into it. Her hand comes up to smooth my hair away but she stops herself at the last second. "I suppose it's my own fault."

This is one of those situations where I don't know what to say, so I don't say anything at all. As usual, it works. She sighs again and keeps going.

"I wish Chloe would yell at me," she says as she tucks her hands in her lap. She stares at her fingernails, which are long and shiny and red. They look like they belong on a witch. "I'd feel better if she yelled. Or ignored me. Or even started throwing things at my head. She's been nothing but nice since I got here."

"Chloe *is* nice," I say.

I don't mention the rest—that I like her best of anyone in the world, and that my heart gets tighter every time I see her crying in the living room after she thinks we've all gone to bed—but I don't need to. I'm pretty sure Mom already knows.

"If you want to be yelled at, you can always ask Trixie," I offer.

Mom's soft laugh shakes the whole bed. "That's true," she says, and then suddenly she's not laughing anymore. "Trixie's beautiful, isn't she? I was only seven years old when she left, which means she's been gone for a big chunk of my life."

"She looks like you," I say, and that makes Mom laugh even less.

"Honey, will you tell me something?" she asks, although she's still looking at her fingernails instead of me. "Why did you call me? I mean, *really* call me?"

That's easy. "I broke my leg."

She tsks and shakes her head. "No, I know that part. I just mean…" Her voice trails off, but I don't say anything then, either. I know she'll pick back up again. She glances down at me with eyes that look just like Chloe's but aren't. I don't know how to explain it. They're the same shape and color, and if I were to draw them, they'd end up being exactly the same, but they feel different.

When Chloe looks at me, I can see the whole world. When Mom looks at me, all I see is her.

"I don't know what I'm supposed to *do*," she says, and in a way that makes me feel uncomfortably like she wants me to be the one to tell her. "Chloe's at work all day while the kids are at school, and you… Well. You're spending every minute of your free time with that grumpy man next door. When you called, you said that you needed me, but you don't. Not really. You all seem to be getting along fine without me."

My uncomfortable feeling only gets stronger.

"I couldn't believe it when the phone rang and your number popped up," she adds as though I'm not sitting here wishing that Todd would come in with one of his jokes and another one of the presents that no one seems to want. "At first, I thought it must have been a prank call, but Todd made me answer. It's so strange. I didn't even know you kids had my number."

That part, at least, I can reply to.

"Chloe found it from the computer at work a few years ago," I say. "She gave it to me in case of an emergency."

Wrinkles start to form around her mouth. "A few years ago? You mean she's had it all this time?"

I dig around in the drawer next to my bed until I find the crinkled scrap of paper. When I hand it to her, her whole arm shakes. She looks at it for so long that I'm afraid I missed something, but when she glances back up, I can tell she's not really in the room with me anymore.

"She never called," she said. "She never even tried. She must really hate me."

I'm back to not knowing what to say again. I don't think Chloe *hates* our mom, but I know she doesn't love her anymore. For some reason, that seems worse.

"She's sad a lot," I say. "And she worries about bills."

My mom throws the scrap of paper back into the drawer as if it hurts her to keep looking at it. "Is that why you called? That's the emergency? Chloe needs money?"

I shrug. Chloe *does* need money, but I'm pretty sure she won't accept any. If she wouldn't cash Jasper's check, then I don't know why she'd bother with one from Mom. Especially since it would probably have to go through Todd first.

All of a sudden, my hands are seized between my mom's. I don't like how wet and warm her palms feel, so I try to pull away, but she keeps holding me. She puts her face so close to mine that I can smell my bubble-gum toothpaste on her breath.

"Would you please talk to me, Noodle?" she asks. "Why did you call? Why did you pull me away from my life? *What do you want?*"

I blink, suddenly wishing I'd never done any of it—punched Aiden in the school bathroom, run away into the forest and tumbled down that ravine, called the phone number so Chloe could maybe have a day or two to herself. I don't have the right words or even the right feelings to make it okay again.

It's a good thing Jasper gave me some, then.

I sit up straighter in my bed and yank my hands out of my mom's. I can tell that her feelings are hurt, but I don't like being touched when my emotions get scrunched up. That's the thing Jasper said at the cabin earlier today—well, that and a lot other stuff I didn't expect, but which helped me all the same.

"It's not okay to hurt people," I tell her, repeating what Jasper said. "When everything feels like it's going to explode and you don't know how to make it stop, you should never let yourself be tricked into hitting someone."

My mom's eyes fly open. "I never once hurt you kids. Not like that."

I know she didn't, but that's not the point. Once upon a time, Jasper *did* hit someone. He told me and Zach all about it. He punched a man who was only trying to do the right thing for a girl they both loved. I didn't hit Aiden over a girl—*gross*—but I did hit him because of what he said about my family.

That our mom didn't love us enough to stick around. That we were trash. That it was a good thing we had each other because no one else wanted us.

I felt awful the moment I closed my fist, and I think I might have run all the way to Canada if I hadn't fallen and busted up my leg, but Jasper says that was just my conscience doing its job.

"*I only hit that man because I couldn't hit the thing I was really mad at,*" Jasper told me, and it made so much sense that even Zach nodded along.

"*What were you mad at?*" I asked.

"*Life,*" he said. "*My mother. My brothers and sisters. All my stupid mistakes and useless dreams. Everything I didn't have and all the things I never would. But mostly I was mad at myself. I've been mad at myself for a very long time.*"

I know I probably shouldn't have asked the next part, but I couldn't help myself. He'd been staring at that picture of the lady on the wall and just looked so *sad*. I had to know.

"*Are you mad at yourself now?*"

Instead of getting upset, Jasper smiled at me—and in a way I'd only seen him when he was reading *Nightwave* with me and pretending he didn't like it.

"*I'm working on it, Noodle*," he said and reached over to ruffle my hair. I usually hated it when people other than Chloe did that, but I didn't mind Jasper. "*Ask me again in a few months.*"

My mom still looks like she's going to start crying, so I try to explain the best I can.

"Jasper promised I can go to his cabin anytime I want," I say. "As soon as my leg's better, I mean. He says it's a nice quiet place to go when my emotions get to be too much, and I can keep my favorite books there like he does."

"I don't understand," she says.

"You left because your emotions were too much, didn't you?" I ask. "Because *we* were too much?"

She opens her mouth and closes it again, looking exactly like Theo when one of his experiments blows up in his face.

"We all feel like we want to run away sometimes," I say and give her hand a little pat. She looks like she needs it. "But not everybody can. *You* did, so that means Chloe has to take care of us now. I don't want anything from you, and neither do Theo or Trixie, but I think maybe you should ask her."

Then I roll over as best I can and pull my blankets up to my chin. Gummy Bear grunts when I accidentally kick him, but my mom stays quiet for a very long time.

So long, in fact, that I'm already asleep by the time she leaves. I don't know where she goes, but I'm pretty sure it isn't to talk to Chloe. That would be the brave thing to do, and even though Mom is beautiful and soft and smells like a department store, she isn't even a little bit as brave as her.

25

—

NOODLE

THE NEXT MORNING, I FIND TODD on the front step with a scraping tool in one hand and a mask over his face.

"Sir? Mr. Aarons? Uh…Dad?"

He stops as soon as he hears my voice. It's hard to read his expression behind the mask, but I'm guessing he's smiling. He's *always* smiling.

"I think we can stick to Todd for now, kiddo," he says with a wink. He lifts the mask from his face and plunks it down on top of his head. "Time enough for all the rest once Ravenna decides whether or not she's staying."

I was right about the smile, which is good, but I don't like that last bit. I never meant for Mom to come here *forever*. I just wanted her to help out Chloe for a little while.

"Todd," I say, rolling his name over my tongue to see how I like it. It feels fine. Not great, but fine. "Can you give me a ride somewhere?"

"Well, now. That depends." He tries peeking over my head to the inside of the house. He's looking for my mom, but he won't find her in there. She slipped out back to smoke a cigarette and play on her phone a while ago. Todd got up early and immediately started doing all kinds of things around the house—fixing the rattling air conditioner in the kitchen, painting over the burn mark by Theo's bed, and now scraping all the rust off the front door—but Mom just keeps trailing around looking sad.

At first, I thought she might have been sad because of all her memories coming back, but mostly I think she just hates this place. She used to look exactly like that when I was a kid, as if something in the air smells bad and she can't escape it.

"She's playing *Candy Crush*," I offer. "I peeked at her phone. She's on level eleven thousand or something."

Todd's smile starts to droop at the edges. Before it can get too far, he tosses the scraper aside and rubs his hands together. The sound is dry and crackly, but not in a bad way.

"In that case, the best thing we can do is go for a drive. A long one. She always plays *Candy Crush* when she's not feeling well."

I hesitate. "If she's not feeling well, shouldn't we stay and look after her?"

Todd steps back as if there's a monster standing right behind my shoulder. "No way, kid. If you want my advice, the best way to deal with a woman like your mother is to give her space."

"Space?" I echo.

"She doesn't like being backed into a corner." He clucks his tongue and shakes his head. "She's like a wild animal that way. In a lot of ways, come to think of it. She says too much responsibility makes her feel trapped."

I want to point out that wild animals have lots of responsibility—that they have to eat and fight and take care of their young to make sure they survive into adulthood—but I don't.

"Does that mean you'll take me to visit Zach?" I ask.

"Isn't that the guy who's Chloe's boyfriend?" Todd says, his brow furrowed.

"He's my friend, too," I say.

I must talk louder than I mean to because Todd raises his hands with a chuckle. "Sure thing, kid. He's a friend of the whole family." As if just now noticing the book in my hand, he nods down at it. "You guys in a book club or something?"

I glance at the copy of *Wuthering Heights* and curl it closer to my body. I don't want to talk about what I'm doing—or why—so I say the first thing that pops into my mind.

"He lives in the woods," I say.

"The woods?"

"Way up the mountain."

Todd blinks. "Are you pulling my leg? Did your brother put you up to this?"

I shake my head. Theo is a good brother, and I like him third best to Chloe and Gummy Bear, but he doesn't always see what's going on around him. I doubt he knows anything about Jasper and Chloe and their books.

"Zach said I could come to him if I needed anything." I hold up the book. "I need him to help me with this."

Todd takes one more peek inside the house. When he doesn't see anything but Gummy Bear sprawled out on the living room floor, he nods once. "Okay, kid. Sure thing. We'll drive up into the mountains and find your friend." As he starts trotting down the front porch steps, I can hear him mutter under his breath, "With any luck, Ravenna won't even notice we're gone."

———

"Aloysius!"

As soon as Todd pulls his car into the dirt parking lot of the survival school, Zach comes running out to greet us. I think he must be in the middle of working because there are a few other people in camouflage standing around, but that doesn't stop him from dropping everything to see me.

That's the thing I like best about Zach. Him and Chloe both. They never make me feel like I'm being annoying when I need extra help. I sometimes feel as if the whole world could be on fire, but Chloe would still be standing in the kitchen and asking us what cereal we want for breakfast.

I know that doesn't sound like much, but when your dad leaves and your mom leaves and the teachers just keep passing you around school because they don't know what else to do with you, breakfast matters.

Zach squats down to my level, his nose crinkled up with worry. "Is something wrong, Aloysius? Are you hurt? Is *Chloe*?"

He says this last bit with a sharp note that makes me feel like I came to the right place.

"I'm okay. She's okay." I cast a quick look over his shoulder, where the camouflage people are loading a bunch of camping stuff into a backpack. "Are you busy? I didn't think—"

Todd clears his throat from somewhere above me. "Sorry for the intrusion, but he was determined to see you. Said something about a book he needs help with. Homework, probably, so it's no use asking me. I was never much of a scholar. Flunked English lit twice, if you want the truth of it."

I set my jaw. As if I'd drag Todd all the way up here for something as silly as school.

"It's not homework," I say. "It's about Jasper. And those notes he and the dead lady wrote to each other."

Zach springs up to a standing position at once—and then he does the thing I like about him, the thing that makes him so much like Chloe. He nods at Todd in a way that seems to magically get rid of him, ushers me to where the other camouflage people are, and gets me comfortably

settled on a log—and all without making it seem like he's done anything
at all.

It was the same when he found me at the bottom of those rocks a few
weeks ago. I was just lying there, trying not to cry, pain shooting like lava
up and down my leg, and there he was. If he hadn't smelled so much like
dirt, his hands warm and strong as he straightened my bone and made a
sling to carry me down, I might have thought he was a guardian angel.

Then again, maybe guardian angels *are* like that.

"Everyone, this is Aloysius Sampson," Zach says as soon as he hears
Todd's car start crunching its way back down the road. He promised to
get me home later, so I don't have to worry about Todd coming back
up here and ruining things. "He's the young man who turned me into
a local hero a few weeks ago. I owe him big time. I can't even walk into
the drugstore now without everyone coming over to shake my hand."

I'm pretty sure he's only saying that to be nice, but the camouflage
people seem to get really excited over it. They pat me on the back and
tell me how tough I am, and then ask Zach all kinds of questions about
what kind of wood he used to frame the splint, and could you also use a
canoe paddle if you had to, and how does canvas compare to Gore-Tex
when it comes to manufacturing a sling?

He laughs and answers their questions, but not before first handing
me a pouch of energy gel. He'd had some in his pockets when he rescued
me and made me suck on one to keep up my strength, and even though it
sounds weird—edible slime in a Capri Sun pouch—I kind of like them.

As soon as he's done talking, he checks his watch. "Right. So everyone has their coordinates, yes?"

The camouflage people nod.

"Then I'll send you out a few minutes early. Remember—speed
is important for this exercise. The longer you leave your partners out
there, the more likely they are to die of exposure." He winks at me just
in case I'm worried about that dying part. I'm not, though. He explained

his job to me—about how he trains pilots to save themselves and their teams if they should accidentally crash—so I know this is just pretend. "Aaaand, go!"

I suck the last of the energy pouch down and watch as the men and women head off into the woods on their training exercise. To be honest, it's kind of making me want to be a pilot when I grow up. The idea of being crashed and alone in the woods for a few weeks sounds nice, just so long as you have Zach to teach you all the things you need to know about finding food and escaping bad guys.

"Shouldn't you go out with them?" I ask as soon as we're alone together. "To keep them safe?"

"Nah. We've got this whole place rigged with deer cameras. My boss can watch everything on his computer." He sits down on the log next to me and pulls out an energy pouch of his own. "Does your sister know you're spending the day with me?"

See what I mean about how nice he is? Instead of asking me if I have permission to be here or making me feel like I'm bothering him, Zach makes it sound like we planned this whole thing together.

"No," I admit. "I'm supposed to be with my mom and Todd."

He's careful not to look at me as he finishes his pouch. "But you don't want to be?"

I shrug and kick at the dirt with my good foot. "Todd's okay, but my mom tries too hard. And then she doesn't try enough." I pause. "Does that make sense?"

He nods. "Yeah. It does. Your sister said something similar."

I nod back, echoing his movements so he knows I know we're on the same page. I also say the thing that's been causing my stomach to tie up in knots.

"Chloe's mad that I called her."

"Not mad," he corrects me. "Just worried, I think. She's afraid you need something she can't give you." This feels like an awfully heavy conversation, so I'm glad when he gets up and tilts his head toward a tent that's been set up off to one side of the parking lot. "How do you feel about discussing this while we make a fishing net out of old parachute cord?"

"Um…amazing?"

He laughs in that special way of his, like Santa Claus before he got old and ate too many cookies. "Then grab those crutches and lead the way, little man. I think you'll like untying all those knots."

———

As I settle into the pile of blankets Zach set up in the tent for me, I can overhear him call Chloe to tell her where I am and not to worry. Even though I don't mind, I pretend I didn't hear anything when he returns with a pile of knotted-up ropes and dumps them in my lap.

"Before we can make a net, we need to get at least ten feet of unbroken cord," he says. "Get those tiny fingers of yours to work."

I'm happy to have something to keep my hands busy while we talk, so I start poking and prodding until I find a loose thread.

"Can you really catch fish when you're all done with this?" I ask as he settles next to me and starts whittling a long, curved stick. "Like, the kind to eat?"

"That's the goal, anyway. Survival at all costs. You'd be surprised how delicious a meal is when you've had a hand in every part of it, catching, killing, and cooking it."

I know I'm supposed to be talking about Chloe and Jasper's book, but this is a *way* more interesting subject. I'm not like Theo, but listening to Zach is almost like reading an adventure story.

"How did you learn to do all this stuff?" I ask. "Like, knowing which plants are safe to eat and how to catch animals and disguising yourself to blend into the trees?"

"Well, now," he says, sitting back in his chair and extending his long legs in front of him. "That's a pretty big question."

I hold up the pile of knots. "That's okay. This is gonna take me forever."

He laughs his Santa laugh again. "Fair enough. Most of this stuff I learned from my dad. He was a big fan of the great outdoors. When I was your age, we used to go camping together for weeks at a time."

"Your dad?" I repeat slowly. Saying those words makes me feel a little lost, but not sad. I don't remember meeting my own dad, even though he technically belongs to both me and Theo. Trixie has a different dad, and so does Chloe, but none of us really care. When all you have for a father is a blank space, it's easy to pretend he's the same blank space for everyone. "What's he like?"

Zach stops to think about it for a second. "A lot like me, actually. Tall. Rough around the edges. Good with his hands. And he enjoys his solitude, but only for a little while. He can spend a month in the wilderness, but then he comes home and spends the whole next month taking my mom out dancing. He calls it life-life balance."

I like that. *Life-life balance.*

"All the men in my family are outdoorsy that way," he adds, watching me out of the corner of his eye. "You could say it's in our blood."

"Books are in my blood," I'm quick to respond. "In mine and Chloe's, anyway. Theo says reading is for people who don't have *Minecraft*, and Trixie would rather talk to people than read about them, but Chloe and me are the same."

Instead of shooting me down, like lots of grown-ups might do, Zach nods. "I agree. You two are very similar." Then he does the thing *all* grown-ups do and tries to sneak one past me. "That's why you came up here today, isn't it? Because of a book? Because of Jasper's book?"

Since I like Zach and I like undoing these knots, I decide to play along. "Kind of, yeah. I stole one from the cabin the other day."

Zach doesn't blink—not even once. "You stole one?"

"Yeah. I should've asked first, but I was afraid he'd say no, so I took the book he was talking about. The one about the lady—*Wuthering Heights*."

Zach blows out a long breath that *feels* like it's not mad. I can tell for sure that he's not mad when he laughs. "You sneaky little devil. I didn't even notice that one on the shelf. Where did you find it?"

"It was just sitting there with all the other books." I find a tricky knot and concentrate on it until it's all the way gone. It must take a while, because when I look up, it's to find Zach watching me with an expression I can't understand. "I don't think he reads that one very much. It was the dustiest of all of them, and the pages aren't bent at all."

"Did you bring the book with you?" he asks.

"Yup. It's full of the writing. I thought you and Chloe might want to see it."

He's quiet again, and this time I don't have a tricky knot to distract me, so I have no choice but to listen to the silence. Eventually, he says, "Can I ask you a question, Aloysius?"

Anytime someone says that, they're going to ask you the question no matter what. But Zach's my friend, so I say, "Sure."

"Why did you bring the book to me instead of Chloe?"

This is a good question—an excellent one, in fact, and I like that Zach knows to ask it.

"Because this will give you a good reason to take her bowling again. You don't have to bring us this time if you don't want to. Theo only gets in the way. Most days, he's a really good brother to have around, but not when you want to be alone." I pause, eyeing him just as much as he's eyeing me. "And you want to be alone with Chloe, don't you?"

At first, I'm afraid he's annoyed I asked, but he eventually shakes his head. "No, I won't do it," he says.

"Do what?"

"Get upset with you for saying the thing we're all thinking. You and Chloe have that in common, too. You cut straight to the heart of the thing. As a man who spends a lot of time avoiding the unnecessary busyness of the world, you have no idea how much I appreciate that quality."

I can tell he's telling the truth, so I set my pile of knots aside and fish the book out of my backpack. I read a little of it when I first brought it home, but I don't think it's for me. Everyone seems to talk in really long sentences, and it takes them forever to get anywhere.

As soon as I put the book in Zach's hands, he breathes out long and slow. His hands move over the cover almost like he's petting Gummy Bear.

"This is really real," he says, but in a voice so low that I'm not sure whether or not I'm supposed to hear it. "So everything Jasper said is true."

I return to the tangled knots, pretending I don't see as he flips open the cover and his eyes start moving over the pages. Even though I don't like the book, I did manage to make it through the first chapter, so I know what he sees when he reaches the first section with the writing.

> I know, by instinct, his reserve springs from an aversion to showy displays of feeling, to manifestations of mutual kindliness. He'll love and hate, equally under cover, and esteem it a species of impertinence to be loved or hated again.

If you read nothing else of these pages, please read this, the pretty handwriting says. *I know you think you're the Heathcliff to my Catherine, and that the only path left to you is a dark and gloomy grave, but it isn't true. Please let yourself be loved again. Please find love again. The best thing you can give me now is a promise that your life will be as full and rich as you deserve.*

I don't know much about the books or the writing or what happened to make Jasper such a sad old man, but I do know that this message is meant for him. Also that it didn't come true.

I used to be afraid of Jasper and what he might do when I accidentally threw Gummy Bear's Frisbees over the fence, but he showed me the closet where he keeps them all so I'm not afraid any more. He apologized and said I could take back as many of them as I wanted, but I'll probably leave them there. I think he likes having all those colorful stacks of plastic in his house.

It's kinda like holding on to that old copy of *Wuthering Heights* for years and years but never actually reading it. He likes knowing how close he is to the things that make life brighter, and he likes being a few steps away from happiness. He also likes not ever actually getting there. It's okay, because I understand. I understand a lot more than anyone thinks.

Because what happens if you reach the thing and you still aren't happy? What happens if you try to do better, but no matter how much of yourself you put in, you'll never be what the teachers and bosses and people in the grocery store want?

"He didn't read this, did he?" Zach asks. There's something in his voice that feels heavy. "He didn't live the full and rich life she tried to give him."

"No, he didn't," I agree. I find another tricky knot and start in on it. Then I say the thing that brought me all the way up here in the first place—the thing I'm hoping Zach can help me with. "But I think maybe, if we try very hard, we can still get him there."

26

—

1960

N THE END, CATHERINE COULDN'T DO it.

She tried to give William McBride what remained of her heart, she really did. She accepted the ring he offered her, a tight band of gold that she had to wear on her pinkie finger thanks to the swelling that seemed to be taking over her body. She planned a discreet wedding with her mother, the two of them poring over magazines to find the best silhouette for hiding a rounded and rapidly growing belly.

She also got to know her betrothed in the time-honored way of overprotected girls everywhere: she sat and chatted politely with him in her parents' living room. The pair of them were always seated in opposite wingback chairs, her mother and father out of sight in the kitchen. She and William couldn't *see* them making cocoa and anxiously stirring their spoons back and forth, but they could hear them just fine.

In fact, she suspected that if her parents had owned one of those old Victorian courting chairs where the couple sat next to each other but was restricted by a wooden barrier that kept decorum at front and center, she and William would have been tied to it.

The whole thing was hilarious, when you thought about it. What did they expect would happen if the two of them were left alone together? That she'd get *more* pregnant?

"Your father found me a great post in Moriarty," William said as he sat with his own cup of cocoa. A dab of it sat on his lower lip, a blob of sugary-sweet chocolate like a mole that was slowly creeping down his chin. Catherine was trying not to stare, but she couldn't help herself.

Couldn't he feel it? Couldn't he feel *anything*?

He grinned, and the blob continued on its downward path. "It's not the most glamorous location, and your mother is afraid the heat of New Mexico might be unbearable as you reach your time, but we'll be able to start fresh, just the two of us. Or three, I guess I should say."

He said this as though he was genuinely happy about the whole thing—a shotgun wedding where he'd fired no bullets, the prospect of raising a child that wasn't his own.

"Moriarty," she echoed. She even managed a smile. "'The spider at the center of the web.'"

With a name like that, how bad could the town possibly be? Granted, she'd looked up the population and found it to be a painfully small seven hundred residents, and she was pretty sure the only thing people did for fun around there was paint scenic backdrops of the surrounding desert, but she'd be busy anyway.

Raising this child. *Loving* this child.

William McBride blinked. "Spider?" he asked. "What spider?"

"The Sherlock stories?" Catherine prompted. "Moriarty? Professor of mathematics? Master of crime?"

"Oh. You're talking about books."

Catherine tried not to let her sudden wash of depression show. She might have even managed it, if William hadn't suddenly brightened and pulled out a flat rectangular gift and handed it to her.

"Speaking of, I got you this. I know how much you love to read."

Something almost like a flicker of hope touched her as she slipped the ribbon off and eagerly tore in, but it was a short-lived sentiment. As soon as she saw the blue dust jacket, she knew she was done for.

"*America's Housekeeping Book*," she said flatly.

If he noticed the sudden plummet of her spirits, he didn't let it show. Instead, he scooted his chair forward, the legs scraping across her mother's carefully waxed hardwood floor. "Since I'll have a higher position at this new post, we'll have to do a lot of entertaining. I'm sure the other officers' wives will be able to pitch in, but this should give you a good solid start."

She let the book sit heavily in her lap, its weight pressing down on her spirits much more than the baby that was starting to show flutterings of life low in her belly.

"Of course, we'll have to live in base housing for a little while, just until we get settled in, but it's never too early to start learning." He flashed his many teeth. "There's a whole chapter in there about getting rid of spots in the laundry. It even has an alphabetical table for stain removal. Can you imagine? All there in one little book."

That was when she ended it. She wished she could have said that she did it with kindness and dignity, that she let William McBride down with the respect he deserved, but it would have been a lie. She stood up so fast that the book fell to the floor with a thud, the pages falling open to something that looked an awful lot like a diagram of a formal place setting.

William jumped with her, ready to come to her aid, but she flung up a hand to stop him.

"No, don't," she cried. "I can't. We can't. I'm sorry."

Her parents came running into the room then, drawn by the sounds of the book falling and the sudden wailing of tears that Catherine could no longer keep back. To their credit, their first instinct was to rush to her aid, but they stopped when they saw her tugging the ring from her finger.

"Catherine, don't be hasty," her mother pleaded.

"Catherine, you need to go to your room and calm down right this instant," her father ordered.

"I don't understand," William said, his glance moving over the inhabitants of the room. The chocolate on his lip finally gave up and fell to the floor, where it landed on the fluttering pages of the housekeeping book. "What's going on?"

Catherine could hear her parents getting ready to intercede, so she forestalled them by holding the ring out in one shaking hand.

"What's going on is that I'm giving you your ring and your promise back," she said. Her voice shook, too, but she had no other choice. She could no more marry William McBride and shackle herself to the same dreary life her mother led than she could marry Jasper Holmes and shackle *him* to a lifetime of self-blame and regret.

Because that was what it would be for Jasper. She knew it just as much as she knew that the Catherine in *A Farewell to Arms* had to die in order for Hemingway's stupid book to have any value. She hated the ending to that book, hated it with a passion she usually reserved for small-minded men living in even smaller-minded worlds, but there it was. If the Catherine in that book had lived—and her child lived with her—then what was the moral? That life could be simple and easy and still worth living? That a man's story didn't have to end when he gave up everything for the sake of an unwanted child?

Catherine had read enough books to know that a happily ever after like that wasn't really possible. Not for people like her, and definitely not for people like Jasper.

"I'm sorry, William," she said, and meant it. "I wish I could be the wife you deserve, but I'm not. And no matter how hard I might try or pretend otherwise, I never will be."

"Catherine Winifred Martin—" her father began, but Catherine only shook her head and pressed the ring firmly into William's hand.

"You're a good person," she said as she squeezed her fingers against his. "And I have no doubt that you'll make some other officer's daughter a wonderful husband. But I don't want to be married to anyone right now. Possibly ever."

"You should've thought of that before you got yourself in trouble with—" her father began again, but this time, it was her mother who stepped up to intervene.

"Perhaps it's best if you walk Lieutenant McBride out, dear," her mother suggested to her husband. She did it in her deceptively sweet way—the way that used to get Catherine's back up, but that now only made her feel sad. Her mom had so much more to offer the world than a clean house and a nicely browned pot roast. In another lifetime, she could have been leading a military installation of her own. "We'll sort through all the details later."

The phrase sounded vaguely threatening, but the moment Catherine caught sight of her mother's expression, she knew it would be okay. Her mom might be angry and would probably try to send Catherine away to a convent for the rest of her life, but she'd never force her down the aisle and into the arms of a man she didn't love.

"Let's talk about this, please," William said. His plea was directed more to her father than to Catherine, which nettled her, but his second plea was even wider off its mark. "Mrs. Martin, you can't let her do this. People are already talking. You know what they'll say if this engagement falls through."

"I don't *let* my daughter do anything," her mom replied, still teetering on that soft, unassuming razor's edge. "And if you think she can be controlled by anything as trivial as small-town gossip, then you have no idea who she is—or what she's capable of."

Her father, sensing defeat, quickly ushered William out of the living room. "Come along, Lieutenant McBride."

"But my future, sir. The posting—"

As they disappeared out of view, Catherine thought she heard her father's reassuring voice promising William that Moriarty was still very much in his future, should he wish for it.

Even though she knew her father was dangling the New Mexico posting as a bribe for William's silence and capitulation, she was genuinely happy for him. Once there, he'd probably fall deep in admiration for another officer's daughter—this time, with one who could see the value in his too-bright smile and even brighter military ambitions. For all she knew, he might even end up loving her.

A wave of relief moved over her at the thought. She sank back in her seat, ignoring the fallen copy of the housewifery book, and settled her hands on the gentle swell of her stomach. Since her father showed no signs of returning, she might have relaxed even further, but her mother's voice stopped her short.

"*Please* tell me you aren't going to marry that woodsman of yours," she said.

"Mom, you make it sound like he's the hunter in 'Little Red Riding Hood' or something. He's not a woodsman. He's a logger. Lots of men around here are loggers."

"I know. That's what I'm afraid of." Her mother scooped up the book and tucked it away out of Catherine's line of sight. "It's a hard life, honey, even for those who were born to it. Haven't you seen the way it ages them?"

Catherine nodded. She'd seen it, all right—of course she had. Wasn't she the one who'd guessed Jasper's age to be a decade more than it actually was? Nowhere in that strong, gruff man was there anything that smacked of a nineteen-year-old dreamer. At least, not until she lay in the circle of his arms, cherished and protected in ways she'd never known were possible. Only then, when he spoke of the books he'd read and the things he yearned for, of the life that had been cruel to him since the day he'd been born, had she understood the truth.

He was a romantic. Possibly the most romantic person she'd ever known. His feet were planted on solid ground, but his heart roamed free.

And if she had anything to say about it, that was where it would stay.

"I'm not going to marry Jasper," Catherine said, her hands still on her stomach. "I can't. It would destroy him."

"Thank goodness for that," her mom said, but with a sideways look that said she wasn't fully convinced. "You'd have been worn down as much as him within the space of two years."

Catherine didn't point out that her decision had nothing to do with her and everything to do with Jasper and the life he was forced to lead. It had been wrong of her, but she'd gone down to city hall to pump information out of Samantha, the chatty blond who worked behind the counter. The girl had plenty to say on the subject of Jasper Holmes, who she'd upheld with starry eyes as a hero who sent half his paycheck home every week without complaint or regret.

"I just want to take that poor man home and feed him a good meal, you know?" Samantha had said with a shake of her pretty curls. "They don't make very many of them like that anymore."

It had been on the tip of Catherine's tongue to retort that they didn't make *any* like him, but she kept her thoughts to herself. She had to or risk breaking out in tears. The sad truth was, no future existed that could fit all the pieces of the puzzle: Jasper, his mother, his siblings, Catherine, the baby…and all the babies she felt sure would follow. Eventually, he'd be forced to choose between them, and she had no doubt that he'd choose her.

And that, she knew, would kill him. Not at first, and not in any quantifiable way, but by the thousand proverbial cuts. Catherine might have enjoyed that kind of spectacle in the pages of a horror novel, but there was no way she'd stand by and watch a man like Jasper suffer.

So it was with a sob lodged deep in her throat that she spoke now.

"I'm not going to marry Jasper," Catherine repeated, hoping the more she said the words, the more she'd grow accustomed to them. "You don't need to worry about that."

"Why do I sense a *but* coming…?"

Catherine managed a weak smile. "Because he won't let me go easily. Not once he knows I've given William the slip. He'll move heaven and earth and probably a little bit of hell to find a way to keep me."

Her mother straightened her posture in a way that Catherine knew, feared, and admired most of all.

"I'd like to see him try and force you to do anything against your will," her mother said tartly. "I don't care if he *did* throw that check away instead of cashing it. We might be backed in a corner right now, but there's still some fight left in us."

Catherine dashed her arm out and grabbed her mother's hand. Her mom looked surprised at the sudden demonstration of affection, but she didn't pull away.

"Thank you, Mom, but that won't be necessary. I already have an idea. I know of a way to get me and the baby somewhere we can be reasonably happy, but you aren't going to like it."

"I don't like *any* of it, dear. That's not the point."

Catherine knew it wasn't. But if her mom had any idea what she was about to propose, she wouldn't be acting so cavalier.

"Then here goes." Catherine took a deep, fortifying breath that didn't fortify her at all. "We need to make Jasper believe I died in childbirth."

Her mother's hand jerked in hers. "Catherine, you don't mean that!"

But she did—with all her heart, she did. The idea was cruel and catastrophic and final. It was also the only way she could think of to save him.

"I know him, and I know what kind of books he reads, so you have to believe me when I say this. If I don't marry William McBride, death is the only other ending Jasper will heed."

She drew a determined breath and prepared to lay out her plans. Hemingway said it best, but he didn't say it first and he certainly wouldn't say it last.

Life isn't hard to manage when you've nothing to lose.

27

—

NOODLE

CAN'T BELIEVE THIS IS REALLY REAL."

Chloe sits on the front steps of the library, her skirt tucked around her legs as she flips through the pages of *Wuthering Heights*. Even though her voice sounds as calm as usual, her eyes are wide and her hands shake as she makes her way through.

She glances up at me—well, probably at Zach, but since we're standing next to each other, it's basically the same thing.

"There's writing on almost every page," she says. She stabs her finger at a line in the second half. "Look. This is the part where Heathcliff and Catherine are sitting up in a tree together. '*He wanted all to lie in an ecstasy of peace; I wanted all to sparkle, and dance in a glorious jubilee. I said his heaven would be only half-alive, and he said mine would be drunk; I said I should fall asleep in his, and he said he could not breathe in mine.*'"

Next to me, Zach doesn't move. He's been acting kind of funny ever since I showed him the book, but not in a way that makes sense to me. He's not mad—that much I know for sure—but I don't think he's happy, either. In fact, the more I think about it, the more he seems like Chloe around Christmastime. She's really good at helping us make decorations for the tree and baking cookies and stuff, but I know she feels bad about how many presents there are. Or aren't.

"What does she have to say about that?" he asks. "Our Catherine?"

I don't think Chloe has noticed how weird Zach is yet. We pulled her out of work on her lunch break, so she's probably busy thinking about book catalogs and story time.

"She says, *'Isn't it funny how unoriginal we are as human beings? A hundred and seventy-five years later, and here we are, living the same lives and making the same mistakes. You're up in the tree, watching the clouds and breathing the air, and all I want is to run away to the next field over. At the very least, I could have been the Heathcliff in our relationship. That would have been a fun switch.'"* Chloe lifts the book so we can see.

"I don't understand any of it," she says before we can read it for ourselves. "Catherine obviously wrote in this book as a kind of farewell to Jasper. She meant for him to read it after she was gone. But why did she leave? And why does Jasper think she died?"

I'm happy to have at least one of those answers. It's not very often that I know something Chloe doesn't.

"Jasper said they were going to have a baby together. He was so upset when she wouldn't marry him that he hit a guy." I pause, remembering his words, and add, "He also said violence is never the answer, and that it's not okay to hurt other people just because you hurt, too."

Chloe's head swivels toward Zach. I get the feeling she didn't really hear that second part.

"Is that true?" she asks. "He proposed and Catherine said no? She was *pregnant*? And you didn't tell me?"

Zach looks as uncomfortable as I feel whenever I have to be polite to grown-ups I don't like.

"In my defense, I meant to," he says. "I was going to tell you the next time we hung out, but you've been so busy with your mom that I haven't had a chance."

Instead of saying something soothing, like she usually does, Chloe narrows her eyes. "You couldn't text?"

"And say what? That Jasper laid his deepest, darkest secret at my feet?"

"Well, yeah, actually. You know how invested I am in this."

Zach's voice gets quiet. "You've got a lot on your plate right now. I didn't want to overload it."

That's when Chloe does a thing I've never seen her do before. She gets mad. Like, *really* mad—the kind that makes your skin turn red and your face get ugly, though I don't think Chloe could ever be that. She also jumps to her feet so fast that her bag spills all over the steps.

"You think Jasper's illegitimate love child is the thing that's going to break me?" she says, and in a voice that's so loud it counts as yelling. "Of all the things I've done in my life—the jobs I've slogged through, the plans I've given up, the mother currently sitting in my living room acting as though she isn't responsible for every last bit of it—you think finally solving the riddle to this book saga is one thing I can't handle?"

Zach doesn't even flinch. He starts picking up Chloe's spilled note-books and ChapStick instead. "I said I was sorry."

"Don't do that," Chloe says as she snatches the purse away from him. She shovels the rest of her stuff in. "I'll clean up the mess. It's the one thing I'm halfway good at."

Zach steps back, looking a lot like he wants the world to open up and swallow him whole—either that, or to run away from these library steps and never come back again. I'm so afraid for this second one that I speak up before Chloe can start yelling again.

"Are you going to show the book to Jasper?" I ask. "Or did you want me to sneak it back on the shelf? I can, if you want me to. As soon as my leg's better, he said I can visit the cabin whenever I want. He'll never know I took it."

Chloe hesitates, and when she looks at Zach, I can tell that she's not as upset anymore. "It's not the worst idea in the world. If he really thinks Catherine's dead and gone—"

"He does," Zach says grimly.

Chloe continues as if he hasn't spoken. "And if he purposely avoided this book because it was too painful—" She waits for another interruption, but Zach stays quiet. She shrugs to match him. "Then maybe the kindest thing we can do is let the broken pieces lie. Take it from one who knows. Sometimes, it's better if the past stays where it belongs. Because once you let it back into your house again…"

Her voice trails off, and I can tell she's talking about Mom. I hang my head.

"I never should've called her, should I?" I ask guiltily. "I'm sorry. I thought she might help, but she's only making stuff harder for you. Theo and Trixie are gone. You and Zach are fighting. I ruined things. I *always* ruin things."

"No. No!" All of a sudden, Chloe is crouched down in front of me. She wants to hug me, I can tell, but she clasps her hands in front of her instead. "Noodle, this isn't your fault, okay? None of this is your fault. You just got caught up in a lot of adult nonsense that never should've been yours to worry about in the first place."

I look to Zach, glad to find him nodding and smiling again. "Your sister is right, Aloysius. I shouldn't have let you get dragged into all this. When I came here, I never thought… That is, I didn't plan—"

For the first time since Zach first came dashing to my rescue, it seems as if he has no idea what to do. I don't like it.

And neither, I think, does Chloe. She reaches out and touches his arm.

"Hey," she says. "That goes for you, too. None of this mess is your fault, and I wouldn't blame you if you disappeared into the woods and as far away from my family as you can get. I know I warned you that we were a package deal, but what I failed to mention is that the package is busted all to hell. Most people would take one look at us and throw it out."

He touches her hand super quick before hopping down a few steps and putting a huge gap between them. That's my first clue that something bad is about to happen. The second is when he takes a big long breath.

I know what that big long breath means. I've heard it so many times in my life that I sometimes think everyone around me has lungs the size of the sky.

"I'd have preferred to save this conversation for a different setting— and a different time—but I don't see any way around it," he says, and so seriously that it makes me feel itchy all over. "I'm afraid we can't put that book back in Jasper's cabin."

My sister blinks. "Why not? Did you already show it to him? Because—"

Zach holds up a hand to stop her from saying more. "No, I haven't shown it to him. I probably *should* have, but I wanted to get my grandmother's take on it first. That was…a mistake."

Chloe's brows snap together. "What are you talking about? What does your grandmother have to do with anything?"

My heart thuds when I see Zach frown.

"I hoped maybe it was all a misunderstanding, but I was wrong," he says.

I'm not sure what this means, but Chloe does. Her face goes white and she drops her purse all over again.

"You have to understand," he adds in a funny voice. I want to ask what's going on, but I don't think either one of them remembers I'm here. "She never really talked about him. She never really talked about any of it. That's why I moved here in the first place. Unfortunately, as soon as I told her about you and your literary scavenger hunt, she booked a flight out here. I'm supposed to pick her up from the airport tomorrow."

"It can't be," Chloe says, her words so quiet they're carried away by the air. "You aren't his—"

"It very much is," Zach says with a grimace. "And I'm afraid I very much am."

PART FOUR

28

—

ZACH

NEVER MEANT TO HURT ANYONE.

It was the one rule I lived by—the one rule I'd *always* lived by—but rules didn't always cut it. Trying not to hurt people and doing it anyway was kind of my family's curse. In fact, I suspected it was part of the reason we spent so much time in the great outdoors. When your only bed was a piece of canvas laid out on the forest floor and your only company was your own miserable self, you couldn't do much in the way of damage.

That's the lie we told ourselves, anyway.

"Wait," Chloe said as she stood on the library steps, her expression torn between confusion and pain. Both of these were important to note: the first, because I knew that discovering Jasper Holmes to be my biological grandfather would be a lot to take in; the second, because only a woman who cared could feel that kind of pain.

Whether it was me she cared about or Jasper, however, remained to be seen.

"This whole time, you knew about her? About *them*?" she asked. The hurt part was starting to win out over confusion, which was no more than I expected. For all that she claimed to be a woman facing dead ends at every turn, Chloe Sampson was pretty damn smart. She'd put the rest of the pieces together faster than most of us could tie our shoes.

"I knew about *her*, yes," I admitted. "But Jasper only existed as a story Grandma used to tell at bedtime. Sometimes, he was the big brave mountain man who worked hard every day of his life, determined to do the right thing by the people he loved. Other times, he was a softhearted romantic who captured Grandma's heart through books. Imagine my surprise when I moved here and saw him for the first time. I ran into him at the grocery store, scowling at the produce section as though the wilted greens were a personal insult."

Instead of getting a laugh out of Chloe, my comment only caused her to furrow her brow deeper.

"You knew she had a baby," she said, still in that accusing, faraway tone. "You knew she broke his heart on purpose and kept it a secret from him all these years."

"It's not as bad as it sounds," I said. Feebly, I suspected, and too late to be of any use. "Until Jasper told me the whole story, I didn't know she'd arranged it to make him think she died in childbirth. Catherine—my grandmother, that is—always made it seem like she and Jasper just ended, that their love story wasn't meant to last. When he first started talking about her dying, I thought maybe it was a metaphor for his emotional loss or something."

Chloe turned a stare on me that could have curdled blood. "A *metaphor*? Zach, he's the unhappiest man I've ever met. He's been nursing a broken heart for over sixty years, and you're bringing the woman who broke it here? Now?"

I winced. Deep down, I knew Chloe was right. Now that I'd met my grandfather for myself and seen the cabin he built like a shrine to my grandmother's memory, there was no hiding it.

"She never wanted me to make contact with him," I admitted. "In fact, she didn't even know I was moving to Colville until I'd already accepted the job with the survival school. And believe me—once she *did* know, she was none too happy about it. It's only now that I'm starting to realize why."

I looked to Aloysius to make sure he was doing okay, but all he did was watch us in that knowing, wide-eyed way of his. That kid saw a lot more than most people realized, but I doubted he understood just what Chloe was accusing me of.

Lying. Omitting the truth. Slapping a fake library barcode on my grandmother's weathered old copy of *A Farewell to Arms* and offering it to his sister as an opening gambit.

Of all the things I'd done, that was the only part I wasn't super proud of. I'd known, from something Aloysius had said when he was half out of his mind with pain in the forest, that his sister recently found an old book with handwriting in it, and that their next-door neighbor had offered to buy it from her. I'd also known, in the way that people in small towns *always* knew, that the laughing, boisterous Sampson family lived next door to my biological grandfather.

At the time, it had seemed the most logical thing in the world to do. I'd wanted to get to know my grandfather better. I'd wanted to get to know Chloe better. Inserting myself into the story with a *literal* story had seemed like the ideal solution.

Until, of course, I realized just how messed up the story was. My grandma had always been a larger-than-life presence, the sort of woman who could hold a room spellbound using nothing but a smile, but this whole situation was starting to feel way too big.

Even for a man built like me.

"Grandma tried to convince me to leave Colville before I exposed myself, but I'd heard so many stories about this place that I couldn't resist." I drew a deep breath and glanced around me—at the unnaturally wide streets of this town, the jagged mountains rising in every direction, so many trees you could stand in the middle of a forest and feel like you were in an ocean. "And then when I got settled in, well…" I let my voice trail away in hopes that Chloe would pick up where I left off.

She didn't.

"I guess I'm more like my grandfather than I'd like to admit," I finished. "Once I set foot in this town, I realized I belonged here. There's something about this place that calls to me."

"Not me," Chloe said, finally finding her tongue. "I've been looking for a way out since the day I was born." Her remark felt barbed, but it was no more than I deserved. I should've been honest with her from the start, but what was I supposed to have said?

Oh, yeah. That bitter old man you're obsessed with? We're related, only he doesn't know I exist. Apparently, he doesn't know my dad exists, either. He thinks we're part of a long-dead past that he buried a long time ago. Also, do you want to go for a hike? I know of a place where we can get lost together.

In the end, it didn't matter, because Aloysius was the one who took her barb to heart.

"You miss going to college in Spokane, don't you, Chloe," he said, stating it as a fact instead of a question. "And only having yourself to take care of."

Chloe cast me a look of such loathing that I could read every word in her big green eyes.

"I'm *exactly* where I want to be, Noodle," she said as she gathered up her purse and held out a hand to her brother. He couldn't take it, obviously, since he had to struggle up the library steps on his crutches, but as she turned her back on me, I knew what she was trying to say.

She blamed me for this mess. For dragging a twelve-year-old into my family drama, for exposing the truth she tried so hard to hide from the three lives that depended on her. But most of all, for taking the side of a woman who'd left this town without once looking back—not at the places she'd left behind, and *definitely* not at the people.

Chloe knew what it meant to be the one left standing, straining to hold all the pieces together. So did Jasper.

And no matter how much I might wish otherwise, I was only one more problem added to a pair of intelligent, well-read curmudgeons who'd been dealt a terrible hand in life...and who never once got an apology or a thanks from those who owed them the most.

29

—

ZACH

AS LITTLE AS I RELISHED THE idea of driving two hours to pick up my grandmother from the airport in Spokane, I knew the alternative—disobeying her—would be worse. Which was why I was so startled when I settled behind the wheel of my Jeep to find the passenger door swinging open and a woman sliding into the seat beside me.

"Uhh…hello?" I said, my hand paused on the key.

"Hey, Zach," the woman said in a laughing voice. I recognized her from the library—she was Pepper, Chloe's best friend. From the way she was looking at me, I guessed she already knew most of our situation. "It's nice to finally meet you—formally, I mean. I hear you're making a trip to the airport."

Since the evidence of this trip would soon be joining us in Colville, I nodded. I also felt a wave of relief. Gossip in small towns tends to flow pretty fast, but this seemed more like the result of a personal conversation. If Pepper knew about my plans, then Chloe was the one who told her.

And if Chloe told her, that meant she hadn't totally written me off. *Yet.*

"My grandmother's flight gets in at ten," I said with a glance at the clock. My boss, a terrifyingly capable retired Air Force pilot who only answered to his call sign of Bones, wasn't happy to give me the day off, but I promised to make it up to him by giving him my dad's secret cricket-and-dandelion soup recipe. "So if you're here to yell at me for lying to Chloe, you're going to have to do it quick."

Instead of being put off by my words, Pepper reached across her shoulder and started buckling her seat belt. "If I come with you, then I'll have all the time in the world to yell," she said, still too cheerful for my peace of mind. "And if you step on it, we can stop at Starbucks on the way. I haven't had a pumpkin spice latte in ages."

I cast her a sideways look, but she was already settled in as if she intended to stay.

"Didn't your mother ever teach you how dangerous it is to get into a strange man's car?" I asked.

She beamed across the console at me, and I could immediately tell why she was such good friends with Chloe. Pepper seemed like the sort of woman who didn't take the word *no* very easily—and Chloe was very much the sort of woman who was used to saying it.

Pepper patted the bag she had tucked at her feet. "My mother didn't, but you can bet your ass my grandma gave me firsthand lessons. Try anything funny, and you're getting a face full of bear spray."

I started the car with a laugh. I might have been caught in the middle of a mess that was only about to get messier, but at least the trip would be a lively one.

"Bear spray doesn't work on me," I said. "The first step in any wilderness training class is learning how to take what you dish out. At this point in my life, I'm practically immune to the stuff."

———

If I was afraid that two hours of driving next to Chloe's best friend would be an agony of interrogation techniques and awkward questions, it was nothing compared to the agony of watching Pepper and my grandmother fall into each other's arms outside the airport.

"My God," my grandmother said as she stepped out of the sliding doors with a train of oversized baggage behind her. From the look of it, she was planning on taking up residence in Washington for the rest of her life. "It's like looking straight through the portals of time. Don't tell me—you *must* be a Pakootas."

"Is it that obvious?" Pepper asked, laughing. She accepted the embrace my grandmother held out to her as though hugging complete strangers was a thing she did every day. "I'd be insulted, but I've seen pictures of Grandma when she was young. She was a serious smokeshow."

"That she was," my grandmother agreed. She turned to me next, only I wasn't offered a hug. If anything, she looked annoyed to see me standing there. "Hello, Grandson. You have some nerve, dragging me back here when I swore I'd never set foot in this state again."

"I'm pretty sure I didn't drag you," I said with a pointed glance at her baggage. "In fact, I didn't even invite you."

"When has that ever stopped me before?" she countered.

That was when I finally got my hug. My grandmother is considerably smaller than me, but she has an energy that makes her feel ten times her size. She smelled, as she always did, like warm vanilla and the musk perfume I'd never known her to be without. That was one of the things that made this whole situation so surreal—my whole *life* so surreal, when I thought about it. For as long as I could remember, Grandma Cathy had been a figure of glamour and sophistication. Dressed in the latest fashions and with chic scarves always swathed about her person, a cocktail in one hand and her cell phone in the other, she was the poster child for a generation that refused to accept old age as anything but a chance to celebrate life. She'd been an unwed single mother at a time when that sort of thing equaled social ostracism. She'd become a book editor in a field that was so male-dominated at the time that she would sometimes find herself not just in a room full of men, but a whole building of them.

To see her in a place like this, where the closest thing to pass for fashion was the newest line of North Face fleece wear and the nearest Michelin Star restaurant was four hundred miles away, felt wrong.

"Well," she said as she eyed my Jeep. It was dirty and battered and ideal for making it over unpaved roads—in other words, a lot like me. "I guess we'd better get this over with."

Abandoning her pile of luggage for me to load, she swung herself into the back seat. Instead of claiming the front for herself, Pepper climbed in next to her.

"I want to hear *all* about your time in Colville with my grandmother and Jasper," Pepper said as she once again buckled herself in place. "And don't leave anything out."

"People always think it's the vain city-dwelling men who are the most arrogant and self-involved, but they're wrong," my grandmother said as I zipped the Jeep down the well-trod highway back home. She spoke in a voice that was meant for me to overhear.

"Do you know a lot about arrogant men, Auntie?" Pepper asked in a voice that was equally obvious. It had taken her all of five minutes to start calling my grandma by the familiar nickname, even less for her to decide that the two of them were destined to be best friends. "I bet you've known your share."

"You could say something like that," my grandmother said primly. Then she laughed and reached forward to pat my shoulder. "But I won't go into details. Poor Zach would run us off the road if he knew about the men I've known in my lifetime—biblically speaking, that is."

I groaned. "This can't be happening."

"See what I mean?" My grandmother tsked. "The real problem with society is men like Zach here—he and his father both, not to mention Jasper, the one who started it all. They act as though they're rough and tough and self-sufficient, but the truth is, they're odiously selfish."

"I'm turning on the radio," I warned, but we all knew it to be an empty threat. Despite my discomfort with the conversation, I found myself interested in what my grandmother had to say for herself. She seemed to have no idea of the devastation she'd wrought when she left this place the way she did, the hearts she broke and the lives she'd left behind.

"They use the manufactured hardship of the wilderness as an excuse for avoiding reality," she continued. "Think about it—we live in a glorious time of human existence. If I pull out my phone, I can instantly access every piece of documented history. We've passed no fewer than fifteen different restaurants since we got on this road, and we can pay for anything we want to eat with a small piece of plastic we carry in our pockets. And that's not even counting the fact that we're sitting comfortably inside a hunk of metal designed to fly over roads using the decayed remains of marine plants and animals that lived millions of years ago. Yet these men pretend that the only thing keeping us alive as a species is their ability to sleep in a tent and skin a squirrel in under a minute."

"You tell him, Auntie," Pepper cheered.

I could hear the amusement in my grandmother's voice over the roar of the engine. She leaned forward and tapped my shoulder. "Back me up, Zach. How often does Bates leave your poor mother all alone in that big house so he can go out and 'commune with nature'?"

"Three or four times a year," I said, understanding my role. Still, I felt compelled to defend my dad. My parents' marriage might have been odd, but it had always been a happy one. "You know she doesn't mind, though. She always ends up painting like six or seven new pieces while he's gone."

My grandmother waved me off. "That's not the point. The point is—"

"Wait," Pepper interrupted. "Your son's name is Bates? Like the butler from *Downton Abbey*?"

I shook my head. Explaining my father's love of the wilderness was nothing compared to explaining the origin of his name.

"Not that Bates," my grandmother said. "The one from *Psycho*. Norman."

"You named your son after the psychotic killer in a horror movie?" Pepper demanded, incredulous.

My grandmother was quick to correct her, which she did with a gentle cough. "No, I named him after the psychotic killer in one of the greatest *novels* of all time."

I couldn't help but add my own mite. "Yeah. The one who lives in an unhealthily codependent relationship with his mother after his biological father leaves them." I laughed at the sudden silence in the back seat. "Grandma has always had a dark sense of humor."

"Bates is a good strong name, and I've never once regretted choosing it," my grandmother said sternly, but then she ruined it by dissolving into giggles. "You should have seen my poor parents when I told them. I think they took the news of my pregnancy better. My mother actually cried."

Pepper breathed out long and slow. "Damn, Auntie. You're next-level badass. Chloe is going to *love* you."

At the sound of that name, my own breath came in a sharp inhalation. When we'd first spoken on the phone, I hadn't said anything to my grandmother about my feelings for Chloe, but her name had naturally arisen—and Grandma had always had an uncanny ability to see beyond the surface of things. I imagine that was what drew her to a man like Jasper Holmes all those years ago. The rest of the world looked at him and saw a confirmed grouch with the social skills of a bear awakening from hibernation; she looked at him and thought, *Huh. He seems sweet.*

"Ah, yes," my grandmother said, careful to keep her tone neutral. "The girl who found the book. The one Jasper has been antagonizing for the past few years."

"I never said he was *antagonizing* her," I protested. "He's been stealing her family's Frisbees, that's all."

I might as well have not been in the car for all the attention the other two paid me.

"Which just goes to prove what I was saying before," she said. "I gave that man the gift of a lifetime. Walking away from him was the hardest thing I've ever done, but I knew it was the only way he'd have a chance at a life of his own. And what did he do with it?"

I had my own answer to this question, but it wasn't the one my grandmother wanted to hear. I'd seen too much of Jasper Holmes and read too many of the lines in those books to believe that his life after her had been anything but a long, lonely slog.

"He wasted it, that's what," she said as if clinching an argument. "He sat in that town and let decades pass without making the least push to improve himself. It's exactly as I said—he's selfish."

I was about to protest again, but Pepper beat me to it. "But Auntie, what if he didn't see your death as a gift? What if his heart was broken and he couldn't find a way to fix it?"

My grandmother grew unnaturally silent. For the longest time, I thought she was going to finally admit that she may have been wrong— that she was, in large part, responsible for the man Jasper turned out to be—but she didn't. At this point, I wasn't sure that she *could*.

"Everyone's heart breaks at least once in a lifetime," she said, determined, as ever, to go her own way. "It's as inevitable as falling in love. The real challenge is deciding what you plan to do about it."

30

—

CATHERINE

MY GRANDSON WAS NO FOOL.

Instead of trying to put me up in a tent out in the woods or booking me into one of the budget hotels that litter the highway, he had the sense to get me an Airbnb in one of the older, statelier homes not far from the white house I once lived in with my parents. I hated to sound pretentious, but I'd been on this planet for over eighty years. In that time, I'd lived in tenement-style building blocks, moldy basement apartments, and a small studio in the heart of New York City, just to name a few. I could rough it with the best of them, but since I was no longer in a position where sleeping in a loft with exactly six inches between my head and the ceiling was necessary, I wasn't going to do it.

Growing old was no picnic, but it had its perks.

"I've checked all the doors and windows, and it looks like everything locks from the inside," Zach said as he prowled about the living room, fidgeting and poking at everything that was even remotely movable. "And I can't see any hidden cameras, but that doesn't mean they aren't here. Don't walk around naked unless you're willing to risk someone recording you from their underground lair."

I laughed and grabbed his cheeks, pulling him down for a quick kiss. "Bless you, child. Anyone who wants to secretly record me in the nude is welcome to it. They'll be feeling the pain of exposure a lot more than I will."

Zach laughed, but in a distracted way that reminded me so much of his father that it made my heart hurt.

Actually, that was a lie. He laughed in a distracted way that reminded me so much of *Jasper* that it made my heart hurt. Bates had always been a chip off the old block, tall and loose-limbed and with those piercing blue eyes that saw so much more than they let on. Zach didn't have the same look of either his father or grandfather, but the mannerisms were there. He was much more outgoing and cheerful—his mother's influence, no doubt—but the vein of seriousness ran deep in these men. They lived and loved hard.

"Do you have the book?" I asked, since it appeared one of us would have to broach the subject first. I held out my hand and waggled my fingers. "I'd like to see it. I don't remember half the things I wrote in there, but I presume it's all sentimental nonsense."

He looked startled. "The copy of *Wuthering Heights*, you mean?"

"Yes, dear," I said, trying not to show my exasperation. "As much as I love you, I didn't fly all this way to catch up on the bugs you've been eating and the constellations you've renamed."

His laugh was a little less distracted that time. So was his smile. If I had to pick one quality that all three of the most important men of my life had in common, it would be that—the devastating quirk of the lips, appearing as if out of nowhere and capable of stopping a heartbeat flat. If this Chloe girl was in any way molded like me, she'd have proven powerless against it.

"Come on, Grandma. I haven't done that since I was a kid."

"The constellations, maybe, but I'd bet every penny I have that you've eaten something from the insect family within the past week."

"But I have to," he protested. "That's literally my job. You'd be surprised how healthy it can be. Mealworms have a really high protein count."

The gag this comment elicited was in no way faked. Jasper always had a touching regard for the great outdoors, and Bates turned recreational camping into a lifestyle, but Zach was the only one who committed himself to it body and soul. I shuddered to think of what would happen if he had a child of his own someday. The poor thing would probably be handed over to the wolves and left to fend for itself.

"And don't try to distract me by telling me all the other disgusting things you've done in the name of your career," I said, lest he get it into his head to try me further. "I came here for the book, and the book I will have. It was never meant for any eyes but Jasper's."

He flushed guiltily, which I took to mean that he read the book and all its notations. I hadn't been lying when I said I didn't remember everything I'd written in those pages. At the time, I'd been five months pregnant and plotting a desperate exit strategy that not even one of the Brontë sisters, with all their love of Gothic drama, would have dared to put to paper. I'd spent every night sobbing into my pillow, wishing upon all the wishes in the world that things could have turned out differently.

Naturally, my literary commentary had gotten a little over the top. If you'd ever been roiling with pregnancy hormones and getting ready to break a man's heart, you'd have been a touch melodramatic, too.

"I don't have it," he said, and with an earnestness that made me believe him.

"You sold it? That seems a touch mercenary."

He ran a rueful hand along the back of his neck. "Of course I didn't sell it. I gave it to Chloe. If there's one person who cares more about how this story ends than either of us, it's her."

I nodded, not displeased with this remark. I didn't know this Chloe person, but I knew her kind. Oh, how I knew it. A librarian who loved books more than she should, a young woman who did what she had to even when it meant cutting out her own heart—you could say that girl still lived and breathed somewhere deep inside me.

That's what I liked to think, anyway.

"Then take me to her," I said as I grabbed my Birkin and headed for the door. "I don't know if you've noticed, but I'm not getting much younger over here."

———

I knew, the moment I met the mother, that I was in for a lot more trouble than I'd anticipated.

"Come in, come in," she said as soon as she caught sight of me standing on the doorstep, my gaze turned as far away from the glorious garden to my right as possible. I didn't know if Jasper was at home, and in my travel-weary state, I wasn't sure I was ready to encounter him, but it didn't matter. I could hardly see anything over the riot of fronds and flowers that erupted out of the yard, spilling out in an orgy of overeager growth.

Oh, Jasper. Channeling all that energy into plants instead of people, building a botanical fortress of literary references as obvious as they were ridiculous. Right away, I noticed a burst of purple wisteria straight from the pages of *A Farewell to Arms.* I had no doubt that if I continued poking around, I'd find roses blooming out of a dung heap a la *Tropic of Cancer* and oleander planted from *The Haunting of Hill House.*

"You must be exhausted," the mother added as she placed a hand on my arm and gently led me inside. "Let me get you a nice cup of tea and a place to rest your bones."

Our destination was a sagging beige lump of a couch that looked like something that had been dragged out of a garbage heap, but that didn't stop her from ushering me into it. From the way she was acting, you'd have thought I was standing around with one foot already in the grave.

"Sorry about the mess," she apologized as she lifted a stack of graphic novels from the couch and tossed them to the table. "We've got kind of a full house right now."

"It's amazing how much space four kids can take up," added a short, nicely dressed man who immediately reminded me of a cross between Willy Wonka and one of his Oompa Loompas. He held out his hand to me in a gesture of friendliness. When I took it, he shook with all the robustness his lady was lacking. I liked him the better for it. "The name's Todd. Todd Aarons. Ravenna here is my wife and the mother of all four, if you can believe it. And looking not a day over thirty herself."

I liked him for that, too. My well-trained eye placed this Ravenna woman on the wrong end of her forties, but with her freckled face and flame of red hair, I could see how one might make the case for her being a decade younger. I could also see how, if the daughter looked anything like her, my grandson had fallen so hard.

"Technically, you only have two of the kids living here," Zach said flatly. He had yet to move into the house, his arms crossed and his stance wide where he stood in the doorway. "Theo and Trixie are still staying at Jasper's."

"Yes, but all their belongings are here, and that's practically the same thing, isn't it?" Ravenna said with a brightness that bordered on the brittle. "I spent the past few years seeing a little something of the world, so I seem to have forgotten how much stuff they have. Clothes, toys, books…"

"*Nightwave*," I said as I picked up one of the graphic novels. "Someone in this house has good taste. This is one of mine."

Ravenna blinked down at me. Somewhere along the line, she appeared to have forgotten the tea, but I didn't mind. Coffee was and always would be my vice of choice. You could thank my father for that.

"No, dear," she said kindly. "That's my son's. Noodle. He loves to read."

I cast my eyes in Zach's direction, begging him to save me, but he was only watching the interaction with a flat press of his lips. It was clear he didn't think much of this woman, whatever he felt about the rest of the family.

"No, I mean I *acquired* it," I explained. "For the publisher. I was only a coeditor on it, since graphic novels aren't my purview, but the moment it crossed my desk, I knew I had to have it. Action with a bit of horror? Flawed heroes you can't help but root for? Yes, please. I've been championing this series from the start."

To the woman's credit, it didn't take her long to put the pieces together. She flipped the book over and scanned the acknowledgments page. "Wait. You mean you're—"

"No way," a voice cried as a boy came bursting through the front door, pushing Zach unceremoniously aside. He hobbled along on a cast, his hair denoting him yet another member of this family. I put his age at around ten or eleven—a few years too young for our projected reader-ship, but I'd been eyeballs deep in H. P. Lovecraft around that same age, so who was I to judge?

"I've read all the *Nightwave* books three times," he announced to me in a voice that bordered on the reverent. "Is there going to be another one soon? Is Ygrit really dead or just pretending? Do you know if they find the Rapier of Wit in time for the final battle?"

I laughed and held up my hands. "Slow down there, young man. One at a time."

"Sorry," he said, his eyes suddenly sweeping down and staying there. "I just really like the books."

I was about to answer his questions in the order they were shot at me, but another figure appeared in the doorway behind him. It belonged to a pretty, harassed-looking girl I assumed was Chloe, since she barely noticed anything but her brother.

"Noodle, for the last time, it's a *walking* cast, not a running-at-full-speed cast. Honestly, I'm starting to think that Theo has more sense than you—oh." She stopped short as soon as she saw me. She also recognized me with a speed that was unsettling. "*Oh!*" she said again, her eyes growing wide.

Since I'd never loved the thought of being predictable, I couldn't decide whether or not to take her reaction as a compliment, but it didn't matter. As soon as an old man entered on her heels, I lost all sense of everything but him.

He was tall and broad-shouldered despite his advanced age, his posture perfectly erect. A full head of snowy white hair brushed the ceiling of the small house, and his clothes, despite being a touch rustic, were well fitted to his strong frame. In fact, if someone had asked me to lay odds, I'd have said he still possessed the strength to fell a whole forest full of trees.

But he also looked beaten. And tired. And so much like the boy I once knew that my heart left my chest.

Especially once he noticed me.

"Jasper, don't—" the girl began, but it was too late. He started to go down like one of those forest trees, every muscle in him collapsing at once.

Every one of my own muscles collapsed with him. I couldn't move—couldn't even react—as he dashed a hand out to grip the doorway. Not that it did him any good. He missed by such a large margin that only Zach's quick thinking and even quicker movements saved him from crumpling into a heap on the floor.

31

—

CATHERINE

THE PAGES OF *WUTHERING HEIGHTS* WERE thick and luscious in a way that no longer exists in publishing unless you spring for a special edition hardback. They were also crisp and virtually untouched despite the fact that I'd left the book on the cabin bookshelf for Jasper to find.

"You were supposed to read this," I accused as I sat next to his bedside. He had yet to wake up from the faint that had sent him tumbling into Zach's arms, but his breathing was steady and he kept muttering in his sleep, so I assumed he'd just collapsed like one of those fainting goats and wasn't ready to face me yet.

The room where I sat over his bedside wasn't his own; Zach was a strong kid, but even he could only manage to drag a man this size as far as the boys' bedroom in the Sampson house. It reminded me a lot of Bates's room growing up. He and I rarely had much money in those early days, since employment opportunities for an undereducated woman in the sixties left much to be desired, but he'd been a collector of all things nature. Rocks, leaves, the long-desiccated corpses of various beetles—if it was filthy and normally found outdoors, he found a way to keep it.

Even a hastily painted-over scar on one of the walls felt familiar. Bates had once tried to light a campfire in the middle of his room so we could have an impromptu weenie roast.

I let the book fall open to a section about halfway through. Chloe had been carrying the copy in her bag, and even though I could tell she was burning to ask me all manner of questions—and to keep the book for herself—she'd willingly handed it over.

"'*You said I killed you—haunt me then!*'" I read aloud from the pages. "'*The murdered* do *haunt their murderers, I believe; I know that ghosts have wandered the earth. Be with me always—take any form—drive me mad! Only* do *not leave me in this abyss where I can not find you!*'"

A sigh escaped me at the passage, especially once I saw what I'd written in the margins.

You can live without your life, J, and you can live without your soul. You have to. For my sake as well as yours, I'm begging you to try.

"Can you believe we were ever this dramatic?" I asked as I ran my fingers over the words. I was pretty sure I could still make out the splotches where my tears had dropped, but that might have been memory turning me sentimental. "I sometimes see kids today, falling head over heels in love and acting as though they're the first ones to ever feel that way, and wish I could get that passion back. Then I recall the agony of those first few years and change my mind. I don't know about you, but I had a rough go of it there for a while. I can't tell you how many times I thought about coming back here to find you."

I might have done it, too, only the radar base closed its doors a few months after I left. My father had been devastated to lose his position, but my mother was more than ready to move on to greener pastures. As soon as they packed up the house and moved to their next posting—in

Philadelphia, if I remember correctly—Colville was essentially erased from their memories.

Not mine, though. It forever lived inside me as the place where I'd learned to stand on my own two feet, even if I'd only managed it because I'd been propped up by the two extra feet I was growing inside me.

"How was I supposed to know you'd leave this book on the shelf for sixty years and refuse to touch it?" I continued with a soft tsk. "It was meant to comfort you, you old fool. I was giving you a ghost to chase so you could live up to your full Heathcliff potential, and you wasted it."

"Get. Out."

The words were dragged out of Jasper's lips as if by force. My gaze flew to his face, but his eyes were still closed and his pallor too white for my liking. He was in good shape for his age, it was true, but sudden frights did strange things to our circulatory systems. A few weeks ago, a car backfired a few streets down from me, and I spent a full ten minutes searching my body for what I felt sure was the bullet hole.

"Hello to you, too," I said as I reached for his hand. Even though his eyes remained closed, he snatched his fingers back before I could make contact. I clucked my tongue. "Well, now. Is that any way to treat an old flame? No wonder why you have this whole town in a quake. If you treat your old friends like this, I can't imagine what you do to your enemies."

He finally opened his eyes and fixed that oh-so-familiar gaze on me. He looked about as deflated as I felt, but the second those clear blue eyes met mine, it was as if the years fell away. I was no longer a retired book editor who was finding the sudden influx of time on her hands a little wearing, no more a devoted mother and grandmother somewhat consternated to find that she'd outlived her usefulness. In that moment, I was nineteen years old again, falling in love for the first time and reck-lessly plunging into the heady, all-consuming delight of it.

"You're dead," he said, still in that voice that sounded as though each word was being wrested from him by force. "You're a ghost."

I couldn't help smiling down at him. "Is this where you're going to start quoting *Wuthering Heights* at me again? *'I have a strong faith in ghosts; I have a connection that they can and do exist among us'* and all that?"

Instead of continuing the quotation or even countering with one of his own, Jasper bolted upright and flung back the blanket I'd been careful to pull over him. He raised a hand and pointed it toward the door, his arm unwavering.

"Get out," he said again, this time with more force. "I don't know what you're doing here or why you've come to break my heart again after all these years, but I want nothing to do with it. Or you."

"Jasper, please," I said. I knew that my coming back here would be a surprise to him, but I'd assumed the years would have mellowed him the same way they had me. That was what time did; it trampled on the dreams and wishes of youth, replaced them with the more substantial, if mundane, realities of life. In the past sixty years, I'd lived and done a lot of things. Some of them—my son, my grandson, my career—I was proud of. Others—the way I'd cut ties from my parents, the too-many hours I'd spent hunched over a desk, a few of my more spectacularly failed relationships—made me long for a do-over.

Regardless, they were all a part of me now. Good and bad, brave and cowardly, my decisions had been made. The only option now was to live with them.

"I know I should have called first," I said, attempting a rueful smile. "Or at the very least, sent a letter. Or a book."

"Chloe!" he called, ignoring me. "Zach! Unless you want to be responsible for my death, you'll get me out of here. *Now.*"

The speed with which the door flew open seemed to indicate that the two young people had been waiting in the hallway for the first sign of distress. And the distance they placed between their bodies as they stepped into the room seemed to indicate that neither one of them had enjoyed the wait very much.

However, either Jasper didn't prepare himself for how much the shock of seeing me and Zach in a room together would affect him, or he hadn't put our relationship together until he saw us standing side by side, because he took one look at the pair of us and blanched.

"No," he said. "Impossible. It's *impossible.*"

"Hello again, sir," Zach said with a slight smile. "Or should I say, Grandpa?"

It was the worst possible thing he could have said in that moment, but I could hardly blame him for it. When Bates had shown little to no interest in getting to know the man who'd sired him, I thought I'd dodged a particularly nasty bullet. It was much easier to close the door on my past than to leave it open a crack, where light and sound and memories could creep in.

But Zach had wondered. Zach had wanted to know. Now the door was thrown all the way open, and there would be no closing it again.

"Please don't be upset with Zach," I said, aiming for peace. It seemed the least I could do after he'd saved Jasper from breaking a hip back there—or worse. "He has nothing to do with my visit. In fact, he tried to talk me out of it, but you know me. The more I'm told not to do a thing, the harder I push to do it."

Jasper ignored this with a tight clamp of his jaw. "A son or a daughter?" he croaked instead.

Now it was my turn to feel the world start to tumble around me. "What?"

"Do I have a son or a daughter?" he repeated, his voice balancing on a razor's edge. "It's a simple question. I'd like to know about the child. *Our* child."

All at once, I felt as though I'd been sideswiped by a red Mustang going too fast down the road. I was all skinned palms and shaking knees, the wheels of my bicycle endlessly whirring, whirring as it fell on top of me.

Zach had his arms around me almost immediately, those strong, capable arms leading me to a rickety chair in the corner of the room, but that only made things worse. Those arms were the same arms that had once pulled me out from under my bike, his smile the same smile I'd once had to drag out of Jasper with all the wiles at my disposal.

"A son," I said, gasping. Zach tried to soothe me with some kind of low-murmured nonsense, but I barely heeded him. "We have a son."

Jasper closed his eyes. For the longest moment, I feared he wasn't going to open them again, but all he did was draw a deep breath before blinking. "A son," he said, and something almost like a smile hovered over his lips. "Okay. Thank you."

Chloe reached out and touched his arm—gently, like someone touching a fragile piece of glass. "Can I get you a glass of water or something, Jasper? Milk? Coffee? A stiff drink?"

"What I want is for you to get them out of here," he said, his voice oddly free of emotion. Then, with a sudden puckering of his brow, he added, "No. You know what? Leave them here. In fact, get that mother of yours to join us."

"My mother?" Chloe echoed. "Why do you need her?"

"I don't need her," he said grimly. "I don't need any of them, but if we're going to start sharing our so-called truths, we might as well do it right. I'll be damned if I'm going to slink away without saying what needs to be said. I did that once in my life already, and look where it got me."

Ravenna must have also been listening at the door, because she popped her head into the room almost at once. "Did someone want me?" she asked.

"No," Jasper said as he struggled to his feet. This time, Zach was wise enough not to help him. "No one wants you—not in this conversation and definitely not in your children's lives. That's the whole point."

Ravenna went suddenly white, her jaw slack. "I beg your pardon?"

"It's not my pardon you need," Jasper retorted. He swept a glance around the room, his thoughts more evident on his face than I'd ever seen them before. When we were young, his expressions had always been impossible to make out, which, if I was being honest, had been a large part of my early attraction to him. A rough, closed-off man who only wakened to vitality in your arms was a heady thing for a girl of nineteen.

The extra lines about his face now, carved as if from stone, were a lot easier to read...even if they had been earned cut by deep, painful cut.

"Look around you, Ravenna," he said, sweeping his arm around the room. "This is what you walked away from. This is what you gave up."

The woman wrinkled her nose as her gaze snagged on a stack of visibly dirty laundry shoved halfway under one of the beds. "My sons' dirty bedroom?"

He practically spit his reply. "No, you fool. Life. Mess. *Family*." Even though he didn't look at me as he spoke, I knew his message wasn't meant for Ravenna's ears alone. "Things were hard. You felt trapped and were trying to make the best of a bad situation. So you left."

"How do you—" Ravenna took one look at Chloe and immediately clamped her mouth shut again.

"I know why you abandoned your kids," Jasper continued. "I know *how* you did it, too. You turned yourself around in all kinds of circles, rationalizing to yourself that you were only doing what was best for everyone. They'd be better off without you. They needed more than you could give. A clean break would be the kindest gift you could offer. It would hurt, obviously, but they had their whole lives ahead of them. They'd get over you and move on, and so easily that you felt pretty sure you'd suffer more than they did in the end."

A hot well of tears sprang to my eyes. I made a motion to wipe them away, but Zach, bless his all-seeing heart, slipped his hand into mine and refused to let go.

"Only that's not how it works, is it?" Jasper asked. His voice had grown so quiet by this time that he held the entire room spellbound.

"You don't get to decide how other people feel. The things you do matter. The way you hurt these children matters. Maybe you genuinely thought you were taking the only path available to you, but the truth is that you took the path you wanted. And you didn't give a single, solitary damn what would happen when your kids tried to run after you only to find that you'd barred the way for any of them to follow."

All at once, two things started happening. Ravenna, who'd gone completely white, started to fold in on herself as if her legs could no longer bear her own weight. And Jasper, equally spent, started to do the same. Since Chloe was the one standing between them, she could only help one.

She chose Jasper.

"Come on, Jasper," she said, bracing her arm under his and helping him toddle to the door. "I think we should get you home before you say something you regret."

He smiled down at her in a way I never thought to see again in my lifetime. That particular twist of the lips, all the more valuable because of how difficult it was to extract, had once been my sole delight and joy.

"I don't regret one word of it," he said. "They don't get to walk away and then come back like it doesn't mean anything. We're human beings, Chloe. Real live goddamned human beings. Not just some side characters who disappear the second they decide to turn the page."

"That we are," she agreed as she led him into the hallway. She paused at the threshold to look at all of us: me and Zach holding hands, Ravenna slowly sinking to the bed. Then she turned her back on us and kept walking. "That we are."

32

—

JASPER

THE LAST THING JASPER WANTED TO do after a day like today was make French toast for the two least grateful children on the face of the planet, but making French toast was exactly what he found himself doing.

"I think it needs more cinnamon," Trixie said from somewhere over his shoulder. She had some kind of god-awful pop singer blaring out of a portable speaker, so he could barely make out the words. "Chloe always puts in a dash of vanilla, too."

"And sugar!" Theo cried as he bounded into the room. Jasper would have yelled at him to slow down, but the blessed boy yanked the speaker out of his sister's hands and switched it off. "No more Taylor Swift," he announced firmly. "*Anything* but Taylor Swift."

"Can I help it if she speaks to my soul?" Trixie countered, but she didn't turn the music back on, so Jasper assumed they were safe. "Do you want me to finish that, Jasper? I don't mind. I'm done with my homework."

"No, I'm happy where I am," he said, and was surprised to find he meant it. The idea of him making breakfast for dinner for a pair of unruly brats while Catherine Martin and a young man who shared his blood were wandering around the town was preposterous in the extreme, but everything about this situation was preposterous.

She's alive. She's been alive this whole time.

"Do you have maple syrup?" Trixie asked as she started yanking open cupboards to pull out plates and silverware. Jasper realized with a start that she was setting the table. Theo, too, busied himself finding the milk in the fridge and pouring everyone out huge overflowing glasses of the stuff. He'd had to buy no fewer than three full gallons of milk since these two had invaded his home, which made him realize two things: one, that Chloe's grocery bills must be astronomical; and two, that he loathed the taste of the stuff.

He didn't stop Theo from filling his cup, though.

"Oooh, he has real maple syrup," Theo announced when he found the little jug Jasper kept stored in the fridge door. "Like, the *fancy* kind that comes from actual trees. Is it okay if we use this, Jasper, or is it only for special occasions? We can always eat it plain. We do at home all the time."

Jasper's chest gave a small heave at the simplicity in the boy's tone. It had been a long time since he'd belonged to those hand-to-mouth days, when something like real maple syrup was an unimaginable luxury, but memories were resurfacing at an alarming rate. He remembered all too well the hunger that was more than just physical need, the determination to make do with what was available, however little it satisfied. Life had never been easy for people like him, but that didn't mean he had to sit back and watch these poor kids get pushed down the same path.

"It's all yours, Theo," he said. "I never cared for that sugary garbage anyway."

"Yesss!" Theo's eyes lit up as he hooked his finger in the jug and carried it to the table. Trixie stopped in the middle of laying out the forks and knives to stare at Jasper. He didn't appreciate such intense scrutiny from a girl who spent as much time in the bathroom as that one, but he could hardly say as much out loud. These dratted children latched onto a weakness faster than a shark following a trail of blood.

"If you don't like sugary garbage, why do you have it?" Trixie asked.

"It was on sale," he lied.

She peeked at the bottom of the jug. "The price sticker says fifteen ninety-nine. That doesn't sound like much of a sale to me."

"That's because it's the Canadian price," he responded, thinking fast. Then, because he could see from her look of doubt that she was about to ask about exchange rates and the costs of shipping, he narrowed his eyes and growled, "Do you always argue this much when someone makes you dinner?"

"Yes," she replied. "It's why I do debate. Otherwise, people just think I'm annoying."

That startled a laugh out of him. If someone had asked him, standing across from Catherine a few hours ago, if laughter was a thing he'd ever consider himself capable of again, he'd have thrown them out of the room. The thing about these dratted Sampsons, however, was that you *couldn't* throw them out of the room. Not for long, anyway. They just kept coming back, and so eagerly that you had no choice but to let them.

Even though Jasper had never admitted it out loud, he liked to imagine that his own brothers and sisters had grown up like this—getting by on the little they had, aware of how unfair their sacrifices were, but still able to find happiness in one other. From the few interactions he'd had with them over the years, he suspected they had.

Not always, obviously. Harriet died during a flu outbreak when she was only twenty-two, and their mother hadn't been too far behind. Uli crushed his hand in a logging accident a few years later, but both he and Olly went on to attend college, so he must have been able to get by without it. Bobby never traveled much further than Aberdeen and, as far as Jasper knew, still lived there in a sad, lonely house like Jasper's, but Tina married young and had a huge crop of kids. He sometimes got cards from a parcel of great-nieces and grandnephews he'd never met. They were polite and cheerful, sending him pictures of faraway places he'd never been and didn't want to visit. Jasper couldn't recite their names to save his life, but it was nice to see them getting on so well.

"What is it, Jasper?" Trixie asked. "Why do you suddenly look so sad?"

He grunted, startled back into an awareness of his surroundings. "I'm not sad," he said. "I was just thinking."

"About what?" Theo asked. He was eyeing the frying pan like he'd never seen food before, so Jasper clicked off the burner and slid the toast onto a platter. Theo and Trixie were eager to pounce on it, but not so eager they dropped the thread of the conversation.

That was another thing about the Sampsons. They were tenacious little monsters, and Jasper liked them all the more because of it.

"You're not still upset about us staying here, are you?" Trixie asked as she watched Theo pour out half the maple syrup onto his plate. She took a decorous amount for herself, but Jasper could tell she wanted a lavish pool of her own, so he picked up the jug and did it for her.

She uttered a short protest before giving in with a giggle. "If Chloe saw this much sugar on my plate, she'd freak out."

"*And* make us brush our teeth three times before bed," Theo added through a mouth thick with French toast.

Trixie wrinkled her nose. "With baking soda, too. It's so much grosser than real toothpaste, but it's cheaper than cavities, so Chloe makes us use it."

Since all four of the Sampsons had excellent smiles, Jasper was forced to agree with Chloe on this one. He was about to say as much when Trixie reached over and touched his hand. "It's okay if you don't want to talk about it, Jasper. We won't make you."

"It's fine," he said. Since this came out as a quick, harsh burst, he coughed and tried again. You couldn't lavish a couple of kids with expensive maple syrup and then get stingy when it came to what really mattered. If he took nothing else away from this mess his life had become, it was that. "I was just thinking about my own brothers and sisters. I was wondering if they were like you guys growing up."

"No way," Theo breathed. "You have brothers and sisters?"

Theo's comment made him want to laugh, but Trixie cut right to the heart of the matter. "What do you mean, you wonder? Don't you know? Didn't you grow up with them?"

He shook his head. "Not really, no. I was about your age when I moved away. Most of their growing up happened while I was gone."

Neither child attempted to smile at this. Theo, for once in his life, wasn't shoveling food into his mouth. He held his fork halfway between his lips and the plate, the syrup falling in gloopy drips.

"You left them?" he asked somewhat blankly. His brow wrinkled. "You mean like Chloe? You moved away for college?"

Jasper was tempted to lie, but something about the boy's wide frank gaze stopped him. These kids were so much more like him than he'd ever wanted to believe. For years, he'd been watching them over the fence with their noise and their activity, their constant go-go-go lifestyle. Seeing them play—and hearing them laugh—always made Jasper feel like an outsider looking in, and he was ashamed to admit that his automatic reaction was to *act* like an outsider looking in.

To admit how much he wanted to be a part of it, of *them*, would be to admit that his entire life had been spent longing for the things he couldn't have. First it was Catherine. Then it was the family he was so close to having with her. Then it was everything else: the ups and the downs, the laughter and the tears, the thousand different worries and joys that made life worth living.

"No, Theo," he said, but with a smile that he hoped would make his situation seem a *little* less bleak. "I left to go to work. Decades of it, in fact—hard manual labor that left me very little time or energy outside of getting by."

Jasper could tell his confession startled them. To look at him now, with his knees protesting every time he get up from the couch and an acid reflux that seemed to flare up the moment he got near a piece of fruit, you wouldn't think that he'd once been a strapping young thing who could chop down a tree in under thirty minutes flat.

"My family was a lot like yours," he said, a little gentler. There was a time and place to describe the hardships of being a logger in the sixties, but this wasn't it. "There were six of us kids. My mom earned a living taking in laundry, but there never seemed to be enough money to keep all of us fed, let alone dressed and shod. I was the oldest, so I had no choice but to earn as much as I could and send it home."

Trixie gently set her fork down and gave him her full attention. Theo wasn't far behind.

"You took care of them," Trixie said, her decisiveness matched by a nod that made him feel as though he was facing his own private Judgment Day. Whatever else happened to this girl in her lifetime, she was going to cut quite a path through law school. "The same way Chloe takes care of us."

"Yes," he said, though he wasn't in entire agreement. Chloe didn't just provide financially for her siblings—she was also the one who washed their socks and made their meals, sang to them when they were sick, and oversaw their homework. That took a kind of strength he'd never possessed. "Unfortunately, there weren't a lot of jobs close to home—not ones that paid enough, anyway. I moved here, sent what I could back to my family, and eked out a living on the rest."

"Is that why you didn't marry that lady?" Theo asked. He resumed eating again. "The one from the books? The one who stopped by the house today?"

Jasper started. "You know about that?"

"Of course." Trixie came perilously close to rolling her eyes at him. "We might be kids, but we're not *children*."

Oddly enough, her words made sense. By age and comparison, the Sampsons would always seem like kids to Jasper, but they'd stopped being children the day their mother walked out on them.

"I didn't marry her for a lot of reasons, yes, but that was the main one," he said. His own plate of French toast had long since grown cold, so he pushed it away. "In those days, women didn't have very many options once they got married and started having kids. There was no way I could've supported her and a family of our own and kept taking care of my brothers and sisters. I had to choose one or the other."

"And you chose your brothers and sisters?" Theo asked—anxiously, Jasper suspected, as though he needed to hear a confirmation that the choice was one he'd make again, if given a chance. That however hard Chloe's life might be, it was the one she wanted to be living. "Even though you didn't get to grow up with them or hang out or anything?"

"No, I didn't choose them," he admitted. At sight of the expression on Theo's face, an old, familiar wave of guilt moved through him. He was quick to clarify. "Not because I didn't *want* to, Theo, but because I didn't *have* to. Catherine made the decision for me."

Once he said the words aloud, the truth of them struck home—and they struck hard. Jasper's early life had been defined by a series of sacrifices he'd been forced into by circumstance. The early death of his father, the precarious financial situation the family had found themselves in, his mother's dependence on a support network that had been placed entirely on his young shoulders—he'd never been given a voice in any of it.

If given another opportunity, however, he would do the same thing over again. Because the truth was, life wasn't always about making good choices. In many ways, it was about *having* good choices. For over six decades, Jasper had operated under the belief that he'd never been given any but bad choices. Would he rather lose the love of his life, or watch his family starve? Would he rather carry the burden of loneliness and hard work for the rest of his life, or soul-crushing guilt?

He realized now that the weight of *those* decisions had never been his to bear. More than sixty years ago, a tiny slip of girl facing social ruin and ostracism had volunteered to bear it for him. She'd given up her home and her family, the comfort of everything she'd ever known, and taken Jasper's choices—both good and bad—with her.

It was the exact sort of thing a young Catherine Martin might have been expected to do. Jasper hated her for it. And, his heart said with a stutter, he loved her for it.

Again. Still. Forever.

"Is it true that you're related to Zach?" Theo asked suddenly. "Noodle said he's your grandson."

Jasper nodded, not trusting himself to speak.

"So if he marries Chloe, will that make you our grandpa?" Trixie asked, her brow knit as she tried to work out the potential branches of the family tree. "Or close enough to count, anyway?"

Theo's eyes opened wide. "We've never had a grandpa before."

"You could take us fishing!" Trixie cried before wrinkling her nose in sudden distaste. "Actually, I don't like fishing, and neither does Noodle, but that's what all my friends' grandpas do. Either that or fall asleep in front of the TV."

"Maybe he could just play Frisbee with us instead," Theo offered.

Jasper held up his hands, warring off a surge of euphoria. He wasn't sure where it was coming from. It could have been the sudden realization that instead of hating Catherine, he wanted to see her again. It might have been the fact that these children were planning their sister's wedding to Zach after an acquaintance of exactly one month.

Then again, it could have also been that the prospect of taking these kids under his wing and throwing a Frisbee with them sounded like something he would very much like to do.

"Wait. Why do you look so sad again?" Trixie demanded. She dropped her fork and ran over to him. Flinging an arm over his shoulder, she squeezed in what could only be termed a hug. Not one to be outdone, Theo was on his feet and crushing Jasper from the other side.

"We don't have to play Frisbee," Theo said. "It was only a joke. We can do all the things you like instead."

Jasper couldn't resist the impulse to ask. "And just what the devil do you think I like?"

He didn't know how or why, but the kids seemed to sense right away that something had shifted...and that the *something* was him.

"Reading stuffy old books," Theo announced proudly.

"Pulling weeds for like eight hours every day," Trixie added.

"Yelling at kids!"

"Making puppies cry!"

"Crushing the bones of your enemies!"

By the time they'd reached the end of their list, the two were about to collapse in giggles. To Jasper's surprise, he wasn't too far from it himself.

"I always knew there was a reason why Noodle is my favorite honorary grandchild," he grumbled as he lifted his fork and begin eating the cold French toast. Lest they get the wrong idea—which their sudden gasps of delight seem to put them in severe danger of doing—he pointed a piece at them and added, "He doesn't talk back like the rest of you."

33

—

JASPER

JASPER KNEW EXACTLY WHERE TO FIND her. At the library, of course. "Here. I brought you these." He reached into his leather cross-bag and pulled out a stack of books: the faded green *Tropic of Cancer*, the battered *A Farewell to Arms*, the well-lined *The Haunting of Hill House*, and of course the barely touched *Wuthering Heights*. "I tried reading the writing in the last one before I came here, but it was so full of maudlin sentiment that I only made it a few pages. Maybe you'll enjoy it more than I can."

Chloe turned to face him, her eyes wide in the way all the Sampsons seemed to have perfected. "Jasper! What are you doing here?"

Since she made no move to take the books, he dumped them on the counter in front of her. She appeared to be doing some kind of data entry on one of the library computers—a thing he felt pretty sure was a waste of her talents and likely the most boring job in existence. But she'd continue in the same way he had when he'd been her age, determined to do her work well and equally determined not to let anyone know what it cost her.

"And before you try giving me all these back again, I should inform you that I came here directly from the bank," he added. "You *still* haven't deposited that check."

Over her shoulder, Jasper spotted two other librarians coming to see what all the ruckus was about. One of them was the girl he'd seen around Chloe's house before—the one who looked exactly like Lonnie Pakootas and who terrified him just as much as that old battle-ax. The other was a waddling scrap of a man that Jasper could already tell he wasn't going to like.

The man arrived at the checkout counter first.

"Chloe," he said in a voice that denoted his status as the overlord of this particular realm. "Is this patron bothering you?"

"Of course he's bothering her, Gunderson," the girl said, hard on his heels. "That's Jasper Holmes. Remember? The guy you told us about? Who killed a woman back in the sixties and then buried her out in his garden?"

The man—Gunderson—almost toppled over in his sudden discomfiture. He coughed and snorted and made a variety of other noises better suited for a barnyard than a library checkout counter. "I never said that," he muttered, unable to meet Jasper's eye. "It was a rumor, that's all. My wife read about it in one of her forums."

Chloe's eyes met Jasper's with a flash of laughter. It had been so long since he'd had that kind of easy intimacy with another person that he found himself sharing her amusement. He also did what he could to get rid of the guy. Suffering fools had never been his strong suit, and no number of Sampsons taking over his life would change that.

"I may not have killed Catherine, but I *was* responsible for her death," he said to Gunderson without a hint of inflection. "Feel free to tell your wife all about it."

At sight of the man's suddenly goggling stare, Chloe rushed to explain. "Don't tell your wife anything of the sort, Gunderson," she said. "The Catherine in question didn't actually die. She just moved away under... Let's call it a cloud of suspicion. A lot of people were led to believe she was dead, but it was all a misunderstanding."

"It's true," the Pakootas girl added. She leaned on the counter, her eyes dancing mischievously up into Jasper's. "You can ask my grandmother about it. She was there at the time."

The Gunderson man opened his mouth and closed it again, clearly at a loss for words—and for the authority to throw Jasper out of the library like he wanted to.

"The dead girl is also staying somewhere in town for the foreseeable future, so if you're thinking about pressing charges, there's no point," Jasper said. He looked down at his hands—deeply veined and liable to ache anytime rain was near—and grimaced. "Although she's not a girl anymore. Everything happened a long time ago."

All of a sudden, Chloe was touching his shoulder, her customary expression of worry back in place. Jasper couldn't imagine why until he realized his hands were shaking.

"Is it okay if I take my break early today, Gunderson?" she asked. "I'd like to see Jasper safely home. There's been a lot more excitement in his life than he's used to lately."

At that—the most understated of all understatements—Gunderson relaxed. "Go ahead, Chloe. We're not busy today."

"And I'll finish inputting the holiday catalog for you," the Pakootas girl added. "I got done with my bookmobile rounds early, so it's no problem."

Chloe took one look at her coworkers and nodded. "Yeah, okay. Thanks, you guys. I know I've been flaking out a lot lately, but—"

"But nothing," Gunderson said. "Patron safety is the most important thing."

This seemed a touch dramatic to Jasper. He might have grown a little shaken when he thought back on all the time that had passed and the

years he'd wasted, but he was built of sterner stuff. He was about to say
as much when Gunderson's gaze fell to the stack of books.

Gunderson reached out to touch the Hemingway spine. "Wait. Are
some of these library property?"

Faced with such a question, there was no other choice. Jasper put a
hand to his chest and groaned as if his every internal organ was about to
explode. "I can't... I'm not..." He pretended to falter where he stood.
"My heartbeat feels faint. I think I need to sit down."

Chloe took her lower lip between her teeth. "You poor thing," she
said in a quaking voice. "There's no time to waste."

With a skill borne of many years of librarian practice, she gathered
the stack of books in one arm. She guided her other arm under Jasper's
elbow as if to support his tottering steps toward to the door. As soon as
they felt the chilly blast of the fall air, she let go.

"Jasper, you wretch!" she said between gasps of laughter. "Gunderson
has almost zero sense of humor. If he were to walk out now and see you
standing on your own two feet, he'd probably fire me."

"A guy like that?" He waved her off, his hands only slightly shaking
now. The outdoors always had a calming effect on him that way. He
didn't know why he hadn't seen the resemblance to Zach earlier. There
were only a few people in the world for whom the fresh air was more
balm than breath, who could find peace and serenity in an environment
that was actively trying to kill you at every turn.

"He won't touch your job without files of just cause and the full
backing of the library board," Jasper added with a grunt. "He'd be terrified of a lawsuit—or, worse, public outcry. His kind always is."

"Huh. I never thought of it that way."

Of course she didn't. Chloe Sampson was in survival mode. She
was so concerned with making it through each day—each week, each
month—that she rarely stopped to breathe. Jasper knew because he'd
done it for almost twenty years. By the time the twins had graduated

from college and the rest of his siblings had started to build lives of their own, Jasper had been treading water for so long that he hadn't realized how close he was to shore.

"Jasper, I can't take these books," she said as they moved down the steps together. "They don't belong to me."

She didn't try to help him, which he appreciated, but he was getting really tired of the books shuffling back and forth. He imagined the books were equally tired of it. They'd carried too many secrets for too long; all they wanted at this point was a place to rest their weary spines.

"Well, they don't belong to me, either," he said irritably. "And what's more to the point, I don't want them."

As they reached the bottom of the steps, Jasper could feel the weight of Chloe's gaze. It was heavy but not uncomfortable, like a blanket on a cold winter's day.

"I'm sorry about Catherine," she said. "It must be hard to see her again after all these years."

Jasper snorted. "Losing her was hard. Believing her to be dead was hard. Watching her waltz back into my life as though the past sixty years never happened is a piece of cake compared to all that." Something like a smile touched his lips. "It's just like her, too. If anyone could be expected to stroll into town, with a son and a grandson and a life full of adventure behind her, it's my Catherine. No one else would have had the nerve."

"Wait." Chloe's nose wrinkled. "You mean you aren't angry with her? You're going to forgive her?"

His laugh was short and sharp, but not to the point of pain. Not anymore.

"I doubt she'll ask for my forgiveness," he said dryly. "Or, to be honest, that she even wants it. The thing you have to understand about Catherine Martin is that she's very much like her namesake, no matter how much she might try to pretend otherwise."

Chloe's eyes dropped to the copy of *Wuthering Heights*. Without having to resort to the pages, she quoted the most apt line of all.

"'*I wish I were a girl again*,'" she said, "'*half savage, and hardy, and free*.'"

Jasper felt his chest grow tight. "She can pretend that she's a grown woman now, with a family and responsibilities, but I know the truth. I always have. She's a beautiful, entitled, cruel whirlwind of a girl, and I love her so much that nothing she says or does will ever change that. Not even death or, worse, sixty years of silence."

Saying the words out loud seemed to give them life—and, by extension, to give *Jasper* life. Chloe, however, only looked doubtful.

"I don't understand," she said, her brow furrowed. "Back at the house, you said that they don't get to walk away and then come back like it doesn't mean anything—that Catherine and my mom can't act as though the rest of us don't matter."

For the first time in Jasper's life, he found himself wishing he wasn't such an obstinate crank of a man, and that his first reaction to pain wasn't to lash out and inflict it in equal and opposing proportions.

"I *did* say that," he agreed carefully. "And you have every right to question the wisdom that comes out of my mouth at this or any other time. But our situations are different, Chloe. Your brother and sister helped me see that. When Catherine left, she did it because she was trying to do the right thing, however misguided. When your mother left…"

He stopped, unsure how far he could push without making things worse. In the end, he decided there was no point.

"She wasn't trying to do anything but make her own life easier," he said simply. "She wasn't thinking about anyone but herself."

Chloe grew very still and equally quiet. "You think I should ask her to leave?"

Jasper absolutely thought that, but he'd have been damned if he was going to tell this girl what to do. He was no more fit to provide life guidance than Theo.

"I think having her in your life would considerably ease your burdens," he said, since it was no more than the truth. "She's feeling enough guilt right now that you could probably ask for anything and get it. And that husband of hers seems like a decent enough guy. Money, housing, food, childcare, even a chance to go back to that college of yours…I imagine none of it is out of the question."

"Oh," she said. Just that—just *oh*—and what remained of Jasper's resolve disappeared. He lifted the books from her hands and stooped to set them down on the nearest step. His back shifted, and he felt pretty sure his knees wouldn't forgive him anytime soon, but he was pleased to find that he managed just fine.

"Chloe, listen to me. Your mom will make your life easier, but you don't need her, okay? Not if you don't want her."

"I don't?"

"No." He put his hands on her shoulders and held them there until she looked up into his face. He didn't know how he'd ever thought she was identical to her mother. Their features were similar, and he was sure Chloe would age just as gracefully, but there was so much uncertainty and determination in those clear green eyes. So much *good*.

"All those things I just listed? The money and the childcare, the soft place to land?" His fingers clenched tightly against her shoulders. "You already have them. I've spent a long time sitting alone in that empty house of mine, watching your family grow. I know I haven't been the easiest neighbor in the world—"

At this, she snorted. He answered her with a chuckle.

"Fine, I've been a royal pain in the ass, but you know what I mean. I'd like to help you—you and Noodle and Theo and Trixie and even that blasted useless dog of yours. You don't have to accept anything you don't want to, and I'd never push myself into your home or life without asking, but I want you to know that I'm an option. If you accept that woman back in your life, do it knowing that you owe her nothing—and that you *need* her even less. Not while you have me."

Instead of addressing the offer, she took her lower lip between her teeth and glanced down at the books. "You really don't want them back? The books? Your love story?"

"I don't need the love story," he said with a lightness he hadn't felt in a long time. Whatever Chloe decided, he felt good knowing that she had options—and for once in her life, they were *good* ones. "Not when I have so many other stories left to read."

34

—

CATHERINE

I COULD TELL THE EXACT MOMENT WHEN Jasper slid into the movie theater seat a few rows behind me.

It would be too much to say that I felt him or smelled him or that the air shifted in a way that only a lover could sense. For one thing, the theater was so dark that I could barely make out the tub of popcorn in front of me. For another, the movie's sound was turned up high enough to send the whole delicate art deco building shattering to the ground.

No, I knew because the old fool was about as subtle as a battering ram.

"You might as well climb up here," I said without turning back to look at him. Just in case he couldn't hear me over the sound of the movie explosions, I raised my voice and added, "We're the only two people at this movie, so you might as well get it over with. This place hasn't changed much in six decades, has it?"

I could tell the exact moment he gave in and joined me, too. His steps were as slow and purposeful as they'd always been, the march of a man who'd never known any beat but his own, but he grumbled the whole way up.

"The security lady is the villain," he said as he fell to the seat next to me with a thump. Kernels of popcorn flew out of the tub and scattered across my lap. "I've seen this one already."

"Of course you have," I said in the voice of a woman who refused to be goaded either by his ruining the movie or the fact that getting butter grease out of my chiffon skirt was likely to prove all but impossible. Trust a man—and this man in particular—to understand nothing about the care and keeping of delicate fabrics. "This town has exactly one theater screen. They show the same movie for two months. You've probably seen it eight times."

To my surprise, the seat shook with a low, friendly chuckle. "You turned into a snob, Catherine. I should have seen that coming."

I turned to him, even more surprised to find that his chuckle was matched by an equally friendly smile. "I beg your pardon?"

"The girl I used to know didn't give two figs about her clothes. In fact, she was happiest when she wasn't wearing any at all." He paused before adding, "Come to think of it, that's when I was happiest, too."

I sat upright in my seat. This time, when the popcorn flew all over, I had no one to blame for it but myself. "Jasper Holmes, you dirty old crow! You can't say things like that to me. I'm a *grandmother*."

"And I, apparently, am a grandfather. It's been a strange few days."

That remark gave me pause—and, if I was being honest, a sharp pang in the region of my heart. It could have been a gastronomic reaction to the unhealthy amount of butter I'd eaten, but it was more reasonable to assume the sensation was one of guilt.

"Jasper, I—"

His hands stole over mine, silencing me before I even knew what I want to say. That I was sorry, obviously, but also that I wasn't. I was sorry for bursting in on him and assuming I'd be welcomed with open arms. I was sorry for letting him believe I'd been dead for all these years, and that our child had died with me.

But that was where the buck stopped. I couldn't regret my son or my grandson. I couldn't regret the places I'd seen or the things I'd done. I couldn't even regret the loss of a love like ours. We hadn't realized it at the time, but it would have consumed us. In many ways, it *did* consume us—only instead of sticking around to watch as we each blew up our lives in a spectacular Brontë-worthy fashion, I left before it had the chance to ruin us both.

"You aren't staying in Colville, are you?" he asked as if reading my every thought.

"No," I said. I squeezed his hand, hoping he'd understand. I knew how much he loved this place. Zach loved it, too, but to me, it would never feel like anything but a small, narrow slice of the world. It was a *beautiful* slice, obviously, and one I enjoyed while I was in it, but not enough to remain forever. "And you aren't going to move to New York, are you?"

That made him chuckle again. "I've always wanted to visit, but no. What would I do there? Offer to take strangers on horse-cart rides through the park? Find a potted plant and hide myself in it?"

"Well, no," I admitted. "But you could always come and stay with me. I have plenty of space these days."

"These days?" he echoed. "You mean there's no husband at home waiting in the wings?"

I liked that he was bold enough to ask the question. I liked even more that only took him a few minutes to do it. "There's never been a husband, Jasper. I found I never had much need of one."

That gave him a moment's pause, which coincided with the sudden flash of the end credits as the movie came to a close. Neither one of us made a move to get out of our seats.

"But you haven't been lonely?" he prodded.

"Not really, no." I admitted. It felt good to say the truth with no need to sugarcoat it. Talking to Jasper had always been one of the easiest things to do. Not because he was a particularly good listener, and definitely not because he was a natural conversationalist, but because I knew myself to be safe in his hands. "How could I be? You've met Zach now, so you know how full my life has been. Believe me when I say that you'll like Bates even more. He says he wants to meet you, but only when you're ready."

The burst of laughter this confession elicited startled me for a second. At first, I was afraid that I might have finally broken Jasper—that mentioning the man he helped create was the straw that would break both our backs—but the laughing narrowed to a warm, rich chuckle.

"*Bates*?" he asked. "Catherine, you didn't."

A gurgle rose up in my own throat. It made me feel almost girlish—a thing I hadn't known I was still capable of. Even though I'd meant it when I said I could never live in this town, I was starting to see the appeal of holding on to the hometowns of one's youth. Even this theater, where I once sat and flirted with Jasper, the pair of us so young and innocent that I could almost feel the ghosts of our past sitting behind us, was so much more than four walls and a faded movie screen.

"I didn't have a choice," I protested. "From the moment I saw his angry, wrinkled little face, I knew it was the only name for him. It could've been worse. I was this close to naming him Norman instead."

He chuckled again, but I could tell his mind was working fast. "I think I *would* like to meet him," he said. "Not right away—I need some time to process first. But in a few months, maybe."

"That sounds perfect. You'll get a kick out of him. I tried for decades to turn him into a suave, sophisticated man of the world, but he turned out exactly like you. He and Zach both. You should have warned me how strong your bloodlines are. I never stood a fighting chance."

When he didn't respond except to continue staring at the thread of movie credits, I was afraid I may have crossed a line. It was too much, too soon. He was catching up on sixty years of history—watching his past rise up from the grave, not just whole, but whole*hearted*. That sort of thing couldn't be easy.

But when he finally spoke, it was with a smile in his voice. "Good. I hope they gave you hell."

"Oh, they did—still do, in many ways. Did you think I came all this way just to see you? I never would've done it if not for Zach. He wanted to see this place, to see *you*, and nothing I said or did could stop him." I risked a sideways peek at him. "I wish I could make you understand, Jasper. The way I left wasn't easy for me, either. I cried throughout my entire third trimester. And afterward, well…"

I stopped. How could I describe to this man the torment of my twenties and thirties? To know that he was still here, working himself to the bone so his family could thrive. To hope against all hope that he'd found a way to move on.

"You don't have to explain yourself to me," he said. I didn't believe him until he rolled his head toward me, his eyes still so bright and blue that it was like looking into a window to the past. In a fit of gallantry he must have picked up far away from this outpost, he lifted my hand to his lips and lightly kissed it. Despite myself and the fact that I was *far* too old for another doomed romance, I felt my heart flutter. "You told me from the outset how it would be. I was just too self-involved to realize it."

I wasn't sure whether it was the kiss or his words that unsettled me most. "I did? When?"

"I gave the books to Chloe, so I can't tell you the exact quote, but I remember it like it was yesterday." He smiled then, but it wasn't a smile meant for me. That was a smile for the boy he once was—the boy who, in many ways, still lived inside him. "'I'm no Hemingway heroine,' you said. You refused to die in childbirth for the sake of the hero's redemption arc. The moment you pulled that ruse, I should've known what you were up to."

A bright, fizzy burst of something flooded my veins. It was the same feeling I used to get whenever I discovered a shiny new manuscript from an unknown author, the same feeling that overtook my weeping sadness the day Bates was born. Like opening the cover of a book for the first time, it was the sensation of the world opening up before me.

"I did say that, didn't I? What an absolute beast I was." I shook my head, lighter in body and spirit than I'd felt in a long time. I wasn't sure I deserved Jasper's forgiveness, and I was almost certain that it came from a place that had very little to do with me, but I planned to take it all the same. "I honestly don't know what you saw in me. I hope you fell in love a dozen times after I was gone."

"Not even once."

The movie credits ended and the lights of the theater came up. As soon as the room was cast into full illumination, I could see the cracks where the plastered walls were falling down, the dirty carpeting and even dirtier stairs. Jasper, however, didn't seem to notice. His gaze was locked on me instead—not sad, but wistful and a little bit sheepish.

"I'm sorry if that's not what you want to hear, but you were the whole story as far as I was concerned," he said. "The beginning, the middle, and the end. I didn't need to open another romance when I already had the perfect one written down."

"Jasper," I said—begged, really. "I wouldn't have made you happy. You have to know that by now. No matter how hard I tried to settle into your life, or how far you followed me into mine, there was simply no place where our lives intersected."

"I do know it," he said quietly. "But I would have done my damnedest to *try*."

I opened my mouth to say more—what, I had no idea—but he wasn't done yet.

"I've never been one of those men who yearned for much," he said. "A roof over my head, food on the table, and a stack of good books were all I needed to live a calm, contented life—or so I believed, anyway."

"But you don't believe it anymore?" I asked. "Because of…me?"

"Not you, precisely." He twisted his lips in a rueful smile. "But because of Zach. And Chloe. And Noodle and Theo and Trixie. Before you go back to New York and your big glamorous life, can I ask you to do me one favor?"

"Anything," I said. I meant the words more than I'd ever meant any combination of syllables before. After everything he'd given me—my freedom, my family, and his forgiveness—there was nothing I wouldn't do for him. "Anything at all."

PART FIVE

35

—

CHLOE

I WAS HAVING A HARD TIME DECIDING whether the book I was reading was more of a comedy or a tragedy. At college, I once took a Shakespeare class where the professor posited that old William's best works were the ones where he fused the two. Real talent, she'd said, was the ability to showcase the light in darkness and the darkness in the light.

I wasn't sure how true any of that was, since I'd had to drop the class halfway through, but I felt pretty sure that when it came to making me want to both laugh and cry, Shakespeare had nothing on a young Catherine Martin.

"What's so funny?" my mother asked as she walked into the living room where I sat with my legs tucked under me and the copy of *Wuthering Heights* open in my lap. "I could hear you chuckling to yourself from outside."

I smiled faintly at her. I had yet to get used to her walking in and out of the front door as if she, well, owned the place, but I was getting better at not showing my strain.

"I'm reading one of the books Jasper gave me yesterday," I said as I held it up. "Catherine wrote all kinds of notes in it for him back in the sixties. Look—right here, it's the part where Catherine is about to die. "'*She's fainted or dead,*' *I thought,* '*so much the better. Far better that she should be dead, than lingering a burden and a misery-maker to all around her.*'"

My mom wrinkled her nose in a way that looked exactly like Theo puzzling over a difficult *Minecraft* build. "That doesn't sound very funny to me. You forget that I've read that book. I remember how it ends."

"It's not supposed to be funny," I explained. "But in the margins, Catherine wrote, '*You already know how I feel about the heroine-must-die-to-save-the-hero trope, but there's truth in this. What's the point of living if all you're going to do is make everyone around you miserable? What are we put on this earth for if not to make life better for those we leave behind?*'"

My mom's frown only deepened. She crossed her arms and leaned against the doorway in a gesture I'd almost forgotten about. She always used to look at me exactly like that whenever she'd come in to find me reading under the covers long after bedtime. "That's not very funny, either."

I sighed and closed the book. "I know, but she was literally staging her own death while she wrote it. She was killing off the heroine—herself—in order to save the hero—Jasper. But instead of going to her grave, she went off and lived the kind of fabulous life most of us only dream of. It might not be *ha-ha* funny, but there's irony in there for sure."

I paused, studying my mother for a long moment. When she'd first arrived at the house, with Todd behind her holding enough suitcases for an around-the-world cruise, she'd looked as though she'd stepped onto the front porch straight from the catwalk. Her hair had been salon-straightened, her nails filed to delicious red points, her heels so tall that she towered over me. Now, a little over a week into her stay, and she looked…different. Everything that had been bright and shiny about her had dulled to a faded, weary gray.

"She was only a few years older than Trixie when she wrote this," I added, since I had to say something. One of us needed to move this conversation along, and as usual, that someone was going to be me. "That's the thing that gets me the most about their whole situation. They were little more than kids at the time, but they carried the weight of the whole world on their shoulders."

"Don't," my mom said suddenly. She flung up a hand as if to keep any further discussion at bay.

I blinked up at her, startled by the vehemence of her tone. "I'm sorry. Is it tedious for me to go on and on about them? I've been a little obsessed lately, I'll admit, but—"

"Chloe. Please."

"I'll stop," I promised, trying not to show how much her words stung. While it was true that I didn't have very many conversational gambits outside books and the kids, I liked to think that I wasn't a *complete* bore. In fact, for a little while there, before I'd learned that Zach was only using me as a way to get close to his grandfather, I even thought I'd had a little dazzle.

I set the book aside and fixed my attention on my mom instead. "What's up?" I asked. Suddenly realizing that the house was awfully quiet for a change, I added, "And where is everyone? I know Theo and Trixie are at school, but—"

"Noodle and the dog are at that man's house. Next door." My mom took a step into the room, changed her mind, and stepped back out again. "And I sent Todd to pick up a few groceries. Just some staples and things. I'd like to leave the house well stocked when we go."

I shared none of my mom's hesitance. I was on my feet and across the room in flash. "Wait. You're leaving? Already? Before Noodle's even out of his walking cast?"

She winced in a way that felt like a slap across the face—though whether it was her face that was being slapped or mine, I couldn't say.

"This isn't easy for me," she said, her voice small and growing smaller by the second. "None of it—coming home again after all these years, seeing how grown up everyone is, how much they hate me…"

I knew it was my job to protest, to reassure her that Theo and Trixie were only struggling with their emotions and hormones and that all would settle down eventually, but I couldn't. Not only would it be a lie, but I wasn't so sure she deserved to hear it.

Less than two weeks. That's how long she lasted this time.

"Please tell me you're at least going to stick around long enough to say goodbye," I said, feeling the ice coursing from my veins into my voice. "They survived it once, but I don't think you realize how close of a call it was. It took me *months* to go through the whole guardianship process and get them back under this roof. In fact, I'm still paying off the legal fees."

"I'll have Todd write you a check to cover them," she said with a complete disregard for the point. "And I'm going to send money home this time—every month, I promise."

I closed my eyes, hoping that by cutting off the sight of her, I might cut off all the rest: how tired and sad she looked, how drained by all the memories this home carried. I also wanted to cut off my understanding.

Because I *did* understand. That was the thing that annoyed me the most. When my mom stood inside these four walls, she didn't see how full of memories and life this house was. She didn't notice the sticky notes set up around the computer monitor where Theo liked to remind himself of all he had planned for his *Minecraft* kingdom: creeper cages, a slaughterhouse for the cows, underground lava tubes in the shape of a pentagram. She also didn't see the stack of books that Trixie kept meticulously piled next to her bed: all of them biographies of famous legal minds, and all of them so far above her reading level that it took her months to get through them. Noodle she still treated like a little boy afraid of his own shadow instead of a young man who was finally coming into himself—soft and sweet and, yes, a little bit strange.

And me, well. Sometimes I thought she didn't see me at all. If she did, she'd have never walked out on these kids without first giving me a heads-up. She had to have known that I'd do anything for them—that I would continue doing everything for as long as they needed me.

Because that's what the Catherines and Jaspers and Chloes of this world did. Sometimes we struck out on grand adventures. Sometimes we stayed home and buried ourselves in books. But we always, always put our love first.

"The money will be nice, thanks," I said, trying not to notice how bitter the words tasted on my tongue. It was killing me to accept such a sad second-rate gift from this woman, but Lonnie and Pepper had been right. As much as I hated accepting help, some things were more important than my pride.

My family was one of them.

"You can also come by and visit anytime you want," I said. "This is your house just as much as it is ours. More, actually. I can't promise the kids will welcome you with open arms, but you're within your rights to try."

"About that." She held up a finger before turning and going to the kitchen, where the sound of rustling papers soon followed. When she returned, it was with a manila folder in one of her manicured hands. She shoved it at me before I had time to do more than blink. "This is for you. It's the deed to the house. I'm only sorry it took me this long to sign it over. I don't think I realized it was still in my name until—" She grew flustered and tried to cover her sudden discomfort. "Well, anyway. It's yours now. Stay here if you want. Sell it and take the kids somewhere else. Just make sure you send me your updated address if you do, okay? I'd like to stay in touch…as much as I can anyway. You get it, right?"

The enormity of what was passing between us wasn't lost on me. She was giving me the house—small and in disrepair, yes, but still worth at least a hundred and fifty grand. She was also giving me a way out of this life, this town. I could take the kids to Spokane if I wanted. Start over near colleges and opportunities. Build something of my own.

But when I spoke, it wasn't about the deed in my hand.

"Until what?" I asked.

She blinked her confusion—and a few wayward tears I pretended not to notice. "Huh?"

"Just now, you said that you hadn't realized the house was yours *until*…and then you stopped. What were you going to say?"

She dashed at her eyes with the back of her hand. Clumps of mascara transferred from her lashes to her skin, leaving a black smear behind. "Nothing, really. Just that I *am* sorry, Chloe. I know it's too little, too late, but you have to understand that this place was killing me. When you lived here and were able to help with the kids, I got on all right, but after you left…" She shook her head in what I assumed was supposed to be a gesture of supplication—maybe even regret—but all I saw was her vanity and weakness, her inability to love anyone as much as she loved herself. "I wasn't built to do this sort of thing alone."

That was when I snapped. I wish I could say that I went off on her in a full blaze of glory, spouting venom like Jasper Holmes at his angriest, letting loose all the stress and anxiety of the past four years—or even that I eloquently reduced her to rubble with a literary quote.

Instead, I severed any remaining ties in my heart and let myself feel the one emotion she genuinely deserved: my pity.

"You were never *alone*, Mom," I said. "That's the thing you got wrong—not sneaking out in the dead of night or abandoning three underage children to the state, not even how long you stayed away without a single word. Your problem was that you had some of the best people in the world living in this house with you, and you never once stopped to think of how lucky that made you."

She winced but took each word as it came. "I know. That's why I'm giving you the house. Your next-door neighbor had a lot to say on the subject. I don't know what you kids did to win him over to your side, but it must have been something big. When I lived here, he was so nasty to me that I used to quake every time I saw one of his lights come on."

"He's still that nasty," I said, the words automatic. "We just learned to look past it to the man he is underneath."

My mom nodded as though she understood, but she didn't—not in any way that counted. If you were to put the two of them side by side, one a cranky old man who had few graces and even less tact, the other a beautiful woman in her forties with a smile that lit up the night sky, everyone would say that they'd prefer the company of the latter.

But they'd be wrong. Jasper was craggy and full of sharp edges, yes, but my mom was a beautiful, ethereal nothing. It had taken me a long journey through Jasper's past to realize it, but life was better when you had something to hold on to. Not memories and not hopes, but something real. Some*one* real.

"He'll take good care of you from here on out," my mom added as if reading my mind. "Much better than I ever did, that's for sure."

She paused then, looking equal parts uncomfortable and hopeful. "Can I hug you, Chloe? One last time before I go?"

I nodded before I'd even had time to finish processing the question—not about the hug, but about it being *one last time*. Maybe she genuinely believed this was the first of many such embraces, but as her arms came around me and squeezed, I knew, deep in my heart, that she wouldn't be back.

"Todd and I will pick up the kids from school," she said as she let me go, her bright color already starting to come back. Now that she'd severed the last of her ties to this place—and to her family—she was a like a bird regrowing its plumage. "We'll say our goodbyes then."

"And Noodle?" I asked, feeling tense.

She fixed her gaze on a spot a few inches above my head. "I'll pop by and let him know we're leaving, but I doubt he'll even notice we're gone.

He's the one who called me to come back, but…I don't know, Chloe. He doesn't have much of a *heart*, does he?"

With that, I realized she was giving me one final gift. By disclaiming all understanding of and for Noodle, she was cutting the last thread of my affection for her. In a way, it was almost like faking her own death and escaping into the night. She would send money home—when she remembered to—and maybe even stamp the occasional birthday card, but we were finally free.

"'*His heart was a secret garden and the walls were very high,*'" I said, one of my favorite *The Princess Bride* quotes rising naturally to my lips. Then I finished with a line of my own. "I'm afraid you just never learned to scale them."

She picked up on the quote almost at once. "We did always love that book, didn't we, you and I?"

"There are worse things in the world to have in common," I agreed, a bittersweet smile touching my lips. "Goodbye, Mom. And thank you."

She looked as though she wanted to add more, but we both knew there wasn't anything left to say. She'd done what she came to do, given what little she had to give, and would disappear as easily as she had the first time.

The only difference was that this time, I knew I was going to be okay.

———

The house felt oddly empty after my mom and Todd finished dropping off the promised groceries and headed out to pick up Theo and Trixie from school. In an act of absolution, they'd gone way overboard, investing in things like gourmet frozen pizzas that I had no room to store and exotic juice blends that the kids would be sure to avoid, but there were several boxes of name-brand cereal in the bags, so my mom hadn't *completely* failed.

I had just finished reorganizing the freezer so that I could cram the last of the groceries inside when I heard a knock at the door.

"It's open!" I called as I pushed against the freezer door with all my weight. I heard a cardboard box tearing inside, but the door managed to latch shut, so that was good enough for me. "And if you're a child coming home from school, please don't dump your backpack on the floor. Put it in your room where it belongs, or I won't hesitate to revoke your internet privileges."

"Is it bad that I like it when you get all authoritative and mean?" called the last voice I expected to hear.

"Zach!" I cried, more to myself than to the man in question. I poked a tentative head out of the kitchen to find him standing in the foyer, looking somehow both sheepish and like a man who'd never feared anything or anyone a day in his life. "What are you doing here?"

He whipped the knit cap off his head and clutched it in his hands like a beggar of old. I didn't buy his act for a single second. No one who looked that good while pretending to be sorry was the least bit trustworthy.

I crossed my arms and glared at him. "If you're here to see Noodle, you came to the wrong house. He's over at Jasper's—I mean, your *grandfather's*."

The venom in my voice was so thick that even I winced a little at the sound of it. Zach glanced quickly up, his expression bleak enough to wring a heart made of much stronger stuff than mine.

"You're really mad about that, aren't you?"

Since I'd already gone this far, I saw no reason to hold back now. "You mean, about that time you lied about who you are and why you live in Colville? About why you sought me out and inveigled yourself into my life and the lives of my brothers and sister?"

"Chloe, please. It wasn't like that, I swear."

I flung up a hand to stop him. I didn't want to hear the way his voice cracked over my name or see the way his lips turned down at the edges. I didn't want to see those crinkles around his eyes, which held so much sadness that I almost—*almost*—believed him.

"I did try to tell you, you know," he added. "That day at the library when I gave you my grandmother's copy of *A Farewell to Arms*. I told you it was from my fairy godmother, but you thought I was joking."

The air constricted around me. "That's not fair, Zach."

"I know it isn't fair. But it *is* the truth."

Something about his simplicity caused me to fight even harder against the pull of him.

"It's not as if it matters either way," I said. "You might find this hard to believe, but I get why you did it. I've lived next to your grandfather my whole life. I know how prickly he can be. You wanted an in, and I provided the perfect opportunity." I smiled then, a little wryly but with genuine feeling. "I'd have probably done the same thing, to be honest. When it comes to doing the tough jobs, I don't think there's a limit to how far I'll go."

He didn't return my smile. If anything, his expression tightened to one of genuine pain. "Do you remember what I said to you that night we went bowling? About how lonely I was growing up? How much I enjoyed being around a family as loud and fun as yours?"

Of course I remembered that night. It was forever burned in my mind as the first time I actually allowed myself to *hope* that my life might be something different. But all I said was, "Sure. Why not?"

He lifted his hands as if to reach for me before dropping them again. "I meant what I said, Chloe. My dad is every inch Jasper's son, even if the two of them have never met before. He's just as prickly and self-contained, an avid outdoorsman like me."

"So? What does that have to do with me?"

"Everything," he said. "And also nothing."

That time, he really did reach for me. He didn't pull me into his arms or anything like that, but he did take both my hands in his own. His fingers were large and rough and capable, and I could suddenly see why a young Catherine had fallen so hard for an equally young Jasper.

"I moved to Colville last year for no real reason other than a curiosity to see the place my grandma used to talk about. She used to say that it was both the best and the worst place she'd ever lived. It was where she'd first fallen in love and learned to stand up for herself—where she'd buried one part of herself and given birth to a whole new one. Obviously, I was curious about Jasper, but that was only secondary to the rest."

"Which was?" I asked. I didn't try to pull my hands away.

"I don't know," he admitted. "I think that's the Jasper in me. As soon as I set foot in the forest here, I knew it was where I belonged. Like my father—and my grandfather—there's something about the wild that calls to me. It's where I feel most at home. But like my grandmother, I also need more than just a few trees and the night sky. I don't mean nice clothes and a high-powered career, but *people*. Siblings and friends and family. Maybe even you."

I tried not to let that last remark get to me, but I was only human, after all. "Does this mean you'll be sticking around for a while?" I asked, watching him through my half-lowered eyelids.

He seemed to sense that I was asking more than just a passing question. "Yeah, I am. I enjoy the town and my work, and Jasper has yet to slam the door shut in my face, so I figure that's as good a sign as any that he's willing to see what we can make of this whole grandpa/grandson thing. I'd also like to see what we can make of this whole Chloe/Zach thing, but I know I'm going to have to work hard to regain your trust. But if you'll be here, I'd like to try." His smile quirked again. "No pressure or anything. Just hope."

My heart gave a sudden, heaving lurch. As fun as it was to indulge in the what-if dreams of selling the house and packing up the kids, of moving to Spokane and finding a way to pay the bills and pick up where my education had left off, the reality was that my life would very much continue the way it always had. Theo and Trixie were deeply entrenched in their respective schools. Noodle was happier than I'd seen him in a long time. I had Lonnie and Pepper to look out for and a job that, despite its low pay and even lower prestige, I genuinely enjoyed.

Besides, Zach was here. *Jasper* was here.

Catherine Martin may have been able to tear herself away and start over somewhere new, but it was like I said before—our Sampson roots drove deep. I couldn't pull them up without damaging the whole lot of us in the process.

"I'm not leaving any time soon," I said, and for the first time, that felt okay. "So you're welcome to do your worst."

He fought to hide his sudden, beaming smile. Although he eventually managed to tamp it down, the damage—for damage it was—had already been done. My heart gave a bona fide pitter-patter. Whatever stops he pulled out to earn my forgiveness were sure to be good ones. Nonsensical, probably, and highly suspicious, but good all the same.

But he wasn't done yet. "In that case, I'm supposed to drag you next door." He tilted his head toward the door. "Jasper's throwing a little going-away party."

"Going away?" I echoed. "For…my mom and Todd?"

"No, for my grandmother. I'm driving her down to the airport first thing in the morning."

My heart gave a sudden, heaving lurch. "Oh, no. She's leaving already? What about Jasper? What about their love story?"

"I think they both agreed that story was better left without a sequel." He extended a hand to me. "Will you come? She really wants to see you before she goes. There's something she wants to give you."

I slipped my fingers into his, drawing comfort from the warm, rough feel of his hand in mine. "If that something is you, I should probably warn you that I prefer my gifts to be of the monetary variety."

"Duly noted," he said, his hand squeezing mine. "But I think you should wait and see. If there's one thing my grandmother's good at, it's giving people the one thing they didn't know they needed most."

36

—

CHLOE

IN THE FINAL STORY OF MY life, it will be written down that my opening chapter started in the year 1960. Long before I was born or even thought of, back when a young woman and a young man fell in love over an illicit copy of *Tropic of Cancer*, events were put into motion. Hearts were broken and babies born, money earned and hard labor performed. A garden was also planted, its seeds taking root in ways that would take more than six decades to bear fruit.

"She's here! She came!"

"It's about time. We've been waiting *forever*."

"Chloe, did you remember to bring over the nondairy creamer I texted you about? I'm making a bomb with it. Just an eensy-weensy one, so you don't need to look like that. It's for Jasper."

I blinked at the scene of mayhem I stepped into, surprised to find not only my own brothers and sister cluttering up the place, but Jasper, Catherine, Lonnie, Pepper, and even Gunderson, who was holding a casserole dish of something green and looking delighted to be invited, well, *anywhere*.

"A bomb for Jasper?" I asked, ignoring the sea of faces to focus on the most salient of all Theo's remarks. "Theo, he's been nothing but nice to us. You can't repay his generosity by blowing up his house."

"I said it's just a small one," Theo protested. "To help him clear out his weeds. He made us pick them all by hand yesterday. Look." He held up his rough, work-reddened palms. "He said if I can find a different way to uproot them, then I'm more than welcome to give it a go."

"I also said you couldn't do more damage to my flower beds in the process," Jasper said in a voice that wavered uncertainly. He cast me an agonized glance. "I meant to make that part very clear."

"Not clear enough," Trixie muttered. "He also thinks we should adopt a goat."

"Can we get a goat, Chloe, please?" Theo asked. "I want to name him the Great Goatsby. Jasper has been reading aloud to us at bedtime."

I laughed, too pleased to find that my siblings were very much up to their usual tricks to care that they were plotting ways and means to build explosives.

"No, we will not be getting a goat, and no, we will not be helping Jasper in any way but with our hands," I said as firmly as I could. Then, aware that all everyone was watching us, "Did Mom and Todd bring you guys home from school today?"

Trixie rolled her eyes. "Yes. And then they drove off into the sunset together. How romantic."

"Does this mean we can go home now?" Theo demanded. "Because Jasper's floor isn't very comfortable."

Noodle drew closer and slipped his hand into mine. "You're not sad about it, are you, Chloe? It's okay if it goes back to just being us again?"

As all three kids stood there, watching me and anxiously awaiting my reply, the tightness that had been in my chest since the conversation with my mom loosened. I wouldn't have chosen to discuss this in front of a gathering of people who could be counted on to ask me questions and poke their noses in my life for weeks to come, but that was the whole point. I'd never be able to raise these children on my own—not the way they deserved to be raised. If I was going to make a success of this, then I needed to admit that I didn't have all the answers…or even very many of the questions.

"I'm not sad," I said. I offered my siblings a watery smile—and then I cast it around the whole room. "I don't need her when I have all of you. It's taken me a long time to realize it, and I know I haven't made things easy, but I appreciate everything you do for us—everything you *have* been doing for a long time."

I might have been overwhelmed by a group hug then, but Catherine spoke up before the collective group could pounce. She didn't raise her voice or even make a big show of speaking, but it was easy to see why she'd managed such a long and varied career. She had presence, this slip of girl who'd once done the impossible—this slip of a woman who was doing it again.

"'*It was not the thorn bending to the honeysuckles, but the honeysuckles embracing the thorn*,'" she murmured playfully. "Now, where have I heard that before?"

Jasper's eyes caught mine and held them for what felt like an impossibly long time. No one else in the room might recognize the *Wuthering Heights* quote, but we certainly did.

"Okay. I think it's officially time to eat." Lonnie broke the sudden silence with a swift clap of her hands. "I don't know about you all, but I haven't been to a good going-away party in ages. Pepper, the music?"

"On it," Pepper said as she whipped out her phone. "Sinatra standards for the olds and Taylor Swift for the rest."

"Wait. Does that make me an old?" Gunderson asked, his face falling.

Pepper slung an arm around his shoulder as her grandmother lifted the casserole from his hands. "Nice try, Gunderson. You're one of us, and you know it. I'm pretty sure I heard you singing all the words to 'Bad Blood' during inventory last week."

He brightened perceptibly. "My daughter Ophelia is nine, Pepper. Of course I know all the words."

"Then there you go. You're a Swiftie just like me."

With a wink meant for my eyes only, Pepper bore him away to the kitchen. Zach, gathering up the children, wasn't too far behind her. I suspected it was a plot to throw Jasper and Catherine together for a private place to say their goodbyes, so I reached for Gummy Bear and prepared to drag him behind me.

Jasper, however, beat me to it.

"I've gotten used to that damned dog following me around everywhere," he grumbled, but with a playful pat on Gummy Bear's head as he led the dog away. "I keep telling him that he needs to learn to keep up, but you can't teach an old dog new tricks." He paused before adding, "Well, you *can*, obviously, but don't go telling anyone I said that. I have a reputation to maintain around here."

"Wait," I called, since it felt strange to be left alone with this woman I understood so well yet barely knew. When Jasper paused and arched his brows, I blurted out the first thing that came to mind. "Are the kids really okay? About our mom leaving again? I was afraid they'd take it pretty hard. The last time…"

He stared at me for a long moment before speaking. In that moment, it felt as though entire libraries passed between us. "The last time, they only had you to look out for them. Now they have us both."

With a duck of his head, he ushered both himself and the dog into the kitchen, where the sound of happily squabbling voices continued. Even though the volume of their conversation didn't change, the longer I stood in the living room with only Catherine for company, the more the sounds receded.

"I don't bite, you know," she said as she settled herself on the couch, one leg crossing smoothly over the other. She looked very much at ease among the creeping vines and bursts of greenery. She patted the seat next to her. "Come. Sit."

I had barely managed to set my bottom on the cushion when she spoke again. "Since you're here, I'm assuming my grandson's apology worked? At least a little?"

I had to fight a roll of my eyes. "Are you surprised? I'm pretty sure that smile could get him out of a twenty-year prison sentence."

"He gets that from his grandfather." Her own chuckle sounded, rich and assured. "Oh, I know they don't look much alike, but the similarities are there all the same. It used to take me *hours* to coax that smile out of Jasper, especially in the beginning, but once I did—whoo boy." She made a fanning motion as if to cool herself off. "To Zach, that smile comes as naturally as breathing. I apologize in advance. You'll have a long, hard life trying to get the better of him in anything."

A flush of heat rose to my cheeks. "It's not like that between us," I was quick to say. "I mean, not yet. Or ever, maybe? I don't know. We're just—"

I was grateful when she leaned across the cushion and pressed a hand on my leg, stopping my babbling short. "I was only teasing. I know it's early days, and your future is still very much unsettled. That's why I wanted to talk to you."

The touch of her palm seemed to exert a soothing effect on me. I let myself relax into the cushions, more curious than afraid.

"Actually, my future is pretty much guaranteed," I said. "For the next decade, at least. Theo's only eleven, and getting him to adulthood with all his limbs intact is likely to take every ounce of concentration I have."

No emotion crossed her face—not even a flutter of her eyelashes. "So you'll work at the library?"

"Yep."

"Shelving books and cashing a paycheck with the occasional envelope of funds when your mom remembers to send one?"

I splayed my hands helplessly. "It's what I've done for the past four years, only without the envelope. Another decade won't kill me."

"No," she agreed. "It won't kill you. It'll hurt, though, won't it?

Knowing you're trapped? Knowing that the great wide world is out there going on without you?"

Even though the question could have easily been taken as a rhetorical one, I gave it serious weight—partly because this woman would be leaving in the morning, so the things I said to her didn't matter, and partly because I'd never given myself an opportunity to really *think* about it before.

"The world has always been going on without me," I said—not sad about it, but calm. Accepting. One might even say *happy*. "Even when I went away to college, it's not like I was out living it up every night of the week. I was buried in books the whole time. They were just different books, that's all. Ones where I didn't already know the ending."

She withdrew her hand from my leg. I thought she might be getting up from the couch, but she reached into her oversized bag, one of those huge expensive things that Trixie is always telling me is essential for a woman who wants to make a splash in the world. When she pulled her hand out again, she was holding a folded piece of paper.

"This is for you," she said, her hand unwavering as I stared at the white square. "It's not a gift—not in the way you're thinking—so you don't have to feel bad about taking it. Go on."

I did as she asked, but when I unfolded it, it was to find a single email address scrawled across the top line. In and of itself, the letters didn't mean much, but the handwriting unlatched something deep in my heart. I knew, logically, that this woman was the same girl from the books—the one whose pretty, scrawling script had once carried so much heart and hope—but it wasn't until I saw the evidence for myself that the truth of it hit home.

Catherine and Jasper. Jasper and Catherine.

"I'm so sorry," I said, sudden tears springing to my eyes. I rarely cried, and even more rarely did it in front of strangers, but I couldn't help myself. I dashed at my cheeks in a belated effort to keep them at bay.

"Don't be sorry, child. You don't even know what the email address is for yet."

It didn't matter. I wasn't crying for myself so much as for all the things that had been given up in this place of shattered dreams and broken hearts. Catherine, walking away from the man she loved for the sake of both their futures. Jasper, spending sixty long years believing himself to be alone in the world. My mom, unable to find happiness in her own children.

Me, trying desperately to find happiness in them for her.

"You know, the thing I've always loved most about books is how they make it possible to live a thousand different lives," she said, speaking as though my heart wasn't leaking out all over my face and dripping onto her expensive purse. "Things in this world rarely go according to plan, and we often find ourselves on roads and in cities we never planned to visit, let alone stay in forever. I take comfort from knowing that I can always pick up a book—a new one, if I want to travel someplace unique; an old one, if I find myself in need of a friend—and make everything feel right again."

"I don't understand," I gasped. "What does this have to do with me?"

She continued on as though I hadn't spoken. "It's why I became an editor. I started out as a librarian, like you, but it wasn't enough for me to simply pull books off the shelf for others to explore. I wanted to be the one putting them there in the first place. That way, I got to control a little bit of my own destiny."

I stared down at the email address again. This time, I saw beyond the handwriting to the actual letters, which contained the name of one of the top publishing houses in New York.

"I think you'll like Payton," Catherine said with a smile. "She's only a few years older than you, but she's already making a name for herself. The internship isn't much to start out with. It's only part-time, and it's mostly wading through the slush pile, but it can be done remotely. And it's paid, so you can pick and choose how you work around your library shifts. She's expecting your email sometime next week."

The paper fluttered down from my hand. "I don't understand," I said, but it was a lie. I understood completely.

She reached over and plucked the paper from midair. This time, when she gave it to me, she crushed it into my hand. "The world isn't what it used to be, Chloe." She gave a short laugh. "Well, that's not true. It's the same relentless, beautiful, soul-crushing place it's always been. But it's bigger now. More connected. If you don't like where you are, you don't have to pack up your whole family and abandon everything you know and love. All you have to do is grab a different story from the shelf."

At the sound of laughter from the direction of the kitchen, she rose to her feet and smoothed the imaginary creases from her skirt. Then she grinned the same grin that I'd seen so many times on Zach's face and beckoned for me to follow.

"'Forget the past,'" she quoted. "'Let the dead bury the dead. Things are working out fine, and that's the only thing you have to remember.'"

Something about her words snagged at a memory. "Is that *Wuthering Heights*?" I asked. I wrinkled my brow as we pushed our way into the kitchen. Everyone was there waiting for us, so full of joy that I thought my heart my burst with it all. "Or—wait. *Tropic of Cancer*?"

"It's *Psycho*, obviously," she said with a laugh. "I never could resist a story with death, decaying matriarchs, and a surprise twist at the end."

KEEP READING FOR AN
EXCERPT FROM LUCY
GILMORE'S *THE LONELY
HEARTS BOOK CLUB*

AVAILABLE NOW!

1
—

THE DAY I MET ARTHUR MCLACHLAN was perfectly ordinary.

I woke up at my usual hour. I ate my usual bowl of oatmeal while hunched over the last few pages of my library copy of *Parable of the Sower*. I can't remember what I wore, but I'm pretty sure it was both machine washable and designed for comfort.

Everything in my closet was machine washable and designed for comfort, but not by choice. Rule number one of being a librarian: You'll leave work every day looking like you waged battle with a league of ancient scribes. Adapt early and adapt often, or your dry-cleaning bills will bury you.

When Arthur first came barreling into my life, I was in the Fiction section restocking a bunch of titles someone had moved for the sake of internet kudos. There was a new TikTok trend going around where people descended on bookstores and public libraries in order to write out sentences using titles. If you ignored the part where *I* was the one who had to put everything back where it belonged, it was kind of clever.

Looking for Alaska Where the Sidewalk Ends
We Were Liars Under the Never Sky
Are You Anybody? I Am No One

I was still chuckling over that last one when I heard the sound of an annoyed cough behind me.

"Young lady, you are blocking the way to Roman History."

Years of practice had me immediately stepping back, an apology on my lips. As I pushed my cart aside, I noticed the man was elderly, his wire glasses perched on the end of his nose and his tweed jacket sporting a pair of suede elbow patches. He walked with the aid of a gold-tipped cane that looked as though it might conceal a sword stick inside.

"Do you want me to look up a specific title for you?" I asked, since he had some way to go to reach the nonfiction shelves. "Anything by Tom Holland is good, but I find I prefer to get my history from Mary Beard. Her approach is wonderfully emotional."

He snorted. "Typical sentimental claptrap."

I blinked at him, wondering what I could have said to cause offense. "I'm...sorry?"

He tapped his cane sharply. "Emotion doesn't belong in history. Emotion belongs in maudlin childhood literature. You should know that, *Pollyanna.*"

I was taken aback but not dismayed by the belligerence in his tone. Strange though it seemed, we had actual library rules about patrons like this. Soothe and disarm, that was the order of the day. Leave them in a better frame of mind than when they arrived. And never, under any circumstances, engage.

"You don't have to read anything you don't want to," I said with a careful smile. "But my name isn't Pollyanna. It's Sloane."

Instead of accepting my peace offering, Arthur tilted his head and appraised me. Something about the intelligent gray eyes behind his rims caught my attention.

"You know what I meant," he said, stabbing a finger at my cart. Sure enough, a copy of Eleanor Porter's beloved childhood tale sat on the top. One of the teens had had the audacity to pair it with John Grisham's *A Time to Kill.*

I held both books up with a laugh. "Don't blame me," I said. "It's *A Time to Kill Pollyanna.*"

He looked pained.

"It's a joke," I explained. "Kids trying to make sentences out of book titles. Some of them are actually pretty good. Maybe I should try my hand at it next time I run into a patron." In an attempt to defuse the tension, I said the first title that came to mind. "*Pollyanna* is *Pleased to Meet You.*"

"Those kids are a plague on the public library system," he said, glaring. "And so, I'm starting to think, are you."

I had no response for this. Well, to be fair, I *had* one, but I knew better than to voice it aloud. One of my greatest skills in this world—some might say it was my only skill—was how good I was at being inoffensive. The trick was to look bland, act blander, and voice no opinions whatsoever. The looking bland part I had down pat, my frizzy brown hair and lightly freckled skin blending into the background so easily that I sometimes felt like a potted ficus. The acting part was easy, too. I could go for days at a time without opening my mouth to say anything but "Yes, of course" and "No, you're right," and no one seemed to think there was anything odd about it.

The opinions part was harder, but working in a public space like the Coeur d'Alene library had taught me the value of tact.

"Well?" he demanded. "Don't you have anything else to say?"

I shrugged, wishing—not for the first time—that I was more like my sister Emily. She'd have known *exactly* how to wrap a grouchy old man like this around her finger. I don't know if it was all the doctors she grew up around or just her natural charm, but she'd had a way of making even the meanest grumps do her bidding. Before she'd gotten too sick to roam the neighborhood with me, we used to visit an ice cream shop a few blocks away from our house. No matter how many fingerprints we left on the glass or how exasperated the shopkeeper got with all our requests for free samples, she always walked out of there with at least one extra scoop.

What would Emily do?

"We could probably incorporate some Roman history, if it helps," I said, thinking of the towering ice cream cones Emily used to carry home with her. She'd never been able to eat the whole thing, but that hadn't been the point. It had been the *triumph* of it she'd enjoyed. In all the years since I'd lost her, I hadn't triumphed over anything.

Or anyone. Not even myself.

Before I could think better of it, I reached for a copy of Toni Morrison's *Beloved* and held it up. "How about *Beloved Pagans and Christians*? You have to admit it's catchy."

I could have almost sworn that Arthur's nostrils flared to twice their size. "So that's how you want to play this, huh?"

I wasn't sure I wanted to play much of *anything*, but I was already in too deep at that point. There was no ice cream at the end of this particular rainbow, but I couldn't help feeling that Emily would have been proud of me all the same.

"*The Roman Triumph Of Mice and Men*?" I suggested, thinking up Roman history titles as quickly as I could. Inspiration struck, and I snapped my fingers. "Oh! I know. *I, Claudius, Journey to the End of the Night*. These are good. I should probably write them down."

Something almost like respect was starting to spark in Arthur's eyes. "You seem to know an awful lot about books on ancient Rome," he said grudgingly. "Why? Are you planning to stab someone in the back?"

This time, I didn't hesitate over my reply. "Only if he deserves it."

A sound somewhere between a bark and a laugh escaped him. "Is that your way of telling me that Caesar got what was coming to him? Is that what it says in your precious Mary Beard?"

"Not exactly," I was forced to admit.

If this conversation kept going along these lines, I was going to have to admit a lot more: namely, that I wasn't nearly as conversant with Roman history as I was letting on. As far as librarians went, I was more of a jill-of-all-trades than a deep scholar. I knew lots of random book titles and could recite the first line from almost every classic piece of literature, but I could only talk intelligently on a subject for about three minutes before my storehouse of knowledge petered out.

"Ha!" he practically shouted. "That's what I thought. You don't know anything about Caesar that isn't written in the back-cover copy somewhere."

This was the point where I should have bowed gracefully out of the conversation. I'd already broken all the rules about not antagonizing the patrons, disorganized my own library cart, and said unthinkable things to a man who was old enough to be my grandfather.

For the first time in my life, however, I didn't bow out. Strangely enough, it didn't even occur to me to try.

"That's not true," I said as I pushed the copy of *Pollyanna* back on the shelf where it belonged. "I just think that anyone who had as many enemies as Caesar did should've been more careful. If he didn't see that knife coming, that's on him. My only enemy is the copier by the south window, and even I know better than to believe it when it says the toner levels are totally fine."

That was when it happened. I wasn't a good enough writer to describe it, but it was as if Arthur decided, right then and there, that I was an adversary worth having.

"I've forgotten more about Roman history than you'll ever know," he said, pointing his cane at me.

"That's probably true," I admitted.

"And I've already read every word Mary Beard has ever written."

"That's…impressive," I said.

He didn't appear to find my return to meekness to his taste. With suddenly narrowed eyes, he added, "And when I want book recommendations from a second-rate Pollyanna who wouldn't know a good book if it landed in her lap, I'll ask for it."

This barb stung more than he realized. Finding pleasure in reading—*losing* myself in a story—was the one thing I did know.

"*The Art of Racing in the Rain*," I said.

He blinked and took a step back, as if even the title of such—what had he called it? *sentimental claptrap?*—had the power to harm him. "What did you just say to me?"

I wore a smile that was only partially faked. He couldn't have been more outraged if I'd told him we were holding a book-burning party down by the lake that made our little city famous.

"If you're looking for a book recommendation, I think you should pick up *The Art of Racing in the Rain*. It's what I suggest to all our regular patrons. I know it has a reputation for being sad, but—"

The spark in his eyes grew almost martial. "Not now. Not ever. Not if it was the only book left in the world. If I want to immerse myself in someone else's pointlessly self-indulgent drivel, I'd give in and listen to podcasts."

I kept my mouth shut. It just so happened that I loved that book. I loved podcasts, too, though that was mostly because I never cared for sitting alone in a silent apartment. There are these really fun ones of people reading classic books in a flat monotone to help you go to sleep. You haven't known true peace until you've drifted off to Proust read aloud in B-flat.

Arthur took himself off after that, muttering under his breath about Roman conquests and literary abominations and librarians who should know when to keep their uninformed opinions to themselves.

And all I could do was smile after him, feeling like I'd eaten a *dozen* scoops of ice cream.

"I can't believe you just tackled Arthur McLachlan and lived to tell the tale," a deep, rich voice said from behind me. I turned to find Mateo, my fellow librarian, watching me with a detached look of awe.

READING GROUP GUIDE

1. *The Library of Borrowed Hearts* follows the lives and POVs of several different characters throughout the course of the book. Who do you consider to be the "main" main character and why?

2. The love story between Catherine and Jasper doesn't end with a traditional happily ever after. Would their lives have been better or worse if things had worked out differently between them?

3. Did you blame Catherine for the end of her relationship with Jasper? Would she ever have been content with a life in Colville? Would Jasper have been content living with Catherine in New York City? What decision would you have made in her shoes? Would that decision have been different if there was no baby involved?

4. Jasper's garden contains several plants and flowers with literary ties. Were you able to recognize any or all of them?

5. Have you ever found writing in the margins of a used book? Does it intrigue you or irritate you? What would you do if you found decades-old love notes in the margins of a novel?

6. The relationship between Chloe and Zach is left open-ended without a promise of anything for the future. Do you think they end up together? Why or why not? How does their potential love story compare or contrast with Catherine and Jasper's?

7. For Jasper, a major revelation is that "life isn't always about making good choices, but about having good choices." How would better choices have impacted his life?

8. Almost all the characters in this book use reading as a way to connect with the other people in their life. How does reading affect your personal relationships? Are there any close friends you've made through a bookish connection?

9. The "curmudgeonly old man" trope is very popular in books and movies throughout history. Why do you think that is?

10. Chloe's situation with her family is similar to Jasper's in so many ways. In what ways do their life choices overlap? How do they differ?

11. Catherine Martin shares a first name with both Catherine Barkley from *A Farewell to Arms* and Catherine Earnshaw from *Wuthering Heights*. What is the significance of this?

READING LIST FROM *THE LIBRARY OF BORROWED HEARTS*

Wuthering Heights, Emily Brontë

Tropic of Cancer, Henry Miller

To Kill a Mockingbird, Harper Lee

The Color Purple, Alice Walker

The Haunting of Hill House, Shirley Jackson

The Hound of the Baskervilles, Sir Arthur Conan Doyle

A Farewell to Arms, Ernest Hemingway

The Old Man and the Sea, Ernest Hemingway

The Lord of the Rings, J.R.R. Tolkien

The Princess Bride, William Goldman

The Iliad, Homer

All Quiet on the Western Front, Erich Maria Remarque

The Red Badge of Courage, Stephen Crane

North and South, Elizabeth Gaskell

Far from the Madding Crowd, Thomas Hardy

The Secret Garden, Frances Hodgson Burnett

The Lonely Hearts Book Club, Lucy Gilmore

The Mysteries of Udolpho, Ann Radcliffe

Little Women, Louisa May Alcott

I Capture the Castle, Dodie Smith

Moby Dick, Herman Melville

Fifty Shades of Grey, E.L. James

Psycho, Robert Bloch

The Documents in the Case, Dorothy L. Sayers

Anne of Windy Poplars, L.M. Montgomery

Pregnesia, Carla Cassidy

Rebecca, Daphne du Maurier

The Woman in White, Wilkie Collins

The Legend of Sleepy Hollow, Washington Irving

Etiquette in Society, in Business, in Politics, and at Home, Emily Post

Lady Chatterley's Lover, D.H. Lawrence

Pride & Prejudice, Jane Austen

Their Eyes Were Watching God, Zora Neale Hurston

"Annabel Lee", Edgar Allan Poe

Breakfast at Tiffany's, Truman Capote

The Tale of Peter Rabbit, Beatrix Potter

America's Housekeeping Book, New York Herald Tribune Home
    Institute

ABOUT THE AUTHOR

Lucy Gilmore is a celebrated novelist in a wide range of genres, including literary fiction, contemporary romance, and cozy mystery. She began her reading (and writing) career as an English literature major and ended as a book lover without all those pesky academic papers attached.

She lives in Spokane, WA, with her family.

LucyGilmore.com
Facebook: AuthorLucyGilmore
Instagram: @tamaratamaralucy